D0407690

TWELFTH

TWELFTH

JANET KEY

LITTLE, BROWN AND COMPANY
New York Boston

Little, Brown and Company
Hachette Book Group
1290 Avenue of the Americas, New York, NY 10104
Visit us at LBYR.com

First Edition: May 2022

Little, Brown and Company is a division of Hachette Book Group, Inc. The Little, Brown name and logo are trademarks of Hachette Book Group, Inc.

The publisher is not responsible for websites (or their content) that are not owned by the publisher.

Library of Congress Cataloging-in-Publication Data
Names: Key, Janet, author.
Title: Twelfth / Janet Key.
Description: First edition. | New York : Little, Brown and Company, 2022. | Audience: Ages 8–12. | Summary: "Twelve-year-old Maren hesitantly enters summer theater camp and becomes caught up in a mystery surrounding the camp's founder."—Provided by publisher.
Identifiers: LCCN 2021027528 | ISBN 9780316669313 (hardcover) | ISBN 9780316669344 (ebook)
Subjects: CYAC: Camps—Fiction. | Theater—Fiction. | Homosexuality—Fiction. | Gender identity—Fiction.
Classification: LCC PZ7.1.K5126 Tw 2022 | DDC [Fic]—dc23
LC record available at https://lccn.loc.gov/2021027528

ISBNs: 978-0-316-66931-3 (hardcover), 978-0-316-66934-4 (ebook), 978-0-316-48574-6 (OwlCrate Jr. edition)

Printed in the United States of America

LSC-C

Printing 1, 2022

For my teachers
In memory of Terry Ogden

CHARLOTTE GOODMAN'S
THEATER CAMP
AMPHITHEATER
COSTUME STORAGE
GIRLS' CABINS
AUDITORIUM
DROP-OFF CIRCLE

Cast List

2015 CHARACTERS:

Maren Sands—a new camper
Hadley Sands—Maren's older sister
Ed Leventhal—Maren's father
Angela Sands—Maren's mother

Theo Templeton—Maren's friend
Graham Axley-Hemple—Maren's friend
Salvador "Sal" Daley—Maren's friend
Allegra Georgina Alvin—prima donna
Nicole "Nic" Esposito and Piper Cohen—
    Allegra's minions

Joanna "Jo" August—owner and manager of
    Camp Goodman; Theater History teacher
Lee August—original owner; Jo's father
Violet August—Jo's mother and Lee's wife;
    deceased
Vincent Cairn—programs director of Camp
    Goodman; Directing teacher
Bernie Del Rio—Tech teacher
Eartha Trails—Movement teacher
Miss Maxine Bradley—Acting teacher

Paul Bradley—Maxine Bradley's son

Rose Batma—Costume and Makeup teacher

Montague "Monty" Martin—Playwriting teacher

Elizabeth Casta—Speech and Diction teacher

Iona Green—Musical Theater teacher

Beth and Louise Axley-Hemple—Graham's moms

Clarence Wood—cafeteria chef

Gabby Johnson—local coffee shop owner

Renee Wallace—owner of Walcorp

Quigley Forrager—film director; Theo's obsession

1940-'50s CHARACTERS:

Charlotte "Charlie" Goodman—an aspiring filmmaker

Rosalie Goodman Jacobs—Charlotte's sister

Herald Goodman (Heinrich Güthermann)—Charlotte's father

Miriam Goodman—Charlotte and Rosalie's mother

Jeremy Jacobs—Rosalie's husband

Emma Bonaventure—an actress

Wayman Wallace—Emma's fiancé

Prologue

In every theater, no matter how large or small, there is one light that never goes off. Long after the actors have bowed and the curtain has closed, long after the audience has left and the sets have been struck and the floor has been swept, there is still one light left shining in the center of the empty stage.

This light is called the ghost light.

In part, the ghost light is left on to keep people from getting hurt in a dark theater. But more than anything, the ghost light is left on because theater people have a lot of superstitions. They believe in things that can and cannot be said, pre- and postshow routines, personal trinkets and tricks and good luck charms. And if they should fail to honor these just so? Well, lights aren't the only type of ghosts in theaters.

The ghost light of this story was shining on the auditorium stage at Camp Goodman, where Miss Maxine Bradley, the Acting teacher, was performing her own pre-camp superstitious ritual. She was wearing a neon-yellow visor over her snowy-white hair, a bright purple unitard, and green leg warmers. As if her clothes weren't loud enough, she was also blasting a song on an old cassette player that leaked through her headphones and into the empty theater. Tomorrow, she would greet another batch of campers, and she liked to dance around the stage a day in advance. It was a ritual she had performed every single summer of the camp's sixty years—and everyone knew Miss Bradley was the oldest instructor at the camp.

She was halfway through her pre-camp dance when something made her pause. She wasn't sure what, exactly. She hadn't heard anything—she couldn't have, over her music—and she hadn't seen anything, either, as the stage was empty. But something made her stop dancing, and that same something made the hair on the back of her neck stand up.

Miss Bradley was superstitious about the hair on the back of her neck standing up.

Slowly, she paused her music and lifted her headphones off. The silence of the auditorium swooped down on her as she spun on the spot, looking first at the stage behind her, then into the backstage wings, then out into the audience. The empty seats before her seemed to have their faces held up to the stage—expectant and waiting.

"Hello?" she called into the quiet.

A buzzing sound came from behind her.

She spun around and gasped as something dark skittered across the floor—then laughed in relief. The sound was just the ghost light, its bulb buzzing away. And the thing that had made her jump? Only her own shadow. She laughed again and shook her head for working herself into such a fright. She was about to put her headphones back on when she realized her shadow was doing something unusual. It was growing darker and lighter, darker and lighter. She turned toward the ghost light again, more curious than afraid now, and saw a remarkable thing.

The ghost light—the light that should never, ever go out—was flickering. Brighter, then dimmer…brighter, then dimmer…and the electric buzz grew louder and softer with it. It was strangely hypnotic to watch, like the gentle pulsing of a jellyfish.

Miss Bradley felt annoyed now. She didn't want to get caught in the dark, and she certainly couldn't safely conduct a class here tomorrow if the lights were on the fritz. She looked over her shoulder, into the dark space off-stage, thinking she might be able to find someone there to help her.

"Hello!" she called again.

As if in answer, the buzzing of the bulb grew louder, the light brighter. It began to pulse even faster than before—bright, dim, bright, dim—almost like a heartbeat. Almost like it were alive. Almost like the light was saying *hello* back.

The hairs on the back of Miss Bradley's neck stood up even taller.

She stepped closer to the light, squinting when it got to its brightest.

"Hello?" she whispered.

This time, the buzz was almost deafening, the light so bright she had to raise her hand to shield her eyes. In the metal frame, she could make out her own reflection, stretched long and thin in the metal—and there was something behind her, something else.

Some*one* else.

Miss Bradley gasped. She would have screamed, but she didn't have time—the floor disappeared from under her and she dropped, silently and heavily, into the square of perfect darkness.

A second later, the trapdoor slid shut.

The stage was empty again.

The ghost light faded back to its usual brightness and shone on.

Maren

June 2015—20 Hours Later
Stonecourt, Massachusetts

"Hey, hey, here we go!" Ed said as they turned off the highway and bumped down a gravel lane, speckled and shady with trees. "We made it in one piece after all!"

He gestured grandly as they passed under a gate with GOODMAN's arching in metallic, spidery script across the top.

The camp sure didn't look like much, Maren thought, as they crawled forward in a line of other cars. Just trees, more trees, and a scattered collection of squat buildings peeking out between them. But then they pulled around the drop-off circle and a building like a glacier suddenly appeared, sparkling in the sun and towering over the rest—the auditorium, Maren realized. Its whole front was made of long panes of glass that gleamed like teeth, reflecting Ed's junky car as it pulled to a stop.

Just as her sister, Hadley, had described it.

Maren's heart started to beat unpleasantly in her throat. The entire drive from Boston, she had felt a slow burn of anger rising off her, as if she were quietly radiating heat. But now that she was really here, at the Charlotte Goodman Theatre Camp in the middle of Nowheresville, the Berkshires, her anger was twisting into something else, something more like nervousness.

Maren's heart beat faster when she caught sight of the kids piling out of the cars around them. One girl had bracelets up both forearms, her mouth triple coated with glitter lip gloss. Another girl had violet hair down to her waist. One boy, who actually seemed to be wearing a magician's black silk cape, was talking to another boy who had drawn scowling rings of black liner around his eyes. These kids made Hadley look, well, *subtle*—and subtle was not a word Maren would have used for her sister.

A short boy with floppy hair that fell to his shoulders stepped out from the minivan directly behind them. He seemed pretty normal, in a T-shirt and sneakers, but no sooner had those sneakers touched the ground than a squeal of "Graham-eee!" went up and a flock of girls enveloped him, tousling his hair and hugging him off his feet.

"Wow," Ed said. "They're...friendly."

He smiled hopefully at Maren. Maren turned away and got out of the car.

Ed and her mother had divorced when Maren was just a baby. He was a bass guitarist and toured around with different bands, popping back into Boston every few weeks to take the girls out on the weekends. It wasn't that Maren didn't love him—she did. It was just that, before this spring, Maren had only ever seen him when they went out for a movie or pizza or ice cream. Before this spring, Maren had never had to sleep on his dumpy couch that smelled like corn chips, or try to scavenge some sort of dinner from his fridge that only had half-empty bottles of mustard and salad dressing. Before this spring, Ed had been a kind of joke she and Hadley shared—their scruffy, incessantly late, never-really-a-rock-star father, who once made the girls ride in the back of his car because his bass guitar was in the front seat. "Guess we know where we stand in comparison to the real leading lady of your life," Hadley had joked.

And now, Maren thought as she popped the trunk, she knew where she stood in comparison to her sister.

"Hello!" came a musical voice, and Maren turned to see a short, pleasantly plump woman walking up with a wide smile. She had a cloud of curly golden-brown hair that frizzed and tumbled at odds with itself. It looked as though her face was emerging from its own dust cloud—in a nice way—and her astounding blue eyes shone all the brighter for it.

"I'm Jo, owner and general manager here—and you," Jo said, stepping away as if to get a better look, "you must be Maren Sands!"

Maren, surprised, only nodded.

"I thought so." Jo beamed. "Your sister talked about you all the time. We're so pleased you're joining us this year."

"Maren's happy to be here, too," Ed answered for her. "Although"—he dropped his voice—"she's been having a *rough time*. See, our family's been through quite a bit...."

Maren scowled and looked away. She wasn't eager to hear her father tell the story of Hadley for the thousandth time, as if it had anything to do with her. Nearby, the short boy, now free from his cluster of girls, was watching her curiously—great, so he'd hear everything, too. Maren glared at him for good measure, then gritted her teeth and turned back, willing the next few minutes to be over with already.

But Jo had put up her hands and was shaking her head. "Say no more," she said. "Summers are for fresh starts, I always say. The only thing I need to know is whether or not you have any allergies."

"Um...?" Ed looked at Maren quizzically. Some father—didn't even know if his kid had allergies. "I don't think so," Ed said when Maren gave him nothing. "Is that a problem?"

"A problem *not* to have allergies?" Jo laughed kindly. "Goodness, no! Just need to know because there's an apiary on the grounds. I came back from there this morning and probably scared a few early arrivals, looking like an astronaut!"

"Sorry, there's a *what* on the grounds?" Ed said.

"Beehives," Maren said automatically.

"That's right!" Jo looked at her with interest. "How do you know that?"

Maren shrugged and looked away.

"Are the bees a problem?" Ed asked.

Jo shook her head. "They're at the far edge of the property. We make sure the campers don't get too close, and we always have EpiPens on hand, just in case. Not exactly standard camp fare, I know, but the hives were my mother's and I can't bear to give them up. Anyway!" She clapped her hands as if to get back on track. "Should we let Maren here head to her cabin, or do you have any other questions?"

"I think we're good," Ed said. "We'll call if anything comes up."

"Remember to try the camp landline first," Jo said. "We're in a bit of a cell phone dead zone up here."

"Really?" Ed tried hard not to look shocked, which made him look extra shocked.

"Oh, you and Maren will be able to talk plenty," Jo

reassured him. "There are computers in the library Maren can use anytime, and the village has more service than we do, so when the campers go into town on Sunday, they wear out their thumbs on their phones. You're welcome to my personal number, too, but I'm not sure how much good that'll do." Jo smacked her hands against her pant legs. "Honestly, I haven't been able to find my phone all day."

"Check the shelf," Maren said.

Ed and Jo looked at her, and Maren bit her tongue. She hadn't meant to say it out loud, it had just popped out. She spoke fast now, hoping to get it over with quickly: "You normally keep your phone in your pocket, right?"

"That's right," Jo said.

"But you wouldn't be able to get to your pocket in a bee-keeping suit. So you must have taken the phone out and put it down somewhere before you put the suit on—I'd guess on the same shelf where you keep your hood and mask."

Jo's laugh came bounding out in a way that made Maren think of a friendly dog. "If my phone is there, I'm going to make sure you get an extra cookie tonight." She beamed down at Maren, then turned to Ed. "That's one smart kiddo you've got!"

"Yeah," Ed said, smiling. "She certainly doesn't get it from me."

Maren looked away again. Ever since she was little, everyone liked to talk about how smart she was. But all being "smart" really meant was she wasn't allowed to make mistakes. And what did it matter anyway, if you still weren't smart enough for the important things?

"Excuse me, Jo?" A nervous-looking woman with a briskly swinging blond ponytail walked up from the minivan. "Graham *does* have a bee allergy, you remember that, right?" The woman pointed to where the short boy was muttering next to another woman, who had blunt bangs and glasses.

"He says of course she knows," the blunt-banged woman called. "He says he's only been here a thousand times!"

"Hi, Louise, hi, Beth!" Jo said, waving to the more distant woman. "And hello to you, too, Graham, welcome back for your thousand-and-first summer!" All three women laughed, but Maren felt a little sorry for the boy, who dropped his gaze so low his long hair swung in front of his face.

"It's not true what they're saying, is it?" the nervous woman said once the laughter had died away. "We saw the new development from the highway, and people say this might be the camp's last year—"

"Just a second, Louise," Jo interrupted. She turned back to Maren and Ed. "Do feel free to ask me any questions, anytime, but if that's all for now, Maren, Mr. Cairn will be here shortly to lead campers to their cabins." With that, and another smile that seemed too big for her face, Jo turned and guided Graham's mom away, talking softly and reassuringly under her breath.

Ed was still squinting at his phone. "I really *don't* have any service. Huh. Weird."

"Tell me about it," Maren grouched, but really, she felt relieved at the thought she might not have to talk to her mom or Ed or anyone else for a while. At home, all anybody ever wanted to talk about was Hadley, and all anybody said was that she was doing "better."

"Hey." Ed sank down until he was level with Maren

and put a warm hand on her shoulder, making it impossible for her not to look at him. "I know this isn't exactly what you wanted. But it's only a few weeks. You can tough it out for a few weeks, right?"

Maren opened her mouth to say she was fine but, to her horror, she felt tears start to build in the space behind her eyes. "Can't I just stay with you?" she blurted out.

Ed's expression fell. "I'm traveling every weekend this month, and you're not old enough to stay at my place alone."

"Well, why can't I just stay in my real room at Mom's?" Maren hated how small her voice sounded. She had promised herself she wouldn't do this, but now that she was here, she couldn't help it. "It's not like Mom's gone more than she normally is at work," she went on. "It's not like I need a babysitter."

"Your mom has her plate full with . . . She's just got a lot to handle," Ed said.

He didn't say *with your sister*, but Maren heard it anyway. Instantly, the tears disappeared, burned away by that angry heat again. Well, fine. If her parents cared more about her sister, then what did she need them for anyway?

"I bet you learn to love it in no time." Ed was still talking, a big smile forced through his patchy beard. "Hadley was always nervous at first, too, but by the end—"

"First-year?" interrupted a crisp voice behind them.

A tall man with a clipboard stared down at them from behind perfectly square glasses. His skin was the color of glassy volcanic rock, and everything about him seemed defined by a sharp, stonelike edge, from his perfectly trimmed mustache to the ruler-straight part in his hair to the expertly folded cravat tucked under his chin.

"Yes," Ed said quickly, standing. "Or, I mean, no?"

The man raised an eyebrow—its arch unsurprisingly sharp.

"It's her first year at camp," Ed clarified. "But she's going into seventh grade."

The man gave a single nod and raised his clipboard to scan it. "Second-year, then."

"*Second*-year?" Ed laughed. "How does that work? My other daughter started coming here when she could barely tie her shoes."

The man gave Ed a look that said he preferred not to waste his time with foolish questions from clueless fathers. "This session is for rising sixth, seventh, and eighth graders. Rising high schoolers will be here next month, and the elementary school session is in August." He turned back to his clipboard. "Sands or Templeton?"

Ed looked subdued. "Sands."

The man made a mark on his paper, then looked over his glasses to consider Maren. For the second time, she had the sense she was being compared to Hadley—only this time, there wasn't much warmth in the comparison. "Very well, Miss Sands," he said after a moment. "I'm Mr. Cairn. The second-year girls' counselor is our Movement teacher, Eartha. She's supposed to be here to help get you settled, but where she is remains to be seen.... As if I didn't have enough to concern myself without Miss Bradley also deciding to take the day off..." He sighed through his nose and removed his reading spectacles with an elegant flutter. "No matter," he said. "I'll take you to your cabin now."

He turned and started down the path without waiting.

Maren looked at Ed, who made a joking grimace. "Yikes," he whispered. "Don't get on his bad side, huh?"

"I'll be fine," she said, and she was almost pleased to hear how cold her voice was. "You should go."

Ed blinked. "Oh, but I don't have to leave right away," he said. "I can help you carry your stuff to your cabin, maybe meet some of your new friends—"

"I said I'm fine," Maren said, loud enough that the long-haired boy, Graham, looked over at her again. "I can carry my own stuff. Just go."

"Okay," Ed said. "Well, have an awesome time, and—"

But Maren had already dragged her sleeping bag, backpack, and duffel bag from the trunk and was walking away, past the fancy auditorium with all those windows that seemed to watch her go. A very small part of her hoped Ed would follow her anyway and insist on helping. A very small part of her knew she wouldn't have stopped him if he had. But a moment later, she heard the rumble of Ed's junker grind to life, and she knew she was on her own.

Camp Goodman had been Hadley's place. She had gone as a camper every year for as long as Maren could remember and, for the past few years, had also been invited to be a counselor for the little kids' camp.

"You should go next year," Hadley had told Maren. It was the end of summer vacation the year before, and Hadley was supposed to be packing up her bedroom for her first semester of college. Instead, they were propped on Hadley's bed, watching a marathon of an old mystery show while Hadley painted their toenails. "You'd love it."

Maren wrinkled her nose. "Why?"

"Because Goodman's is totally the best," Hadley said. She leaned back to study the blue polish on her toes. "The kids there are all weirdos—you'll fit in great."

"Hey, look who's talking!" Maren pretended to be offended.

"Exactly!" Hadley grinned. "I'm saying that as a compliment. Who wants to be normal?"

Maren rolled her eyes but couldn't help smiling: "Weirdo" did feel like a compliment from Hadley. Even just lying around the house, Hadley always looked in some way *magnified*. That day, she was wearing huge red cat-eye glasses and a vintage velvet smoking jacket over her pajama bottoms. She was the sort of person who filled a spotlight like it had been custom-made for her. Maren, meanwhile, wore regular glasses and jeans and had remarkably unnoticeable brown hair. She was the sort of person the spotlight passed right over, and, mostly, she was okay with that.

"Being in a play, it's hard to describe how special it is," Hadley went on. She straightened her leg and then pulled Maren's foot toward her. She held up first a green, then an orange polish bottle next to Maren's toes. "Playing Emily in *Our Town* was just magical for me...." Hadley's gaze got far away. When she spoke again, it was with a lilting accent and dramatic enunciation. "*Goodbye to clocks ticking—and my butternut tree! And Mama's sunflowers,*" she intoned the lines. "*And food and coffee—and new-ironed dresses and hot baths—and sleeping and waking up.*"

"*Oh, earth,*" Maren chimed in—she had helped Hadley practice the lines so often that she, too, could repeat them without even trying. She clutched her heart melodramatically, *"you're too wonderful for anybody to realize you!"* Then pretended to faint back on Hadley's pillows.

"Ha-ha," Hadley said, rolling her eyes. She selected a raspberry color and, after carefully edging the brush against the bottle, started painting Maren's big toe. "Man, it's annoying how quickly you memorize stuff. Guess that's why you're the smarty-pants of the family."

Maren felt something inside her shrink. She pretended to watch TV while Hadley focused on the work of polishing.

Maren picked things up quickly. That's how she thought of it—not that she was smarter than her sister or the other kids in her class, just that she figured things out faster. It had never seemed like something Hadley minded (or even noticed, really) but, last fall, Hadley had trouble with the SAT and hadn't gotten into the college she wanted. It was fine, Hadley kept telling everyone, because she was still going to school in New York, and a theater school at that, which was what she had really wanted—but Maren knew the disappointment cut deeper than her sister let on. Maren also knew she had no reason to feel guilty, but with their mom working long hours at the firm and Ed being Ed, it had always been her and Hadley against the world. So what would happen if Hadley decided she didn't like "smarty-pants" Maren so much anymore?

As if reading her mind, Hadley said, "The least you could do is put those smarts to good use."

Maren glanced at her sister cautiously.

But Hadley only smiled and nodded at the TV screen. "Who did it?"

Maren bit back a smile and shook her head.

"Oh, come on, Seaweed," Hadley wheedled "I know you know!"

When Maren still wouldn't tell, Hadley took the nail polish and intentionally brushed a line across the top of Maren's foot. Maren screeched as the cold paint tickled her skin, and then she and her sister were wrestling—as much as you can wrestle with wet, freshly painted toes—across Hadley's bed, sending her pillows and books and magazines sprawling.

The paths through the woods were long and windy and branched off to other, smaller paths every once in a while. At every intersection, Mr. Cairn informed her, there were wooden signs that pointed in different directions—the one that pointed back where they had come from was labeled AUDITORIUM, another said CAFETERIA, and one, pointing straight up, JUPITER. By the time they stepped out into a clearing at the end of the GIRLS' CABINS path, it felt like Maren *had* walked to Jupiter. Her hair was plastered in dark sweaty streaks to her forehead, her glasses kept skidding down her nose, and the straps of her backpack dug uncomfortably into her shoulder. She tried to wipe the sweat away as they moved toward the cabins, conscious of some girls sitting on the grass out front.

"It's so not fair they make us wait to learn what play we're doing," one girl was saying, swinging her honey-colored hair to the side so she could adjust the straps of her blue halter top. "How are we supposed to know what audition to prepare?"

"You don't need to worry about auditions, Allegra," piped up another girl. She had wide, watery eyes and a small, rabbity mouth, and was leaning toward the first girl, Allegra, as if begging to be patted on the head. "You're sure to get a lead—you always do."

Allegra narrowed her eyes. "*A* lead?"

"*The* lead, I mean," the girl corrected herself quickly, and the way her mouth worked as she stumbled over the words made her look even more rabbity. "Whichever lead you want."

"Plus, we're third-years now," said another girl in a dull monotone. She was drawing a black ring of barbed wire around her arm with a pen. "They always give the good roles to third-years."

"As well they should," Allegra sniffed. "I haven't been coming to this camp since I was five for nothing." Her face shifted to sickeningly sweet when she caught sight of Maren and Mr. Cairn walking past. "Oh, hiiii, Mr. Cairn," she simpered.

"Miss Alvin," Mr. Cairn responded without slowing his pace. "Welcome back."

"We were just wondering what show we're doing this year," Allegra oozed on, pinning Mr. Cairn with a smile that seemed more like a snarl to Maren. "They won't tell us, but surely you know, don't you?"

"Of course," Mr. Cairn said, a hint of satisfaction creeping into his voice. "And I'm sure you'll perform admirably for your audition."

Allegra swelled with pleasure. Maren fought hard not to roll her eyes. Something of her thoughts must have shown on her face, however, because Allegra's gaze snagged on her, and her eyes narrowed coldly. Maren turned and hurried to follow Mr. Cairn to one of the cabins set deeper in the trees, nodding as he pointed out the squat cement restroom, but feeling the gaze of the girl on her back the whole time.

What was spectacular about the cabin was absolutely nothing. In fact, if Maren had been told to close her eyes and imagine a run-down old camp cabin, this would have been pretty much what she would have come up with: creaky wooden floors, chipped paint on the stained walls, windowsills frosted with a thick layer of dead flies. There were two sets of bunk beds and dressers, one on each side of the room, though one set was already occupied.

"Miss Sands, these are your cabinmates, Miss Lorna McCall and Miss Katie Yang." Mr. Cairn stood in the doorway and nodded in turn at the two girls.

Lorna and Katie smiled at Maren.

"Hope you don't mind," said Lorna, who, with her almost invisible eyebrows, looked perpetually surprised. "We picked our bunk first." She gestured to a bed half-hidden under stuffed animals and fuzzy pillows, the bedposts strung with beads, and the wall speckled with pictures. A lot of the photos, Maren noticed, were of Lorna and Katie from the time they were kids, always with their arms around each other.

"We're switching top and bottom every night," Katie added, a mouthful of bright blue braces jutting out when she smiled, "so that way it's fairer."

They stared at Maren, as if waiting for her to tell them what an awesome idea it was.

"It's awesome," Lorna said, when Maren didn't respond.

"You're over here," said Mr. Cairn, fluttering a hand toward the bunk on the far side of the room. "And it looks like your bunkmate already selected the top bed."

This was an understatement. Based on the clothes flung about, it looked as though Maren was sharing a bunk with a small tornado.

"Go ahead and unpack," Mr. Cairn went on, turning to go. "A brown-bag dinner will be available in the cafeteria for the next few hours as campers continue to arrive. Then there's the opening night ceremony in the auditorium precisely at eight, which is *man-da-tor-y*." He hammered out every syllable of the word, as if relishing each one. "You should be able to find your way easily enough, if you stick to the paths, and be sure to—"

But whatever Maren needed to be sure to do was drowned out by a strange, warbling whistle. A moment later, a huge shadow filled the doorway behind Mr. Cairn.

"Where are the loons?" the shadow cried and clomped into the cabin.

Maren's first thought was that this woman had enormous feet. Then she realized the woman was wearing thick wooden clogs painted with daisies. Then she realized that, actually, her feet were enormous inside the enormous clogs, too. All of the woman was enormous. She was probably over six feet, and seemed even taller in her drapey, blockish dress, with a long gray braid swinging behind her.

"I went searching for the loons," the woman continued, smiling to reveal a gap between her two front teeth. "But my call may be out of tune."

She made another strange whistle. Mr. Cairn gave a tight smile.

"Girls, meet your counselor, Eartha Trails." He turned and addressed Eartha. "You need to go farther north to find nesting loons."

For a moment, Eartha looked devastated, but her expression bounced back half a second later. "Hey!" she cried and stooped in front of the girls, bringing her hands to her knees as if they were much younger children. "How about *we* become the loons? They can be our collective animal familiar for the cabin!"

Maren snuck a sideways glance at Lorna and Katie. She was relieved that they, too, seemed overwhelmed by the gigantic physical and energetic presence of Eartha Trails.

"How about we let the girls settle in before choosing a cabin mascot, shall we?" Mr. Cairn said, turning for the door. "Girls, we'll see you tonight. And remember to follow the trails." He paused before he went down the front steps and added, "You can't possibly find trouble so long as you follow the trails."

When they were gone, Lorna and Katie immediately turned to each other and began whispering, the word "loon" floating up between giggles. For a moment, Maren felt the urge to join in, but she hesitated.

Her gaze drifted back to the photo collage wall. They didn't seem to need anyone else. And anyway, if they'd been coming to camp this long, would they know Hadley? Would they ask about her? The last thing Maren wanted was to have to keep explaining about her sister.

Maren dragged her duffel and backpack over to the

dresser by her bunk. She began unpacking her clothes and other stuff into the bottom two drawers. Eventually, Lorna and Katie wandered out to get some dinner, but Maren, still full from snacking on gas station junk food during the drive, grabbed a notebook from her backpack and flopped back on her bunk with a sigh.

In addition to being smart, Maren had always been called quiet—a label that felt unfair. Just because she wasn't always pushing to be first in line or the loudest in the room the way Hadley was didn't mean that Maren had nothing to say. At school, she could get by just answering questions when she was called on and sitting with some of the other nice, "quiet" girls at lunch. But at home, it had always felt as if Hadley soaked up all the talking time, all their parents' attention, all the breathing space. She bickered endlessly with their mother, and she set the tone of either sarcasm or silence whenever they saw Ed. Maren sometimes felt like in order to be the good kid, the peacekeeper, she *had* to be the quiet one.

"It's such a relief," their mother had once told Maren with a sigh, "having at least one kid who doesn't have to share every feeling."

As if Maren didn't have feelings *she* wanted to share, too.

Instead, Maren had taken to writing what she felt in a notebook or journal, a place where she was allowed to say as much as she wanted about anything she wanted—although recently, she hadn't had a lot to say there, either.

She closed her notebook again. She reminded herself there was exactly one thing she wanted from this summer:

to get through it as quickly and painlessly and *invisibly* as possible. She didn't expect a camp full of Hadley-like people to make much space for her to join in anything; by this time, she had stopped expecting it of even Hadley. But she was fine by herself. She wasn't Hadley, and she certainly didn't want to be.

⤳⤳

When Maren sat up again and looked out the open door, she saw that the sun had started to set. The gaps between branches glowed bright orange and pink, as if the trees were drooping with fantastic fruit. It was probably time to head to the auditorium. Maren pulled a hoodie on and moved to the door.

But no sooner had she stepped out of her cabin than she was distracted by a shrill shriek: "God, get away from me, stalker!"

Unsurprisingly, the voice belonged to Allegra. She and a few more girls were still sitting on the grass, only now the rabbity one was braiding a little girl's hair and Allegra was making a very ugly face. She raised one hand to shield herself from a boy standing nearby with a small, handheld digital recorder.

"Stalk her?" said the boy with the camera. "I barely know her!" He laughed an oddly high, hiccupping laugh, like a broken wheel squeaking on a shopping cart. He had the worst haircut Maren had ever seen, short and bowl-like around his face so that it seemed like his entire head was covered with bangs, and was wearing a button-down vest covered in shamrocks.

"I said stop filming me, creep." Allegra swiped an

annoyed arm at the boy's legs, but he quickly danced out of reach.

"Relax," the boy said, aiming the camera around the group. "I'm not interested in you. Blonds are so Hitchcockian, totally passé."

Allegra squinted. "What did you just call me?"

"I'm just saying, I need a heroine with a bit more cojones."

He aimed his camera at the little girl in the center, who smiled and gave a playful shake to her braids—*his* braids, Maren realized with a jolt. The girl in the center was actually the boy Graham, who Maren had seen at drop-off. This would have been surprising enough, but even more surprisingly, the boy with the camera suddenly spun in Maren's direction and shouted, "Bunkie!"

Startled, Maren looked over her shoulder. No one there. She looked back.

"The stalker's your bunkmate?" Allegra said, smirking at Maren.

"I don't know," Maren said automatically.

"You don't *know*?" Allegra said, smirking wider. "You don't know who you're bunking with?"

The other girls in the circle adopted similar smirks. Graham, frowning, started tugging out his braids.

"I grabbed an early dinner, then started shooting establishing footage, so we haven't met yet," the camera boy— or, camera *girl*, Maren realized—explained with another grin. "I'm Theo."

"Honestly," Allegra said, shaking her head and making her voice a fake, ugly sort of innocent. "Can you believe Goodman's lets people like *her* into the *girls'* cabins?"

A soft, hissing laugh rose from the group, like a venomous puff of smoke.

Theo's expression went carefully blank. "Actually," Theo said, "I prefer 'they.' It's better to ask than make an assumption about someone else's gender pronouns."

"What?" Allegra made an even uglier face.

"My pronouns. I use 'they, them, their,' please," Theo went on as if she—they—hadn't noticed. "So if you want to insult me, you'd say it like: 'Can you believe Goodman's lets people like *them* into the girls' cabins?'"

Allegra rolled her eyes at the correction. "Oh, you're one of *them*," she said. "Everyone knows *they're* just doing it for attention. My mom says it's obviously a phase."

Maren expected Theo to get mad or embarrassed, but they only laughed their squeaky-wheel laugh.

"Sure," they said sarcastically. "*I'm* the one who likes attention." They pursed their mouth and pretended to toss a long sheet of hair over their shoulder—a deadly accurate impersonation of Allegra. A snicker moved stealthily through the group. Allegra's eyes flashed.

"We should probably get going, right?" Graham said, shaking out the last of his braids and standing. "Don't want to miss the show announcement."

Allegra's attention instantly switched. "I swear, they better pick a play with some good female leads. I didn't grow out my hair all year to have to play a statesman in *Julius Caesar* or *Hamlet* or something."

Seeing her chance to escape while Allegra was distracted, Maren turned and hurried toward the path while the others were still standing and dusting grass off themselves. She heard footsteps following after her, and a moment later Theo appeared jogging beside her.

"For the record, I think I'd be an excellent statesman," they said, huffing under a huge backpack clattering with key chains. "And I do love a good death scene, so *Julius Caesar* would be right in my wheelhouse."

Maren made a noncommittal sound and kept walking.

"Lots of people think that, you know," Theo said. "Think that kids like me use different pronouns to get attention, because we want to be different or because it's a phase or whatever."

"I don't think that," Maren said defensively. In truth, she had never really thought about it at all until now.

"But I'm just being myself," Theo went on as if they hadn't heard. "I don't need attention for being different—I *am* different. I just have to accept who I am. And so does everyone else."

Maren didn't know what to say, slightly awed by Theo's self-certainty. Had she ever said anything half so confident? She decided to change the subject. "Why do you have your backpack with you?" she asked.

"My equipment bag? It's for my camera." Theo smacked the clattering hump fondly. "I wanted to go to film camp but couldn't find one for under high school ages. It's cool, though. I've decided to make a documentary about Goodman's. Mind if I ask for your opinion on the rumor that it's shutting down after this year?" They raised their camera and aimed it, its lens flashing and winking, at Maren.

"Yes, I do mind," Maren said, then walked faster.

Theo lowered the camera but hurried to keep up. They

rambled on about what kind of camera they used and why, as well as an in-depth analysis of how even the best contemporary directors—including the famous auteur and Theo's personal favorite filmmaker, Quigley Forrager—now used digital instead of traditional film, and how Austin, Texas, Theo's hometown, was particularly advanced when it came to digital filmmaking.

While they spoke, Maren watched them out of the corner of her eye. She had heard the terms "trans" and "nonbinary" before but had never met anyone who identified as either. Most people Maren knew were either a boy or a girl and had never felt any kind of anything about it. Not that Maren minded—if Theo wanted to use "they," it was fine by her—but even so, Maren hoped Theo would find someone else to befriend before too long. Theo might not care about attention, but they certainly got plenty of it, and they'd make it hard for Maren to stay under the radar this summer.

With Theo's help, they both managed to get hopelessly turned around on the paths, and the sun was setting in earnest by the time they arrived at the auditorium. Inside, the lobby had royal-blue carpet and the walls were covered with gold frames of old people who looked rich; when Theo and Maren followed the other kids into the theater itself, however, it was clear the camp had seen better days. The velvet fabric on the seats was threadbare in places, and the beat-up stage floor was scarred with layer upon layer of scuff marks, deep gouges, and electrical tape.

Jo, the camp manager, was sitting on the stage in the light of an antique-looking lamp, swinging her feet over the edge. She had pulled a fluffy orange sweater over her overalls, which, combined with Jo's normal cloud of hair, made her look as if she had her own gravitational field. Maren slid into a row near the back and ended up wedged between Theo and a boy tugging at a strip of rubber peeling from his sneakers. When the rest of the campers had maneuvered into one seat or another, Jo raised an arm, signaling overhead. The lights dimmed to a spotlight around her, making her hair look even bigger in the glow.

"If theater be a mirror to life?" Jo called out over the audience.

Maren jumped in her seat as the auditorium exploded with a single shouted phrase: "THEN PLAY ON!"

This incomprehensible announcement was followed by stomps, cheers, whistles, and outright screams. Even the boy next to Maren gave up ripping apart his shoe to shout, "Oh yeah!" and pump his fist a few times. Theo grinned as they panned their camera across the cheering audience. Maren sank further in her seat.

"Did you know that this is Camp Goodman's *sixtieth* anniversary?" Jo said when she could be heard over the cheers. "My father, Lee, was the first manager of the camp." She stretched out an arm in front of her to the right, where a stooped figure wearing a baseball cap sat in a wheelchair in the first row. "And for sixty years, we have been honored to watch so many talented young people grow into their own onstage. When I say that you all are part of our family, I mean it truly—and how about you meet the amazing instructors that lead this family!"

The crowd kept clapping and cheering as various

names were called and adults stood from their seats for their introductions. There was Mr. Cairn, who offered a tight, military wave when Jo announced he was teaching Directing, and Eartha, who waved both arms over her head, as if imitating a butterfly, when her name was called—appropriately, she taught a class called Movement. The rest Maren hadn't met yet: A rosy-cheeked woman named Ms. Green taught Musical Theater, and a scruffy-haired man named Monty taught Playwriting; a short woman named Ms. Casta taught something called Speech and Diction, while a large man named Bernie was the "tech master." Costume and Makeup was being taught by Rose, a woman so tall and beautiful, with dreadlock braids down her back, that Maren thought she must be a model.

Maren clapped along politely as the names were called, and she was just starting to zone out when Jo said in conclusion, "And Miss Maxine Bradley is our Acting teacher, of course, but she couldn't be with us tonight." Almost without taking a breath, Jo immediately plowed on to discuss rules and expectations...but there was something in the way Jo breezed past Miss Bradley's name that made Maren sit up straighter. Adults were always doing that to her these days—thinking that if they said something fast enough or casually enough or cheerfully enough, Maren wouldn't notice and understand. But it was normally those things that ended up being the most important. Maren looked around, wondering if anyone else had noticed anything unusual.

"What's up?" Theo whispered.

When Maren turned to them, she saw their camera was aimed at her.

"Nothing," Maren said, leaning away. "Nothing."

"Well, now that we have that out of the way," Jo finished her speech and blew a relieved breath into the microphone. "I bet you're dying to know what show you're going to be making so great this summer, aren't you?"

The room went silent, breathless with anticipation.

"As I said, this is our sixtieth-anniversary celebration. And in honor of our camp's history, we have decided to perform the first play ever performed here."

With that, a projection lit up the back of the theater, and Maren squinted to read it. A digital banner unfurled in fancy lettering:

1955–2015 CAMP GOODMAN PRESENTS: TWELFTH NIGHT.

"Excellent!" Theo cried as the rest of the audience erupted in cheers.

Maren clapped along. She had heard of William Shakespeare, of course, and knew some of the more famous plays: Hamlet to-being or not, Romeo and Juliet dying for love, even the wild island of *The Tempest*. But she had no idea what *Twelfth Night* was about, and she had never met kids her age who were so excited about putting on a play before.

"Is there a good death scene?" she surprised herself by joking to Theo.

"Not really," Theo said back, "but there's always room for improvement."

In the lobby, there were two tables set up—one stacked high with white binders, the other with a punch bowl and plates of cookies. Theo charged straight for the snacks, but Maren opted to stop and pick up a white binder first, which, it turned out, held a large-print copy of the *Twelfth Night* script. At the second table, the woman with rosy cheeks was passing out single cookies wrapped in cellophane packets while Mr. Cairn policed the glasses of punch with a hawklike gaze.

"Chocolate chip or—wait." The red-cheeked woman paused when Maren got to the front of the line. "Wait, are you Maren?"

Surprised, Maren just nodded.

The woman smiled, her cheeks seeming to glow all the brighter, and picked up a specific cellophane packet with *two* cookies.

"Hang on, Ms. Green, we have to make those last," said Mr. Cairn disapprovingly.

"Jo's orders," Ms. Green insisted. "This young lady apparently helped her find her phone."

Maren accepted the package, muttered her thanks, and scooted out of the line. She might have been imagining it, but she thought she felt Mr. Cairn's gaze follow her as she walked away. She wound through the lobby, where everyone clustered off in twos and threes, until she made it to a relatively quiet corner. There she leaned against the wall, toying with the cellophane wrapper. She hadn't meant to eavesdrop, but she suddenly heard someone say, "You don't think it's true about Jo closing the camp, do you?"

She looked up at the three people standing in front of her—two boys and a girl with round, earnest eyes inside an equally round, earnest face.

"Oh, I heard she's sold it already," said one boy, with extra nonchalance. "I heard it's only a matter of time before this whole place becomes a Walcorp parking lot."

"She wouldn't do that!" the girl said. "Would she?"

"Not if the ghost has anything to do with it," said the other boy, and he gestured at the wall behind them, where there was a small, framed portrait.

The first boy laughed, but the girl's eyes got rounder with worry.

"Don't even joke about that," she said.

"Joke about what, the Goodman ghost?" the other boy said, grinning wickedly. "Don't worry, you don't need to be scared...so long as you don't anger it!"

"You going to eat those?"

Maren jumped as Theo appeared next to her. Their finger was aimed at Maren's cookies. Maren shook her head quickly and held the packet out.

"Really? Neither of them?" Theo seemed astounded, but they had already opened the package, lifted out both cookies sandwiched together, and taken a large bite, crumbs snowing down their vest.

Maren tried to turn back to the conversation about the camp, but the two boys were talking about some video game, and the round-faced girl had wandered away. Hadley hadn't mentioned anything about a ghost—but then, Maren thought with unexpected bitterness, Hadley had a way of not telling Maren the important things.

Maren took a step toward the framed picture on the wall to study it closer. It was of two girls standing on some cement steps. The girl on the left looked like a living doll, with a big flouncy dress, a perfect smile, and dark curly hair pulled back in an enormous bow. The other, taller girl was also wearing a flouncy dress, but she smiled with her lips closed, her head cocked at an angle, as if considering the photographer. There was an inscription along the bottom: *Rosalie and Charlotte "Charlie" Goodman.*

Maren looked again at the taller girl. So this was Charlotte Goodman. Along with her closed-lip smile, there was something about the thoughtful angle of the girl's head that made it look as if Charlotte had a spectacular secret.

There was a sudden hacking sound, and Maren turned just in time to see Theo spit something into their palm.

"Yeesh!" Theo shook their head at the pile of half-chewed cookie they held. "Who puts fortunes in with chocolate chip cookies?"

"A fortune?" Maren couldn't help leaning closer and looking at the mess. Half buried in the soggy clump was a damp piece of paper, a bite mark along one corner. "I don't think they put it in the cookies so much as between them," she said. *And didn't expect anyone to shove them both in their mouth at once,* she thought but didn't add.

"Here—" Theo pulled the scrap free and, before Maren could protest, forced it into her hand. "Maybe it's lucky."

Maren made a face as she pinched the damp paper with her fingernails. She was about to ask Theo if there had been a fortune in the other cookie packets, but she looked up at the exact moment they cupped the pile of spat-out cookie back into their mouth. They grinned at Maren while their jaw worked, and Maren decided her question wasn't worth seeing Theo's chewed food again.

She looked back at the paper. It was about the size of a business card, made of the same sort of thick, creamy paper with gold around the edges. The message there was in a swirly cursive—handwritten, probably, based on the way the ink ran where Theo had bitten it. As Maren squinted to make out what it said, she felt a sudden shudder rise along her spine—as if the words meant more than they seemed. As if it were some puzzle for Maren to figure out.

In my stars I am above thee;
but be not afraid of greatness: some are
born great, some achieve greatness, and
some have greatness
THRUST upon them.

Charlie

Long before Maren Sands was born, long before Camp Goodman opened, Charlotte Goodman was ten years old and gripping her father's hand.

"Ach, not so tight, Charlie!" her father teased as they climbed the stairs to the studio. "I cannot feel the blood in the tips of my fingers!"

Though he had lived in America for more than twenty years, she loved the way her father's accent stretched and resculpted words into a new landscape: *tips of fingers* instead of *fingertips*.

Charlie tried to nod, but she wasn't sure she managed to with all the distractions around her. Since they had first stepped foot on the lot, the people around them seemed to be moving at double the normal speed. Everyone had somewhere to go and something that needed to get there— loops of wires or shimmering gold fabric or big light bulbs cradled in their arms like glass babies. Everywhere she looked, someone was rushing by, looking important and busy and, most of all, *beautiful*.

They were on a movie set for *Dance, Girl, Dance*, where both her parents worked—her mother as a dancer, her father as a set dresser and painter. Normally, Charlie and her little sister, Rosalie, were at school or left in the care of their neighbors when her parents went to work, but Charlie had begged and begged and *begged* until finally her father relented and agreed to take both girls as a birthday present for Charlie.

"It's not going to be what you think," he had warned last night. "When you are watching a movie, you live in the magic. But making a movie, you learn the tricks, like a magician—and the magician knows it's not really magic."

"She's too old to believe in magic anyway," her mother had added, her gaze remaining on the rags she was rolling into Rosalie's long, dark hair.

Now, Rosalie was holding their father's other hand as they walked through the halls, her perfect rag curls bouncing with every step. The door to the dressing room was open, and inside women were seated or standing in front of a wall of mirrors, wearing sparkly black leotards with short, frilly dancing skirts. They had top hats, too, which some spun on their fingers or tried to fix over their hair at a jaunty angle.

One of the women disentangled herself from the others and turned around to face the door. "Darlings," she cried loudly, holding her arms open wide.

It took Charlie a moment to recognize her mother. Not because she looked all that different—her mother's dark hair was still in the same perfect wave, and she always wore makeup, even though now it was heavier and oddly flat. It was because her mother was performing a part—the role of warm, loving mother—that made Charlie grip her father's hand tighter.

Rosalie must have sensed this difference in their mother, too, but instead of shying away like Charlie, she ran forward into her mother's open arms.

The roomful of women cooed and awwed.

"Oh, just look at those curls," said one of the dancers, crouching down level with Rosalie and flashing the gleaming white rocks of her teeth. "Why, this child is prettier than Shirley Temple and then some!"

"She dances better than Shirley Temple ever did," their mother said, smoothing Rosalie's skirt, which was still as stiff as it had been when she had starched it that morning. Rosalie's cheeks flushed prettily at the compliment, as if to better coordinate with her pink dress.

Encouraged, Charlie followed her sister and stepped up next to her mother's chair.

"And this one..." The actress turned toward Charlie.

Charlie stood up straighter, awaiting her appraisal. She knew she wasn't as pretty as Shirley Temple—she wasn't even as pretty as Rosalie—but she also felt that here, basking in the golden light of all these beautiful women and the glamour of the movies, she might just be something special too.

But the actress burst out laughing. "Why, she's so *serious!*"

Whatever hope had been blossoming in Charlie's chest punctured with a pop.

"Oh, that's just Charlie," her mother said lightly, tugging Rosalie into her lap.

More actresses and dancers crowded around to admire the pretty mother and daughter: "She looks just like you, Miriam!" "Only eight and already a beauty queen!" "Oh, how precious!"

Charlie stepped farther and farther back, ducking her head and resisting the urge to tug at her braids. Her hair wouldn't hold a curl for anything. Her dress was already wrinkled in the back where she had sat on the ride over. And she could never stay still like a lady. "You need to at least put in an effort, Charlotte," her mother always said, but it wasn't that Charlie wasn't putting in an effort. She was always trying, and trying too hard, even when she didn't know what she was supposed to be trying so hard *at*, exactly. No, the problem was that everyone seemed to already know something about her. Something bad. Something off. They already knew she wasn't like them, and no matter how hard she tried, they didn't like her because of it.

Her father's hand reappeared in hers. He leaned close and whispered, "Want to see what your papa's been working on?" His cheeks twitched, so Charlie knew he was smiling behind his mustache.

Charlie nodded and let herself be tugged toward the door. The sound of the women in the dressing room behind her faded, their laughter distant but still bright, like exotic birdcalls. Charlie couldn't help but hunch her shoulders against it, as if afraid that at any second one might swoop down and attack.

"My work is not all that glamorous as your mama's," her father was saying as they moved down the hallway beyond, "but somebody's got to paint the sets."

Her father paused at an enormous set of steel doors. He pointed to an unlit light above the doors, surrounded by a wire bracket cage.

"If it were red, we would have to wait outside," he explained. "But now, with any luck, everyone will all be at lunch."

He eased one of the doors open, peeked inside, then ushered Charlie in with his finger to his lips.

Charlie would have been quiet even if she hadn't been instructed to be. There was something about the space, so big and open, that demanded silence, almost like going to church. Also like a church, there was the sense of a miracle in progress. Inside, the room had been made to look like a city street. Charlie's mouth hung open as she walked on a floor that had been painted to look like a cobblestone street, past flat boards painted to look like fake buildings with nothing behind their front doors, even around a plywood cutout that had been painted to look like a car.

"Up there," her father whispered, pointing. "That's my best work."

Charlie gasped. There, where there should have been a ceiling, was a gauzy pink and soft lavender sky speckled with shining stars.

Her father laughed and tapped his finger under her chin. "You'll catch flies, you leave that open too long."

"It's beautiful," Charlie breathed, and meant it.

"Ach! Well!" Her father waved away the compliment but sounded happy. "It is a bit tricky to paint a morning sky with stars," he admitted. "And see that star? That one brighter than the others?" He took her hand again and aimed her finger at a star that hung just a little higher than the others. "That's the North Star. The director tell your papa, make sure the North Star is like something someone can wish on!"

"And he painted a star that could *grant* a wish," someone said from behind them.

"Ms. Arzner," her father cried as he spun around. "Charlie, this is the director! She's in charge of the whole movie!"

Charlie's mouth, which she had just managed to close, fell open again.

Wearing a wide tie loosely knotted under a crisp white collar and shirtsleeves rolled up to the elbow, the person behind them looked in every way like a director…except in one: The director was a woman.

"I've told you a thousand times, please call me Dorothy," the director—Dorothy—said to Charlie's father with a grin. She jerked her strong chin back up at the morning sky. "It's a shame the audience won't get to see that gorgeous peachy glow, what with the film being in black and white."

"Yes, but you see the real deal with your camera," Charlie's father said. "So the audience must see my work through yours."

Dorothy laughed. "I'll do my best." She looked down at Charlie with an inquisitive expression. "And who's this? An artist in training?"

"My daughter, Charlie." Her father dropped an arm around Charlie's shoulders and gave a squeeze. "A *director* in training, I think!"

Charlie felt her shoulders tense, preparing to shield herself from the woman's laughter, the way the women in the dressing room had laughed at her.

But Dorothy Arzner only nodded. "We can always use more of us," she said and winked at Charlie.

Her father and Dorothy talked on about the scene

that would be shot that day, the dance they would do, the two lead actresses—but Charlie could barely pay attention. Charlie had decided the movies *were* magic after all. And Charlie had just learned what a magician could look like.

Maren

"I'm always starving," Theo said the next afternoon at lunch, as if Maren hadn't noticed. "I'm trying to establish a working relationship with Clarence, the cafeteria chef, early." Theo waved at the pasty-looking man behind the serving counter, his long, scraggly goatee clouded behind the haze of a hairnet.

He didn't wave back.

Maren wasn't surprised. After less than a day together, it was already clear Theo frequently had this effect on people. When Eartha had handed out the schedule that morning, Theo asked how settled she was on the loons being their spirit familiar ("I've always thought I was more of a capybara"). When Jo had led a tour through the auditorium and Black Box theater and backstage spaces, Theo tried to start a competition with the group on who could name the most songs about space ("*WIDE-OPEN SPAY-CEZZ!*" they sang—or really, howled). The rest of the morning was filled with the worst sort of camp activities and games imaginable: "dinner party," where Theo pretended to be murdered; "freeze," where they pretended to murder anyone they were in a scene with; and finally, "trust falls," where, unsurprisingly, Theo almost dropped Maren.

By the time the campers gathered in the cafeteria for

lunch, there was a wide berth around Theo—and Maren. Everyone seemed to have decided that Maren was Theo's best friend, a decision Maren hadn't had much of a say in. She couldn't help but feel the injustice of this. It wasn't her fault her bunkmate was so entirely, unapologetically themselves. At school, Maren had never been popular, but she had also never been unpopular; and being unpopular, she was learning, was very different from being invisible.

"Class selections," Mr. Cairn announced as he clicked his shining oxfords into the cafeteria while holding up a pile of papers. "Read the descriptions, turn in your selection here, and then report to the auditorium by one PM for the play read-through."

He dropped the papers on the table and stepped back as a bunch of kids hurried over to snatch them—Theo among them.

"What does he mean, classes?" Maren asked when Theo returned with an extra handout for Maren. "We have to take classes at camp?"

"Of course," Theo said, straightening their vest covered with sunflowers. "We get to pick three theater subjects to learn more about. Didn't you read the brochure?"

Maren looked down at her own paper to avoid answering. She didn't remember Hadley talking about taking classes but, based on the descriptions, Maren would make her choices based on what she *didn't* want to do. Musical Theater? Ms. Green, the pink-cheeked lady, was nice, but Maren would rather die than have to sing onstage for an hour each day. Acting didn't sound much better, and Directing was out, too, since Theo had already gouged a deep black circle around it on their paper. She was disappointed that

Costume and Makeup were put together—she might have been okay with costumes, but makeup? No, thanks. Movement Maren skipped over since she suspected she'd be getting way more of Eartha than she wanted, and Speech and Diction she eliminated because she had no clue what that was.

"Done!" Theo smacked their pencil down as if they had been taking a test, then leaned over to look at Maren's paper. "Hey, you should take Directing with me!"

"Maybe," Maren lied. "But you go ahead, I'm still thinking about it."

"Don't take too long," Theo warned as they stood. "I'll save you a seat for the read-through!"

Maren tried to smile, though it was probably more like a cringe. She dropped her head and took her time studying the rest of the page. She finally drew a soft circle around Tech. Building sets and working lights couldn't be too bad. After a moment, she also marked Theater History, which was taught by Jo. That left only one choice she hadn't decided against: Playwriting. Maren paused, her pencil hovering. She had never shown anyone the stuff she wrote before—not that she had ever written anything more than an odd scribble or two in her journal. What would it be like, putting her ideas on paper for someone else to read?

"Last call for lollygaggers," Mr. Cairn called, and Maren could feel his words hover over her. She hurried to circle Playwriting, then turned her paper in.

Maren had just pushed open the door to the auditorium when she heard an earsplitting scream from somewhere inside. Her heart exploded in her chest. Without thinking, she ran the rest of the way in.

The stage was still empty, but there were some kids already sitting in the auditorium seats. Everyone's attention was turned on—who else?—Allegra.

Of course Allegra.

Allegra stood in the front row and looked around, as if to confirm she had everyone's attention, then screamed again and pointed at—who else?—Theo.

Of course Theo.

"Miss Alvin, what on earth," Mr. Cairn said—much more calmly than he would have if it had been Maren screaming, she thought—as he swept out onto the stage.

"Theo said it," Allegra said, still loud enough for the entire theater to hear. She seemed both scared and satisfied. "Theo said the name of the Scottish play! In a *theater*!"

All eyes swung from Allegra to Theo. They tried to shrug but looked a little unnerved.

"She asked me what my favorite Shakespeare play was," Theo said. "So I told her *Titus Andronicus*, and then she asked me what my second favorite was, so I said *Henry V*, and then she asked me what my *third* favorite was, so I told her *Mac*—"

"You aren't supposed to say it!" Allegra cried. "You aren't supposed to actually say the *name* of the Scottish play!"

Maren had the feeling that getting Theo to say *Macbeth* was exactly what Allegra had been trying to do.

Mr. Cairn sighed. "Oh, not this again." He waved to the group. "Everyone! Come sit in a circle on the stage, please! Let's get this foolishness out of the way."

When everyone had gathered, Mr. Cairn took a deep breath, as if demanding patience from himself. "Theater people are, by and large, superstitious," he began. "And there are some who believe that saying the name of a certain play—a play by Shakespeare that we refer to as the Scottish play—in a theater is bad luck."

A few kids gasped, as if retroactively shocked. Theo shrank a little bit, a worried dip appearing in their brows.

"But keep in mind," Mr. Cairn went on, "that though there may have been *coincidences* in the past, there has never been proof of any so-called curse."

"Oh, if you're going to tell the story, do it right, Vincent!" Maren turned to see Jo enter, her broad face eager.

"I'll leave the honors to you." Mr. Cairn sighed again and crossed his arms, as if indulging a child, as Jo hurried to sit on the floor next to him.

"Well!" Jo sat and leaned forward, then made her voice softer: "It all began on the play's opening night, in Shakespeare's own time, on August 7, 1606…."

Supposedly, Jo told them, the boy who was going to play Lady Macbeth died unexpectedly backstage. People assumed it was a fluke, but mishaps kept occurring every time the show was produced. And then, in 1934, four actors who were playing Macbeth *died in a single week*.

"But why?" someone asked in a whisper. "Why is the play cursed?"

"Better ticket sales," Mr. Cairn said drolly.

"No one knows why," Jo answered as if she hadn't heard Mr. Cairn, then dropped her voice mysteriously. "But some say it's because Shakespeare put real dark magic in the incantations of the three witches, the Weird Sisters."

In spite of herself, Maren felt a shiver ride up her spine.

"And some," Mr. Cairn said, "say it's nothing but a hazing ritual to torture new actors."

"Oh, really?" Jo grinned. "I noticed *you* called it the Scottish play."

Mr. Cairn leveled a look at her that could have frozen Hawaii. "That is out of respect for people who are superstitious."

"Uh-huh." Jo smirked. "Well, out of respect for superstitious people, *whoever they might be*"—Mr. Cairn looked away haughtily—"we will, as a group, refer to it as the Scottish play whenever it comes up in conversation. That said…" Jo paused on Theo as she smiled around the circle. "No student has ever caused or been hurt by a curse at Goodman's."

"Of course not," Mr. Cairn added. "And no one has ever claimed *Twelfth Night* is cursed—in fact, it's one of Shakespeare's happiest comedies. So, now that these shenanigans have been dismissed, shall we begin reading it?"

"Absolutely!" Jo clapped her hands and dug her script binder from her bag.

Most kids began to follow suit, satisfied with the story, but some still looked worried. A few cast nervous glances at Theo, as if expecting them to burst into flames. Allegra wore an arch, knowing expression, while Theo seemed uncharacteristically subdued.

"Remember," Mr. Cairn said, "the parts will be assigned randomly for this reading and will switch with every act, so don't think that just because you're reading a character now, you're going to be cast as that person later, all right? Auditions aren't until tomorrow, people."

Finally, the mention of auditions seemed to drive away the last of the thoughts of Theo's mistake, and the students dove into their scripts as the reading began.

Maren hadn't been sure what to expect with the play, but she had to admit, *Twelfth Night* was—well, it was pretty wonderful. The story is about Viola, who washes up on a foreign shore after surviving a shipwreck that killed her brother. She hears of Duke Orsino, who is in love with the beautiful Lady Olivia. Viola, dressed as a man to be able to work, agrees to serve as a go-between for Duke Orsino to try to convince Lady Olivia, who is in mourning for *her* brother, of the duke's love. But Olivia instead falls in love with the disguised Viola, "Cesario," while Viola falls in love with Orsino, and—just when it seems there's no way any of them can be happy—it turns out Viola's twin brother, Sebastian, actually survived the shipwreck as well. There's a lot of mistaken-identity jokes, where people think Viola dressed as a man is Sebastian and Sebastian is Viola, but eventually they work it all out and Olivia and Sebastian marry so that Viola and Orsino are free to be in love.

Sometimes it was hard to keep track of who was actually who in the story, and sometimes it was hard to understand what was happening because the language was all poetry. But Maren found she was enjoying it. Reading Shakespeare was a bit like a mystery: She had to pay special attention to where the words were placed to understand what the characters were saying, and just when she thought she knew what was coming next, there'd be a twist and something else would happen instead. Plus, there were a lot of funny side bits, especially in the feuds and pranks played among the servants. One pompous servant named Malvolio got tricked into thinking Olivia loved him when her maid forged a letter in Olivia's handwriting. Theo read that part, and they were actually really good.

"*'To the unknown beloved.'*" Theo read Malvolio's letter in a pompous, nasally voice. "*'Be not afraid of greatness: some are born great, some achieve greatness, and some have greatness thrust upon them.'*"

Kids in the group laughed, but Maren sat up straighter.

Her so-called fortune, the one that had been in with her cookies, was a quote from *Twelfth Night*? What did that mean? Maren looked around the circle, but everyone else was still focused on the script. Maren looked back at the page and read the quote again: *"Be not afraid of greatness..."* The lines didn't make any more sense in the play than they had when she read the scrap of half-chewed fancy paper. What was the point of giving it to Maren? Had someone even meant to give it to her at all, or was it just an accident? Still baffled, Maren shook her head and tried to refind her place in the script.

The read-through took most of the afternoon, and when they were finally done, Jo asked what they thought the play was about. "If you had to summarize it in one or two words," she said, "how would you describe it?"

Maren, along with the others, stayed quiet. It seemed impossible to put a play where so much was happening into a few words.

"Comedy?" a third-year girl said finally.

"Con*fusion*," added a boy.

Everyone, including Jo, laughed. "Sure," she said. "There's a lot happening in the plot, and it's funny to see the characters so confused."

"I got pretty confused, too," the boy said, flashing dimples and a bright smile as everyone laughed again.

"There's time to work that out." Jo smiled. "What else is the play about?"

"Love," Graham said, promptly blushing as a lot of the group giggled. Allegra reached over and ruffled his hair as if he were a little kid.

"This play is absolutely about love." Jo raised her voice above the giggling. "Love in all its forms and love regardless of gender. Isn't it astonishing that in Shakespeare's day, he wrote a play where Viola dressed as a boy could attract the love of both Olivia *and* Orsino? Isn't it amazing the way the audiences just accepted the characters falling in love with who they loved, regardless of gender?"

No one said anything. A few campers seemed to be fighting back more giggles, but others were nodding along seriously—Graham among them. Maren remembered his two moms at the drop-off circle.

"And keep in mind," Jo went on, "this was at a time when all the characters, including the women, would have been played by male actors, so the gender-bending in this play would have been even more noticeable."

"Is that how you're going to cast it, too?" asked Allegra's friend, the rabbity girl, sounding nervous. "Gender...bent?"

"Of course," Jo said without hesitation. "I'll hear anyone read for any part, regardless of the gender of the character or the gender of the actor."

"Right on," Theo said, holding up the fist that wasn't already holding up their camera.

"Right on," Jo agreed, and raised her fist back. "So, back to *Twelfth Night*. Is there any other word we could use to describe what the play is about?"

"Grief," Maren said. She hadn't meant to say it, but suddenly the word was out of her mouth, hanging heavily over her. She could feel the stares of the other kids and wanted to slink into the shadows.

"Grief," Jo said, and she said the word tenderly, as if she were cupping it in her palm. "That's right, there's a lot of loss leading up to this play. Viola and Sebastian each think the other has died. Olivia's brother is dead. Orsino's love is unrequited. But there's more to it than just grief. Anyone know why it's called *Twelfth Night*?"

No one answered.

"It's for Christmas," Jo said, "the twelfth night of Christmas and a celebration of new birth. It's about celebrating in the darkest part of winter. So, yes, these characters have lost a lot. But still, they are finding cause to celebrate. The play might be about loss, but it's about *overcoming* loss. And finding new life afterward."

Maren could feel Jo's eyes on her, but she kept her gaze aimed at her script—kept it there until Jo finally announced it was time to break for dinner.

⤜⤏

Like Sebastian, Hadley hadn't died. She had only become unrecognizable.

After she left for college, things were a whole lot quieter. Suddenly, Maren and her mother were able to eat dinner and watch TV in the evenings without any arguments about who had or hadn't gotten their homework done. Maren and Ed went to movies that Hadley would have rolled her eyes at, and sometimes did puzzles or played games Hadley would never have had the patience for. Whenever Maren or her parents tried to call or FaceTime Hadley, she'd always say she was great—she was *great* but so, so, *so* busy—and hang up after five minutes. Maren missed her sister, but she'd be lying if she didn't admit that it was kind of a relief, too. It felt as if some part of her she had unknowingly been trying to keep small was finally able to stretch out.

But things changed again when Hadley came home for Christmas break. She seemed a little different—a little skinnier, maybe, her eyes a little less bright—and she slept a lot. Soon after, news came that Hadley had failed out of her college classes. She had just stopped going to them.

"I didn't see the point," Hadley said when their mom demanded an explanation. "I didn't see the point of any of it," she added to Maren later. "Everyone there was so competitive, so intense. They seemed to know everything already. I was hopeless."

"But you've always wanted to go to New York," Maren argued. "You've always wanted to be an actress."

Hadley just shrugged. "It wasn't how I thought it would be."

Maren had heard the word "depressed" before, but it was strange to associate it with someone like Hadley— someone who had always seemed so full of life. All spring, their mom scheduled appointments with therapists and psychiatrists during the day when she and Maren were at work and school. Hadley said they were helping, but eventually they learned this was a lie, too—Hadley hadn't been going to these appointments, either. When their mom yelled, Hadley shrugged and disappeared back into her room as soon as possible.

And maybe Hadley really had stopped seeing the point of anything, because, in the months that followed, she stopped *doing* anything. She stopped calling her local friends and going to plays and reading poetry books. She stopped getting dressed and getting out of bed. She stopped taking showers and coming down for meals. She stopped leaving her room at all.

She stopped being Hadley.

If Theo had been unpopular before the whole *Macbeth* thing, now they were downright disliked and avoided. Maren saw campers shooting them dirty looks as the group piled into the cafeteria, shaking off the first drops of the rain that had just started.

Theo, for their part, seemed unconcerned. "I think this will be the new focus of my documentary," they said resolutely as they stood in line with their tray, then turned their camera on Maren. "What do you think? Do you believe in the curse?"

"I don't know," Maren said nervously, ducking away from the camera lens.

Ever since the read-through, she had a knot of dread in her gut, a feeling something bad was going to happen. She tried to ignore it, but soon after everyone had gathered their food and sat down, Jo came in with a few of the other instructors. Every one of them wore an expression of barely masked concern that instantly set Maren on edge.

"There's been a slight change in the schedule," Jo announced, then waited as the chatter in the cafeteria slowly faded. "Because of the rain, the only activities we can offer tonight are board games in the library with Ms. Green—"

"Excellent!" Theo cried, even as most of the room started grumbling. They nudged Maren. "Want to play Clue? Dibs on Colonel Mustard!"

"Or," Jo's voice rose over the conversation in the room, "you may return to your cabin and remain there. I'm afraid we must insist you pick one of these two in case the weather worsens, and we will be coming by for bunk checks before lights-out. Thank you."

Without further explanation, Jo left, Mr. Cairn right after her with his usual brisk clip, followed by the other instructors.

"I should get seconds now," Theo said, and Maren nodded distractedly as they hurried back to the line.

"What's going on, Nic?" she heard a familiar voice ask behind her. She shifted slightly in her seat until she could see Graham, leaning across the table to talk to one of the girls in Allegra's clique, the bored girl now drawing a pentagram on the back of her hand.

"Allegra heard Mr. Cairn say that Miss Bradley is still missing," Nic said. "He said her car is in the lot, so she must be, like, wandering the woods or something."

"That's terrible," Graham said. "Do they think she's okay?"

"Who knows?" Nic shrugged as she circled the star.

"But Allegra says with all the instructors out searching, it's a primo opportuno to give the curse a Scottish Welcome." She raised one eyebrow suggestively and jerked her head to the side.

She was referring, Maren saw, to Theo, who currently had their camera trained on a group of wide-eyed first-years—interviewing the group for their documentary, or perhaps enlisting a board game team. Maren felt the knot in her stomach tighten. She wasn't sure what a *Scottish Welcome* meant, but she doubted it would be good. When she looked back, she saw some of the same fear on Graham's face.

"I don't know," Graham started to say. "With the rain and everything—"

But Nic shushed him, looking directly at Maren. Maren flushed, embarrassed to be caught eavesdropping, and turned back around just as Theo returned.

"Good news." Theo, carrying an extra plate, threw themselves back down next to Maren. "Chef Clarence is warming up to me—and to think, he was going to throw this out!" They gestured at the plate they had brought back, where sad, wrinkled carrot coins swam in watery tomato sauce. "Do you think they have backgammon? Maybe we can get a tournament going or something. What should we call it?"

"Actually, Theo," Maren said softly, "I think I'm going back to the cabin. Maybe you should, too."

Theo made an appalled face and swallowed. "And miss out on the Super Spectacular Best Backgammon Tournament? You can't leave! We have to!"

"I don't *have* to do anything," Maren said, feeling a

little testy. Why wouldn't Theo take a hint? Why did they keep insisting Maren wanted to do everything they did? Clearly, Theo thought the same thing about her that everybody else did: that Maren was "quiet," that she'd go along with what everyone else wanted. Before she could think better of it, Maren announced, "It's not like we have to do everything together."

Something in Theo's face closed, like a door swinging shut. Instantly, Maren understood that she had hurt their feelings. So much for speaking up for herself.

"I just meant," Maren tried to start over, "I just meant that I don't feel like games tonight, is all."

"Yeah, no, I get it," Theo said haughtily, stabbing at a carrot. "We don't have to do everything together. It's whatever."

"But"—Maren shot another quick glance at Nic— "maybe with the whole curse thing, maybe you should come back to the cabin with me."

"I said it's whatever," Theo said loud enough that others at their table looked over. "It's *fine.*"

Maren felt her face redden. "Well, *fine* yourself, then," she snapped, and gathered her tray to take it to the trash. If Theo wanted to get creamed by the mean girls, that was their problem. Maybe this way, they'd leave Maren alone, too.

⌇

The rain was really coming down as Maren ran along the path to the cabin. She kept her bag pressed against her chest, hoping her script didn't get too wet, but couldn't resist checking on it once she was finally inside. The little card slipped out of the pocket where she had been storing it and fluttered to the floor. Maren stooped to pick it up and studied it again. Now, standing alone in the empty, old, leaky cabin, she felt silly for thinking the card meant something important. It was just a quote from the play. Maybe it had been put there accidentally after all. Or, worse, maybe someone had heard about Hadley and was trying to cheer her up, as if the quote were the theater camp version of an inspirational poster of a kitten, telling her to *hang in there*. She sighed and shoved the paper back in the binder pocket. Who cared about greatness anyway? Right now, she felt anything but great.

She lay on her bunk and tried to read her script again but couldn't focus. The rain beat even harder. Why was she worried? Maren had tried to warn Theo, hadn't she? She had tried to convince Theo to come back to the cabin.

Yeah, sure, she thought guiltily. *You were really nice in your convincing.*

An hour must have passed before she heard the sound of footsteps pounding up the cabin stairs. In spite of herself, she felt relieved. Theo was fine, and Allegra was all talk. Maren snapped her binder closed and sat up, but when the door was thrown open, it wasn't Theo standing in the doorway, or even Lorna or Katie. It was Graham.

"Is Theo here?" he said between heavy breaths. There was rain dripping off his hair, and he had clearly been running.

For a moment, Maren could only stare at him in confusion. "Theo?" she managed eventually. She stood up and crossed her arms. "They're playing board games. Why?"

Graham's face fell, as if he were afraid of this. "See, there's this joke? With the Scottish play curse thing? That some kids do?" Graham said between breaths, sounding miserable. "Normally the cursed kid has to step outside the auditorium, spin around three times, quote a line from Shakespeare, and then wait until someone invites them back in."

"Oh, right," Maren said, guessing the obvious: "And then I bet no one invites the kid back in." Graham nodded and Maren rolled her eyes. What a dumb prank—and mean, especially in the rain. But still, it didn't seem that serious. "So Theo got a little wet," she said. "What's the big deal?"

"The thing is," Graham went on, "that by the time... someone did invite Theo back in, Allegra had taken Theo's camera bag and hidden it. And now Theo's out there, looking for it, and it's almost curfew."

"Well, Theo's smart enough to be back in time," Maren said. "I'm sure they're on their way."

But Graham shook his head. "Allegra hid it in the costume storage."

"So?"

"So, do you know how big the costume storage is? Or how long it'll take Theo to look through it? Or how fast Mr. Cairn will kick them out if he catches them there?"

Maren took a sharp breath. So it wasn't just a dumb prank after all. Allegra really was trying to get Theo kicked out of Goodman's. The thought made the place behind Maren's eyes feel hot and tight. "Right," she said, reaching for her flashlight. "Where's the costume storage?"

Maren ran down the path in the woods, cursing the rain smudging her glasses, the mud splattering her sneakers, and her luck. She was panting hard by the time she got to the outdoor amphitheater, where the path branched into several more paths. She followed a smaller one to the left, as Graham had described, and thicker woods closed over her, making it harder to see outside the narrow focus of her flashlight's beam. Maren expected Mr. Cairn to step out of the shadows at any second and haul her back to the cabin by the collar. Graham had promised to try to intercept him, but she didn't have high hopes about Graham's capabilities. He hadn't exactly stopped Allegra, had he?

Maren shook her head at herself. Just when she was starting to think Goodman's wasn't the worst place in the world, here she was, risking getting kicked out—and for Theo, of all people.

Yes, for Theo, said a surprisingly firm voice in her head. *The one person who's actually been trying to be your friend here, Theo.*

She forced herself to run even faster.

Eventually, there was a gap in the trees ahead of her, and she ran out onto a small patch of gravel. There she found a one-story building made of bland, gray cinder block with a heavy metal door. It looked a little like the bathrooms next to the cabins, except it had no windows. She went to the door and tried the handle. Unlocked. Carefully, she pulled the door open, the hinges whining a long, rusty squeal, and shone her flashlight inside. She felt her heart drop.

The inside was packed, floor to ceiling, with racks and racks and *racks* of clothes. In the entryway alone, she saw a rack of square-shouldered soldier uniforms, a rack of primly layered Victorian skirts, and a rack of wedding dresses, the clouds of white silk and tulle ethereal and eerie in the beam of her flashlight. When Maren stood on tiptoes, she could see even more racks: brightly colored zoot suits, flapper dresses dripping fringe and pearls, Greek togas, Dracula capes, and oh so many Elizabethan doublets. Even the walls were lined with overflowing shelves of stacked hats, shoes twinned up in cubbyholes, and belts draped or coiled like snakes. Near the ceiling, gloves dangled limply from a clothesline, waving slightly in mute applause.

Maren took a deep breath. She could look for two straight *years* and never find a camera bag in all this—or Theo, for that matter.

Just then, a deep voice came from somewhere inside the building: *"Stay where you are, if you want to live."*

Maren hesitated, then called out, "Theo?"

There was a surprised yip. A moment later, Theo appeared, wearing what looked like a pope's hat over a forehead flashlight. "Oh, hey, Maren!"

"Was that a movie quote?" Maren raised a hand to shield her eyes from the beam of Theo's headlamp.

"Yep, from the most famous auteur ever, Quigley Forrager, duh!" Theo beamed. "Hey, want to try on a banana suit?"

"We don't have time, Theo," Maren said—even as she wondered what a banana suit was. "Allegra's going to tell Mr. Cairn about us being back here, and if we're caught after curfew, we're definitely getting kicked out."

"A setup!" They fell into an accent again and raised their fist. *"Why, I outghta!"*

"We need to go now," Maren said.

But Theo shook their head, looking serious for the first time. "Not without my camera. I'd sooner leave my left arm."

Maren sighed. "Can't we just come back for it tomorrow? It's going to take us forever to find it in here."

"You think I don't know that? I've been hunting for ages!" Maren shook her head in exasperation as Theo started listing all the places they'd checked already—which didn't seem like many, given how they kept getting distracted by costumes. She looked around, trying to think of where Allegra might have hidden the camera. As full as the racks were, every single costume was hung on a wire hanger. Would a thin hanger be able to support a bag as heavy as Theo's equipment bag?

"—and then I got lost somewhere back by the giant monkey head," Theo was saying, "but it didn't have a body to go with it, isn't that weird? And then there's the dress with dinosaur spikes on the shoulders—"

"Listen," Maren interrupted. "I've got an idea of where Allegra might have hidden the camera, but if it's not there, I'm leaving without you. Okay?"

Theo shrugged. "An idea is more than I've got. Where to?"

"We need to look for a mannequin."

"You mean a dress form?"

"A what?"

"A dress form—or, a dress*maker's* form is the official name," Theo said pretentiously. "It's like a mannequin but for draping fabric when you're—"

"Sure," Maren cut them off. "Sure, yes, look for one of

those. Your bag is probably too big for a hanger. It'd have to hang off something bigger to support it."

"That makes sense! Onward!" Theo cried, and charged back into the racks.

Maren followed, though she tried to be more systematic. She thought of costumes that might be big and intricate enough to deserve a dress form. First, she checked by a rack with the wedding dresses, then a rack of astronaut suits, and then what looked like a yeti costume—but they were all strung on one or more hangers, no dress forms. Maybe it wouldn't fit in among the racks. She pushed her way toward one of the walls and began walking the periphery. The room got even more crowded the farther back she went, and darker around her flashlight beam.

Finally, at the very end of the row, she found what she was looking for: a headless, armless figure of a dressmaker's form, propped up at the end of a row of racks. Its back was to Maren, and she had to duck under a whole collection of tutus to get to it, but she finally managed to squeeze and climb her way over and spin it around. The form was wearing a silvery gown with lace sleeves. Draped around the neck, hanging in the center of the dummy's chest, was Theo's camera bag.

"Found it!" Maren cried.

Happy shouts rose in answer, though at the opposite end of the building. "Where are you?" Theo called.

"Here!" Maren shouted, then held the bag up and started shaking it. All the key chain flash drives clattered, and soon enough, Theo had followed the sound there.

"Oooooh!" Theo squealed as they took the bag and hugged it to their chest. "Thank you, thank you, *thank you*!"

"No problem," Maren said. She hesitated, then added, "And this evening, at dinner? I just wanted to say…"

"No problem," Theo said.

For a moment, they both just stood there, smiling at each other.

"We have to get back," Maren realized. "Before Mr. Cairn finds us."

"Right! Front's that way, I think—" Theo started, but their words fell off mid-sentence, their eyes suddenly wide.

Maren heard it, too, a sound that made her stomach drop: the front door squealing open, then the sound of fast pattering footsteps darting inside.

Without thinking, Maren grabbed Theo and dragged them to the nearest rack full of wide hoop skirts. Each ducked under one, huddling inside the layers of fabric. Maren flipped off her flashlight and Theo did the same, just as they heard the door slam closed.

Maren held her breath, her heart hammering in her ears. She waited, expecting to hear Mr. Cairn or Jo or even Allegra. But nothing happened. She could hear movement somewhere ahead of them, but whoever had come in wasn't saying anything. What was going on?

Just then, there was another sound: the hum of a car arriving, followed by the slap of a car door opening and closing, and feet on the gravel.

When the costume storage door squealed open and slammed shut a second time, Maren could have sworn she heard a muffled, frightened animal yelp somewhere nearby. *Did they bring dogs to find us?* she thought wildly. She tried not to breathe as heavier footsteps tromped deeper into the room. The heavy footsteps paused, and a moment later the person was whispering in a hushed growl. It was too low to tell whether it was a man or a woman, and, even stranger, they seemed to be making nonsense sounds.

They were speaking another language, Maren realized. Speaking another language *on a cell phone.*

She leaned toward where she thought the door was, straining to hear more. Her shoulder accidentally brushed against the dress she was under. The skirt rustled, and the hanger above rattled noisily on the rack.

Instantly, the person stopped speaking.

Through the thin fabric of the dress, Maren could see the beam of a flashlight jump to life, then watched in horror as its ray bounced around the room. She held her breath and cowered closer to the floor. Next to her, she felt Theo do the same, hugging their bag to their chest.

The footsteps began to move slowly and carefully through the room, the beam of the flashlight tracing arcs across the empty rows of clothes. Maren shut her eyes and hoped against hope that the flashlight wouldn't land directly on them. Would their silhouettes be seen through the skirts? Her heart beat faster. She didn't know why, but something told Maren that she and Theo were in a lot more danger than just getting kicked out of camp. The steps came down their aisle and stopped nearby. Maren took a chance and raised her chin a fraction of an inch off the ground, trying to get a glimpse of whoever was out there. All she saw was a pair of work boots, big and made from heavy, dark leather. The boots stood there a moment longer as Maren struggled not to move, not to breathe, not to panic, even as every nerve in her body was screaming.

Finally, the boots turned and walked back down the

aisle. Soon after, Maren heard the door slam shut, but she stayed huddled against the floor until she heard the car pull away. She waited a moment longer, then eased out from her hiding place. The room was pitch-black. She fumbled with her flashlight. The beam of light trembled when she finally got it on, and she was surprised to realize her hands were badly shaking.

"What was that?" Theo whispered from nearby, flipping on their headlamp and crawling out from under their skirt.

"I think you mean *who* was that," Maren said. She swallowed hard, trying to clear a knot in her throat. "Whoever it was, I don't think they cared about us being out after curfew. I don't think they were looking for us at all...."

Slowly, she spun her flashlight at the costumes around her. What had made that animal whimpering sound? And was it still in there with them? For a moment, all she heard was the patter of the rain and the harsh breath of the wind outside. Then there was something else, something so incredible and out of place that she had to look at Theo and see if they heard it, too.

"Is that..." Theo whispered, their face reflecting Maren's dumbfounded shock. "Is that *music*?"

Maren held a finger to her lips as her flashlight continued its course along the racks. Nearby, a row of sleeves seemed to be moving ever so slightly—as if someone was breathing behind them. Maren's heart pounded. She looked at Theo, then pointed at the rack of clothing and gestured that she was going to push it away.

Theo nodded, their jaw clenched, and joined Maren in position behind the rack, their hands out.

One, Maren held a finger up. *Two*, she raised a second.

"Three!" Theo shouted out loud, and together they pushed the rack away.

Maren screamed.

Theo screamed.

The old woman who had been hiding behind the rack screamed.

It was so confusing that Maren stopped screaming, and then Theo stopped screaming, and then even the white-haired lady stopped screaming. She wore a neon-yellow visor, a bright purple unitard, and green leg warmers, but her clothes were disheveled and streaked with mud. She fumbled with an ancient cassette tape player, the music leaking from the foam headphones before she managed to turn it off.

For a moment, they all stared at one another, mouths abandoned open.

"Please!" The woman found her voice first. "Please, you have to help me! Please take me to Jo August of Goodman's camp! I'm a teacher there. Do you know it? Are we still close?"

Theo and Maren shared a look of wide-eyed amazement.

They had found the missing Acting teacher.

Fifteen minutes later, Theo and Maren were standing in the entryway of Jo's house, dripping wet from the long walk in the rain. Jo was kneeling beside Miss Bradley, who was laid out on the living room couch, her visor pushed back so one hand rested over her forehead.

"I didn't tell them anything," Miss Bradley moaned softly, her eyelids fluttering. "Not a thing."

"There, there, Maxine," Jo said gently, though she seemed as baffled as Maren felt. "We've called your son. He'll be here soon."

"Not a hooting thing," Miss Bradley repeated as Jo adjusted a crocheted blanket over her.

A floorboard behind Maren creaked, and she jumped. An old man in a wheelchair was there, wearing a shirt buttoned all the way up and an ancient baseball cap. This was Jo's father—Lee, Maren remembered. Silently, he held some towels out to Maren and Theo, his arms shaking slightly from the effort.

Maren took a towel printed with faded poppies and whispered, "Thank you."

Theo only managed a jerky nod of thanks.

Lee wheeled past them to Jo and touched her lightly on the shoulder. Jo looked up. For the first time since Theo and Maren had appeared on her doorstep with Miss Bradley draped between them, Jo seemed to remember they were there.

"Theo, Maren, I'm so sorry," she said, standing. "Please, come in."

Maren took a few tentative steps deeper into the room, and a moment later Theo followed. Jo's living room reminded Maren very much of Jo herself: warm but a little messy, overflowing with books and mementos and pictures lining every shelf and wall. There was a piano in one corner, stacked high with sheet music, and a small fire crackling in the grate. Miss Bradley lay on the big, squashy, floral-print couch, so Maren and Theo each took a velvet armchair, having to shove some embroidered pillows out of the way first.

"I'm going to need you two to help explain what

happened," Jo said. Her voice wasn't angry but solemn, and she looked between the two of them with an intense gaze.

Maren took a breath, wondering where to begin.

But before she got a word out, she heard footsteps pounding up the porch, and a moment later a bald man wearing a beige raincoat over blue-and-white-striped pajamas threw open the door without knocking.

"Mother?" he called.

"Paul!" Miss Bradley said, raising her hand from her forehead and holding it out tremulously. "Here, darling!"

Paul hurried over to the couch, palming the rain from his scalp, and dropped to his knees in front of his mother. "Thank goodness! Where have you been? What happened?"

"I was just waiting to hear that myself," Jo said, turning again to Theo and Maren, but Miss Bradley's voice had returned.

"I'll tell you what happened!" Miss Bradley cried and struggled to sit up. "I was *kidnapped*! Taken against my will and thoroughly questioned!"

"Kidnapped?" Paul goggled at his mother. "Questioned?"

"They wanted to know about the ring!" Miss Bradley clutched at Paul with one hand and Jo with the other. "They wanted to know where the ring was hidden! They thought I knew because I've been here the longest, but I didn't tell them a thing, not a single hooting thing!"

Theo made a sound, and their hands twitched.

"Ring?" Paul seemed incapable of doing more than repeating everything his mother said with a question mark. "Hidden?"

"Did you see who it was, Maxine?" Jo asked calmly. "Did you recognize them?"

"I know *exactly* who it was!" Miss Bradley cried, her voice lifting to such a powerful shriek, the flames in the fireplace grate seemed to leap higher. "I saw the reflection in the light! I saw it as clearly as I see all of you right now." Miss Bradley took a moment to look around at each of them in turn, her round eyes red-rimmed and cloudy with age but filled nonetheless with a dramatic glint. "It was"— Miss Bradley dropped her voice to an impressive whisper and closed her eyes—"*Charlotte Goodman.*"

Whatever response Miss Bradley had expected from this impressive statement, it wasn't what she got. A very confused silence followed. Maren looked to Jo for an explanation, but Jo only raised her eyebrows at her father, who coughed into his fist.

"Charlotte Goodman?" Paul Bradley said, sitting back on his heels. "The namesake of the camp, Charlotte Goodman?"

"That's right." Miss Bradley nodded without opening her eyes, her voice soft. "It was Charlotte Goodman."

"Isn't Charlotte Goodman dead?" Paul said bluntly.

"That's right," Miss Bradley said again, her voice insistently ethereal. "Charlotte Goodman *is* dead."

The fire crackled loudly in the grate, and for a moment the atmosphere of mystery and suspense returned. Maren felt a chill ride dangerously up her spine, and Theo's hands twitched again.

But Paul Bradley gave a derisive snort. "So a ghost did it?"

Miss Bradley's eyes snapped open, her expression unmistakably annoyed. "Yes! Charlotte Goodman! She must have heard the camp is in danger of closing down!"

"What makes you say that, Maxine?" Jo said seriously.

"I know what Charlotte Goodman looks like, for heaven's sake, after working at this camp for how long! I saw her, she looked just like that."

She pointed to a picture on the mantel. It was another black-and-white photo—though this one was clearly from several years after the one in the auditorium, and much less formal. In it, two young women were standing side by side, their arms slung around each other. One of the girls had long, curly dark hair and a sweetly dimpled smile, while the other's hair was cropped short and she was wearing a plaid shirt with the sleeves rolled up. Even without being told, Maren knew instantly from her slight smile and the angle she held her chin that this second girl was Charlotte. You couldn't have called her pretty—in fact, you might have called her handsome—but there was something intense in her gaze that made Maren like her. She stared down the camera, her expression somewhere between challenging and mischievous, as if now eager to share a joke.

"She looked just like that," Maxine insisted again. "Just the same—with that short, wild hair and that boy's shirt. I'm telling you, she's trying to find the treasure before the camp closes and it's too late!"

"Oh, great, a teenage, treasure-seeking ghost kidnapped you." Her son turned to Jo with an impatient huff. "What is going on here?"

"I can't say I know about this kidnapping, but your mother is referring to an old legend about the camp," Jo began. "It goes back to when Rosalie Goodman Jacobs—"

"*Rosalie* Goodman?" Paul interrupted. "I thought we were talking about a Charlotte Goodman."

His mother shushed him.

"Rosalie was her sister," Jo explained, pointing to the other girl in the picture. "Charlie—that is, *Charlotte* Goodman—was a talented film director who died very young, in a fire. Her sister, Rosalie, founded the camp and named it after Charlotte in her honor."

"Oh. Sorry," Paul said, managing to sound not sorry in the slightest.

"By coincidence," Jo went on, slower now, as if she were weighing her words carefully, "another woman died in the same fire, a woman who owned a rather important piece of jewelry, a diamond ring. The ring was very valuable and belonged to a very important, wealthy family. They insisted that Charlotte had had the ring at the time, but it was never found in the wreckage."

"Fine," Paul said. "What does that have to do with the camp?"

"They thought Charlotte hid it here," Maren said suddenly. She felt everyone looking at her, but she didn't care. The mystery was lining itself up in her head, the pieces snapping into place. "People thought she gave it to her sister to hide here. Right?"

Jo nodded. "That's the legend, at least," she added.

They were all quiet a moment, only the fire crackling.

"Well?" Paul broke the silence. He looked at Jo first, then his mother. "*Is* there some sort of, I don't know, hidden treasure here?" Maren couldn't help but notice he seemed less dismissive of his mother's story now that there was the possibility of a payout.

But Jo shook her head. "My parents and I have been

here since the camp opened, when I was just a toddler." She gestured to her father, who sat impassive in his wheelchair, the firelight reflecting off his smudged glasses. "We've never seen or heard anything that suggested Charlotte or her sister hid anything here."

"But that's just not true, Jo!" Maxine insisted. "Your mother believed in the ring more than anybody! Why, in the last years of her life, she said many times that the ring was hidden in the theater! Tell them, Lee!"

Paul Bradley's eyebrows rose as he appraised the old man, and Maren saw Jo cast a concerned glance at her father, as if she expected the mention of her mother to upset him. But Lee only smiled faintly at Maxine Bradley, unbothered.

"See!" Maxine exclaimed.

But Jo's voice was firm: "My mother never claimed the *ring* was in the theater."

"But—" Maxine piped up, but Jo silenced her with a hand.

"And more to the point, my mother wasn't well during that time," Jo went on, her tone somewhere between pained and annoyed. "By the time she died, she was having trouble separating the past from the present, and reality from fantasy. After she passed, my father and I searched every inch of the auditorium, top to bottom. We never found anything."

"Then why did you pick *Twelfth Night* as the show for this year?" Miss Bradley jabbed a bony finger at Jo, as if she had caught her at something. "Why, if not because your mother said it was the key to finding the treasure!"

"Maxine, you know very well I picked *Twelfth Night* because it's the camp's sixtieth-anniversary year—if not our final year," Jo added with a sigh.

"Which is why Charlotte came back as a ghost! She was giving me a warning!" Maxine insisted. She had ripped her visor off her head and waved it to punctuate her point. "She's come to give us the ring just when her camp is in danger of closing!"

"And had to kidnap you to do it?" Paul said, his sarcastic tone returning.

Miss Bradley gave him a solid whack with her visor.

"Ow! Mother!"

"I'm telling you, it was the ghost of Charlotte Goodman!"

"Ghost or not," Jo said, raising both hands as if to separate Miss Bradley and her son, "it's more than possible that someone believes the stories enough to search for the ring. Maxine, you've been missing for over a day, so something's clearly happened. What's the last thing you remember?"

Miss Bradley shot her son a satisfied glare. Not even he could argue with that. "I was on the main stage," she began, and she draped herself languidly back on the couch. "I was doing my traditional pre-class dance when the ghost light started acting strange. I went to investigate, and suddenly the trapdoor opened and I fell smack right on through! That dark"—her voice dropped to a whisper, and she shuddered—"that dark, it swallowed me up. After that, it's just flashes. I remember a small room, and someone asking questions about the ring. Then I was alone, so I squirmed until I finally got free of the chair I was tied to. It was so dark outside, but I ran! I ran so far, through so much mud, stumbling and falling and running again, so very far...."

"Oh, I see," Paul said, his face clear with understanding. "I get it now."

Everyone looked at him.

He nodded definitively: "Head trauma."

Miss Bradley whacked him again with her visor.

"It makes sense!" he said, rubbing his arm. "You fell through a trapdoor, hit your head, and have been wandering around, insensible, ever since."

"Can we see your head, Maxine?" Jo asked.

Maxine looked flustered. "Well, there might be a bit of a goose egg...." She turned her head to the side. It was obvious, even under her white hair, that there was a significant bump. Paul just shrugged smugly.

"But there *was* someone," Theo piped up, their voice high and nervous. "Someone came into the costume storage, looking for her."

"The costume storage?" Jo's eyebrows shot up. "What were you two doing in the costume storage?"

Theo's mouth snapped shut again, but Miss Bradley had found a second wind.

"That's right! Witnesses!" she cried, pointing wildly at Theo and Maren. "They saw Charlotte Goodman, too! They saw her following me!"

"Theo? Maren? Is this true?" Jo asked.

Theo looked at Maren, their face pale, their mouth floundering.

Maren swallowed hard. "We didn't see Charlotte Goodman," she admitted, "but we did see someone." Keeping her gaze mostly on her lap, she told the story of going to the costume storage to find Theo's camera, seeing the boots come in and leave, and then finding Miss Bradley hiding.

"Someone was *hunting* me!" Miss Bradley said, triumphantly slamming her bony fist into the couch cushions when Maren had finished. "Searching for me after I made an escape!"

"So..." Paul said slowly, his eyebrows dipping in confusion. "So someone was after my mother after all?"

But this time, it was Jo who shook her head. "I'm afraid there might be an explanation for that," she said. "Mr. Cairn and most of the other counselors have been walking the grounds tonight looking for you, Maxine. Most likely it was one of them."

"Right." Paul's expression swung back to smug. "So there you have it. You hit your head, imagined a ghost, and were running from the people who were trying to help you." Paul sighed. "You're just too dramatic for your own good sometimes, Mom."

"But...but I know what happened..." Miss Bradley said softly, turning to each of them in turn, searching their faces, pleading for an ally. "I know it."

Maren said nothing. While there was no doubt in her mind that someone had been responsible for Miss Bradley's disappearance, she couldn't see how the ghost of the long-dead namesake of the camp could be involved. She felt Theo twitch next to her.

When Miss Bradley flopped back against the pillows again, it was without a dramatic pose. She looked, for the first time, as old and frail as she must have been. "I'm tired," she announced, turning away from them. "I need to rest."

"Sure, Mom," Paul said. "I'll take you home."

She let him pick her up, sagging in his arms like a wilting flower.

"You'll get someone to look at that bump, won't you, Maxine?" Jo said, following them to the front door. "Paul? You'll take her to a doctor?"

"Of course," Paul said, magnanimous now that he felt he had been proven right. "Thanks for looking after her, Jo."

Jo stood in the doorway watching them leave, raising a hand in goodbye as the car pulled away. She came back into the living room and fell onto the couch with a groan, rubbing her eyes. Her father wheeled over and dropped his veiny hand onto her shoulder.

"Can you believe it?" Jo looked at him and shook her head. She laughed a single, cynical bark. "The *ghost* of Charlotte Goodman."

Her father smiled. They sat like that for a long moment, something important held between them.

Theo twitched again, and it was enough to break the spell.

"Right." Jo took a breath and stood, smacking her thighs. "It's late. Let's let Mr. Cairn know you're safe and escort you two back to your cabin."

"Does this mean...?" Theo squeaked. "Are we not going to be kicked out?"

Jo studied them for a long moment. "I don't know how you managed to find yourself in the costume storage tonight. But I think, for now, we can just be grateful that you were there. And," she added, her voice growing even more serious, "I must insist you honor the curfew from now on. We believe in giving students freedom at Goodman's, but the rules exist for a reason, and if there's any truth behind Maxine's story..." Her sentence trailed off as she again fell into thought.

"Do you think someone really is looking for the ring?" Maren asked, the question slipping out before she lost her nerve. "Someone really believes it's here?"

Jo considered her, then smiled wanly. "Who can say what people believe in the theater?" she said finally. "We are a very superstitious bunch."

Charlie

December 24, 1944
Los Angeles, California

The black velvet dress was too short, too tight, and too hot for the LA sunshine, even if it was almost Christmas. It had a high lace collar that scratched at Charlie's neck and two flouncy sleeves that didn't quite make it all the way to her wrists. It had been a gift from her grandmother the year before.

"Aren't you going to say something?" her grandmother had said when Charlie lifted the dress out of the wrapping.

"Thank you," Charlie had said, but she quickly dropped the dress back into the box.

Her grandmother had merely sniffed and looked away, her mouth like the knot at the bottom of a wrinkly old balloon.

Now another year had passed, and it was almost Christmas again, only there would be no new presents this year. Their graceful, beautiful mother had died in a car accident—a tragedy, everyone said—and their father hadn't gotten out of bed for the past week. Rosalie was wearing a matching dress as she sat next to Charlie, their hands clasped tight together. Without even being asked, Charlie had put on the old dress that morning and told Rosalie to do the same. They were the only black clothes they owned anyway.

"Well, I suppose it could have been worse," their grandmother was saying, sitting opposite them. "None of Miriam's so-called movie friends could make it, I see, but at least we had a good, proper service, the way Miriam would have wanted."

She glared as if daring Charlie to disagree.

Charlie wanted to—the idea that her mother, who had never once taken her daughters to church, would want a funeral service that excluded her Jewish husband would have been laughable, if it hadn't been so sad. But before she could say anything, Charlie felt Rosalie give her hand a quick squeeze. *Don't make this harder than it already is*, the squeeze seemed to beg, somewhere between a warning and a show of allegiance against their grandmother. Charlie returned the squeeze and swallowed her words. She forced herself to look out the window at the street rushing by with the sunshine cruelly burning down, as if nothing had changed.

It was the thought of Rosalie—and their father—that had kept Charlie sane through that impossibly long, bleak day. Now they were finally being driven home, and Charlie could barely fight back the wave of engulfing sadness that had been threatening to overtake her all day.

She suddenly became aware of the radio—the driver was listening to the news, and the announcer was saying something about the war.

"Wait!" She jerked forward in her seat. "Will you turn that up, please?" she asked.

The driver reached a gloved hand forward and spun the dial. The volume slowly rose as the announcer's words washed over the back seat. *"It's being called the bloodiest battle of the war thus far,"* the announcer said, *"as our boys on the*

European front find themselves outnumbered by German forces at the siege of Bastogne. But even now, as a harsh and brutal Christmas dawns, the Germans find American stubbornness and courage a force to contend with. When they demanded Bastogne's surrender, one US general is said to have replied, 'NUTS!' "

"That is quite enough of that," her grandmother snapped. "There's no need to hear of violence *and* that language, thank you very much—and on the radio, no less!"

The driver turned the volume down again, and Charlie threw herself back against her seat. There was a tightness in her chest, and she wasn't sure if she wanted to cry or scream or break something. "I wish I were over there," she said softly. "I wish I could do something."

"Don't be ridiculous, child," her grandmother sniffed. "The front line is no place for a lady."

Charlie wanted to point out that the women in Europe had no choice but to be on the front line, but again Rosalie squeezed her hand. Resentfully, Charlie squeezed back. She pictured herself in the olive army uniform she had seen soldiers wearing before they were shipped out, hunkered down in the cold and firing at the Nazis. At least there, she could take this feeling and *do* something with it. At least there, she would be fighting for her country, her family, her life. . . .

She didn't even realize her grandmother was still talking until she heard, "Aren't you going to say anything?"

Charlie blinked at her. "What?"

Her grandmother inhaled and drew herself up in her seat. "*What* is very rude! You say, 'I beg your pardon' or 'Excuse me' like your mother's daughter should!"

Charlie set her teeth. "I beg your pardon," she managed.

"I *said*"—her grandmother resettled like a disgruntled hen—"I'm going to pay for you and your sister's private school tuition. Don't you have anything to say to that?"

Charlie forced herself to smile, to say, "Thank you."

She expected her grandmother to sniff and turn away, as usual. But instead, her grandmother snapped, "It's more than you deserve, wicked child."

Beside her, Rosalie shifted in shock. Charlie could only stare at her grandmother as the old woman's face flushed unevenly.

"You worried your mother to an early grave," her grandmother accused. "You and your father both. You think she would have been out that night, at some party with those wild friends of hers, if she hadn't had her Jew husband and you, you…*unnatural* child to drive her away from home?! She knew what you are, and mark my words"—her grandmother pointed a gnarled finger right in Charlie's face— "you won't be allowed to keep at it in Catholic school! No, little Miss, you will not! The nuns will beat it out of you if they have to! What do you have to say to *that*?"

There were many, many things Charlie wanted to say to that.

She wanted to tell her grandmother that there was a difference between manners and kindness and that, for all her grandmother had of the former, she would never know or have any of the latter. She wanted to tell her grandmother that she didn't care what the priest said about good and evil; in her book it was evil to refuse to let a man go to his wife's funeral because he was Jewish. She wanted to tell her grandmother that whatever she was giving them,

Charlie didn't want it—not her school, not her church, not her money. She wanted *nothing* from her grandmother.

But she could feel Rosalie looking up at her, Rosalie's hand tight in hers, Rosalie's silent plea that Charlie keep quiet. Rosalie's face was just starting to show the woman she was growing into—like their mother but sweeter, the hard edges softened by their father's kindness and by her own gentle spirit. Rosalie had many more years to go in school. What would it be like for her if Charlie told her grandmother exactly what she could do with her money?

All at once, the tide of sadness broke over her, drowning her anger in a wet blanket of sorrow. She swallowed hard. "Thank you," Charlie said.

Maren

"Someone is *definitely* searching for the ring, all right," Theo muttered as they fussed with arranging the five or six pancakes they had piled on their plate. "They kept saying, 'The diamond this, the diamond that, she doesn't know where the diamond is.'"

"All I heard was someone speaking another language," Maren said, then paused, her bagel halfway to her mouth. She realized it was a detail she had forgotten to mention to Jo, but since Jo didn't believe the rest of the story, it hardly seemed important to add now.

"They *were* speaking another language," Theo said. "French."

"They were speaking French?" Maren stared at them. "Wait, *you* speak French?"

"Not exactly, but I speak Spanish, and the word for diamond—*diamant* in French, *diamante* in Spanish—is pretty much the same. It sounds like the English word, too, if you know the context." Theo shrugged modestly. Their vest today was patterned in dancing vegetables—carrots, broccoli, radishes—which seemed to jig excitedly with the movement.

"Did they say anything else?" Maren asked.

"Not that I heard, but to be honest, I was kind of freaked out."

Maren nodded. "The thing that freaks me out the most is—"

Theo made a sound and shook their head, their eyes fixed over Maren's shoulder. A second later, someone clomped up behind them.

"Class schedules!" Eartha cried, throwing herself so enthusiastically next to Maren on the cafeteria bench that it jumped under them. "Looks like you both have Tech first. Want me to walk you over to the woodshop?"

"No, thanks, we'll be fine," Maren said, and she held out her hand to take her schedule.

"Oh, but!" Eartha held the paper out of reach, then gave a frazzled laugh, as if she had surprised herself. "I only meant, are you sure you don't want help? The woodshop can be kind of tricky to find your way around....No? Well, okay."

Maren and Theo exchanged a confused look as Eartha passed over their schedules and busied herself with the other papers in her hands.

"I see my other loons are in Movement with me!" Eartha said. "Perhaps Katie and Lorna would like to do some introductory chanting before classes start."

Maren watched Eartha hurry away. "Was she blushing?" Maren asked.

But Theo was already leaning over their schedules, comparing pages. "We're in Tech together, that's cool," Theo said. "But I have Costume and Makeup while you're in Theater History, and then you have Playwriting while I have Directing."

"Wait, what?" For the second time, Maren could only stare. "*You're* taking Costume and Makeup?"

Theo bristled. "Why shouldn't I? You think it's too girly for me?"

"No, I thought it was too girly for *me*," Maren admitted.

Theo relented with a laugh. "Well, I can't help it that I have impeccable fashion sense and skill with a sewing machine." They pointed at their vegetable vest—which, Maren noticed, even had vegetable-shaped buttons.

"You make those?" Maren said, impressed.

"Yep. My mom and I have been sewing since I was a kid."

"That's really cool, Theo."

"Thanks." Theo shrugged modestly. "Plus, in Makeup, we're going to work with specialty makeup—like, old-age makeup, monster makeup, fake blood and gore makeup...." Theo wiggled their eyebrows.

Maren laughed. "That sounds more like you."

"Right?" Theo crossed their fingers. "Here's hoping I get to make Allegra look like an old woman. Or better yet—an old woman zombie!"

Maren laughed again and glanced over at Allegra, who was still glaring at her cereal. She had nearly spit out her Cheerios when Theo and Maren walked in—Theo's camera held high to capture her shocked expression.

"Anyway, what were you saying?" Theo upended the syrup over their pancakes. "About last night?"

"Oh, right." Maren leaned forward and lowered her voice. "What freaks me out is the person was talking on a cell phone."

Theo frowned as they struggled to saw their knife through the fat pile on their plate. "What's so scary about a cell phone?"

"It means there's more than one person in on it, if they were talking about it on the phone with someone else."

"I didn't even think of that!' Theo's mouth fell partly open, and they used the opportunity to shove in a giant bite.

"Plus, we're in a dead zone, remember?" Maren went on. "Most cell phones don't work here."

Theo swallowed hard and said, "Of course!" They slapped themselves in the forehead, sending a spray of maple syrup across their neck and over their shoulder. "It sounds obvious once you say it," they added, wiping at the sticky spots with a napkin. "So we're looking for at least one person with a super-duper, spy-worthy cell phone who speaks French and wears big boots. But that could be pretty much anyone, right?"

"Actually," Maren said slowly, frowning at her bagel, "I think it was an instructor."

Theo's eyes widened. "Plot twist," they whispered, setting down their fork to grab their camera.

"Well, think about it," Maren went on uncomfortably. "Jo said Miss Bradley was last seen the day *before* camp started. It would have been pretty empty then. People would have noticed a stranger around."

"That makes sense," Theo allowed.

"And Miss Bradley said it was her tradition to dance in the auditorium—that means someone knew her well enough to know she would be there and set up a trap."

"And dress like Charlotte Goodman!" Theo finished excitedly.

"Well, maybe," Maren allowed, though privately she thought the ghost part might have been Miss Bradley's more-than-ample imagination at work.

"Um, about that..." Theo glanced around. "Should we

be worried about a pair of booted French mystery people coming and smothering us in our sleep?"

"I don't think so." Maren tried to sound confident, even though she had been wondering the same thing. "I mean, no one besides Jo and her dad and Miss Bradley and her son know we were there, right?"

A shadow appeared over her again. Maren glanced over her shoulder, expecting to see Eartha. Instead Mr. Cairn glowered down at her.

"Miss Sands," he said. "I see you have your schedule there. A schedule for a student in *good* standing at Goodman's." He leaned closer so only Maren and Theo could hear him. "Jo may have let you off the hook this time, but one more misstep and I will see to it personally that you both are packed up and sent off before you can say *iambic pentameter*. Do I make myself clear?"

Both Theo and Maren nodded mutely.

"Wonderful." He straightened. "Oh, and Templeton? I look forward to seeing you in Directing class."

Theo shrank in their seat as Mr. Cairn's large, highly polished shoes clipped away. Together, Theo and Maren shared a look as the reality of their situation crashed down on them: Even if the night before was still a secret from the other campers, the counselors would have been told. And if it *had* been a counselor who had kidnapped Miss Bradley— a counselor with large feet, no less—then they would know exactly what had happened. They might even be hoping for a chance to get back at them....

"I understand if you don't want to keep investigating," Maren said quietly.

Theo looked offended. "Are you kidding? It's the new

subject of my documentary!" They held up their camera like a defiant fist.

⁓

Maren couldn't help but feel jumpy the rest of the day as she looked at the adults at camp and wondered about them. Even if Mr. Cairn did seem like the best fit for a villain, he certainly wasn't the only one who could have filled the literal boots. The tech master, Bernardo Del Rio, was a large, bald man with a sprawling black beard. He wore a pair of thick safety goggles and kept his thumbs hooked in his suspenders as he rocked back and forth in his steel-toed boots.

"Welcome. I am Bernie," he said at the beginning of class, though Maren had to lean forward to catch his words. For such a large man, he had an incredibly soft and gentle voice. "If you're here, it's for Tech, and if you're here for Tech, then you're here to work. Understand?"

No one spoke.

"Good. Questions?"

No one raised a hand.

"Good. Then we begin."

As promised, Tech *was* a lot of work. They started by painting the backdrop a flat white and hauling lumber from the loading dock and then had to clean the dirty paintbrushes and sweep the floor—all of which was much harder than it sounded. Maren was exhausted at the end of the hour when she said goodbye to Theo and slumped to Theater History on heavy legs. The class was technically supposed to be in a rehearsal space, but no sooner had Maren arrived and taken a seat than Jo's head appeared around the door, surrounded by her normal halo of frizzy hair.

"The Greeks!" she sang. "They invented our idea of Western theater, and they didn't do it inside, so come on, today we're going to the amphitheater!"

Outside, the morning was bright and hot. As they walked down the path, Jo explained how the Greeks used to put on plays for the festival of Dionysus, where everyone wore masks and stood together in a chorus.

"Except for a man named Thespis," Jo said as she shifted to the side to let the group walk down the steps to the amphitheater, where the white stones gleamed like pearls. "He stepped forward and played a singular character. That's why actors are called 'thespians.'"

For the rest of the class, they took turns saying lines on the amphitheater stage, speaking a few words to hear the way the outdoor space naturally resonated. At one point, Maren noticed Graham standing nearby. He offered her a shy smile, but Maren looked away as if she hadn't seen. Even if he hadn't been the one to play the prank on Theo, he hadn't done much to stop Allegra, either. She didn't need him trying to be friendly now.

This class, too, passed quickly, but Maren hung back afterward, offering to help Jo carry her things back to the auditorium.

"How's Miss Bradley?" she asked softly as the rest of the class pulled ahead on the trails.

Jo sighed. "Apparently, the doctor says she's fine, but she's still shaken up. It's especially hard, at that age. I saw something similar happen to my dad a few years ago with his stroke. His body has mostly healed, and he can speak when he feels like it, but his spirit? That takes a little longer."

"Jo," Maren said slowly, "why *did* you pick *Twelfth Night*?"

Jo's face instantly went defensive. "I know what Miss Bradley thought about the play and my mother and this ridiculous ring." She couldn't keep the exasperation out of her voice. "But it has *nothing* to do with that. We picked the play because it was the first play the camp ever did, and because kids can stand for a little Shakespeare every now and again. Whether they think they want it or not."

Maren smiled, then had an idea: "You thrust greatness upon us?" she said as casually as she could, though she watched Jo intently. She still had no idea why the quote was given to her or what it meant, and Jo leaving it for her made as much sense as anything.

But Jo groaned—not exactly the response Maren was anticipating.

"Sorry," Jo said when she saw Maren's expression. "I just hate how that line is always taken out of context."

"What do you mean?"

"The idea that you can just have greatness thrust upon you, it makes it seem as if success is an accident or given to you by someone else," Jo said, with surprising passion. "It gives people permission to not try for what they really want."

"Why would people want permission to not try?" Maren asked.

Jo shrugged. "Fear of failure, maybe. Or fear of being seen. Or a desire, when things get hard and you do fail, to just give up because it doesn't matter anyway, you weren't meant to do something great if it wasn't thrust upon you."

Maren nodded automatically. They were quiet for a moment but for the sound of their steps landing on the dry summer grass.

"You know, Maren," Jo began again, and Maren could feel her eyes on her. "We have a counselor on call for the camp, if you ever need to talk to someone."

Maren looked at her, surprised. "What?"

"Well, with Hadley and now Miss Bradley, I just want you to know there's someone you can talk to about everything that's been going on, if you want." She looked a little flustered. "I'm here, of course, but I understand if you want to talk to someone else, a professional, instead."

Maren felt her face grow hot, though she wasn't sure if it was with tears or embarrassment. Just when Maren was starting to forget the raw ache of pain, someone or something reminded her of Hadley, and that she was always going to have her sister to live up to or against. "Thanks," Maren said firmly. "But I'm fine."

‽

Maren said goodbye to Jo when they returned to the auditorium, then headed to rehearsal room 2, where her Playwriting class would be. Maren was surprised to see it was set up almost like a classroom: There was a whiteboard along one side, but instead of desks, there was a circle of plastic tables with chairs. Maren took a seat in an unobtrusive corner, far from the whiteboard but not at the head of the circle, either.

"Don't you think it's weird we have classes at camp?" said a voice next to her. Maren glanced up and saw a boy in the adjacent seat, his face hidden as he dug around in his backpack. "It's summer. I didn't know I was signing up for summer school."

Maren opened her mouth to agree, but just then a

group of girls spilled in the door, doing what looked like a combination belly dance and mime. "Is there anything about this place that isn't weird?" Maren said.

The boy laughed. "Fair point."

Maren turned back to him and felt her cheeks flush.

He had smooth brown skin, high cheekbones, and a pair of dimples bracketing a luminously bright smile. She remembered him making jokes during the read-through. Now he held out a hand. "Sal," he said. "From New York."

"Maren," Maren managed, swallowing hard and trying to smile back with suddenly dry lips. "Boston."

"All right, East Coast, you can't be too bad." Sal flashed another megawatt smile. "How've your classes been so far?"

"Pretty good, just Tech and Theater History. You?"

Sal groaned. "I picked Movement. And that teacher? You know about her yet?"

"Oh yeah." Maren couldn't help laughing. "Eartha's the second-year girls' counselor."

"Ah, man! I just sat through an hour of trying to open my chakras with her!"

"What are chakras?"

"I don't know, but mine are *definitely* still closed."

Maren laughed again and started to tell him about Eartha choosing the loons as their spirit familiar, when she was interrupted by a high, girlish shriek.

"Oh, thank *God*, Sal!" Allegra slid into the chair on Sal's other side.

"Hey, what's up, Allegra," Sal said. "I thought you were taking the Acting class."

"Ugh, so did I!" Allegra looked around the room with

a vague sweeping glance, as if to confirm that there was nothing more interesting around before turning back to Sal. "But Jo just told us that Miss Bradley isn't going to be *up to the challenge* this summer." Allegra put five or six air quotes around the words.

"Seriously?" Sal asked. "What happened?"

"What happened is she's like a hundred years old? I mean, Miss B adores me, so I can't say anything, but Jo said there's no time to find a replacement, so the Acting students have to be split into Playwriting or Directing, and I'm like, I don't want to do either? But then I figured there'll probably be less *damaged* people in Playwriting." She paused only long enough to toss a flirty smile in Sal's direction as she wrangled a tiny journal with a fuzzy purple cover out of her bag. "It's got to be better than the Directing class anyway. That seriously psycho second-year keeps talking about how she's going to be the next Quigley Forrager, and it's like—"

"They're," Maren said.

Allegra looked at her as if for the first time. "What?"

"Theo uses *they*, not *she*," Maren said, then added, "As in, '*They're* still at camp, even though someone tried to get *them* kicked out.'"

Allegra smirked, but before she could say anything, Sal nodded. "Word. One of my cousins is trans, and we've always known she's a she, you know?" He shrugged lightly. "No big thing."

"Oh. Yeah." It was almost fun to watch Allegra's face as she struggled to find the right expression. "Totally."

The door slammed open and a man breezed in, papers

fluttering in his arms. He had a pleasantly scruffy look about him, with a crumpled plaid shirt, a slight beard, and hair that looked as if a painter had tripped mid-stroke—a wild dash swooped up and then in all directions.

"What is it?" he asked mid-stride. "What do characters in a play *need* in order to be strong and dynamic?" He turned when he got to the front of the room and looked at the class with good-natured intensity, pushing his sleeves up his arms, as if ready to dig into something.

"A name?" guessed a boy with freckles sitting across from Maren.

"A name?" The instructor seemed to be genuinely considering this. "People do need names—and mine is Monty, by the way—but do characters? Shakespeare sometimes has characters named ghost or captain or soldier, so maybe not. What else?"

"A character needs, like, to have a good character?" a first-year girl guessed shyly.

There were a few snickers around the room, and the girl slumped in her chair. But when Monty laughed, it was kind, as if she had been trying to tell a joke.

"A character needs character! That's totally right! But how does the audience know who a character is? What's the one thing we *need* to start writing characters?"

There were some other guesses after that: Characters needed love, characters needed families, characters needed to live somewhere. Allegra announced to the class that, as an actor, she wrote a full history for the characters she played, including where they had been born, what their favorite color was, and what their pet was named.

"That's great." Monty nodded amiably. "But an audience wouldn't want to sit through an entire history of a single character, even if your character has a neon-green hedgehog named Cuddle-butt."

Everyone laughed. Allegra smiled and started playing with her hair again. Apparently, she had moved on from wanting Sal's attention to Monty's in the blink of a cuddle-butt.

"You're overthinking it!" Monty said after a few more guesses. "You know this already, I promise. What do characters *need*?"

He looked right at Maren then—maybe because she was one of the few who hadn't guessed yet, or maybe because he knew that she knew the answer. And she did know. It was obvious, the way Monty kept leaning on the word "needs."

"Needs?" Maren said. She kept her eyes on Monty as she felt the rest of the class turn toward her. "Characters have to have needs?"

Monty smacked his hands together, then spun in a whirlwind and went to the whiteboard behind the table. "Needs!" he said over his shoulder as he scrawled out the word with a squeaky red marker. "If characters don't need things, they'd just mope around onstage. Instead, some characters *need* certain things, other characters *need* other things, and conflict is created. Go ahead and free-write for a few minutes about a time you needed something and couldn't get it—and remember, it's not dramatic to write about needing ice cream and then getting some. Write about something real, something big, something important."

Maren felt her stomach tense as she stared down at the

blank page in her notebook. What did she have to say that was real, big, or important? What did she need? Everything she could think of seemed stupid or too little to bother putting into words.

Then she thought about Hadley.

She let her pencil hover over the page for a millisecond longer before she wrote:

I need you to open the door.

She took a breath and studied the words, then let the pencil carry out a few more words, and then a few more. Something in her relaxed, like a muscle she hadn't even known was tense. Her memories fitted themselves into words and the words into sentences, and then, almost by accident, the page was almost full. She couldn't have said whether it was ten minutes or ten hours later when Monty finally clapped to call the class back to attention.

"So," he said and peered around at them. "Who's ready to share theirs?"

Now Maren felt as if her stomach didn't just drop—it fell all the way through the floor. She glanced back at the page and felt her cheeks grow warm at some of the words written there. She had forgotten that she was in class and had written as if to herself in her journal. There was no way she could read this in front of a roomful of people! What had she been thinking, writing these personal things down?

Unsurprisingly, Allegra's hand had flown up.

"Great! Come on up here!" Monty sat down and folded his hands, looking as if he'd never been more fascinated in his life.

Allegra walked to the stand in front of the whiteboard.

"'My Needs' by Allegra Georgina Alvin," she read,

looking up to smile alongside her name. She cleared her throat and began in a highly dramatized voice:

> *What I need most in the entire world is a new phone. I'm about to be in high school. In high school, things matter. People look at you and care about how you look. Right now, I have an old phone, and even though it's in an exclusive case my dad brought back from Japan, where he travels for business, I had this phone last year and people are going to notice if I have the same phone. I need a new phone and asked for one for my birthday. My mom said we'll go shopping when I get back from camp. The End.*

There was some applause as Allegra took an elaborate bow before returning to her seat.

"Great!" Monty said, taking his place back at the front. "So, what do we know about this character, who are they?"

"They're about to be in high school?" said the shy first-year girl again.

There were some laughs, but Monty nodded along. "Great point: This character is pretty young. What else? How would you describe them?"

"She's shallow," a boy said.

Allegra glared at him.

"Well, now, that's not fair," Monty said. "We all want cool new stuff, and phones are important to talk to the people we love. But why does *this* character need a phone?"

The class was quiet.

"We don't know yet," Monty agreed. "So that's your

assignment for next time, Allegra. Keep building your character, give them a strong reason why they need this phone—maybe to talk to their dad who travels internationally a lot, or maybe another reason."

Allegra gave Monty her best smile and nodded.

"Right," Monty said, "so who's next?"

Maren watched the clock as, one after another, most of the class stood up and read their monologues. She felt worse as, one after another, it became clear no one had written anything as horribly honest as hers. Most were like Allegra's—needing a good grade on a test, needing to get on the soccer team, needing their own room. The class talked about the monologues as if they were no big deal, as if there was nothing personal about them at all, and then Monty gave an assignment on what to work on. Nobody seemed upset or all that uncomfortable, but just thinking about someone hearing her monologue made Maren want to crawl into her backpack and disappear. The only one who didn't write about something stupid was Sal, but his made Maren feel even worse about hers in a different way. When Monty called Sal to the front, he bounded up without even his piece of paper.

"This is a poem," he said, "but it doesn't have a title yet. Okay, here goes." He shook out his shoulders, then launched in:

> *Teacher says to write about my needs and*
> *I think—*
>> *Hold still, got my fill*
>> *Plenty of pills*
>> *Rough to swallow*
>> *Feel so hollow*

Try to focus on tomorrow
But tonight
When I turn off the light
My thoughts chase my dreams away
When dreaming is the only place I stay
Maybe I use them up, just getting through
the day
    Can't fall asleep
    Can't count those sheep
    Maybe I'll just count my needs
    Instead

"Great work, and fantastic commitment to the performance!" Monty said as the class cheered. Maren expected Monty to say it was perfect and there was nothing they could do to help a monologue like that, but instead he asked the same questions, including who the character was and why they needed sleep. "*Specificity*, Sal. Give us a little more of the story." Monty grinned. "I think Shakespeare will be a great model for you, too—no one knows how to rhyme a story like Shakespeare."

Sal nodded and made notes.

"Right. Anyone else ready to go?" Monty looked around, his gaze landing directly on Maren. She looked down.

"Okay," Monty said after a moment. "Well, I think there are a few shy folks left, but maybe they'll share something next time. Have a good lunch, everybody."

There was a sudden scraping of chairs as the group got up to leave.

"That was *incredible*, Sal," Allegra squealed as she leaned closer to him. "Where did you learn to do that?"

"Thanks," Sal said. "There's a slam poetry club at my school. I got really into it last year."

"You going to lunch?" Allegra said, standing. "We can walk there together."

"Yeah, okay, cool," Sal said, and he slid the rest of his stuff in his backpack. "Maren, you in?"

"She can meet us there," Allegra said before Maren could answer. She slipped her arm through Sal's and practically hauled him out the door. "I'm sure you're going to get cast *majorly* in the play—maybe you'll even be Orsino."

Maren waited until they were gone, then ripped the page out of her notebook and folded it into a teeny-tiny square, and shoved it in her pocket. Tomorrow, she promised herself, she would write about something small and dumb so no one would know what a terrible person she was.

"So you're Maren?" She turned to see Monty packing up an ancient, battered leather bag. "The kid who helped Jo find her phone?"

Maren felt her face burn. "Yeah, I guess."

"Huh. Good to know." He squinted and seemed to study her. "How long did you know the answer was *needs* before you spoke up?"

"I don't know," Maren lied.

"Sure you do," Monty said as he straightened and headed for the door. "Next time, don't make me work so hard, okay?"

He shot her a grin on his way out.

"Auditions!" Mr. Cairn trumpeted when the campers had all gathered in the auditorium after lunch. He gestured to the plastic tables set in the front row, laid with several stacks of papers. "Select a side, study it, and we'll call you in to read for us alphabetically."

"What are sides?" Maren whispered to Theo as the others surged forward and scrambled for the papers. To no one's surprise, Allegra was at the front of the group.

"Just parts from the play you read for your audition," Theo explained as they joined the back of the line. "Who do you want to be?"

"Haven't thought about it," Maren said honestly. After everything that happened with Miss Bradley, auditioning for some play had been the furthest thing from her mind.

"I'm hoping to play to my comedic strengths." Theo bounced on their toes, making the vegetables on their vest dance. "Like maybe Sir Toby or Sir Andrew or Malvolio. Hey, you should audition for Maria! Then we'd be in a lot of scenes together!"

"Maybe," Maren said. The character Maria was funny, and being onstage with Theo would be better than being onstage *without* Theo. But still, if Maren absolutely had to pick a character she wanted to be, if she absolutely had to say the character that felt the most like her...

When she got to the front of the line, she picked up the side marked *VIOLA*.

Theo raised their eyebrows.

"It's just for the audition," Maren said defensively. "It's not like I actually want to be a lead or anything."

"Hey, it's cool," Theo said, and that was all they said.

The two of them followed the others out to the hall-way, where they would practice and wait to be called in to read on the stage. Theo immediately sat against a wall and started muttering their lines under their breath. Maren joined them and looked over her page, trying to focus. The Viola monologue was the moment when Olivia sends a ring after Viola, and Viola knows Olivia has accidentally fallen in love with her.

VIOLA:

I left no ring with her. What means this lady?

Fortune forbid my outside have not charm'd her.

She made good view of me; indeed, so much

That, as methought, her eyes had lost her tongue,

For she did speak in starts distractedly.

She loves me sure; the cunning of her passion

Invites me in this churlish messenger.

None of my lord's ring? Why, he sent her none.

I am the man. If it be so—as 'tis—

Poor lady, she were better love a dream.

It was interesting, Maren thought, that there was a ring in the play and the legend of the ring at the camp. Maybe that was why Miss Bradley had thought the play was some sort of key? Maren read the monologue a few times, enough that she memorized it, but couldn't see how it had anything to do with the camp or a ghost. Still, she mouthed the words "she were better love a dream," liking the way they bounced in drumbeats off her tongue. About half an hour later, Mr. Cairn came out and announced they were about to get started.

"When we call your name, line up against the wall." He checked his clipboard. "Up first: Alvin, Axley-Hemple, Berrington, and Cagney."

"Break a leg, Grahamie," Allegra said to Graham as he got in the line behind her.

Graham muttered something and looked at his feet.

"Why do people say 'break a leg' in the theater?" Maren wondered aloud.

Theo said, "It's another superstition, to say the opposite of what you mean. Which reminds me: *Hey, Allegra!*" Everyone's gaze went to Allegra, who turned and glowered at Theo. *"Good luck!"*

The afternoon seemed to go very slowly and very quickly at the same time. Every few minutes, Mr. Cairn would come out and call a few more names to wait backstage. They returned one by one—some looking satisfied, even smug, while others pushed through with lowered or teary eyes, looking upset. In spite of repeatedly telling herself she didn't care, Maren started to feel nervous.

Finally, Mr. Cairn came out and called, "Richards, Roberto, Sands, Tan, and Templeton." Maren and Theo stood and lined up with the others.

"Wait here," Mr. Cairn instructed when they got backstage. "We'll call you one at a time." He walked back into the audience.

Moments later, "Ramona Richards" was called, and a very tall Ramona Richards walked out onstage, her legs trembling like a newborn fawn. Soon enough, she was hurrying back past them and Mr. Cairn was calling, "Emil Roberto." A boy with a very stretched-out shirt collar loped onstage. Emil Roberto took a little longer—they had him read the monologue he had chosen and then read a second monologue they assigned to him. He looked pretty confident when he was finally released and breezed by Maren just as she heard "Maren Sands!"

Maren took a deep breath and started across the stage but stumbled mid-step. In the front row of the audience, a whole group of instructors sat—not just Jo and Mr. Cairn but also Eartha, Ms. Green, Ms. Casta, and Monty. Eartha gave her an encouraging smile as Maren tried to refind her footing. Her heart now beating uncomfortably hard in her throat, she finished walking to center stage, then lifted her paper and opened her mouth.

"Say your name and who you're reading first," Mr. Cairn said, just when Maren had taken a breath.

"Oh, Maren? I'm Maren Sands?" She looked down at her side, feeling foolish. "And I'm reading Viola."

Jo nodded and gestured for her to go ahead. Maren raised her paper again—not because she needed it so much but because she didn't want to look at them. She took a breath and started talking. She tried to speak slowly and steadily, to make sure each point was clear and the poetry came through, but her nervousness tripped her up and made her go too fast. The words sounded flat and wooden, and before she knew it, it was all over.

"Great, thanks, Maren," Jo said.

Maren nodded and turned to go, her face flushed.

"Just a moment," she heard, and looked back to see Monty raising a hand. He smiled up at her. "Maren, I was wondering if maybe you'd read something else for us really quick?"

"Okay," Maren said, thinking of Emil having to do the same before her.

"Something, maybe, you wrote yourself?" Monty said.

Maren felt as if all the air had been sucked out of the room.

"Maren wrote a monologue today in Playwriting class," Monty explained to the other teachers. "I thought maybe she'd be willing to read it to us now."

The other teachers looked at her expectantly.

"Go ahead, Maren," Monty insisted. "It doesn't have to be perfect. Let's hear it."

She had no choice. Miserably, Maren dug the paper out of her pocket. Her fingers trembled as she unfolded the page, and then the words poured out:

> *I need you to open the door.*
> *I come home from school and I know you're*
> *there. But you're not in the living room watching*
> *TV. You're not in the study on the computer. You're*
> *not in the kitchen, making us a snack of apple*

slices and peanut butter sprinkled with cinnamon,
the way you used to do, because the cinnamon is
a little bit of extra magic. You're not doing any of
the things you used to do.

You're in your room, with the door closed.
You're always in your room, with the door closed.
If I knock, the way I used to knock, you
wouldn't tell me to go away or that you're busy.
You probably wouldn't even look at me. You'd just
stay there, in your bed.

Whatever door you've closed isn't just to your
room. It's to the rest of you. And you don't care
that I need you to open it.

I walk by your closed door, going to my own
room. Fine, I think, and I close my door, too.

There was silence in the auditorium when she was done. Maren folded the paper back up and, without looking at any of them, turned and walked quickly off the stage.

"How'd it go?" Theo asked. Their eyes got wide as Maren pushed past. "Are you crying?"

Maren just shook her head and plowed on, hopeful Theo would understand it wasn't about them. She hustled out to the hall and grabbed her bag, then ran, as fast as she could, outside.

Maren barely looked up from her feet running along the path, but her feet, thankfully, seemed to remember the way back to her cabin, and thankfully she didn't see any of the other campers along the way.

It's not so bad, she tried to tell herself when she reached the path for the girls' cabins. *You didn't want to be in the play anyway... did you?*

Whether she had wanted to or not, it didn't matter now. She knew her audition hadn't gone well from the start, but having to read her monologue in front of a bunch of people who knew Hadley—they'd never see Maren as anything but a pitiful younger sister now.

At this very moment, Hadley was checked into a special clinic, where she would stay and get treatment for her depression. Their mom spent every evening with her, and sometimes she and Ed and Hadley all went to a "family counseling session." Her mother had told Maren this as if that word, "family," didn't include her. Both her parents said this was a good thing—that Maren didn't need to worry about Hadley, that Maren should be grateful because now Hadley could work through her issues with a professional, that Maren should celebrate Hadley was on her way to getting better.

But Maren didn't feel so celebratory. As much as she tried to feel grateful that Hadley was getting the treatment she needed, Maren still couldn't help but actually feel... angry. She was angry at Hadley for disappearing into herself. Angry at Hadley for not asking for help sooner, and angry at herself for not realizing her sister *needed* the help. And, if she was honest with the deepest, darkest, most selfish place in herself, she was angry that, just when Maren should have finally been allowed to explore what she wanted, just when she should have finally had the time and attention of their parents, Hadley took it all back and Maren got shuffled off here, to Hadley's old camp, where everyone already knew her and everything was already claimed by Hadley.

Maren had finally reached the girls' cabins. She wanted nothing more than to climb into her bunk and pull a pillow over her head and pretend like she had never heard of Goodman's... but something made her pause on the path. There was a rustling sound of footsteps moving through the leaves on the far side of the cabin, but Maren couldn't see anyone.

"Hello?" she called.

There was the sound of some more footsteps, and she expected Lorna and Katie or even Graham to come around to the front. But no one came. Maybe it was another prank, Maren thought—maybe Allegra was crouched back there, with rabbity Piper and bored Nic and all the other wannabes, holding their hands over their mouths and trying not to laugh. Well, if they thought they could mess with Maren, they had picked the wrong day. Before she could change her mind, Maren took a breath and ran around to the other side of the cabin.

No one was there.

From deeper in the woods, she heard the crack of a twig, the trill of insects, the wavering notes of birdsong. She squinted into the underbrush but saw nothing. *Maybe it was a squirrel*, she thought. She almost made herself believe it, but then she looked down and saw a fresh footprint in the mud—patterned like a running shoe or a sneaker, with a design along the bottom.

But whose was it?

On instinct, Maren raced around the front of the cabin again, pounded up the steps, and burst through the door.

The cabin, too, was empty, but there was a charge in the air, a swirl to the dust motes. Someone had been there a moment before—she was sure of it.

But who? And *why*?

Quickly, she looked around the room to see if anything was different. Her eyes caught on her dresser. There was something small and white with gold around the edges sitting on the top. Slowly, she walked over and picked it up. It was an envelope—made out of the same paper as the card that had been in her cookies—and Maren knew immediately that the two were a matched set. Hands trembling, she picked up the little envelope and turned it over. On the back was some writing in the same fancy cursive scrawl, and as soon as she read the words written there, she understood:

There *was* a ring.

The play *was* the key.

And someone, for some reason, wanted *her* to find it.

Wear this jewel of me

Charlie

October 26, 1947
Los Angeles, California

Charlie was stretched out on the living room floor, listening to an advertising jingle on the radio. One hand was idly plucking at a stray thread along the bottom of her blouse, which she had already untucked from her uniform skirt. Her knee socks lay in a crumpled heap next to the saddle shoes she had stomped out of without bothering to untie, and her toes were still wiggling, as if trying to soak up the freedom.

On the couch sat her younger sister, Rosalie, her blouse still tucked in, her knee socks still up to her knees, her feet daintily crossed at the ankle. Their father was also sitting on the couch, though he was almost hidden under layers of blankets. Every now and then, the whole pile would shudder with a cough and Rosalie would reach over to fuss the corners back into place.

A commercial for baking soda ended, and the radio program began. Charlie's breath caught as she heard the gruff voice of the announcer insisting, *"Hollywood Fights Back!"* followed by a dramatic blast of drums and horns. She felt a shiver of excitement run down her spine. This was happening for real, right now.

One by one, famous movie stars and directors came on and introduced themselves:

This is Judy Garland.
This is John Huston.
This is William Holden.
This is Lucille Ball.

"Ah yes," their father said. He raised a finger from his blanket nest, and a sharp grin flashed out from his sallow face. "Now they will listen to the lovely Lucy. She will tell them why what they are doing is no good."

Charlie smiled and spun the dial to turn the volume up. Even though she hadn't met Lucille Ball on the set of *Dance, Girl, Dance*, she had always felt proud knowing that the actress had been in the same space and worked on the same movie as her parents. There was even a scene where her mother danced in a chorus line behind the redheaded star.

"All of us agree that the Constitution of the United States must be defended," Lucille Ball said over the radio. *"But the way to do this is not by shutting up the man you disagree with. You must fight for his right to speak and be heard. All civil liberties go hand in hand, and when one goes, the others are weakened."*

"Hear! Hear!" their father cried, before falling into a hacking fit.

The radio program lasted half an hour, with even more stars coming on. They all spoke about democracy and freedom of speech, and how the House Committee on Un-American Activities was wrong in conducting hearings against accused Communists in Hollywood. Charlie nodded along so much that, by the end of it, her neck was sore. She glanced back at their father and saw he was smiling. He didn't know any of the Hollywood Ten personally, but he had more than a few friends who had been let go from the studios due to suspicion of so-called "Communist activities." They weren't really Communists, he explained, but they were fired because they were in the labor unions and wanted fair pay. Or because of their foreign accents.

The program ended, more commercials started up, and Charlie turned the radio off. She rolled over on her back with a satisfied sigh. "That'll show 'em," she announced to the ceiling.

"Yes," their father agreed. "The Congress cannot help but listen to all these important and valuable people now."

"But Papa," Rosalie said carefully, her big eyes even bigger with worry. "If the Communists are bad…I mean, if they're trying to bomb us…then *shouldn't* they leave the country?"

"Didn't you just hear the program?" Charlie glared at her sister. "These hearings aren't about Communists, they're about free speech!"

"Communist, not Communist, that's not the point." Their father shook his head seriously. "The point is that this is America, and in America you are allowed to believe whatever you want to believe."

"Still," Rosalie muttered, and tugged nervously at her hair.

Charlie's heart sank. If someone like Rosalie—who was as good-hearted as they come—still wasn't convinced that the House Committee on Un-American Activities hearings were wrong after a string of movie stars explained it to her, then what hope was there for the rest of the country?

Their father hacked carefully into a handkerchief, then cleared his throat. "When I first came to this country," he said, "one of the first things I see and hear was a man in a bar criticizing the president. I could not believe this— an ordinary man in an ordinary bar, openly criticizing the leader of the country? I was so scared for him! But you know what happened to this man?"

Rosalie shook her head.

"*Nothing*," her father finished. "Because that man is allowed to think what he want and say what he want here. The Communists, they might think differently than us, they might say things we disagree with, but if we take that away from them, what will stop others from taking it away from us? We cannot be so quick to trade this freedom to think and say what we want." He got a distant look in his eyes. "May you never know what it's like when you don't have right to speak or think."

Rosalie blushed, and even Charlie looked away. As a child, Charlie hadn't understood why her father moved to America, but now they both knew that their father had been incredibly lucky to leave Europe. After the war began in 1939, he had tried to help his two brothers and their families get out, but they hadn't been so lucky. They all died in the concentration camps.

Rosalie went into the kitchen to begin fixing dinner. Charlie flopped back with another sigh, but this one was less satisfied. The war had ended two years before, but she had never stopped wishing she could have been one of the young soldiers to land on the beaches of Normandy, or to ride onto the streets of Paris, or to liberate the concentration camps. Whenever she felt scared or helpless, she'd imagine herself in that olive uniform ... only to realize how silly she was, wanting to fight in a war that was long over.

"I wish I could have been born earlier," she said to the ceiling. "I wish I could have been there, fighting." What she really meant was *I wish I had been born a boy.* Or maybe just *I wish I could be the way I see myself.*

Her father was quiet a moment, perhaps understanding.

"My Charlie," her father said again, and there was a soft ache in his voice. "I think there will be many battles left for you yet."

Maren

June 2015
Stonecourt, Massachusetts

"Okay, let's just say the quote is a clue to finding the ring. Who do you think gave it to you?" Theo asked the next morning at breakfast. They were wearing a vest with a lot of little cactuses—or, cacti?—and they were managing to leverage spoonfuls of oatmeal up with one hand while the other kept their camera trained on Maren. "And why?" they added after they swallowed.

"I don't know," Maren said honestly. "Maybe it was someone who knew I was good at finding stuff, who heard about me and Jo's phone or you and your camera case. Maybe they need help." She knew she was reaching, but she also knew, without being able to explain exactly why, that she was right: The quote was a clue to finding the ring. And someone wanted her to find it.

"You think it was Jo, then?" Theo asked.

Maren shook her head. "Couldn't be. She and a bunch of the others were in auditions. It also couldn't have been Eartha, Ms. Green, Mr. Cairn, Ms. Casta, or Monty, either."

"It could have been Bernie or one of the tech crew, I guess," Theo said. "Or, what about Jo's father? He was there the night we found Miss Bradley—maybe he left it!"

But Maren shook her head again. "I saw a footprint, not a wheelchair tire mark."

Theo groaned. "Why do things only seem obvious once you say them?"

"And besides, the clue itself said—" Maren started, but something a few tables down caught her eye.

Allegra was pretending to cry fat, ugly sobs, while her minions giggled and kept flicking glances at Maren. Graham was bent so close to an orange he was peeling, his nose was practically touching it. Maren looked away and ground her teeth. She hadn't told anyone, not even Theo, the real reason she had been crying—about having to read the monologue she had written. It was easier to let them think she had just been embarrassed by her audition. Or at least it had seemed easier, before Allegra found out.

"Forget about them," Theo said under their breath. "It's just to get back at us."

"I know," Maren said. She pretended to focus intently on stirring her oatmeal. The raisins looked like little crawling beetles.

"Plenty of kids have bad auditions," Theo went on. "And it's not like you wanted a role anyway."

"Theo, I *know*," Maren snapped. "Can we please just drop it and get back to the clue!"

"Okay, okay," Theo said. "Are you going to eat the rest of that?"

Maren slid over the solidifying remains of her oatmeal, beetle-raisins and all.

"So," Theo said as they dug in, "what do you think the clue means? All that about greatness, I mean."

Maren didn't answer right away. The truth was, even if the envelope referenced a jewel, Maren had no idea what the quote about greatness on the earlier card meant. But she didn't feel like admitting that to Theo right then. "The word 'thrust' is underlined," she said, remembering. "That's probably important."

To her surprise, Theo snickered. "Yeah, but isn't it like..." They made an embarrassed face. "A dirty joke? You know, *thrust*." Theo wiggled their eyebrows lewdly.

"I don't think someone gave me a dirty joke for a clue," Maren said, hoping her voice was as icy as she was aiming for.

"Well, it's a joke in the play anyway." Theo shrugged. "You know what I think?" they said, now scraping up the last of Maren's oatmeal—it was amazing, really, how fast and thoroughly they could eat. "That clue is just clueless."

Maren avoided Theo during Tech class after that, even though she privately agreed: If it was a clue, it was remarkably empty of help. Maybe that was why someone gave it to her in the first place—it was a mystery they couldn't solve themselves. She kept zoning out in Theater History, where Jo was talking about commedia dell'arte masks, and got to Playwriting early.

"What's up, Boston?" Maren felt a jolt as Sal took the seat next to her. "You all right? Didn't see you at dinner last night."

Maren gave him a look. "You mean you heard about my audition."

Sal nodded, but thankfully his face was free of pity. "So what happened?"

Maren hesitated. She hadn't told anyone at camp about Hadley yet, much less shared the monologue she wrote, but looking into Sal's warm brown eyes, she found she wanted to.

"Today's the day!"

Maren and Sal both jumped as Allegra dropped into the seat on his other side.

"The day for what?" Sal asked.

"Um, casting? Only like the most important day of the entire summer?"

"Really? I would have thought the show was the most important day," Sal teased.

"O-kaaaaay." Allegra rolled her eyes. "The second most important day. What role are you hoping to get?"

"I auditioned for Feste," Sal said.

"Feste? You mean the *fool*?" Allegra looked at him in shock.

"That's the joke, though, see. He's the 'fool' because that's like his job, but really he's the smartest, savviest character in the whole play. He's the ultimate player!"

"I guess," Allegra said, sounding unconvinced.

"Plus," he added, turning to Maren, "he's the one with the songs. I asked in my audition if it'd be all right for me to rap them."

"Cool," Maren said.

"I love rap!" Allegra quickly leaned forward to regain Sal's attention.

"Really?" Sal said. "Who are you into?"

Allegra's smile turned stiff, but she was saved from answering as Monty swept into the classroom with his usual whirlwind. Maren felt a heavy, sickening thud in her gut. Would he make her read her writing again? What if she cried—in front of everyone?

"Conflict!" Monty announced, attacking the white-board with a marker and writing the word there. "So far, you've written for one person, with one need, telling their side of a story. But if two people want different things and are in conflict about it, there's the question of who's going to get what they want." He dropped his voice to a whisper. "And that's called..."

Maren felt the whole class leaning forward, waiting, and then waiting a moment longer. Monty opened his mouth, closed it, grinned, opened it again...then turned and wrote the word "SUSPENSE" on the board. Maren laughed with the rest of the class.

"Okay, freewrite—start a scene where two characters have separate needs and this creates the conflict. Remember, there's more than one side to every story."

There was a flurry of papers as everyone set to work. Maren had just put her pencil to the page when she heard Monty add, "You can use the character you've already created in your monologue or create two new characters."

Without meaning to, Maren looked up at him, and their eyes caught. For the tiniest fraction of a second, Monty seemed to pause, like he wanted to say something else, but instead he turned away before Maren had time to blink. Her stomach dropped again as a new thought hit her: What if he had hated her monologue? What if, on top of humiliating herself by crying, she had humiliated herself by showing what a terrible writer she was?

She looked down at her paper and resolved today that she wasn't going to write about anything personal or important. She made up two businessmen arguing over a promotion. But unlike yesterday, when the words had seemed to flow naturally from her hand, today the words kept stalling, feeling stiff and awkward and clunky. What did she know about being a businessman? And, more importantly, what did she care?

A little while later, when Monty asked for volunteers and picked a few kids to read, he didn't even look in Maren's direction. Good thing, too—by the time Monty had said the hour was up and it was time to change classes, Maren had only written a few lines and scratched almost all of them out. She snapped her notebook shut in shame as the other kids—who probably had amazing, thrilling, incredible ideas—were busy packing their brilliance away.

"Maren?" She turned to see Monty standing behind her chair. "Can we step outside in the hallway and talk for a moment? It's nothing bad," he added in a hurry, when he saw her face. "Just need a quick word."

Monty headed for the door, and Maren, her legs suddenly feeling heavy and stiff as she dragged herself out of her chair, followed as best she could. From the corner of her eye, she saw Sal was watching, looking concerned, but so was Allegra, a smirk curling unpleasantly on her lips.

Outside, Monty was waiting for Maren at the far end of the hall, one hand tugging absentmindedly at his beard. He straightened up and cleared his throat as she walked over.

"First of all," he said, his voice still low, even though they were the only ones in the hall, "I just want to say I'm really sorry for asking you to read your monologue yesterday. This is my first year here, so I didn't know about what you and your family are going through, but no matter what, I shouldn't have put you on the spot like that."

Maren nodded at her feet, unsure what to say. She had never had a teacher apologize to her before.

"But I also want to say"—Monty paused until she looked up—"I want you to know that you wrote a really fantastic, powerful piece."

Her expression must have looked as shocked as she felt, because Monty laughed a little bit, and after a second, so did she.

"I don't want you to feel obligated to share something you're not comfortable with the class," he went on, "but also, that monologue was powerful because it *meant* something to you. All of us, all the counselors, everyone, felt that. That's exactly what good writing is supposed to do— make people feel things." He looked for a second as if he were going to launch into one of his excited lectures, but he reeled himself back in at the last second. "Anyway. I guess I'm trying to say that, if you want to share in the future, this is a safe space. No one is going to judge you or laugh. I'll make sure of it. And even if you don't want to share, I'd like to challenge you to keep writing about your sister and all the other things you're struggling with. Don't be afraid to let all of it out on the page. Who knows, you might find others who feel exactly as you do, who need to read it. Okay?"

Maren nodded again. Her limbs felt slack, her hands numb and sweaty, but another feeling was growing in her chest. "Okay," she said.

"Okay," Monty breathed, looking as relieved as she felt.

The classroom door opened, and the other students poured out. Monty tipped an imaginary hat to her as he joined the throng of people headed to lunch. Maren watched him for a moment, then turned back to the rehearsal room to get her stuff.

Sal was waiting by the door. "Everything good?" he asked.

"Yeah," Maren said. The relief continued to seep through her with a slow, delicious warmth as she replayed Monty's words: He had called her writing *fantastic* and *powerful*. She felt herself grinning. "Yeah, everything is good."

Sal looked as if he had more questions, but then just grinned back at her. "Well. Cool. See you in rehearsal this afternoon, then?"

"Right," Maren said. Feeling a little giddy, she added sarcastically, "It is the most important day of the summer."

Sal's laughter made her feel even better.

⟡

The cafeteria at lunch was abnormally quiet. Even Theo seemed slightly less hungry than usual, and they kept adjusting their cacti vest, as though the spines were pricking them. Twenty minutes before the end of lunch, people started standing by the door. At fifteen minutes, Mr. Cairn came in and announced that the cast list was posted on the front door of the auditorium. Immediately, the horde of kids shot past him, Theo jumping up and joining them as they crammed through the door. Maren started to follow but couldn't make herself rush. She took her time finishing her soup and clearing her tray, then slowly wandered over. By the time Maren walked up to the auditorium, Theo was one of the few students lingering out front.

"Guess what?" Theo cried, skipping over to meet her. "I got Malvolio!"

"Theo, that's awesome!" Maren said, and she meant it. "He's totally the funniest character—you'll be great."

"Yeah." Theo spread their arms out happily as if to hug the sky. "Now I get to make Allegra act revolted."

"So she's Olivia?" Maren asked, though it wasn't a question so much as a confirmation. "Well, you'll show off your acting abilities by pretending to love her."

Theo let out one of their squeaky-wheel laughs. "The rest of the cast is okay, though," Theo went on, even though Maren was close enough to read the paper herself now. "Greg Galanis is Orsino—he's a third-year—and Sal got Feste, which is perfect, and Graham is Sebastian! He does kind of look like Piper's brother."

"Awesome," Maren said again, a little less heartily than before, as she stared at the rest of the cast list.

Piper—the rabbity-faced girl, one of Allegra's minions—was cast as Viola. It was stupid to feel disappointed, Maren told herself. She knew she really had messed up her audition. Still. If this were a story or a movie, she would have been cast as Viola. If she had been Hadley, she would have been cast as Viola. And a tiny, *tiny* part of Maren had maybe even hoped to be Viola. She ran her finger down the rest of the list until she found her name.

Stage Manager: Maren Sands

"Stage manager," Theo said, studying Maren's face for a reaction. "That's a pretty important job."

"Yeah," Maren said, taking a breath and then forcing

herself to smile. "Yeah, it's perfect. This way I can keep studying the script for clues while you rehearse."

"Oh, that's right!" Theo's eyes brightened. "You'll know the whole play by heart soon enough!"

"Only downside," Maren said as she heaved open the door for Theo, "is now I have to try to *manage* all of you."

Theo let loose another laugh, and Maren smiled.

There was a big square of plastic tables set up on the main stage of the auditorium when they got there, and kids were being directed into different groups by Mr. Cairn.

"Cast members, take a seat around the table," Mr. Cairn said, pointing at Theo. He added to Maren, "Stage manager, you go sit by the director."

Theo plopped into an open chair beside Graham and Sal on one side of the circle, while Maren walked around to where Jo was standing.

"Stage manager, excellent," Jo said distractedly. "You're going to be taking notes for me on the script today. Sound good?"

Maren nodded and dug out a pencil and her script binder.

"All right, folks!" Jo called the group to attention when everyone had arrived. "You ready to get this show on the stage?"

The group cheered and Maren clapped along, trying not to look at Allegra's self-satisfied face.

The afternoon went fast as they were given instructions about what rehearsals would be like. For the rest of the week, Jo explained, the cast would be split up to work with different counselors—some with Jo on the main stage, others with Mr. Cairn or one of the other counselors in the rehearsal spaces—and everyone, even those working as crew, would go onstage at some point in the performance. The kids assigned set crew would also be responsible for staging the storm that happened before the beginning of the play, using a dance or movement piece. Eartha was already warming up, waving her arms back and forth as if she were doing synchronized swimming, and getting glances from Bernie. The kids on costume and prop crews would design and be onstage for the celebratory feast at the end, the music arranged by Ms. Green, so that Feste the clown could sing the last song.

"Make sure it's a good party," Sal called out.

After the crew left, there was another read-through of the play, now with the actors in set parts. Greg was funny in a melodramatic sort of way as the lovesick Duke Orsino, while Emil, the boy who had auditioned before Maren, had gotten the part of Sir Toby and clearly loved pretending to be drunk all the time. Theo did a great Malvolio, making their voice nasally and arrogant, which worked well next to Nic's droll Maria, who read the lines in the same bored way she spoke in real life. At the part where Malvolio is imagining being married to Olivia, Theo even brought out their Allegra impression again, sending more than a few snickers down the table. Allegra glared, and she read all of Olivia's lines to Malvolio with outright contempt, though she oozed affection at Graham's Sebastian, as fake in her lines as she was in real life. Graham's naturally quiet voice really did sound baffled by Allegra, but it was Sal who ended the play with a flourish, putting a hip-hop beat behind his song "The Wind and the Rain."

The only sour note in the whole thing, Maren thought, was Piper as Viola. Maren wasn't a fan of the weepy, moany way Piper read her first scene, or the overly dramatic way she protested her innocence at the end, and she pitched her voice laughably low when Viola was dressed as Cesario. Still, Maren reminded herself, glancing several times at Jo to try to gauge her response, it was just the first rehearsal.

By the end of the read-through, it was almost dinnertime.

"I think we can leave a little early today, don't you?" Jo said, stretching and shuffling her hands through her cloud of hair. "Great work, everyone. Tomorrow, we're going to get on our feet and start blocking some scenes."

There was a round of applause, and then a commotion as kids gathered their things. "Hang back a second, Maren," Jo said when Maren made to join them. "After rehearsals each day, we'll go over the schedule for the next day."

Maren sat down and opened her binder again. Theo, fussing with their camera bag, raised their eyebrows at her in question. Maren just smiled and jerked her head at Jo. Theo nodded, then followed the others out to dinner.

"So!" Jo said as the last students filtered out and the auditorium door banged shut behind them. "Tomorrow, we break into scenes. I'll start at the beginning in here, to make sure all the characters in act one are ready to go. Mr. Cairn will run lines on the letter gag in the Black Box. Everyone else should be sitting in the audience in here, working on their lines quietly. They have to check in with you if they're going to leave, so you know where to get them when I'm ready for them on the stage. Yes?"

"Got it." Maren nodded, double-checking to make sure she had the list of who was rehearsing where correct.

"And remind me to ask Ms. Casta to come in and work with the kids in the Black Box. That's the Speech and Diction instructor," Jo said, noticing Maren's blank expression. "She'll work with them on projection, though it'll be different in the thrust versus the proscenium."

The note Maren was scribbling jerked wildly across the page. "What did you say?" she asked.

"Just different types of stages." Jo didn't seem to realize she had said anything extraordinary, preoccupied as she was gathering her things. "The main stage is a proscenium stage, with the audience only in front. The Black Box has seating on three sides."

"But," Maren said, trying to keep her voice calm, "what kind of a stage is the Black Box? What is it called?"

Jo looked at her with interest. "A thrust stage. Why?"

"No reason." Maren's voice sounded breathy and weak even to her. "Just curious."

༄

When the campers had been given a tour, Jo had explained that most theaters actually have two different stages in them: The first is the main stage for the big shows; the second is a smaller, simpler space called the Black Box. While the main stage gets all the fancy sets and lighting, the Black Box is less adorned but nonetheless manages to make the magic of a story come to life.

Hiding the treasure in the Black Box was perfect,

Maren thought, and she couldn't wait to search it. But it was a couple of days before she got the chance. Mornings were jam-packed with classes—from Tech, where Bernie was militant in observing them use the equipment, to Theater History, where they jumped forward through several centuries at a time, to Playwriting, where it felt like Maren learned something new every day.

"Don't forget, conflict doesn't always have to be loud," Monty said once after a third-year boy, Travis, read a scene that was mostly just shouts and fistfights. "Sometimes conflict is quiet. Sometimes it's internal, a character struggling with themselves."

Maren knew exactly what he meant—she spent most of the class debating with herself whether or not to read her writing out loud, but ultimately couldn't bring herself to do it.

Rehearsals in the afternoon were even harder. Maren's time was spent running between the different rehearsal spaces and the auditorium, trying to make sure everyone was where they were supposed to be, and taking notes for Jo. Maren's script pages were full of scribbles: about which character should go where, when they should cross, when a light or scene change should happen, and general notes to remind Jo to do something later. By the time evening rolled around, Maren was too tired to even contemplate sneaking out.

But on Friday, she finally got her chance—Jo decided to let the group, including Maren, go to dinner early. Even hurrying, she just barely managed to catch Theo before they headed for the cafeteria.

"Hang on," she said, grabbing Theo's arm and pulling

them out of the current of kids. She lowered her voice and added, "Let's search for the you-know-what in the you-know-where while everyone else is at dinner."

She had told Theo all about the revelation that the Black Box was a thrust stage, and Theo had agreed to help her search. But now, Theo hesitated.

"I don't know," Theo said, looking longingly toward the path. Their vest that day was covered in tropical hibiscus flowers, as if the fabric had meant to end up on a bathing suit but had gotten lost along the way. "Maybe we should wait for another time."

"We might have waited too long already! Someone kidnapped Miss Bradley to find this ring, and with rumors of the ghost, they might have already—"

Theo cleared their throat pointedly and Maren turned around.

Graham was there, his eyes bouncing between the two of them. All week, he had been trying to ingratiate himself back in their good graces, and even though Maren had remained firm in her resolve to give him the cold shoulder, so far he hadn't taken the hint. Now, Maren glared at him. How much had he heard?

"Hi," he said uncertainly. "You two heading to dinner?"

"Hey, Graham," Theo said. "Yeah, in a minute. We'll meet you there."

Maren said nothing.

"Okay," he said. "See you there."

"See you," Theo said.

After another long moment, Graham finally turned and walked away. Maren waited until he was out of earshot, then whispered, "We have to look now. Who knows when our next chance might be?"

"Is it worth the risk, though?" Theo started. "What with breaking the rules and Mr. Cairn and all..."

Maren suddenly understood. "You don't believe me about the ring, do you?"

"I believe you," Theo said, sounding anything but certain, then shrugged, uncomfortable. "But it's just that there's really no saying how long Chef Clarence is going to have enough baked ziti for dinner and I—hey! Where are you going?!"

Maren had turned and was heading back into the auditorium. "You don't want to risk it, fine," she said over her shoulder. "I'll go by myself."

She threw open the door and strode through. A moment later, Theo appeared at her side.

"I'm just saying, Italian is my third-favorite type of food of all time," Theo huffed. "And I really don't trust Mexican food this far north, which makes Italian temporarily my second favorite, so they better not be out of ziti when we get there."

"If we find the ring," Maren said, "I'm sure they'll give you as much ziti as you can manage."

This idea seemed to perk Theo up considerably.

Maren had never been in the Black Box except in a group before, and there was something a little unnerving about all that open, empty, silent space.

"Hello?" Maren called softly from the door. No answer.

Not that she had been expecting any, she reminded herself as she stepped the rest of the way into the theater. She felt Theo's camera follow her with its recording eye, a feeling that didn't help with the creep factor.

"If you were an expensive ring," Theo mused, panning around the room, "where would you be hidden?"

"Come on," Maren said, dragging out her flashlight and shining it to the side. "Let's start looking under the seats."

The seating rose into three levels like bleachers, creating a wedge of hallway-like space underneath. These were used for actors to cross under and through without the audience knowing, and over the years, the actors had written names and messages. Maren held up her flashlight and studied the old graffiti etched into the unpainted wood there:

EW + GG

RED AND GRAY 2005!

DAMN YANKEES—GOOD OLE DAYS

MISS ALTMAN IS THE BEST! 2013

It would have been easy to hide codes in the graffiti, but the earliest date she saw was 1988, and no mentions of *Twelfth Night* to be found.

"I don't think it's under here," Theo said after a while.

"I think you're right," Maren said, stepping back out onto the stage and looking around. With new sets and props for every show, everything out here would have moved around too much for there to be something hidden in it. But what *wouldn't* have changed in sixty years? There wasn't a curtain, and the chairs in the audience were old red and orange plastic, but not sixty years old.

"How does the rest of the quote go?" Theo asked, joining her.

"*In my stars I am above thee; but be not afraid of greatness,*" Maren recited. "*Some are born great, some achieve greatness, and some have greatness—*"

"Yeah, yeah, thrusting, yeah." Theo waved the rest of the quote away. They were staring upward. "*I am above thee.*"

Maren let her head fall back so she, too, was looking up.

"Of course!" She laughed. "The lighting grid!" Any changes that happened up there would be to the placement of the lights—but the grid itself wouldn't have moved. "How do we get up there?"

"Come on," Theo said, and Maren followed them to a metal ladder tucked into the far corner behind the stage.

It was kind of like a fire escape, Maren thought as she started climbing after Theo. It shouldn't be too scary, she told herself.

She was wrong. Her hands were shaking by the time she pulled herself up onto the grid. She wiped them on her jeans, trying to hide her nervousness from Theo, who seemed perfectly comfortable and was already halfway across to the lighting board.

As its name suggested, the grid was laid out in a series of intersecting wooden walkways, like streets—called cat-walks, Maren remembered from the tour. Thankfully, there was no fly system like in the auditorium, where ropes and pulleys were used to lift and lower backdrops and curtains, but there were still plenty of pipes and wires and rigging that Maren didn't know what to do with. The only safety measure was thin black handrails that looked like they couldn't have prevented anything from plunging to the stage below, but she gripped them as she stood up, and again with every step. She sighed in relief when she finally joined Theo at the lighting board, where the grid widened and there were some chairs. She took one and leaned against the wall, trying to steady her breathing.

Theo was peering down at the complicated equipment. "You do realize Bernie will legitimately kill us if we mess with any of this stuff, right?" they said.

"It's too new to be what we're looking for anyway," Maren said. "It's got to be..." But she didn't finish, distracted by the bright yellow fluorescent tape that marked the edges of the grid. Probably for the tech crew to move around in the dark during the show, Maren thought...but then, why was there glow tape on the black ceiling? "Why is there tape up there?" she mused out loud.

"It's the constellations," came a voice from behind them.

Theo yelped and Maren whipped around, feeling dizzy as she remembered how high up she was. Graham stood by the ladder, blinking his long hair out of his eyes.

"It's the constellations," Graham repeated, and he started pointing. "See, there's Orion. And Cassiopeia. And Taurus and Aries and Cancer—"

"What are you doing up here?!" Maren shouted, recovering first.

"I saw you two climbing," he said shyly. "And I thought—"

"You thought, *What a great way to get Maren and Theo*

in trouble?" Maren cut him off. "You thought, *I bet Allegra will love it if I catch them—*"

"I *thought* I could help you find the ring," Graham said.

Maren and Theo shared a surprised look.

"I've been going to this camp practically my whole life," Graham hurried on. "I've heard all about the ghost of Charlotte Goodman and the ring hidden in the theater. I can help!"

"We don't need your help," Maren said, turning away.

"Hold on," Theo said. "We kind of do."

Maren looked at them, appalled. "Are you kidding? After the prank with Allegra, how can we trust him?"

"I think, since I'm the one who got pranked, it should be me who gets to decide whether or not Graham can help," Theo said firmly. "And I say Graham can help." They cast a glance at Maren. "Okay?"

Maren sighed. "Fine." She gritted her teeth and turned to Graham. "Where's the Big Dipper?"

Graham's face lit up. "This way!"

He clattered down the row to the opposite corner, Theo following quickly after. Maren walked in slow, measured steps while gripping the handrail to join them.

"There," Graham said, pointing to the familiar diamond shape and then above it. "And there's the Little Dipper, too, and the North Star."

"Why the Big Dipper?" Theo asked.

"Malvolio gets tricked into wearing yellow, crossgartered stockings," Maren said, pointing to the four stars that made up the "cup" of the Big Dipper and then drawing connection points in the air with her finger. "If you connect the points of the stars at diagonals, then—"

"It's like a cross!" Graham finished, understanding.

"Or *X* marks the spot!" Theo cried. "But how could the ring be *in* the constellation?"

But Maren was looking at the North Star. There was something about it that made Maren lean closer....

"I think it's here, actually," she said. "I think the four corners of the Little Dipper—yes, they're the points of a ceiling tile! I bet it lifts up!"

"I'll get it!" Theo said, and they clambered up to stand on the safety rails.

"Careful!" Maren gripped the back of their T-shirt, and Graham grabbed another fistful of shirt as Theo stretched out and leaned forward. Their fingers just grazed the tile, and they pushed at it to reveal a sliver of space beyond.

"I think I see something," Theo whispered, their voice hushed with excitement as they strained even farther forward, their fingers disappearing in the dark. "It's like a... I think it's a...a...oh, I can't believe I'm not getting this on camera!"

"Just grab whatever it is and let's get out of here," Maren groaned.

"Got it!" Theo said.

At the exact second they stepped away from the ledge, the door to the Black Box theater opened and someone walked in.

❧

In one movement, Maren, Theo, and Graham all dropped flat against the floor of the grid. They stared at one another in horror as the sound of footsteps tromped to the center of the stage and then stopped. Holding her breath, Maren lifted her head just high enough that she could peer over the edge of the grid. She saw the top of someone's head— someone with a perfectly straight part.

It was Mr. Cairn.

"Excuse me?" he said into the theater. "Is someone here?"

Almost as if he felt Maren's gaze on him, Mr. Cairn looked up. Maren flattened back down, her heart pounding.

"Hello," Mr. Cairn said again, his voice becoming brusquer. "Come out immediately, please."

This was it, Maren thought. They were going to get kicked out. She pictured Mr. Cairn's righteous expression as he escorted her and Theo and Graham in a parade of shame past the other campers. She pictured Ed's hapless annoyance, her mother's disappointment, and Hadley...

Then she heard a second set of heavy footsteps coming from backstage, and a moment later someone else shuffled into view.

"Mr. Del Rio?" Mr. Cairn voiced the campers' confusion as the tech master, Bernie, appeared.

"Sorry to surprise you," Maren thought she heard Bernie say, though it was hard to hear his soft voice from so far away. "I thought you were someone else."

"I see. Are you waiting for someone?" Mr. Cairn asked.

"No," Bernie said too quickly. "Are you?"

"No," Mr. Cairn said.

There was a long moment during which the two men seemed at a loss. Mr. Cairn cleared his throat and patted at his hair while Bernie shuffled his big feet.

"Right," Mr. Cairn said finally. "Well, perhaps we should join the others at dinner, then."

"We should, only I must return to the woodshop first," Bernie said. "I'll see you there, Mr. Cairn."

"Very well, Mr. Del Rio."

And with that, the two men set off speedily in two different directions—Mr. Cairn back toward the lobby, Bernie toward the backstage hallway.

As soon as Maren and the others heard the separate doors swing shut, the three kids were on their feet and hurtling for the ladder. Graham led the way, and Maren climbed down so fast after him she didn't even have time to be afraid. She waited until Theo landed next to her, then they all ran for the door.

They had almost made it through the lobby when Graham grabbed both of them by the arms and yanked them back, practically dragging them behind the box office podium. Maren was about to protest, but just then she heard a new set of footsteps approach. She held her breath, but whoever it was passed right by their hiding place without even slowing their pace. Maren peeked over the rim of the counter. She recognized the long, swinging gray braid immediately: Eartha. She was walking uncharacteristically quickly, then turned the corner toward the Black Box and was gone. Maren waited an extra second after she had disappeared, just to make sure, then breathed a sigh of relief.

"All the adults are annoyingly active this evening," Theo whispered Maren's thoughts. "Shouldn't all old people be asleep by now or something?"

"Forget them," Maren said. "Show us what you found!"

"Oh!" Theo smiled and pulled something out of their pocket. "You mean this?"

They held out a cream-and-gold envelope. It had a *2* drawn on the back.

"You do the honors," Theo said. "I want to get this on camera."

Maren looked at the envelope, then shook her head. She turned to Graham. "You're the one who knew about the constellations. You should open it."

Graham's eyes went wide. After a moment, he took the envelope with trembling hands and peeled it carefully open. They all clustered around to read the card inside:

Be you his eunuch, and your mute I'll be
When my tongue blabs, then let
mine eyes not see

Charlie

November 7, 1950
Los Angeles, California

This stupid party should have ended hours ago.

The guests' fancy clothes were crumpled and sagging, their foreheads beaded with sweat, their hair drooping. The red, white, and blue confetti had been dropped and was now trampled into streaks and stains across the parquet dance floor. The hors d'oeuvres were down to crumbs, and the drinks were finally, thankfully, running out. But still the remaining guests just wouldn't call it a night. They insisted on singing along to the new senator's theme song, "Happy Days Are Here Again," one more time and asking Charlie for another round.

Charlie was exhausted. Her arm was so sore from carrying around trays of champagne that she wasn't sure she'd be able to lift it tomorrow, and her cheeks were cramping from the effort of keeping a smile plastered on her face. Not that anyone looked at her. No one ever seemed to look at Charlie too closely. Not while she kept her hair as short as a boy's and wore a boxy white shirt and trousers instead of a skirt.

It had started as a game, dressing up like a boy. When they had been cleaning out their father's room after he died, Charlie had secreted away some of his clothes without

Rosalie noticing, and she started wearing them whenever she found herself alone in the house.

Then it had become a necessity. As soon as Charlie graduated from high school, their grandmother gave them an ultimatum: Rosalie was to go live with her, to be brought up "right," or there would be no more money coming in for either of them. Rosalie had refused, and Charlie was happy. She would never, not in a million years, have condemned Rosalie to live with that bitter old woman, but they both suddenly had a very real, very urgent need for money. They sold the house and moved into a small apartment. That took care of them for a while, but slowly the funds dried up and their budget got tighter and tighter. Charlie tried to get a job, but it seemed the only work available for women was either as a typist or as a shopgirl. She was fired after only one afternoon typing, when she accidentally typed "severely yours" instead of "sincerely yours" at the end of her boss's letter, and whenever she asked for an application at a shop counter, the girls there looked at her the way her mother once had: as something wrong and, most likely, unfixable.

One day she got desperate and, not sure what else to do, found herself sneaking out before dawn, before the neighbors woke up to see her in a too big blazer and pleated pants. The first place she applied—a caterer's—she was hired on the spot. It had been thrilling, to realize that a *costume* was all it took to change how people saw her. She walked a little taller and with her hands in her pockets, secretly elated. Let people think what they wanted, she thought. Underneath, she was still the same person, but dressed as a boy, she worked evenings catering and could still pull in the odd job during the day, painting fences and any old thing to keep some money coming in for her and her sister. She even occasionally got some work on movie sets—always sweeping under the director's chair, never sitting in it, but still.

But something had started to weigh on Charlie. It wasn't that dressing as a boy felt dishonest—not any more dishonest than trying to wear a skirt, anyway. It was that it still didn't feel like *her*. It didn't feel like she was seen. Maybe she never would be. Maybe there really was something about her, something wrong, something that made people's gaze slide right past.

At someone's insistence, the band picked up "Happy Days Are Here Again." The last holdouts of the party sang along drunkenly.

Charlie gritted her teeth. She was glad her father wasn't alive to see this: Richard Milhous Nixon winning the California Senate seat. Nixon, who had been on the House Committee on Un-American Activities that had labeled progressives as Communists. Charlie didn't care what Rosalie said about their father's illness; he had died, Charlie was sure, after having to watch the country he loved abandon the ideals he cherished. He died of a broken heart. And here Charlie was, having to watch people literally sing the praises of the politicians who did it.

As if speaking Charlie's thoughts, she heard a bitter, angry voice next to her say, "What unbelievable idiocy."

Charlie turned and felt her face flood with heat. Next to her was the most beautiful woman Charlie had ever seen outside a movie set. Her hair was short and bleached a pale, silvery blond, her skin was tan, and she wore a gown of

gleaming silver sculpted to her body so precisely, Charlie expected to see rivets. Her mouth, painted an oxblood
color, was perfect—even though, at the moment, it was
twisted in disgust.

"Helen Gahagan Douglas was the first honest, decent
politician California ever had," the woman went on, "and
she gets beaten by this potato-faced fraudster."

Charlie opened her mouth to agree.

"That's Senator Potato-Face now," said someone on the
woman's other side, a plume of cigar smoke rising with his
words.

Charlie's mouth snapped shut as she faced front again.
Of course the woman hadn't been speaking to Charlie,
hadn't even seen Charlie. Without moving her head, Charlie tried to study the woman's date out of the corner of her
eye. The man had an unmistakable look of arrogance about
him, mostly because of his extraordinarily large forehead
and the way he was constantly angling it to look down his
nose.

"Besides," the man went on, gesturing with his cigar,
"you really want some *actress* sitting in the Senate?"

"Why on earth not?" the woman said. "She did a great
job in the House of Representatives. For *three* terms, thank
you very much."

"Yes, well." The man made a dismissive sound before
popping his lips around his cigar again, taking a quick puff.
"She got elected during the war, when the men were away
fighting. It was all well and good for the ladies to show
support then, but the real men are back now and ready to
run our country again."

"Nixon? A real man? He's so slimy, he should be used

to grease engines," the woman shot back. "Do you know the sort of campaign calls Mr. Nixon's office ran? They would call up a person on the telephone and say, 'Did you know Helen Gahagan Douglas is a Communist?' or 'Did you know Helen Gahagan Douglas is married to a Jew?' and hang up!"

The man waved his cigar dismissively. "That's just a rumor."

"I got two calls myself!"

"Well, Mrs. Douglas did herself in when she was soft on the Reds," the man said. "Not like Nixon. He took care of the Communists, that's for sure."

"*Accused* Communists."

"Accused Communists, Communists—what's the difference?"

"Nixon was *doing* the accusing!" The woman was shaking with anger. "Take my word for it," she went on, and her voice was so icy Charlie was surprised the man didn't shiver. "Nixon will get his comeuppance some day or other."

"Take *my* word for it"—her date refused to be shown up—"that man will go far. Daddy says he has the full support of the Republican Party. He says he wouldn't be surprised if Mr. Nixon gets on the presidential ticket someday."

"Oh, well, if *Daddy* says so," the woman mocked. "I'm sure *Daddy* and his money will do more than their share to put Mr. Nixon on that ticket."

The man just laughed. "You didn't seem to hate his money so much when it brought us out here."

The woman's brow furrowed and she turned away from him. Her eyes, a bright and magnificent blue, caught and held Charlie's. A bolt of electricity shot through Charlie so that her very fingertips tingled with warmth. For a moment, no one—not the partygoers, not the band, not even her date—mattered besides Charlie and this woman.

"You're just a sore loser," the man said. "But don't think I've forgotten our bet."

The woman broke her connection with Charlie, turned to face forward, and sniffed. "I don't know what you're talking about."

He chuckled. "Oh, I think you do. You lost a bet, Missy, and now it's time to pay up." He tapped his cheek with his hand holding the cigar. The woman waved the smoke away, her nose crinkled in disgust.

"You know I can't stand how you smell after those things."

"Pity's for you, because a bet's a bet and you have to kiss this smelly old potato."

He tapped his cheek again, and Charlie realized he was waiting for a kiss. The woman refused to acknowledge him for a moment, her jaw working in anger. Then she turned and leaned toward him, her mouth grimly puckered, preparing to offer a perfunctory kiss. But the man turned and caught her mouth with his, pulled her to him, held her there. Charlie had to look away, but not before she had time to see the enormous diamond, the size and shape of a glacier, winking from the woman's left hand. An engagement ring. The warmth Charlie felt a moment before disappeared, snuffed out, without even a whiff of smoke remaining.

"There," the man said, finally letting the woman go. "Was that so hard?"

Maren

June 2015
Stonecourt, Massachusetts

"What I don't get," Maren said thoughtfully, "is what *Twelfth Night* has to do with Charlotte Goodman. Or the ring, for that matter, even if there is one in the script."

"Well," Graham started, "the legend goes—"

"Wait, wait!" Theo said, gripping his forearm. "This is my favorite part!"

It was Saturday night—movie night—and they were sitting in the back of the outdoor amphitheater, watching *Singin' in the Rain* projected on the loose white backdrop draped across the stage.

Maren glanced at the screen. "You say that about every part," she accused Theo. "All I see is more of Gene Kelly and that other guy tap-dancing."

"*That other guy?*" Theo sounded appalled. "Donald O'Connor is a *legend*!"

Maren rolled her eyes. "Oh, sorry, Mr. O'Connor, sir." She pretended to bow toward the screen. "Your legendary-ness."

Graham laughed, but Theo didn't seem to pick up on her sarcasm.

"Jeepers, does it get any better than *Singin' in the Rain*?" Theo sighed when the song had finished. "I mean, a meta musical *and* a portrait of Hollywood history from silent films to talkies? Got to be my favorite movie, ever, of all time."

"What about Quigley Forrager?" Maren teased. "I thought he was your favorite."

"He's my favorite *auteur*," Theo clarified.

"You keep saying that like I know what it means," Maren said.

"It basically means a director," Graham said.

"A director with *vision*," Theo insisted. "Especially because, in addition to being an artist, he's also a cinephile and a dedicated preservationist."

"Preservationist?" Maren couldn't help asking.

"Someone who makes sure old movies don't get destroyed. He'd totally approve of *Singin' in the Rain*."

Maren and Graham smiled at each other. As much as Maren had been resistant to letting him join in on the hunt for the ring, she had to admit she was warming up to him.

"You were starting to say?" she whispered to Graham while Theo was enraptured by the screen. "About Charlotte Goodman?"

"Right, so, Charlotte died when her movie caught on fire."

Maren started. "How does a movie catch on fire?"

"Celluloid film burns hot and fast," Theo said without taking their eyes from the screen. "Super dangerous, back in the old days. Haven't you heard of the Fox vault fire? A bunch of films were being stored in bad conditions, and they *spontaneously combusted*."

Maren gave them a look. "You're making that up."

"I am not!" Theo was offended enough to look away

from the screen. "The film put off a gas and it built up and then—BOOM!"

Graham's eyes went so wide, they practically reflected the stars dancing on-screen. A few campers sitting down lower in the amphitheater turned around to see where the sound was coming from. Among them, Maren wished she didn't notice, was Sal, sitting with Allegra and her friends. She quickly shushed Theo.

"Anyway," Theo said, slightly quieter. "A lot of silent movies are completely lost because of that fire, no existing copies, and that's what made people realize the need for film preservation. Quigley Forrager supposedly has a huge, temperature-moderated facility where he keeps a bunch of early-era celluloid—"

"Yeah, yeah, Quigley Forrager, we know," Maren said. She turned back to Graham. "Go on."

"Well, the legend has it that the movie Charlotte was working on, the one that went up in flames? It was an adaptation of *Twelfth Night.*"

"Really?" Maren felt her heart speed up. "What about the ring?"

"There's two stories about that, actually," Graham said, leaning forward again. "Some people say Charlotte had run out of money to make her movie, so she stole a diamond ring from the actress who was playing the lead. The actress went there that day to confront Charlotte about it, and Charlotte set the fire as a distraction to try to get away—only neither of them made it out."

Maren wrinkled her nose. She didn't really like the idea of searching for a stolen ring, or of Charlotte Goodman as a thief. "What's the other story?"

"Well, some people say the actress was going to leave her fiancé," Graham said. "She asked for Charlotte's help and gave her the ring to sell for money to make a getaway. Only he caught them before they could...and he murdered them both in the fire."

"Wow!" This had managed to draw even Theo's attention. "Now *that's* a story."

"Yeah," Maren said, then slumped back with a sigh, "except neither helps us figure out what this new clue means."

"What, you mean there aren't a lot of mute eunuchs around?" Theo joked.

Graham snorted, but Maren ignored them both.

"It's from the part in the play where Viola dresses like a man and the Captain agrees not to say anything," she said. "But last time, 'thrust' referred to a part of the stage. Graham, are there any tongues or eyes onstage?"

Graham shrugged. "There's the lip of the stage, I guess—you know, the part that juts out into the audience. And sometimes, the backstage parts are called wings, but—"

"Wait, wait!" Theo held out an arm to silence them. "This is the best part!"

Maren and Graham exchanged another look, this one less fond, as the three actors danced around, singing about what a good morning it was.

"But," Graham went on after the song ended, "I've never heard of anything in a theater being referred to as a tongue or an eye."

Maren nodded. She hadn't thought so, but it was worth asking. This clue seemed more like a proper riddle, one that would be in a jokebook or told by someone's uncle:

What has a tongue that goes mute when its eyes can't see? She had tried to doodle some ideas about the clue during her free moments in rehearsal that day—could "mute" have something to do with microphones? Or the mention of eyes and lips refer to putting on makeup in a dressing room?—but none of them made perfect sense.

As if reading her mind, Graham said, "Maybe we could ask the instructors for help. I bet they'd have some ideas."

"We can't," Maren said firmly. "Not until we know who kidnapped Miss Bradley."

"It's obviously Mr. Cairn, isn't it?" Theo said, raising their eyebrows. "He was in the Black Box, and he threatened to get us kicked out."

"No way." Graham shook his head vehemently. "Mr. Cairn is great, he's just strict. He made a kid cry one year for spilt milk—literally."

Now Maren shared a look with Theo. They seemed to agree that Mr. Cairn was far from *great*, but both knew they wouldn't be able to convince Graham otherwise.

"We can't rule Mr. Cairn out," Maren said fairly. "But Eartha and Bernie were there, too, and they both wear big shoes. So until we know for sure, we can't ask any instructors for help."

"At least tomorrow's Sunday," Theo said. "We can spend all day searching if we want."

"Well, yeah…" Graham said. "Except, maybe, first? We should go to the village really quick? Neither of you have seen it yet, so maybe you should check it out?"

Theo and Maren looked at him.

"I have to call my moms," he admitted. "Otherwise, they'll worry."

"Oh, right, cell service!" Theo smacked their forehead. "Yeah, my mama will catch the next flight up if I forget to give her the weekly call."

"Yeah, mine would, too, I guess," Maren said. She pretended to become interested in the movie then. It had only been a week, but she had gotten so used to being unable to talk to her family that the idea of calling them made her feel nervous.

"We can go into town really early," Theo was saying, "so there'll be plenty of time for treasure hunting later."

"Good idea," Graham agreed. "Plus, if you get to town early enough, the chocolate shop sometimes has free samples out."

Theo looked as if they were ready to leave right then.

⟳

The next morning, Theo and Maren dressed quickly, making sure they took their wallets and phones for once, and tiptoed out of the cabin while Katie and Lorna were still asleep. Graham was waiting for them in front of the cafeteria, and they were among the first to gather their trays. Chef Clarence even gave Theo an extra portion of scrambled eggs since so many people were clearly taking the Sunday morning to sleep in. Maren watched Clarence's large, hairy hand shuffle a spatula around the egg pan. She had a sudden idea, but she waited to tell the others until they were all sitting down.

"Do you think it could be Clarence?" she whispered when he had his back turned, busy rooting around in the giant, industrial-sized fridge. "He probably has time between breakfast, lunch, and dinner to poke around clue-hunting."

Theo immediately shook their head. "Can't be," they said.

"Why?" Maren demanded. "You think he can't be an old-lady-napper because he sometimes gives you extra food?"

"No." Theo swallowed. "Because he only ever wears Crocs." They took another forkful.

Sure enough, when Clarence came out from behind the buffet to refill the apples stacked in the basket, Maren saw that his feet were covered in rainbow tie-dyed Crocs.

"Good idea, though," Graham said kindly.

Maren shrugged, a little embarrassed, and pretended to focus on her breakfast.

As soon as they had all eaten their eggs—and, in Theo's case, yogurt and a banana and a piece of toast with peanut butter, and an extra banana grabbed for the road—Graham led the way to a new path, where he said the route to town started.

"It's not a long walk, but we'll have to sign out and in with a counselor," he explained.

Sure enough, Jo was sitting in a lawn chair when they arrived, her legs stretched long, a clipboard resting on her lap.

"You three are up early," Jo said, looking over the rims of her sunglasses.

"Ahead of the crowds, that's us," Theo said.

"Oh, I see," Jo said, grinning. "You want to get samples from the chocolate shop."

"Right in one," Theo said. "I'm starving."

Jo laughed. "Well, Graham knows the drill, but just so everyone's clear: You check back in with a counselor as soon as you return, and you're back no later than six PM," Jo told them as they wrote their names on the sign-out sheet. "If I hear any complaints, you lose Sunday village privileges for the rest of camp. Understood? Great, then enjoy!"

It was about a twenty-minute walk to town, most of it on the same sort of shady, tree-lined walking paths they used all over camp. At one point, though, the trees fell away, and they were confronted with a bulldozed plot of mud. There were two trailers with WALCORP printed in big letters along their sides.

"Walcorp? Gross." Theo gave a dramatic shiver, their camera already out and panning across the torn-up soil.

"This used to be camp land," Graham said with a frown. "I guess it's true what they say, that Jo had to sell off some of it."

Maren didn't say anything. She was looking at the trailers, trying to remember what Maxine Bradley had said about her kidnapping. For the first time, Maren wondered where she had been held before she made her escape....

"You ready?" Theo interrupted her thoughts.

"Yeah," Maren said, turning away. "Yeah, let's get out of here."

A few minutes later, the walking trail became a house-lined sidewalk, and a minute after that they were strolling through the brick-lined streets of the village. For years, Maren had heard Hadley's stories about going to the village of Stonecourt on the weekends—going shopping for handmade candles and hand-knitted scarves and home-made fudge—and had always wondered why the campers were allowed to go there alone. Now Maren understood: It would be pretty hard, in a place this small and with so many grown-ups around, to find any trouble to get into.

"There's normally good cell service at the benches," Graham said. "We can make our calls from there."

"Oh, right," Maren said, remembering with a fresh swoop of nervousness the phone calls.

Graham led them down a side street of closed shop fronts to what looked like an old-time town square. There was a cluster of benches there, one of which was already occupied by an elderly couple sharing a bag of toffee.

"Perfect," Theo said, gesturing to the chocolate shop ahead, an open sign in the window. "Let's get the parental check-ins over with and then hit those samples."

They had no sooner dialed and raised the phone to their ear than Maren heard a thick Texas drawl burst from their phone: "Oh my word, it's our little baby butt calling from fancy theater land!"

"Hey, Mama," Theo said. "Guess what?" Their voice quickly rose to the volume and excitement of their mother's. "I got cast as Malvolio! I get to make the lead actress disgusted—isn't that *awesome*?"

Maren turned to share another smile with Graham, but he already had his phone out and held up in front of him.

"Hey, Mommy," he said softly to the two women whose faces were mashed together on the screen. "Hey, Mom."

"You look a little pale!" cried the woman with the golden hair Maren had seen at the drop-off circle. "Are you getting enough vitamin D? You need at least ten minutes a day in the sun."

"Be careful how you answer that, kiddo," joked the woman with blunt bangs. "If you say you're getting enough sun, her next question is going to be if you're applying enough sunscreen."

Maren felt a tight twinge of jealousy in her chest as she pulled out her own phone. It was as if Theo's and Graham's mothers were competing to see how loudly they could announce their love for their kids. She scrolled down to Ed's number and pressed call. The phone rang. She started to get nervous, realizing she hadn't really thought about what she was going to say, but her call went to voice mail anyway.

"Hey," Maren said, then hovered after the word, not sure whether it'd be weirder to call him *Ed* in front of the others or *Dad* to him. "So, I'm good," she went on. "At camp. Just in town with some of my friends." She was quiet for a moment, trying to think of something else to say. Why was she even bothering, when Ed didn't care enough to answer his phone? "Anyway," Maren continued to the emptiness of the voice-mail box. "I was just supposed to let you know that I'm fine. That's it, so...okay, bye."

Graham and Theo were *still* talking to their parents—Theo laughing so loud, the elderly couple stood and drifted away from the benches. Realizing there was no way to avoid it, Maren took a deep breath and pulled up her mother's number. She held her phone to her ear, listening to the dull electronic tone.

Her mom picked up in the middle of the third ring. "Hey there, Mare-bear," she said, and her voice sounded warm and quiet—like she was sitting at the breakfast table, sipping her first cup of coffee. "How's Goodman's treating you?"

"Hey, Mom, I'm good," Maren said, and she was surprised to find herself smiling.

"That's wonderful," her mom said. "Your dad mentioned you weren't the happiest at drop-off, but you know, between work and your sister, I just couldn't—"

"I'm fine," Maren interrupted. "Really."

"Well, what show are you doing?" her mom asked after a slight pause. "Who are you cast as?"

"*Twelfth Night*," Maren said. "But I'm not in it, I'm just the stage manager."

"The Stage Manager?" Her mother laughed. "You know, that was actually a character in *Our Town*. You remember, the play your sister did?"

Maren said nothing.

"Well, your sister is doing great, too," her mom went on, as if Maren had asked. "The doctors are really positive about her recovery. They say she's making good steps."

Maren said nothing.

"Her therapist thinks she's still on target to be back in school next fall. They think—well, I should let her tell you, of course. She has phone privileges now, if you want to call back and talk to her later this evening?"

"I can't," Maren said. "I'll be back at camp by then."

"That's too bad. I'm sure she'd love to hear from you."

Maren swallowed, her throat suddenly tight with tears.

Her mother sighed. "You shouldn't be mad at her, Maren. It isn't her fault. You know mental illness is a sickness like any other. There's enough stigma around depression without Hadley having to feel judged by her family."

Maren felt the heat rise to the space behind her eyes, tears threatening to spill over now. So she was "family" after all, but only whenever it was convenient? She knew objectively that her mom was right—that it wasn't Hadley's fault—and yet, why should *their* mother think only of Hadley's feelings? After all the sadness and scares Hadley had put them through the past few months, why shouldn't

Maren feel mad? And shouldn't her mom care how she felt, too? "I should go," Maren managed, her voice croaking on the last word.

"So soon? I still want to hear all about camp," her mother said quickly. "You still have to tell me all about your new friends, and what you're doing—"

"I'll call you next week," Maren said. "Love you."

She didn't even wait to hear her mom say it back. She hung up and stared down at her phone. A small, painful part of her hoped her mom would call back, but the phone stayed silent, the screen black. She waited a moment longer, then jammed her thumb against the power key and shut the phone all the way off, shoving it back in her pocket.

Unbelievably, Theo and Graham were still talking away on their phones. Maren looked around, hopeful of finding someplace open to go. She saw a little sign pointing the way to the coffee shop down the street. Maren waved until she caught Theo's and Graham's attention, then gestured at the shop.

Theo gave a thumbs-up and carried on their conversation, now drifting into a string of rapid Spanish, but Graham frowned. "What about samples?" he said.

"You got trampled?" came the voice of one of his moms from his phone.

"I'll be back," Maren mouthed, then turned and followed the sign's directions around the corner.

The coffee shop's front door was bracketed by two azalea bushes blossoming a lurid neon pink. Maren saw the elderly couple from the bench slowly climbing the stairs. She bounced up after them, catching the door right before it closed.

"It's those camp kids," she heard the elderly man complain to the woman behind the counter. "They're about to invade the town again, the hooligans."

"Every summer, every Sunday," the elderly woman added.

"I don't know," the woman behind the counter said, catching sight of Maren and smiling at her. "They certainly liven up the place."

"Liven up the place?" The elderly woman shook her head. "They'll be the death of us!"

She noticed Maren behind her then, scowled, and turned back around. Remembering Jo's threat about complaints, Maren was perfectly behaved while the elderly man and woman each ordered a cappuccino, paid, and collected their drinks. When they walked away, the woman behind the counter raised an eyebrow threaded by a silver ring and grinned conspiratorially.

"Don't mind them," she said quietly, nodding as the couple settled into some seats by the windows. "Most of the town is on the far side of fifty, if you know what I mean. I've lived here my whole life, and they used to say the same about me—still do, sometimes." She grinned, a silver stud glinting in her nose. "How about a hot chocolate on the house, from one hooligan to another?"

Maren couldn't help but smile. "Thanks," she said.

The woman, whose name tag said *Gabby*, winked and set to work steaming the milk. Her hair, which was piled on her head in an uneven bun and held back with a bandanna, bobbed along as she drizzled some chocolate sauce in the cup, then poured the milk over it and stirred with a long spoon.

She was just passing the drink to Maren when the door chimed. Gabby's face—which had been so friendly—fell into a stiff, flat mask. Confused, Maren turned to see exactly what could have caused such a sudden shift.

The answer wasn't *what* but *who*: An extraordinarily skinny woman, swaying on tall high heels, was using her bony elbow to push open the door. She wore a steel-gray suit, a pair of fat, expensive-looking sunglasses, and an expression that said she had better things to do—with the surprising added touch of a yellow construction hard hat.

"Renee," Gabby said, her tone polite but infinitely frostier than it had been seconds before with Maren. "What can I get you?"

"Americano," the woman, Renee, sighed without looking up from her cell phone, where she was rapidly texting. Her nails were a striking pale blue and shaped into points, like cat claws. "You can manage that, can't you? Whoever was working the counter yesterday definitely only gave me three shots of espresso instead of four, and I practically *choked*, it was so revolting."

"Three shots are standard," Gabby informed Renee as she got another cup and wrote her name on its side. "An extra shot will be an extra fifty cents."

Renee sighed again and drew off her sunglasses as if throwing down a gauntlet. Her eyes, now revealed, were a pretty pale green, but it was hard to see them through the giant sticky spikes of mascara. "Fine," she said, "I guess I'll pay extra, since four shots is the only way to make it tolerable."

Maren wanted to thank Gabby again but, after seeing a muscle twitch in her cheek, decided it would be best to do it later. She took a seat at a table in the corner, as far as possible from the elderly couple as she could, and watched, sipping carefully, as Gabby filled Renee's order. When Gabby set the drink down, Renee handed over her credit card with a bored flop of her wrist. Gabby looked annoyed at a sign that read CREDIT CARDS ON PURCHASES OVER $5 ONLY, but seemed to prefer getting rid of Renee to forcing this point.

Renee, unfortunately, wasn't so easy to get rid of—she took her drink to an open table next to the elderly couple, put her phone up to her ear, and began a conversation. The elderly couple exchanged the same look they had at the benches, and Maren fought the urge to laugh. She guessed she couldn't be too offended, since they clearly thought the adult Renee was a hooligan as well.

Maren was so distracted that it took her a moment to realize something: Renee was speaking *French*.

Maren's heart started to pound. Could Renee be the person who was on the other side of the conversation that night in the costume storage with Miss Bradley?

If only Theo were here to translate! Maren dug out her phone to text them, but realized it was no use. They were probably still talking to their parents and wouldn't see the text in time. She could leave now and run and get Theo, but Renee might be long gone by the time the two of them got back. She had to know what Renee was saying!

Maren had an idea.

As casually as she could, she gathered her hot chocolate and her phone and wandered toward the woman's table. There was a bulletin board with flyers for local museums and art galleries behind her. Maren paused in front of it, pretending to study the notices. She pressed the home key on her phone. Nothing. She wanted to scream—why had she turned her phone all the way off? Hurriedly, she jammed down the power button. The screen took its time rebooting, its progress agonizingly slow, and Maren felt every painful second as more French words unspooled and disappeared, unknown, from Renee's mouth. Finally—*finally*—her phone was on. She quickly found the voice memo app, then hit record.

For three, four, *five* whole seconds, Maren held her phone out, hoping against hope that she was close enough to catch Renee's words.

And then, out of nowhere, Maren's phone started ringing.

Maren jumped. Renee spun around in her seat. Their eyes met. Renee studied Maren, squinting, her mascaraed lashes as sharp as the teeth of a bear trap. Maren turned away quickly, fumbling with her phone.

"Hello?" Maren answered. She kept her eyes latched to the bulletin board even as she felt Renee's continuing to study her.

"Hey, hey, Merry Mare!" Ed's voice was still scratchy with sleep. "Sorry I missed your call earlier! What's up? How's camp?"

Maren's panic turned suddenly into a surge of anger. How very like Ed, to first miss her call, then call at the worst time possible. "Fine," she said, trying to keep her voice calm. "I'm fine. Just at a coffee shop."

Out of the corner of her eye, she saw Renee turn back around in her seat. She was speaking faster and quieter now and seemed to be wrapping up her conversation. Maren would miss her chance to record anything else.

"A coffee shop, huh?" Ed was saying. "Man, I've got to take you to 1369 Coffee House when you get back to Boston! It's got some great coffee, and desserts, too, if you—"

"It's not really a good time," Maren interrupted him.

"Oh," Ed said after a surprised pause. "Oh, sorry, I just got your message and wanted to hear a bit more about the camp and all. When your sister was there—"

"Why does everyone want to talk about when Hadley was here!" Maren must have said it loudly, because now Renee, Gabby, and the elderly couple were all looking at her. Maren blinked back tears of frustration and shame. She knew it wasn't her father's fault and she shouldn't have yelled at him, but she couldn't help it. Why did everyone think she wanted to hear about Hadley's experience at camp? She wasn't Hadley! She closed her eyes and took a breath. "I only called because the camp told us to. I'm fine, that's all."

She hung up just in time to hear Renee say "Au revoir." Renee stood and looked over Maren at Gabby.

"You should really think about putting up an age minimum for customers," Renee announced. "Might help you keep the wrong sorts out of here."

Maren felt her cheeks burn.

Gabby just looked back at Renee coldly. "Age doesn't seem to be a factor when it comes to the wrong sorts," she said.

Renee made a *humph!* sound and clacked out on her high heels.

"You okay?" Gabby asked Maren gently when Renee had gone.

"Fine," Maren muttered, rubbing away her tears. Just

as quickly as her anger had risen up, now it disappeared entirely, leaving her feeling embarrassed. "I'm sorry, if anyone complains, I'll—"

"Don't you worry about that, honey," the elderly woman piped up from the corner. When Maren looked at her, surprised, she offered a reassuring nod.

"That's right," the man said. "No corporate suit is going to chase away our campers!"

Maren felt more tears forming, these grateful, but she shook them away and asked, "Who was that woman anyway?"

Gabby gave an angry sniff. "Only her royal whiny-ness, Renee Wallace, the owner of everything, aka Walcorp."

Maren was so confused she felt dizzy. "As in... like, the store Walcorp?"

"The multibillion-dollar devil that's finally trying to build in the Berkshires—yep, one and the same," the man said.

"The company has been buying a lot of property around here for a while," the woman added.

"They keep trying to buy this place out from under me." Gabby scowled. "But I pay my mortgage, thank you very much, and nothing she says or does at the bank is going to change that!"

"But..." Maren looked out the window, where she could just see Renee Wallace disappearing down the sidewalk. "But, I mean, why is *she* here personally?"

"Another great question. No one knows why the founder's daughter keeps hanging around, but..." Gabby leaned across the counter and regarded Maren with a serious look. "But the word is, what she really wants is the camp."

Maren's head was spinning as she left the coffee shop and started on the trail back to camp. What was Renee Wallace, the rich daughter of the founder of one of the biggest companies in the world, doing in the middle of Nowheresville, Massachusetts? And why did she want the camp's land?

Because she's looking for something, a voice in Maren's head answered. *Because she's looking for the ring.*

Maren's steps slowed, then dragged to a stop completely. If Renee Wallace was the person working with an accomplice within the camp, she had been behind the kidnapping of Miss Bradley—she was trying to find the ring. But that was crazy! Why would a wealthy woman like Renee care about one ring? And who was she working with? And did they know about the clues in the play?

Maren took a deep breath. She was getting ahead of herself. If Theo were here, they would remind her that she was making assumptions—but, speaking of Theo, they were still in the village. Maren realized with a start that she had left without telling Theo and Graham where she was going. Actually, did *she* know where she was going? Maren looked around. She thought she was on the same trail as the one Graham had led them on that morning, but she didn't remember passing the Walcorp plot. Maybe she had taken a wrong turn somewhere and forked off in the wrong direction? She was about to turn around and retrace her steps back to town when she heard someone call out.

"Hey, Boston!" Sal jogged toward her, both dimples on display. "What's up? You get lost or something?"

"A little turned around," Maren admitted, returning the smile. A warm thrill at running into him filled her chest. "You?"

"I was about to head to town when I saw somebody stomping around in the woods and thought I might finally catch the ghost." He grinned wider. "You do realize you're creeping behind the boys' cabins, right?"

"Oh no, really?" Instantly some of her thrill turned to blistering embarrassment. "I knew I took a wrong turn somewhere. I should probably go find Jo and tell her..." She realized something else Sal had said. "Wait, did you say something about the ghost?"

"Ghost *story*, more like." Sal shrugged. "A few guys have said they've seen someone sneaking around back here, but it's probably just talk."

"Around here?" Maren looked around her feet at the path, but there weren't any fresh footprints to see. "Did they see where it went?"

Sal shot her a quizzical look, then pointed off to one side. "I mean, this one guy Tony thought he saw the ghost go that way but—hey! Wait up!"

Maren had already started in the direction of his finger.

The path here was narrow and cluttered with leaves and fallen branches. She could hear Sal panting and trampling sticks behind her.

"Does this ghost owe you money or something?" he called at one point, but Maren just plowed on ahead.

After a few more minutes, the path opened up into a clearing. There was a shed, a glassed-in greenhouse, and a bench stacked with empty flowerpots. On the far side of the shed was a meadow of high grasses, spotted with a few small, square wooden structures. Even farther, Maren could just make out the distant Walcorp diggers and trailers.

"Those must be the beehives," Maren said to Sal when he caught up. "Jo comes back here to tend them. She said something about it on the first day. They probably saw her in her beekeeping suit."

Sal laughed. "Man, I knew those kids didn't see any ghost."

"I don't think we're allowed around here," Maren said, turning away, feeling disappointed. "We should probably head back."

"Are you kidding? We can't leave now—this is like from a fairy tale or something!" He walked around the outside of the greenhouse and whistled. "Come on, let's go inside."

"I don't know," she said, thinking of Mr. Cairn's stern face.

But Sal didn't seem to hear her. "You coming?" he said, holding the door. He gave her another dimpled smile.

She felt that slight thrill again. "Yeah, okay," she said, and she started forward before she had a chance to change her mind.

Inside, it was twice as warm as outside, and so humid the glass was streaked with condensation. All around the glass walls were shelves stacked with pots, every one of them overflowing with vibrant, exotic-looking flowers.

Sal whistled again. "Somebody must love these," he said, bending down to examine a particularly beautiful orange flower. "Orchids are really hard to grow. I tried to grow one with my mom once, but it was so fussy, it died in like two days."

Maren looked around with a fresh sense of curiosity. If the flowers were so hard to take care of, then, considering that every adult she knew was in rehearsal all day, who had the time?

"Check out this one," Sal said, crouching next to an enormous orchid in a pot on the floor, each white flower on the arcing branch as big as a teacup. "Wonder if Ms. Casta makes them do tongue exercises."

Maren froze. "What did you say?"

"Just a joke," Sal said. "In Speech and Diction, Ms. Casta makes us do all these tongue twisters to warm up. Like, *You know New York, You need New York, You know you need unique New York—*"

"*Be you his eunuch, and your mute I'll be / When my tongue blabs, then let mine eyes not see,*" Maren said, staring at the orchid.

"I don't know that one...." Sal made a face. "Wait, what about a eunuch now?"

"These flowers!" Maren grabbed his arm. "They have tongues! And they don't speak!"

"That's right," Sal said slowly. "Flowers *don't* speak...."

"Eyes," Maren muttered to herself, looking around, "what has eyes in a greenhouse?"

"All I know is, if it has anything to do with being a eunuch, I'm out," Sal joked, but Maren's mind was racing.

"Vegetables! Vegetables have eyes! Sal, we need to look for a plant that's out of place—a carrot or cucumber or a potato plant."

"What would a potato plant be doing in an orchid greenhouse?"

"It shouldn't be!" Maren laughed. "So help me find it!"

It took a good fifteen minutes of searching the many, many plants, but eventually Sal called out, "I don't know what kind of plant this is, but it's not an orchid."

Maren raced over to where he was, almost upsetting the big white orchid plant on the floor. She crouched next to him in front of a medium-sized pot. The plant sprouting from it had wide leaves with broad, trumpet-shaped purple flowers. There was what looked like a bumper sticker wrapped around the outside of the pot, the writing obscured and crusted over with soil. Maren brushed at it with her thumbs until she could make out what it said.

"*Don't blame me,*" Sal read. "*I voted for Helen Gahagan Douglas.* Who's Helen Gahagan Douglas?"

But Maren had spotted a small label stuck in the soil itself and pulled it out: *Solanum tuberosum.*

"How much you want to bet that means 'potato' in Latin?" Maren breathed.

"I really wouldn't bet anything right now," Sal said.

Maren was dimly aware he was looking at her like she had lost her mind, but she just dug two fingers into the soil and started feeling around.

"Whoa, hey, just because it's not an orchid doesn't mean you should *hurt* the poor potato!" Sal said, but Maren had already felt the edges of something hard and flat. She screamed a little in excitement and pulled out a cream-and-gold envelope wrapped in a cloth bag, scattering more dirt on the floor in the process.

"What," Sal whispered, "is that?"

Part of her thought maybe she should wait for Theo and Graham, but she was too excited. Maren plucked off the bag, opened the envelope, and took a satisfied breath.

"Our next clue," she said, then held out the paper for him to see.

And yet, by the very fangs of
malice I swear,
I am not that I play.

Charlie

August 12, 1951
Los Angeles, California

Charlie stood behind the closed door at the end of the church aisle. Next to her, her sister, Rosalie, half buried in her lace-and-satin explosion of a dress, trembled and gripped her arm.

"You'll stay with me the whole way?" Rosalie whispered as they watched a chorus line of twelve bridesmaids, Jeremy's many cousins and sisters, all wearing matching peach fluffy dresses, begin a slow, sauntering promenade down the aisle. "You won't leave me?"

Charlie smiled. If she had thought for a moment that Rosalie didn't want to marry Jeremy, she would have thrown her sister over one shoulder and carried her out the door. But she knew Rosalie loved Jeremy and that her nerves were more a product of having to stand in front of Jeremy's very large, very opinionated, very wealthy East Coast family. Rosalie's new family was, Charlie had been repeatedly told, one of the prominent social families of New England. Jeremy's father had a seat on the Boston City Council, and one of his uncles was a front-runner for governor. It had been a minor scandal to the family when Jeremy, a shy, gangly man who blushed almost constantly behind his glasses, moved out to Los Angeles and fell in love with Rosalie, but his family eventually learned what Jeremy realized immediately and Charlie had known always—that there was no one sweeter, kinder, or more wonderful than Rosalie.

"I'll be here," Charlie assured her sister. "Now and always." She smiled as relief swept over her sister's face.

In the chapel, the wedding march began playing. An usher stood nearby, ready to open the door and reveal Rosalie to her future husband.

"Ready?" Charlie asked her sister.

Rosalie stood up straighter and nodded. The usher took this as his cue and pulled the door open. Rosalie squeezed Charlie's arm, and they took their first steps forward.

At the other end of the aisle—flanked by those peachy bridesmaids on one side and tuxedoed young men on the other—was Jeremy, squinting in their direction. His mother had demanded, no doubt, that he take off his glasses for the ceremony, but when they got close enough for poor nearsighted Jeremy to see, his face split into a wide grin. Charlie felt Rosalie's grip on her arm loosen and knew she was happy. At the front, Charlie lifted Rosalie's veil to give her beaming sister a kiss on the cheek, then took her seat in the front pew. Jeremy's mother gave Charlie an approving nod before turning back to observe the rest of the ceremony with a militant intensity. Charlie knew she should be grateful for even that. If Jeremy's mother had known the truth…

When Rosalie had introduced Charlie to Jeremy and his family, she had called Charlie "my brother." It was something they had decided on together, after Charlie was caught wearing a blazer by their old landlord and they were asked to leave their first apartment. When they moved into their new place, Charlie wore men's clothes all the time.

But there was a big difference between telling a land-lord or a neighbor or even a boss that Charlie was a man, and Rosalie having told her future in-laws this lie. Charlie always comforted herself that, if she were ever found out, there was always another apartment, another job, a fresh start. But this was Rosalie's new family—and, by exten-sion, Charlie's too. She was going to have to see them for holidays and weddings and birthday parties. What would happen if *they* ever found out?

Soon enough, the rings had been exchanged, the vows said, and Rosalie and Jeremy were presented as man and wife. Charlie stood with the others and clapped as her sister and her new husband passed back down the aisle, beam-ing. After the ceremony, Jeremy's mother had coordinated a lavish reception at the home of a family friend—or, really, at the *mansion* of a family friend. It was massive and ornate, decorated with the most expensive, fashionable furniture, and every corner blossoming with peach roses. Tables had been set up in the sprawling garden and laid with a beautifully catered meal, while the cake towered like a miniature fairy palace in the gazebo by the pool. Charlie sipped at her punch and tried not to seem too out of place.

"Hey, Charlie!" Her new brother-in-law beamed and waved her over where he stood with one of the party guests. "Wayman here was just talking about getting into the movie business! I told him my new brother-in-law is a cracking good director." He draped an arm around Char-lie's shoulder and gave it a comradely shake.

"I'm not a director yet," Charlie said, embarrassed.

Even after years of working as a grip or camera techni-cian, she had only just recently managed to work her way up to film cutter. She loved getting to pore over the reels every day, studying each film frame by frame and watching the editor make choices about when the story shifted between actors. Cutting and editing were, she knew, the same way Dorothy Arzner had really gotten her start in the film business—but Arzner hadn't directed a movie in nearly a decade, and most studios would have laughed at the idea of a woman behind a camera. Another reason why her secret felt increasingly dangerous.

She hurried to take a sip of her drink, trying to swallow her nerves.

"Well, you *should* be a director!" Jeremy was saying, his enthusiasm refusing to be dimmed. "You'll get there one day!"

Charlie couldn't help but smile. She was grateful to Jeremy, whose genuine happiness made her feel a little more at ease.

"And Wayman here is thinking about getting in the producing game," Jeremy said, turning to another man. "Isn't that right, Wayman?"

"It's not me who's interested," said a haughty voice, and Charlie looked up to see Jeremy's companion. He was a man with an enormous forehead, puffing on an even bigger cigar. He looked familiar, though she couldn't place him. "I personally can't wait to get back to New York," the man was saying, "but my fiancée here insists on trying her hand at acting before we get married. She's the reason we're staying in this den of iniquity, aren't you, my sweet?"

And there she was, walking up to them with a tight, humorless smile, still the most beautiful woman Charlie had ever seen. Suddenly, Charlie knew exactly where she had seen her and the man—the political party from the year before. Today, the woman was in a dress of spring-green silk with pearl buttons that went in a diagonal line instead of straight down, and her unnaturally blond hair was styled in waves to make her look like a movie star. Charlie looked away, feeling herself blushing.

"Yes, *she* likes this den of iniquity," the woman said. "And for the millionth time, *she* doesn't like being called *sweet*."

"Apologies." Wayman turned back to Jeremy and Charlie. "Jeremy, you've met my *sour* fiancée, haven't you?"

"Of course, so good to see you, Emma!" Jeremy leaned forward and kissed the beautiful woman on the cheek.

"Oh, Jeremy, you're glowing even more than the bride," Emma teased.

"I'm the happiest man in this den or any," Jeremy agreed. "And the luckiest. I really can't thank Wayman enough for hosting our reception at this lovely home—"

"Jeremy's brother-in-law, Charles here, is a movie man," Wayman interrupted, and gestured at Charlie with his glass. "Perhaps, darling, he'd be able to help you with your little Shakespeare project."

"Really?" Emma said, and just like that, her startlingly bright eyes spun around and landed on Charlie.

Charlie felt like a moth, stuck straight through her heart and pinned in place. She was certain, in that moment, that Emma saw her—the real her—and recognized her. A flicker of confusion passed over Emma's face and her perfect bow mouth opened, perhaps ready with a quick-witted barb about the men's blindness.

Charlie cast a panicked glance at her sister. Would her

secret be revealed so soon? What would happen to Rosalie? When Charlie looked back, she saw that Emma had followed her gaze. Impossibly, she seemed to understand—seemed to sense that Charlie's was a secret that needed keeping. Her mouth closed and lifted into a smile.

"It's very nice to meet you—Charles, is it?" Emma said.

Charlie swallowed. "Just Charlie," she said, her voice raspy in her throat.

"Well, very nice to meet you, Just Charlie," Emma repeated. She held out a hand gloved in cream satin.

Charlie took the hand in hers. She held it.

Maren

"Wait, wait, wait, wait," Theo said, holding up a hand at breakfast the next morning. "What do you mean, the coffee shop lady just *gave* you a hot chocolate?" They looked at Graham aghast. "Did you know the coffee shop lady just *gave* out hot chocolates?"

"Kind of missing the point, Theo," Maren said. She had just told them everything about Renee Wallace, the phone call in French, and, most important, finding the third clue in the orchid greenhouse. But naturally, Theo was fixated on something else.

"I'm just saying," they said, "we spent ages in the chocolate shop, and all we got were three teensy-tiny chocolate-covered raisins! Raisins, Graham, *raisins!*"

"It's not like we bought anything," Graham reminded them. "And we only stayed in there so long because we were waiting for someone." He purposefully avoided Maren's gaze.

"I am really sorry for ditching you two," Maren repeated for probably the tenth time. "I just needed to think, and then Sal and I were talking about the ghost and found ourselves at the greenhouse, but I didn't mean to find the next clue without you."

Graham shrugged, still not looking at her, but Theo

flapped a friendly, dismissive hand. "Clue, schmoo, I'd rather just skip to the finding-the-ring part."

"Well, we're not there yet." Maren looked around to make sure no one was eavesdropping, then pulled the newest quote out of her binder. "Any idea what this one means?"

She held it out to Graham, but he didn't take it.

Theo leaned over and snagged the card. "*Fangs of malice*, huh?" they mused. "Sounds like a horror movie. What do you think, Graham?"

Graham just kept poking at his English muffin, a half-melted pat of butter sitting on the sharp points like snow on mountain peaks. Maren frowned. How many times was she going to have to apologize?

"Or not!" Theo said, their voice a little too chipper. They slid the clue back across the table at Maren. "What did Sal think?"

"Well—"

"So you told him everything?" Graham broke in again, his voice sharp with very un-Graham-like bluntness. "You told Sal everything?"

Maren looked at him, surprised. "I mean, I kind of had to—he was there when I found the clue." She looked from Graham to Theo, who was starting to look uncomfortable. "Why? Is that not okay?"

"Sal's a good addition," Theo said. "Just, from now on, the four of us should vote before we let anyone else in on the Twelfth Team."

"Then maybe we should also vote on the name the Twelfth Team," Maren joked. "It sounds like we're the *twelfth* team, like the team after the eleventh team."

"Given my lack of athletic talent, I would be honored to

be on the twelfth team of anything," Theo said in a mock-haughty voice.

Maren laughed. "Anyway, maybe Sal will have some ideas at lunch. He said he'd sit with us today, and he's good at that sort of—"

All of a sudden, Graham stood up. "I should get going," he said.

Maren and Theo looked at him, then at each other.

"But we all have Tech class first," Maren said. "Don't you want to walk over together?"

"I have to do a thing first," Graham said as he headed for the door.

Maren watched him go, then looked at Theo.

"Don't worry about him," Theo said, reaching over and snagging the abandoned bunch of grapes from Graham's plate. Their vest today had thin rainbow stripes—horizontal on one side, vertical on the other—and made Maren think of an optical illusion. "He's just jealous."

"He's jealous that Sal and I figured out the greenhouse clue without him?"

Theo gave her a look that almost seemed impatient. "Not jealous of the *clue*, no."

"Then what?"

"Nothing. I don't know." Theo plucked the grapes from their stems and popped them in their mouth, then pointed at Maren's plate. "Are you going to finish that?"

Graham continued to avoid Maren for the rest of the morning. In Tech, he got assigned to a different work crew than Maren and Theo, and in Theater History, where Jo was discussing Japan's Kabuki theater, he picked a seat on the far side of the room. He practically ran out of class at the end. In Playwriting, Sal tried to start up a conversation about the clue, but Maren shushed him. Allegra was right there, fiddling with her fuzzy notebook and pretending not to listen, and Maren didn't think any of them would want Allegra to join the Twelfth Team.

Maren had almost given up on Graham by lunch, but he appeared just when she, Theo, and Sal found seats on the grass outside the cafeteria.

"I just want to say one thing," he announced, holding his tray high. He looked down at all of them seriously, some of his scowl from this morning returning, and took a deep breath. "I think we should agree right now that if we find it, the ring goes to Jo. It isn't ours to keep, and if it's worth anything, the money should be used to save the camp. Agreed?"

"Absolutely," Maren said.

"Yep," Sal said.

"Right on," Theo said, moving the camera to catch everyone.

"Also," Graham went on as if he hadn't heard, "we should agree to do this as safely as possible. Renee Wallace and someone else *kidnapped* Miss Bradley to find this thing. If it seems like it's going to get too dangerous, we go tell Jo right away. Deal?"

"Deal," Sal said.

"Deal," Theo agreed.

Maren nodded but turned away, pretending to struggle with her cell phone. She didn't like thinking of someone else taking over the search for the ring, even if things did get dangerous. Anyway, Jo didn't believe in the ring, she comforted herself. If they gave her the clues, she'd probably just ignore them. "That reminds me," Maren changed the subject. "Theo, want to tell us what Renee Wallace was saying in French?"

Graham took a seat, and Sal slapped his back, while Theo pressed play on the audio file. They squinted as a few seconds of French piped out, then abruptly cut off. Maren ground her teeth, remembering Ed's sudden interruption—and how mean she had been to him. She forced the thought away as Theo played the recording a few more times, but in the end, they just sighed.

"There's not a lot I can make out," they admitted, passing Maren's phone back. "Renee says something about raising money—*levée de fonds*—like *fondos* in Spanish."

"Well, finding the ring would raise money, all right," Graham said.

"And I think I heard something about a *cuisine*? She said something like *petite cuisine*."

"Theo, no offense, but you hear food for just about everything," Sal joked.

All of them laughed. Maren meant to ask Theo if *cuisine* could mean anything else, but she didn't get a chance. Somehow, they got to laughing about this YouTube video of a cat they'd all seen, and then laughing as Theo recorded Sal doing tongue twisters from Speech and Diction—"red leather, yellow leather, red leather, yellow leather"—with his mouth full of olives, and then, impossibly, lunch was over and it was time for rehearsal.

Maren looked up aghast as the campers started making

their way to the auditorium. "We haven't even talked about what the clue means yet."

"Don't worry about it," Sal said. "There'll be plenty of downtime during rehearsal when we can talk about it."

But there was no downtime at rehearsal, after Jo announced that actors had to be "off book," their lines memorized, by the end of the week.

"That's camp for you, people!" Jo called over the grumbles. "We move *fast*!"

For the rest of the day, Theo, Graham, and Sal were working with either Jo or Mr. Cairn, blocking their scenes, and in the rare moments when they weren't onstage, they had their heads bowed over their scripts, learning their lines. Maren was the busiest of them all—running back and forth with messages between Jo and the other counselors, keeping track of where actors were, learning everyone's name, and managing the running and break times. When she was finally able to sit, it was usually to make notes for Jo of where every single character was at every moment onstage. Her script was so full of "Olivia crosses here" and "Orsino moves upstage" that there was no room for her to jot ideas to herself about the clue.

Tuesday flew by at the same frantic pace. In Tech class, they had begun to build the hull of a ship that could be broken in half for the storm at the beginning of the play, and in Theater History, they were learning about Elizabethan drama in Shakespeare's time—"Just think of it as the time when *Hamlet* was the *Hamilton* of the day," Jo said.

In Playwriting, Monty wrote the words "TEXT" and "SUBTEXT" on the board.

"A character can say, 'You're the worst,' and really mean, 'I wish you loved me,'" he said, "Or, 'This is the best chicken dinner ever,' and mean, 'I'm dying inside.'"

The class laughed, but Monty raised his eyebrows.

"Are you telling me that you say exactly what you mean all the time?" He seemed astounded. "Sometimes we don't know how to say the things we need to say to the people we care about the most."

A quiet settled over the class then, one that felt fragile, as if it had been spun from glass. Maren wondered what they were all thinking about right then; she was trying her very hardest *not* to think about her sister.

"Freewrite," Monty said. "I want you to write a scene where two characters never say what they're actually fighting about. I know, it sounds tricky, but"—he shrugged and grinned—"you might find your characters sound a whole lot more like real people."

He was right—it was tricky.

After the freewriting, Sal shared the scene he had written about two men discussing what the phrase "I love you, man" meant, but no one could guess what they were really talking about. Allegra's scene was all too obviously about one woman stealing another's boyfriend—though the "charming and beautiful blond" forgave the other.

"Good work again," Monty said when it was time for lunch. "Looking forward to hearing more tomorrow."

Maren fiddled with her bag so she didn't have to meet his gaze. True to his word, Monty never made Maren read aloud what she wrote. But sometimes he looked at her when he asked if anyone had anything they wanted to share, as if to let her know he hoped she would. Sometimes she surprised herself by wanting to share, too.

During rehearsals, while the others were onstage or studying, Maren tried to think up answers to the clue, but so far, this one was proving to be the hardest yet. The phrase "fangs of malice" meant lying, she learned, but Maren couldn't see how that related to any of the other clues or a location at the camp. She found herself gritting her own fangs when she had to watch the scene where the line came from—where Viola and Olivia first meet. Onstage, rabbity Piper prattled through the words, while Allegra batted her eyelashes and clasped her hands as in super-fake, totally melodramatic love.

"Bring that down a little bit," Jo directed during rehearsal.

Allegra lowered her clasped hands.

"No, not the hands," Jo said, "I mean the intensity. Don't *perform* being in love."

Allegra made a face. "But I'm supposed to be in love, aren't I?"

"See, the problem is you're thinking about how you *look* instead of how the character *feels*," Jo explained as she held up the script. "Just look at the line here: *Stay: I prithee, tell me what thou thinkest of me.* Why do you think she's asking Viola that?"

Allegra tossed her hair over her shoulder. "She wants Viola to notice her."

"That's exactly right. And do you know what that feels like?" Jo asked. "To have a crush on someone who doesn't notice you or think of you that way?"

Maren almost scoffed out loud. How could someone like Allegra know anything about unrequited crushes? But to Maren's surprise, Allegra gave a single, tight nod in answer. Then she quickly looked around, as if daring anyone to laugh at her.

"Well, remember how that feels when you say your line," Jo said. "Try again."

When Allegra read the line again, she stopped trying to make it look like she was in love, and this, somehow, made her seem more in love. Jo smiled her encouragement, and even Maren was a little impressed. She spent the rest of the rehearsal not entirely hating Allegra, though that didn't last long.

"As many of you know," Jo said at the end of rehearsal, "the Midsummer Gala is next week. This is a pretty special opportunity to raise money for the camp and for the members of the community to meet all of you, so there will be snacks and all kinds of party stuff."

There were some excited murmurs in the room. Maren couldn't help grinning at the expression on Theo's face when they heard "snacks."

"Jo?" Allegra's hand was in the air even though she had already started speaking. "Have you made a decision about who's going to perform?"

"Thank you, Allegra, I was just getting to that," Jo said with a patient smile.

Maren felt a new tension in the room grow.

"Every year, we choose a scene from the play to be performed for our donors—just to show them what we do here. I know any of you would do an amazing job representing the camp, but I can only choose a small group to perform. So…"

Jo took a breath, and the tension became almost unbearably high. "I'll be making my decision about which scene after seeing who is off book by Friday. Sound good?"

The group nodded, successfully motivated. Allegra smirked at Piper and Nic—confident, no doubt, that she was going to be picked.

By Thursday, the news of the gala performance selection and the upcoming off-book deadline seemed to have whipped everyone into a panic. The cafeteria was silent at breakfast, and everyone seemed distracted during classes— Bernie actually raised his voice to tell Greg to put his script away or it would be taken. Maren was distracted as well, but not because of the play. She still hadn't figured out the clue, and who knew how many more clues came afterward? They were running out of time—to figure out the clues, to find the ring, and to save the camp from Renee Wallace.

At lunch, Theo, Graham, and Sal were gathered in a weary huddle at a table, all of them slumped over their open scripts, blindly shoving food in their mouths.

"Does anyone have any ideas about the *fangs of malice*?" Maren said as she laid down her tomato soup and grilled cheese with care.

"What's that?" Sal looked up from his script. "Oh yeah, right, the clue—let me think...." He paused and squinted into the distance.

The other three looked at him curiously, half expecting him to snatch the magic answer out of thin air.

"Yeah, no, I've got nothing," Sal said, then dropped his gaze back down to the pages in front of him.

"I don't think I'll ever have ideas again," Theo groaned, grabbing their hair at the temples. They were wearing a rather plain vest today—just a black-and-white checkerboard pattern—and for once, they didn't have their camera out. "My brain is a fried egg—a fried egg on top of burnt toast—a fried egg on top of burnt toast with ground sausage on the side." They hesitated. "Also, I think I'm still hungry." They gave Maren's tray the side-eye until she handed over a corner of her grilled cheese.

"I've been thinking about the *I am not that I play* part," Graham said. "Like, does *play* mean the play?"

"That's a good idea," Maren said hopefully. "You have parts in a play! Is there any way the play is not what it seems?"

"Yeah," Sal grumbled. "It didn't *seem* like it was going to kill us, but it's definitely killing us."

"Ain't that the truth," Theo said. "It doesn't matter how many times I repeat the words, Malvolio's lines just aren't sinking in."

Maren sighed and sipped at her soup. So long as the others were focused on the play, there was no chance they were going to work out the clue. It was up to her. "I'll see you guys later," she said, putting down her spoon and standing.

"Now?" Theo asked. "I was hoping you could help quiz me on my lines."

"Sorry, can't," Maren said, grabbing a triangle of grilled cheese. "But I'll see you in rehearsal. I'm sure you'll be fine."

"In that case, are you going to eat your—" Theo started, but Maren had automatically pushed her bowl of soup in Theo's direction.

Maren ate the rest of her sandwich as she hurried to the main building. She realized she hadn't tried the internet yet, and though she didn't exactly expect Google to have a map to the ring, she thought it was still worth a search.

The camp's library looked like any school library, full of colorful tables and beanbag chairs, as well as a section of tables set with computers. There was one slight difference, though: Most of the shelves in this library were filled with the slim-spined volumes of plays, tucked together like the lines of a barcode. Maren ran her finger along a few as she made her way over to the computers. There were some people already sitting there—a girl on costume crew, Jameela, Skyping quietly in the corner; a pair of first-year boys, Anton and Will, playing a video game; and, to Maren's surprise, Monty, typing away—but no one looked up as Maren found an empty computer and signed in.

She decided to check her email first, and she wasn't surprised to find one from her mom and one from her dad. She wrote back a one-sentence message to her mom that she was fine, she'd call on Sunday—it was easier to write something than have to deal with her mom worrying. She read her dad's message about touring with a Bob Dylan cover band in Vermont but didn't know what to say back, so she left it alone. She was about to sign off when another email appeared.

Hey seaweed read the subject line.

Maren snatched her hands away from the keyboard, as if she had been burned. There, sitting innocently in her in-box, was an email from Hadley. It had been sent only moments before. That meant, on the other side of the state, her sister was online at the exact same second she was. Her fingers trembling, Maren reached out again and moved the cursor over the email, but she didn't click on it. Did she really want to see what Hadley had to say to her?

With a quick swipe, Maren moved the cursor over and hit delete. The unread email disappeared instantly, as if it had never been there. Maren sighed. It felt almost good, as if she had chopped off a bad spot on an apple and tossed it away.

That done, she opened a search engine and typed in "play." The results weren't hopeful: a definition of play as "to engage in enjoyable activity or sport" and, of course, theatrical plays. She tried searching "twelfth night play" and came back with links to buy copies of the script. On a whim, she typed in "Charlotte Goodman." The camp website came up, but not a lot else. She clicked on a page that claimed "read old newspapers here!" and opened an article from a Los Angeles paper.

RISING DIRECTOR AND STARLET MUSE DIE IN REEL BLAZE, read the headline.

> The Hollywood stars hang a little lower tonight, as they mourn the death of Charlotte "Charlie" Goodman and rising starlet Emma Bonaventure, who died when the iconic Crandolf Building burned down on the Global Studio film lot.
>
> While the exact cause of the fire is unknown, a single spark could have set the celluloid film there into the fierce blaze that soon overwhelmed most of the building. By the time the fire brigade arrived, it was too late

to save the structure or its contents, though at this time there is no evidence of foul play.

Emma Gertrude Bonaventure, rising starlet and social darling, is survived by her fiancé, Mr. Wayman Wallace, who managed to escape the burning building and alert authorities that his fiancée was still inside.

"She was radiant," the obviously distressed Wallace told your trusted correspondent. "You couldn't take your eyes off her."

Mr. Wallace seemed particularly distraught that he won't be able to lay his beloved to rest in his family's plot, but authorities insist the building is so unstable and damaged, a search for remains would prove impossible.

Mr. Wallace further asked your trusted correspondent to inform all readers that he is still searching for the engagement ring he gave his beloved Emma, desperately seeking it "for sentimental value," and is offering a reward for its return. At the mention of Miss Goodman, however, Mr. Wallace's handsome face turned to a sneer, though he refused to give further details or to respond to comments he supposedly made about the director while seen imbibing at the Mango Room earlier that evening.

This was to be the debut film of director Charlotte "Charlie" Goodman, though studio sources also aren't responding to rumors that the fire comes on the heels of a major fallout between investors and the studio.

> Charlotte Goodman is survived by her sister, Mrs. Jeremy Jacobs of Stonecourt, Massachusetts. There will be a memorial on the Global Studio lot on Thursday.

Maren stared at the names.

Then, her fingers trembling, she opened another page with the search engine and typed "Wayman Wallace." There were pages and pages of results, each one making Maren's heart beat faster. She clicked on the first, an online encyclopedia page, which confirmed in the first sentence what she had been thinking:

> **WAYMAN WALLACE** (September 9, 1922 – October 19, 1987) was an entrepreneur and business magnate best known as the heir and later CEO of what became known as Walcorp Industries. The eldest son of tycoon Horace Wallace and his wife, Paulina, Wallace inherited his father's majority share in the chain of convenience stores bearing the family name in his early twenties. He went on to invest in the entertainment industry, producing over a dozen films, owning a record company, and investing in profitable real estate, most notably as an early developer in Las Vegas. In 1960, he married Esmée Antoinette Martin Deschamps, an aspiring singer whose career he managed until his death nearly three decades later. Wallace died after the "Black Monday" stock market crash of 1987, when he saw the value of his company

plummet. Believing that the empire his father had built had been overstrained by his breadth of investments and that Walcorp would have to declare bankruptcy, Wallace died as a result of a fall from the ninety-seventh floor of the Walcorp Building in New York City. He left no note. Following his death, his brother acted as interim CEO of the company until being replaced by Wayman Wallace's daughter, Renee Wallace, as CEO fifteen years later.

Maren stared at the screen, the pixelated letters burning against their white background.

Wayman Wallace was the founder of Walcorp.

Wayman Wallace was Renee Wallace's father.

Wayman Wallace was there the night Charlotte Goodman died—and the ring went missing.

Something moved behind her, a flit of shadow she caught reflected in the monitor's screen. Maren spun in her seat, heart pounding. Her eyes roved over the shelves of books behind her, darting from one brightly colored volume to the next, peering into the space between, half expecting to see a pair of eyes peering back at her. But no one was there. No one was anywhere, she realized when she saw all the computers were empty, and a glance at the clock explained why—rehearsal started two minutes ago.

As quickly as she could, she shut down the computer, grabbed her things, and flew from the library. Halfway down the stairs, she realized she hadn't cleared her search history and almost turned back—but there was no one there, she comforted herself, and besides, she hadn't done anything wrong.

Maren managed to drop into her seat just as Jo was calling the group to attention for rehearsal. Jo gave Maren a raised-eyebrow look but only said, "Last day with scripts in hand! Let's get to scene assignments."

Maren tried to focus as groups were split up: Orsino and Viola were working in the Black Box with Mr. Cairn, the chorus with Ms. Green in the rehearsal space, and so on. Jo wanted to work on the first part of act 1, scene 5, which meant that Sal and Theo were on the main stage—along with Emil, who played Sir Toby, Nic as Maria, and, unfortunately, Allegra as Olivia.

Maren flipped to the scene in her script, feeling like dinner couldn't come soon enough. She thought the hardest part of the afternoon would be having to hold on to the secret until then, but, as it turned out, the hardest part was having to watch Theo struggle onstage. It was still obvious Theo was a talented performer—they were fearless and funny, making large gestures and playing up Malvolio's voice. But the problem was, Theo didn't know their lines. At all.

The other kids weren't perfect yet, either, and would frequently glance at the script from time to time to remind themselves of what they were supposed to say. But Theo still had to read every word, and unfortunately for them, this was hard to do when they were acting. They kept making big gestures or getting so wrapped up in the character that they would lose their place in the script, stumble on the words, and struggle to find their place again.

"Great choices, Theo," Jo kept calling to them. "But don't lose the line in the action."

Theo would nod, their bang-length hair bouncing, as they flipped through pages. When they started up again, things would go on smoothly for a little while, but then Theo would get too much into it, gesture too broadly with the hand holding the script, and lose their place all over again. Maren saw Sal wince as Theo traced their finger all over the page, while Allegra looked more and more satisfied.

By the end of rehearsal, Maren was gripping her pencil so tightly she thought the wood might snap. Finally, Jo sighed and called the group over for notes.

"Really great work, team," she said. "But focus on the fundamentals. A lot of my notes are getting repeated—Nic, remember Maria's got some sass to her, but she keeps it light. Allegra, pull back for now, focus on the internals of the character. And Theo? Get those lines memorized for tomorrow."

Allegra, who was smiling and whispering to Laurence, the guy who played Sir Andrew, brushed off her note, but Theo's gaze stayed on their feet. They took off like a shot as soon as Jo dismissed them for the evening, but Maren knew she couldn't go after them until Jo ran through the next day's schedule. Ten minutes later, Maren had just pushed through the front door and stepped out into the last of the sunlight when she heard someone call: "Hey, Maren! Wait up!"

Maren turned to see who it was, and promptly almost tripped over her own feet in shock.

Allegra was casually loping toward her—*Allegra*.

"Hey!" Allegra said too brightly. "How's it going? You going to dinner?"

It took a full ten seconds for Maren to respond. That was how long she considered the question, looking at it from all angles and trying to find the intended insult. "Yes," Maren said eventually, unable to keep the suspicion from her voice.

"Per*fec*tion! Let's walk together," Allegra said, then started down the path, chatting on as she went. "God, don't you just hate how grumpy everyone's been? It's like, yeah, we get it, acting is hard work, sorry to, like, interrupt your summer, but why did you bother to come to a theater camp, you know? I was just telling Nic the other day..."

And on she went. Maren felt as if she had stepped into an alternate reality. She imagined all the explanations Theo would come up with: Allegra had been subbed out by aliens. Allegra had been hit by a mysterious bolt of super lightning that magically changed her personality. Allegra had time-traveled and now, knowing the error of her ways, was allowed to go back and try to make amends to everyone she had wronged.

"I mean, it's like with your sister," Allegra was saying, suddenly snagging Maren's attention, "when she was Emily, she stayed in character and didn't—"

"Wait, what?" Maren pulled up short. Allegra paused along the path and looked back at her, blinking her big eyes. "You know Hadley?"

"Oh yeah!" Allegra showed Maren her mouthful of perfect teeth. "Hadley was a counselor here when we were in the elementary school session. Didn't Graham tell you?"

Graham obviously hadn't told her, but worse, Maren hadn't thought to ask. She remembered being afraid when she met Katie and Lorna that they might remember Hadley, but now it seemed strange that Graham hadn't mentioned it. "I didn't realize," she said, before she slowly started walking again. "Why haven't you ever said anything?"

"I don't know." Allegra shrugged, matching Maren's stride. "But you're right, we should talk more—maybe you should sit with us sometime. We could talk about Hadley, or I'd actually really love notes from you about the show— it'd be interesting to hear what you think, what Jo says about the performances, which scenes are the best...."

All at once, Maren realized why Allegra was talking to her. She almost laughed out loud. "I don't know who's going to be picked for the gala," she said bluntly.

Allegra's footsteps faltered for just a split second. "Oh."

"Jo hasn't said anything, if that's why you're talking to me," Maren said, feeling emboldened now that the cafeteria was within view. When Allegra didn't respond, she added, "Even if she had, I wouldn't tell you."

"Glad I didn't waste too much of my time on you, then." Allegra's voice had its usual bite back in it. "A little bit of advice, though?" She paused as they got to the cafeteria door. "You're being *so* obvious about Sal. It's actually kind of sad."

Maren felt her cheeks grow hot, but she held Allegra's gaze. "I think it's sad you care so much about performing in the gala," she said. "Especially because Jo will probably pick a scene with Malvolio."

Allegra's face cramped before she forced her mouth into a smile. "Maybe," she said under her breath, her eyes glittering nastily, "except your freak friend can't seem to get *her* lines down, now can *she*?"

Maren felt blood pounding in her ears. She opened her mouth to say something, but Allegra had already turned and breezed into the cafeteria, waving at Mr. Cairn standing just inside the door. Mr. Cairn nodded, his eyes moving to latch onto Maren.

After a moment, Maren forced herself to follow Allegra. She was so angry she didn't even remember the walk to the table where Theo was already sitting.

"Hey, will you ask for an extra baked potato when you get your tray?" Theo asked as Maren threw herself into the seat across from them. "Chef Clarence, aka the potato protector, cut me off at two, but everybody knows carbs are brain food and—whoa." They had noticed Maren's expression. "What happened to you?"

"Nothing," Maren said, her anger solidifying into resolve. "You know what I'm going to do?"

Theo raised their eyebrows. "If it starts with 'getting' and ends with 'Theo another baked potato,' then you'll officially be my hero."

Maren couldn't help but laugh. "Fine, after I get you that potato—"

"*Yes!*"

"I'm going to help you memorize your lines tonight."

"Really?" Theo seemed shocked. "I thought you would want to do clue-figuring stuff."

Maren hesitated. Again, she thought about everything she had learned about the Wallaces, and the clue still unsolved in her bag, and the fact that camp and her chance to find the ring ended in a week...but there was nothing that couldn't wait another day. "What I really want," she said, grinning, "is for you to get chosen for the gala over Allegra."

"Well-a-day that you were, sir," Maren prompted Theo.

"By this hand, I am," Theo said, holding up one hand and pointing at Maren with the other. *"Good fool, some ink, paper and light; and convey what I will set down to my lady: it shall advantage thee more than ever the bearing of letter did."*

"That's really good, Theo!" Maren said, then went on reading: *"I will help you to't. But tell me true, are you not mad indeed? Or do you but counterfeit?"*

Theo shook their head twice as they said, *"Believe me, I am not; I tell thee true."*

"Nay, I'll ne'er believe a madman till I see his brains. I will fetch you light and paper and ink."

"Fool, I'll requite it in the highest degree: I prithee, be gone!"

"Perfect." Maren beamed at Theo as they made it to the end of the scene. "Theo, you didn't look at the script once!"

Theo shook their head in amazement. "I can't believe my brain is actually holding all this stuff. I'm kind of worried it's going to start leaking out my ears."

"It's not going to leak out your ears," Maren said, closing her stage manager's binder and pulling her breakfast tray toward her. She and Theo had worked late into the night and woken up an hour early to run Theo's lines, but other people were starting to trickle into the cafeteria now, and soon enough the day would begin. She grabbed her egg-and-sausage breakfast sandwich and explained through a bite, "You just had to memorize the words with the actions you wanted to do naturally, and now you have it."

"How did you know that?" Theo said, sounding almost shy. "How did you know I could do it?"

Maren shrugged. "People learn in different ways—audio, visual, and physical—so you've got to mix it up. I used to help my sister memorize stuff, too." The words came out so simply Maren felt a bit shocked at herself. Had she ever talked about Hadley to Theo? She didn't think so. She crammed the rest of the sandwich in her mouth, just in case Theo decided to ask questions.

But Theo was still too fixated on the memorization techniques. "Yeah, physical movement really helped. That, and watching the recordings of myself." They had used Theo's camera to record them saying their lines, then played it back; for some reason, seeing themselves on-screen had helped Theo remember their lines. Now, though, they toyed with their paper napkin nervously. "I still might not get chosen for the gala," they announced as their eyes moved to the door.

Maren followed their gaze and saw Allegra walking in. She was talking seriously with Piper and Nic, no doubt instructing them on their scene today—Nic looked as uninterested as ever, but Piper was nodding so fast it looked like her head might rocket free from her body and go nodding around the room by itself.

"That's true, you might not get picked," Maren said after she swallowed her giant mouthful. "But you also might *get* picked. And anyway, you're off book, that's the important thing."

"Right," Theo said, then hesitated. "But what if I forget

my moves and then forget the words and then no one knows I learned them in the first place and then—"

"You won't forget," Maren said firmly. "All you need now is practice to build your confidence. Do you want to run another scene?"

"Let's do the letter scene," Theo said. "But let's do it in the woodshop—it's probably quieter there. It's getting crowded in here."

"Sure"—Maren started gathering her things—"though I don't think anyone has ever called the woodshop *quiet* before."

Theo gave a squeaky-wheel laugh, and after they had grabbed one, no, two more apples for the road, they and Maren headed for the door.

Outside, it was hot and humid again, but Maren found she didn't mind so much today. More kids were making their way up to breakfast now—most still looking half-asleep, but a few were studying their scripts as they went, their mouths moving as their feet wobbled on the uneven dirt path.

"Poor things," Theo said with a satisfied sigh. "Still trying to memorize only visually."

They were both surprised to see Eartha standing outside the woodshop when they got there, her back to them as she softly closed the door.

"Hey, Eartha!" Theo called as they and Maren strolled up. "What are you doing here?"

Eartha jumped about a foot in the air and spun around, her long braid cracking through the air like a whip.

"Oh! Little loons!" Eartha let loose a high, hysterical laugh when she saw the two of them. "Oh, I didn't see you there! Well, of course I didn't see you there, you can tell I didn't, of course!"

Maren and Theo shared a look.

"It must be late if you're already on the way to class!" Eartha said.

"No, it's okay," Maren said. "We're just—"

"I didn't mean to take up your Tech teacher's time," Eartha jabbered on as if she hadn't heard. "But Bernardo and I were just discussing a possible clog venture, shoe design, woodcutting, Dutch things, all that, must go get ready for my class, bye!"

And with that, she took off down the hall, her fat gray braid swinging behind her.

"That seemed a little suspicious," Maren said under her breath as they watched her go. Eartha had never been at the top of her suspect list for the accomplice, but seeing her there now made Maren wonder again.

"No kidding," Theo said, making a face. "Who thinks wooden clogs are a good fashion venture?"

"Says the kid who brought a vest a day to camp?" Maren joked. Today, Theo was wearing a red vest patterned like a bandanna with tiny cowboy-hat buttons.

"This is my power vest," Theo said, tugging it straight. "I'm wearing my power vest today for extra oomph."

"What makes it a power vest?" Maren asked.

Theo stood taller and put their hands on their hips. "I do."

"Off-booking we go!" Jo announced that afternoon when they had all gathered in the auditorium. "Let's start from the beginning and work all the way through." She winked. "That'll give those of you who don't appear until the later acts time to do more last-minute studying."

Only Allegra laughed, obviously fake and entirely in line with her acting abilities. The rest of the cast took seats around the auditorium, waiting for the scene before theirs to go backstage, while Jo and Maren sat in the front row.

Jo leaned over to Maren. "Make a light tick mark by lines missed or messed up," she said softly. "Just so I can see the scenes that are the most ready to go."

Maren nodded, poising her pencil over the page.

The first scene had Duke Orsino with some of his men, and Greg held up manageably well, only missing a line or two. The same could also be said of Piper, who had a lot of lines as Viola in scene 2, along with Hee-young, who played the Captain. In the third scene, too-cool Nic as Maria got flustered when she made a tiny mistake, and the fourth scene, between Orsino and Viola, was pretty rough. Maren ticked the missed lines with her pencil, feeling a little flick of satisfaction for each one. Then came the fifth scene—the first time Sal and Theo would be onstage, along with Emil and Laurence as Sir Toby and Sir Andrew, as well as Nic, Piper, *and* Allegra.

Maren felt herself stiffen in her seat as Sal and Nic came on and went through their first lines. A moment later, Allegra and Theo joined them. Allegra, as expected, had her first few lines absolutely perfect. Worse, though, she was the one who had to prompt Theo's first line, and soon enough Maren heard the cue:

"*What think you of this fool, Malvolio?*" Allegra said. "*Doth he not mend?*"

She turned to Theo, already smirking. Theo hesitated, and the pencil shook in Maren's hand. But a second later, Theo rocked back on their heels.

"*Yes,*" they said, "*and shall do til the pangs of death shake him.*"

Allegra's jaw went slack. She couldn't have hidden her shock if she had tried. Theo went on, not missing a single word: "*Infirmity, that decays the wise, doth ever make the better fool.*"

Sal was late coming in for his next line—"*God send you, sir, a speedy infirmity, for the better increasing your folly!*"—but he was smiling hard.

Allegra tried to recover, and she delivered her next line, "*How say you to that, Malvolio,*" like a challenge, already preparing to gloat should Theo mess up on the long monologue that followed.

But Theo had that monologue down, every line, every word, and finished it with an extreme flourish on "*fools' zanies!*"

Jo laughed, and Allegra noticed.

"*Oh...* um... *oh, you are sick with self-love, Malvolio,*" Allegra struggled and stammered, "*and... taste with a... tempered appetite!*"

The line was supposed to be *distempered appetite.* Making a mark in the script where Allegra got it wrong gave Maren so much pleasure, she nearly tore a hole in the paper.

The run-through took all afternoon. It was far from perfect, with a tick mark or twenty appearing by everyone's name in Maren's binder, but even with the mistakes, Maren couldn't help but be impressed by how much work everyone had done—and how great her friends were. Sal missed a few of his lines, but it was the first time Maren had gotten to hear some of his songs, and they were amazing. Graham also seemed to have most of his lines memorized, though, Maren admitted, sometimes he spoke too softly to tell. Best of all: Theo. Theo lost their place once or twice, but they were always able to recover, and their longest scene—where Malvolio has to "read" an entire letter—was so perfect that afterward Jo actually leaned over and looked at Maren's script, as if to confirm that not a single line had been marked. Maren was more than happy to show her the clean page, and Jo shook her head in amazement.

Only Allegra, in Maren's opinion, struggled to recover from some kind of a shock.

By dinnertime, they were only in the fourth act, but Jo announced they were done for the day.

"Excellent, *excellent* work." She beamed. "I know you're all eager to hear about the gala, and I'm ready to make my decision."

Everyone went so still that Maren could have sworn some kids were holding their breath.

"I know all of you would do a wonderful job representing our camp," Jo said, "but this year, I've decided it will be an excerpt from act two, scene five."

There was some buzz and flurry as campers tried to figure out what scene that was, but Maren recognized it immediately and knew exactly who would be performing—

"That means," Jo went on, "that we will be represented by Nic, Laurence, Emil, Siobhan, and Theo."

Maren couldn't remember the last time she had cheered so loud—and she wasn't the only one. Most of the cast were on their feet clapping and shouting. She heard Sal whoop enthusiastically and thought she even heard Graham above the others. Nic had trouble keeping her bored expression free of a smile, and Theo blinked hard and had to duck their head out of sight. Allegra, Maren noticed with pleasure, had already turned away.

The walk to the cafeteria was perhaps the happiest moment Maren had had at camp thus far. Sal kept pumping his fist, Graham couldn't stop smiling, and Theo laughed their squeaky-wheel laugh. But Maren should have known it was too good to last. No sooner had they gotten their trays and found seats than Mr. Cairn came marching into the cafeteria. Conversation fell away as he glared down at them.

"You may have noticed," Mr. Cairn said, his words clipped and furious, "that the library is no longer open. That is because the internet is a privilege—a privilege that *someone* took advantage of when *someone* used it in an inappropriate manner." Mr. Cairn landed on the *someone*s as if hammering his fist against the word. "So now, everyone will have restricted computer privileges."

Whispers circled around the group, soft protestations that it wasn't fair, as well as some snickers about what Mr. Cairn meant by "inappropriate." Maren could feel Theo trying to catch her eye, but she kept her gaze fixed on Mr. Cairn, her expression politely surprised.

"From now on, there will be a counselor observing the lab at all times. Should anyone be caught on inappropriate sites again"—Mr. Cairn paused, his silence dangerous, then finished—"expect to be severely reprimanded."

Finished with his threats, Mr. Cairn clipped away and

started speaking with the servers behind the counter. Conversation returned to the room slowly after that, in tentative tones.

"They've never restricted the internet before," Graham said, leaning forward. "What do you think that's about?"

"I think it was me," Maren said, trying to keep her voice low, but feeling it waver with her hammering heart. "Theo and I were so busy with their lines yesterday, I didn't get a chance to tell you all that I used the computer to do some research."

Sal bugged out his eyes. "Yowza, Boston, that's what you call research?"

"No, I wasn't actually looking at...!" Maren's face flushed, but she shook her head seriously. "I mean, I looked up stuff on *Charlotte Goodman*." Quickly, she told them what she had learned about Charlotte, the actress Emma Bonaventure, and Wayman Wallace.

Sal snapped his fingers. "So that's why Walcorp is all over this place! The Wallace family wants that ring back!"

"Yeah, and I didn't have time to clear my search history," Maren said. "Someone must have seen it."

"It has to be the accomplice from the costume storage," Graham said, his eyes wide. "Maybe there'd be something about Wayman Wallace that would lead to them, like a connection or something, and they couldn't risk you figuring it out."

"So they invented a story so you can't learn more," Theo said darkly. They turned their camera toward themselves, pointing a finger at the lens. "It's the first step of any good cover-up—distraction and isolation from the truth!"

Maren shushed them as Mr. Cairn walked by.

"We have to watch our backs," Sal continued more quietly when he had passed. "Next thing you know, there'll be random bag checks, like at school."

"Goodman's isn't like that," Graham said defensively.

Sal shrugged. "You said yourself, they've never monitored the computer lab before."

Graham looked ready to disagree, but Maren interrupted him. "What we need," she said simply, "is to figure out this clue, and fast."

Charlie

Charlie was poring over the script pages they were shooting that day when there was a knock on the office door.

"Come in," Charlie called out, then looked up just in time to see the door swing open.

There was Emma—decked out in green velvet pantaloons, a flouncy lavender blouse, and an embroidered doublet doing a less-than-perfect job of concealing her womanly figure. It was hard to believe it was possible, but Emma looked more beautiful every time Charlie saw her.

"What do you think?" Emma laughed. She entered the room with a spin. "How does Viola—I mean, *Cesario*— meet your approval, dear director?"

"You look nice," Charlie managed, hoping her voice didn't give away how much she felt as she struggled to find the right words. "Your hair...looks nice."

"You think so?" Emma fiddled with her floppy Renaissance cap self-consciously. Her soft, golden-brown hair was swept up boyishly but for a few stray tendrils that broke free down her neck. Without the constant ironing and products Emma had used on her hair, her natural curls seemed to expand at her touch, as if stretching after a long nap. "It's been so long since I've been anything but Jean

Harlow blond, I'm afraid my natural color will look dull on camera."

"No, I like it," Charlie insisted. "It's not dull at all, it's like the color of—the color of toast."

Emma gaped at her. "*Toast?*"

"In a good way," Charlie hurried to say, but Emma had already thrown her head back in a laugh.

"I think that's the best compliment I've ever received," Emma said, gasping for breath between giggles. "Toast-colored hair! Oh, Charlie, you're a natural charmer with the ladies."

Charlie felt her face flush and turned away. She pretended to fuss with some of the pages from the script on her desk.

"Hey," Emma said, and suddenly she was standing next to Charlie, her hand warming Charlie's shoulder. "You know I didn't mean anything by that."

"No, no, of course." Charlie hurried to stand. "Are you ready to head to set, then?"

"Almost." Emma smiled. "I wanted to give you a little something." She dug in her pocket and pulled out a small box wrapped tidily with a red bow.

"What's this?" Charlie asked.

Emma shrugged coyly. "Call it an early Christmas present."

Charlie could only stare down at the box. "I don't like Christmas," she said before she caught herself.

"You don't like *Christmas*?" Emma's mouth fell open, and Charlie thought she might laugh again, but she just shook her head and forced the box into Charlie's hands. "Well, I *love* Christmas, and you've already given me the

gift of directing this movie, so here, call it a good luck gift."
Emma beamed. "Open it already, will you!"

With numb, slightly trembling fingers, Charlie undid the ribbon and eased the lid off the box. Something small glittered up from a bed of white stuffing: a single silver charm strung on a chain.

"It's a viola!" Emma clapped. "Get it?"

Charlie's throat was suddenly tight with emotion. She closed her eyes, the memory of her grandmother's prim, disgusted face suddenly looming beside her mother's disappointed, embarrassed one. It was like this, sometimes—like it didn't matter how old Charlie got or how much she achieved. Her mother was always there, telling her she must try harder. Her grandmother was always there, telling her she didn't deserve what she got. She swallowed hard and opened her eyes again. "Thank you," she said softly. "It's very nice." Charlie started to put the lid back on the box, to seal the treasure away so she could look at it later, in private.

"What are you doing?" she heard Emma say. "You have to wear it for luck!"

Before Charlie could stop her, Emma had plucked the box from her hands, the necklace from the box, and reached up around her neck. Charlie could feel Emma's breath, warm and tickling, against her neck. She forced herself to keep her eyes on Emma's ear, on a freckle just below it; she was afraid what her eyes would betray otherwise.

"There!" Emma smiled. She stepped back, but only far enough that she could hold the charm out on her palm. With her other hand, she pulled Charlie's collar up and dropped the chilly silver charm inside so it was hidden by her shirt. "So you can remember us," Emma said softly. "Because we're both Viola in a way, aren't we?"

Charlie held Emma's gaze, her heart beating hard. She could smell Emma's face powder and the starch in her costume and something floral beneath it—lavender water, Charlie realized. Emma didn't step away. She just kept watching Charlie, a curious expression on her face, like she was waiting for something. Charlie took a breath, unsure what she would say, when another lingering scent hit her: cigar smoke. Wayman's arrogant face drifted up in front of her, breaking the spell. It was true, Wayman Wallace was the producer for the film. It was true, his money had allowed them to buy the equipment they needed and hire the crew, and it had even given Charlie the director's chair she had wanted so desperately. But still, Charlie didn't like him any more than she had the first time she met him. She still thought he was horribly stuck-up, pompous, and rude. But Emma had chosen Wayman. She chose to stay with him, she chose to marry him, and, no matter what Charlie thought, she clearly chose to love him.

It was Charlie who stepped away first. "I suppose we should go, then," she muttered.

Emma blinked. "I suppose so," she said quickly and spun away, out the door.

Charlie followed more slowly. She reminded herself that she was lucky—she was finally a real movie director, and she got to spend every day working with the woman she loved. So what if Emma couldn't love her back the same way? Charlie should be happy with what she had, she told herself firmly as she followed Emma onto the movie set. Maybe this was as happy as she was allowed to be.

Maren

June 2015
Stonecourt, Massachusetts

Since the next day was Saturday, they had agreed to all get up early and meet at breakfast to talk, but Maren was still a little surprised when she and Theo showed up and the boys were already there.

"So," Maren said, keeping her voice low just in case anyone was eavesdropping. "*And yet, by the very fangs of malice, I swear, I am not that I play*—any thoughts?"

Sal said, "I got it," at the exact second, Theo said, "Way ahead of you."

They looked at each other.

"You worked it out, too?" Sal said.

"You bet I did." Theo beamed. "Shall we say it on the count of three?"

"All right. One—"

"Two—"

"Three!"

Sal said, "The sound booth!" and the same time, Theo said, "A stuffed animal."

They looked at each other again, this time in perfect bewilderment.

"It's got to be a sound booth," Sal insisted. "*I am not that I play*? The things that play other things are in the sound booth! Got to be!"

"What about the 'fangs' part, though?" Theo said. "What do the fangs mean, other than an animal?"

"The 'fangs of malice' just means telling lies," Maren said, "or acting like something you're not."

"See?" Sal looked victorious. "And what do you tell lies through? A microphone. Which would be in the sound booth."

Theo rolled their eyes and looked at Graham. "Are there any stuffed animals around here?" they asked him.

"Like teddy bears?" Graham said, confused.

Sal snorted.

"No, not like *teddy bears*," Theo said, their voice dripping with disdain. "Like . . . like mounted antlers or a boar's head or something."

"You know whose head is really bored here," Sal muttered, and Maren ducked her head to try to hold in her laugh.

"I'm *talking* about *taxidermy*," Theo announced stiffly. "Think about it—the eyes literally meant the eyes of a potato plant, so why couldn't fangs literally be, you know, fangs of an actual animal!"

"There's probably a lot of stuff like that in the prop closet," Graham said.

They all turned to look at him.

"You know, props? The stuff people use onstage that isn't part of the set or the costumes?" he said.

"We know what props are," Maren said. "But I've never heard of the prop closet."

"It's basically the theater's attic," Graham said. "I've only been up there once, years ago, when everyone had to carry down a bunch of books for this scene in *Blithe Spirit*, but I think I remember seeing a giant stuffed bear. I bet there's a lot of stuff like that up there."

Theo shot Sal a smug look.

"Great, if the bear's name is Malice, then you're in business." Sal rolled his eyes.

"So we'll have to split up and search both," Maren jumped in before Theo could say anything back. "Graham will go with Theo and check out the prop closet, and I'll go with Sal and look in the sound booth."

"No way," Theo said, so firmly that the others looked at them in confusion. "No offense, Graham, but I want Miss Sherlock on my side when we find the clue in the prop closet."

"Fine," Sal said, throwing his arm around Graham's neck, and Maren's heart sank. "You can get Maren's help all you want. Graham and I are *still* going to find the clue, because it's *obviously* in the sound booth."

"Wanna bet?" Theo said.

"Okay, okay!" Maren held up both hands. "Only problem is, *when* are we going to be able to search these spaces? Someone is onto us, remember? It's not like the counselors are just going to let us roam around."

"Easy," Graham said. "We sneak out during movie night tonight."

For the second time, they all turned to stare at him.

"What?" Graham self-consciously rubbed at his nose. "The counselors will be distracted. No one should notice if we slip out in the middle, so long as we make it back before the movie ends."

Now they all gaped at him.

"I thought it was a good plan," he mumbled.

"It's a *great* plan," Sal said, slightly awed.

"Oh, Grahamie," Theo said, their voice slipping into Allegra's squeals, "how did we bring you to this life of crime?"

They went to ruffle his hair, but he was too quick for them and ducked out of reach.

Rehearsals went all day on Saturday and kept everyone busy. First, they finished the off-book testing of act 5, where everyone was onstage. Allegra seemed to be responding to the disappointment of not getting the gala by refusing to look at Theo. It was so obvious that eventually even Jo had to call out, "Come on, Olivia, sound like you mean it when you say Malvolio has been wronged!"

After a tense dinner, during which Theo ate theirs and most of Maren's portion of chicken tetrazzini, they came out of the cafeteria and discovered it had started to rain.

"Inside," Mr. Cairn shouted over the grumbles, standing on the path under a wide-brimmed black umbrella. "Everyone, movie night has been moved to the auditorium. We're showing the movie there."

"What do we do now?" Theo muttered to Maren under their breath.

"We stick to the plan," Maren said softly. "If anything, now we don't have to run so far to make it to the prop closet and back."

"It'll be easier for them to notice we're missing, too," Theo pointed out, but together the two of them joined the crowd heading in the direction of the auditorium. Inside, Bernie was fiddling with a projector set up in the middle of the seats, while the large white screen was pulled across the stage. Theo and Maren took seats near the door, and Maren casually glanced around, trying to find the other two. Graham and Sal were sitting in a row alone, but directly in front of them was Allegra and her crowd. Maren felt a spike of concern. What if Allegra noticed when the boys tried to slip out? But there was nothing Maren could do. She took a seat next to Theo and tried to look calm as she waited.

After what felt like forever, Bernie stepped away from the projector and Mr. Cairn announced it was ready to go. The lights went down, and the movie started.

"It's *Little Shop of Horrors*," Theo cried, as always, too loudly. "It's got to be among my top five—no, top *three* favorite botanical horror movies."

"You do remember that we're not actually going to stay and watch the movie, right?" Maren whispered.

"Oh. Right." In the light from the screen, Maren could see Theo's face fall. "Well, I guess that's okay. My *first* favorite plant horror movie is Quigley Forrager's *Stalked*, where there's this greedy sunflower that—"

Maren nodded along, thinking that Theo's sunflower vest suddenly looked a lot less friendly. She was grateful Theo was wearing a vest patterned with stars and moons tonight.

Half an hour into the movie, the sound suddenly cut out.

"Oh, but I love this part," Theo groaned along with the rest of the crowd.

"Um, Theo?" Maren reminded them. "That's our cue."

"Oh. Yeah."

It wasn't hard to slip out. Plenty of kids were on their feet, grumbling or trying to get a better view of Ms. Green and Monty, who were gathered around the stereo to inspect it, while others had taken this as a good opportunity for a bathroom break. Maren took one last glance over her shoulder—Bernie, she noticed, wasn't anywhere to be found. Neither was Eartha, and neither was Mr. Cairn.

She and Theo met up with Graham and Sal in the stairwell.

"Nice work, Graham." Theo patted his shoulder.

"Thanks, but it won't take them long to figure out that I kicked the cord and unplugged it," Graham said.

"We should hurry, then," Sal said.

"And be careful," Maren added. "Bernie, Eartha, and Mr. Cairn weren't in the auditorium when we snuck out, and any one of them might already be looking for the next clue."

They agreed to meet back in ten minutes, then hustled up the stairs. At the third-floor landing, the boys peeled off to go into the sound booth.

"Just keep climbing," Graham said as they left. "You can't miss it."

Theo and Maren had two more floors to go and were both panting by the time the stairs ended abruptly in a solid metal door. It was unlocked.

"That's lucky," Maren said, though really, she felt the exact opposite. She took a deep breath. "Well, shall we?"

Theo, still panting, just gestured with one hand to go ahead. The other hand had already lifted their camera.

The prop closet was a long, narrow space with a low, slanted ceiling. The middle of the room was a walkway just wide enough for one person. One side of the room had giant filing cabinets, while the other was open shelves. Maren flipped the light on, and it buzzed dully as she peered to look at some of the labels on the file drawers. "Dishes—plain" was one, while another was "Dishes—patterned," under the topmost drawer, which read, "Bells—jingle, dinner, and cow."

"Well, at least everything is labeled," Maren said with a sigh.

She walked to the far side of the room, eyeing the cabinets, while Theo followed right behind, tilting and panning the camera up and down the shelves.

"Now we just need something labeled 'Fangs, Malice' and we're set," Theo joked.

"Let's look for anything that says 'animal' to start," Maren said. "And let's hope we find some fangs before the movie ends."

Maren and Theo each took one side of the room. Maren checked a drawer marked "squirrel" to find a very battered-looking hand puppet, and another labeled "hamster" to find a perfectly situated cage, complete with wood chips, water bottle, and plastic wheel, though thankfully without the actual animal inside. She put her hand tentatively into the puppet and shook the wood chips around until she saw the bottom of the cage, but she found no slips of paper with gold edges.

"I've been thinking," Theo said. "Doesn't it feel like this whole thing is made for someone?"

Maren turned to look at Theo, who was stroking the feathers of a large, stuffed raven contemplatively. It had come from a shelf labeled "Poe."

"I don't know, maybe," Maren said. She shook out a

quilt patterned with Noah's ark while she thought about it. The truth was, she had been thinking of the clues as hers for so long, she didn't like the idea that they could really belong to someone else. "What makes you think that?"

"I don't know...." Theo pulled out a tiger-printed rug from the lowest shelf by the floor, complete with a fake stuffed tiger head. They wrapped it around themselves so the head perched on one shoulder. "Just, I can't help thinking this has to be about something more than a ring."

"More important than a diamond ring that can save the camp?" Maren huffed as she struggled to stuff the blanket back into its drawer. "What's more important than that?"

"Love," Theo said simply. "This feels like it was done by someone who really loves someone else. Someone who would know if *play* means the sound booth or *fangs* the prop closet."

Maren raised her eyebrows at them. "You didn't seem to think it was possible it was the sound booth earlier."

"Yeah, well, I'm just looking out for the Twelfth Team." Theo took the tiger rug off and ran a finger in its mouth to check for the clue. "Nothing pulls a group apart like romance."

Maren paused. "What does that mean?"

"Do you have a crush on Sal?"

"What? No! What? What are you talking about?" Maren said, but she turned away so Theo couldn't see her burning cheeks. She tried to sound casual as she opened a drawer and dug out a papier-mâché turtle.

"What about Graham?"

"I don't have a crush on Graham," Maren said, completely honestly.

"I know you don't," Theo said. "But Graham likes you."

"What?" Maren's cheeks were burning even hotter as she spun back toward Theo. "How do you know?"

Theo rolled their eyes. "Aren't you supposed to be the girl wonder detective here? You really haven't seen the clues?"

"Not really," Maren said awkwardly.

"Well, I'm just saying, all this lovey-dovey loony business shouldn't interrupt our mission."

"Interrupt it how?" Maren said scathingly. "Like, by making us gossip when we should be searching?"

"Fair point." Theo shrugged and opened a new drawer.

Maren tried to go back to work, too. But now her brain was buzzing with more questions. Graham had a crush on her? What was she supposed to do with that? She looked at Theo, ready to demand more details, when another question popped up.

"Do you..." she started.

"What?" Theo said.

"Do you have a crush on anyone?" Maren said. "It doesn't matter if you do or don't," she hurried to say when Theo didn't respond. "I just didn't want to make assumptions, so—"

"I'm only interested in QF."

"Oh," Maren said. It was another moment before she confessed: "I don't know what that means."

"QF for Quigley Forrager!" Theo laughed their squeaky-wheel laugh. "I'm only interested in cinematic brilliance!"

Maren rolled her eyes. She was about to say that all these crushes made her think of *Twelfth Night*, but before she could, she heard something that made her stomach drop: There was the unmistakable clatter of footsteps on the stairs.

Someone was coming.

Maren flew for the lights and snapped them off. She turned to where she thought Theo was—only to realize with horror she knew *exactly* where Theo was.

"Theo," she hissed, "your vest glows in the dark!"

Theo looked down at their very apparent torso covered with stars and moons, shining a vivid electric green in the pure dark of the storage space. "Oh yeah," they whispered, and they sounded almost proud. "It's this special fabric paint that my mom and I—"

In one quick swoop, Maren snatched the tiger rug and threw it over both Theo and herself, wedging them both onto the lowest shelf. A second later, the door swung open and the lights snapped back on. The footsteps that clicked in were sharp and crisp, as was the voice that followed: "I demand an explanation for this!"

Maren's heart seized.

"I have called twenty times in the last *day*," she heard Mr. Cairn say. "What do you mean his family took me off the list? Carlos's family isn't—" His words fell away. "I'm sorry, you mean to tell me his brother is there?"

There was silence as the person on the other line spoke.

"His brother, Stefan, who Carlos hasn't spoken to in fifteen years? That brother is suddenly controlling the list of who is allowed to know about his care? Yes, but... yes, but... I realize he's a blood relation, but Carlos is on my plan, what about that? How am I—" The conversation went on for a while, with Mr. Cairn interrupting whoever was on the other side of the line to ask specific questions, but he seemed to get nowhere. "This will not be the end of this conversation," Mr. Cairn said finally. "I expected better from you all, given how many years we've trusted your health care system. Good day, Nurse Beverly!"

Mr. Cairn hung up, but then he stood there for a long time. Maren thought she might have heard a sniffle, or a sigh, but the idea of Mr. Cairn *crying* kept her even more frozen in place. Finally, Mr. Cairn seemed to gather himself. His shoes clicked away, the lights snapped off, and the door closed. A moment later, they heard his shoes march back down the stairs.

Maren threw the tiger rug off her, breathing hard.

"No freaking way," Theo whispered.

Even in the dark, Maren could see their eyes, as bright as the stars on their vest and wide with shock. Maren knew her own eyes must be the same size, but there was no denying what she had seen and heard:

Mr. Cairn had been using a cell phone.

"Not possible," Graham said for the millionth time.

Theo and Maren shared a look. Sal just shook his head. As expected, the news that Mr. Cairn had to be Renee Wallace's accomplice hadn't gone over well with Graham. It hadn't gone over at all, actually, since Graham was still adamant it couldn't have been him. During the entire walk into town the next morning, when Theo and Maren explained for the millionth time about hearing him on the phone—"A cell phone, Graham!" Theo said. "One that worked!"—Graham still refused to believe it.

"So Mr. Cairn has a special phone or something, that doesn't mean anything." Graham jumped, grabbing at a high, green acorn. The whole branch swung down with his weight, then snapped back with a crack as the acorn broke free. He rolled it in his fingertips, spinning it from knuckle to knuckle. "Just because he's strict doesn't mean he'd try to steal from Jo and the camp. In fact, he's more likely *not* to be the accomplice, because that would mean breaking the rules."

"Well, who else, then?" Maren said, trying to be fair. "Did you see Bernie or Eartha or anyone else do anything suspicious last night?"

To her surprise, Graham's scowl only deepened.

"See, the thing about that is..." Sal said carefully. "There was a reason Bernie and Eartha weren't around to help with the movie issues last night. Right, Graham?"

Graham just kept scowling.

"Turns out," Sal went on, and Maren could hear a smile at the edges of his voice, even as he was fighting to keep it from his face, "they had another engagement, if you know what I mean."

"I don't," Theo said, their camera aimed at him. "What do you mean?"

"They were in the sound booth when we got there," Graham said dully. "They're kind of, um, dating. Or something."

"*Something* is right," Sal said, unable to repress a grin now.

Maren felt her jaw drop. She remembered how flustered Eartha had been when they caught her coming out of the woodshop, how she had wanted to walk them to Tech the first day of classes, the way Bernie looked at Eartha warming up on the stage.... Maren felt a laugh building in her chest. She tried to swallow it down, but it broke loose, and she heard Theo and Sal start, too. Eartha and Bernie? It was all just too weird.

Theo spun their camera on themselves. "PLOT TWIST!" they shouted into the lens. "This action-adventure movie just got a romantic subplot."

"But that doesn't mean Mr. Cairn is involved." Graham raised his voice above their giggles.

"Graham..." Sal started.

"No, seriously!" He turned and faced them, blocking the path. "The accomplice you saw in the costume storage was wearing boots. Mr. Cairn doesn't wear boots."

"It was raining that night," Maren pointed out. "He probably put boots on for that."

"Okay, but he wasn't speaking French when you over-heard him on the phone."

"We don't know that he can't, though," Theo jumped in. "He's very cultured."

"But he wasn't searching the prop closet for a clue!"

"As if there was a clue to find in the prop closet," Sal said. Theo looked offended, but Sal held up both hands. "Not that it was in the sound booth, either. We didn't find anything in there... even after we were able to search when Bernie and Eartha finally vacated their secret kissing spot."

The three of them cracked up again.

Graham shook his head furiously. "Mr. Cairn has been at the camp for years. You think he would just *suddenly* betray Jo and her family? Why now?"

"He needs the money for hospital bills," Maren said.

Graham looked at her. So did Theo and Sal.

"I didn't know that," Theo said in surprise.

"He was arguing about insurance stuff." Maren had heard her parents talking about a lot of the same things for Hadley. "Sorry, Graham. People do crazy things when someone they love is sick. He probably couldn't resist getting paid by Walcorp. Meanwhile," she sighed, "we now have less than a week to figure out this clue."

"Well, that's why we're here, right?" Theo said.

Maren nodded and looked up at the Stonecourt church, its famous broken clock set above a pair of arched wooden doors. There was a plaque along one side that Maren stopped to read: The clock dated back to the 1760s, though it hadn't worked since a lightning storm in 1915. After it was determined to be unfixable, the parish had decided that both hands should be left pointing straight up to 12—"to heaven," the plaque said.

"You know what they say about broken clocks," Theo said, their camera aimed at the clock.

"They're right twice a day?" Maren said.

"Oh, is that what they say?" Theo paused thoughtfully. "That's actually better than what I thought they said."

"Do you think there's a service going on in there?" Graham said.

Maren shook her head and pointed at the bulletin below the plaque: The church service didn't start until 10:30 AM. "Let's check it out before people arrive."

She pushed open one of the doors, which gave with the slightest squeal, and held it open for the others. Theo followed with their camera, then Sal, then Graham, hovering far enough back to make it clear he didn't really want to be there.

The church—or chapel? Maren wasn't sure which name was correct—was small but well-kept. The pews were a dark, rich wood, and there was a huge stained glass mural behind the pulpit. The colors were just starting to glow in the morning light, and Maren could imagine how magnificent it was in full blaze.

"Beautiful," Theo murmured beside her.

Maren nodded again. Even though she didn't grow up religious, she instantly recognized the familiar scene: the baby in the manger, the adoring parents bent over him, the clustered animals and shepherds and wise men, all underneath the bright star and angel at the top. It *was* beautiful, though it did seem a little strange to look at a Christmas Nativity scene now, in the summer.

"Hey!" Sal called in a low voice. He waved them all back over to the doors, where there were some handouts and flyers alongside them. He had one open to a map of the church and cemetery grounds. He pointed to a tiny square. "I think I found the grave."

"We're not going to do anything...you know," Graham asked when they were again outside and trooping along the gravel path through the graveyard.

Maren couldn't help rolling her eyes. "We're not going to break into a grave, Graham."

"Yeah," Sal said, "this is really more about paying our respects to our girl Charlotte."

"How do you know *they* identified as a girl?" Theo said.

"Fair point," Sal said. "Then we're paying our respects to our friend Charlie Goodman."

"Hear! Hear!" Theo nodded, satisfied.

The Stonecourt historical cemetery had gravestones stretching back to the seventeenth century—some older than America itself. Maren and the others picked their way respectfully among them until they got to an ornate mausoleum. Maren had never seen one up close before, but she thought it looked like a very fancy garden shed. Beneath two outstretched angel wings, Charlotte's name was etched in the stone:

CHARLOTTE GOODMAN
JULY 23, 1930—JULY 6, 1953
Si hoc somnium
me dormient

"What's that say?" Sal pointed to the words at the bottom, half covered by dark green moss.

Theo squinted at the letters. "It's Latin, I think," they said.

"You speak Latin, too?" Sal asked.

"No, but it's the root of all the Romance languages, so I can figure out some of it. 'Si' would probably mean 'if' here. And 'dorm'…that's like *dormir*, to sleep, I think. But what I don't get is the 'somnium.'"

"It sounds like somnolence," Maren said, "but that's another word for sleep."

"So it says, 'If I'm sleeping, let me sleep'?" Graham said.

"That's how I feel every morning when I hear that wake-up call," Sal said. "If I'm sleeping, let me sleep!"

The boys cracked up. Theo kept squinting at the stone, but finally they shook their head. "*Dorm* and *som* must have slightly different meanings, but I don't know them."

Maren was only half listening, her brain already puzzling over something else: "Hang on," she said slowly. "I thought the article said they couldn't recover the bodies."

"They didn't," Theo said.

"So if there are no bodies, then what is this here for?"

"I think it's just kind of a memorial thing?" Graham said delicately. "My grandma still has a carved headstone next to my grandpa, even though her ashes were scattered, just so my mom has somewhere to visit."

"You'd think naming a whole camp after Charlie was memorial enough," Sal said.

"I don't know that it's ever enough," Graham said. "Not when you lose someone you care about like that."

They all stood another moment, looking at the mausoleum in respectful silence. Maren felt a twinge in her chest. She knew that Charlotte Goodman had died a long time ago, and she didn't believe in the ghost, but Charlie had begun to feel like an old friend, someone who was looking out for Maren and the others. Seeing the gravestone made Charlie's absence feel real in a way it hadn't felt before.

"Look at this," Sal called. He was standing a little way off, pointing to another headstone. "Aren't these Jo's parents?"

VIOLET AUGUST
AUGUST 6, 1927–
SEPTEMBER 3, 2002

LEE AUGUST
APRIL 1, 1930–

There was a fresh bouquet laid along the stone— orchids, Maren recognized, from the greenhouse. She wondered if Jo took care of them after all.

"Speaking of parents..." Theo finally broke the silence. "We should probably head into town for our phone calls."

Graham and Sal agreed, and Maren nodded, following the others even as she felt like turning and running in the opposite direction.

As soon as they got to the benches, the other kids were immediately on their phones—each welcomed with loud proclamations of love and being missed. Theo started recounting what sounded like some of their Malvolio lines in rapid-fire Spanish. Sal was laughing at something his little brother had said. Graham was nodding at his mothers' pressed-together faces. Self-consciously, Maren stepped away and dialed her mother's cell phone. She was relieved when it went straight to voice mail, where she quickly told her mom she was fine. After a moment's hesitation, she went ahead and dialed Ed's number, assuming she'd get his answering machine, too.

But to her surprise, he picked up after the first ring. "Maren?"

"Hey," she said. "Yeah, hey, Ed, it's me."

"Hey, I thought you might call around this time again." He sounded awake, even pleased. "So what's the good word? How's that camp turning out for you?"

"It's good," she said. And then, to her even greater surprise, she actually started telling him about it—about being stage manager, the play itself, helping Theo learn their lines and them getting picked for the gala performance....

"That's awesome," Ed said, when she had wound down. "You sound happy there."

"Yeah," she said. "Yeah, it's okay." She paused, then plowed on. "You know, the show is next week? A lot of parents come out for it and stuff. You don't have to come, obviously," Maren hurried to add. "I mean, I know you've got your own shows—"

"You kidding?" he cut her off. "Of course we'll be there."

Maren felt something expand in her chest, something warm. "Yeah?" she said.

"Definitely," he said.

Maren felt herself smiling. "Hey, Ed?" she said suddenly, then looked over her shoulder to make sure she was alone. She wasn't sure what she was doing, only that it probably couldn't hurt to try: "When I say, '*By the very fangs of malice, I swear, I am not that I play,*' what does that make you think of?"

"Is this like a riddle or something?"

"Kind of."

"Well, I don't know anything about 'fangs' or 'malice,'" Ed said. "But you say the word 'play,' I think of ten different instruments I want to get my hands on."

Maren stood perfectly still, her brain suddenly whizzing.

"Hello? Maren? You there?"

"Yeah!" she breathed. "Yeah, I'm here."

"I'm sorry, I'm no good at riddles."

"No, that helped." Maren was smiling again. "Thanks, Dad. See you at the show."

She had already hung up by the time she realized what she called him.

"*It's the final countdown!*" Monty sang as he breezed into Playwriting class on Monday. "Hard to believe it, I know— the summer always flies by."

Maren gave him a smile, though he was hardly the first

to have reminded them they were officially in the last week of camp. Mr. Cairn had said so no less than three times at breakfast, Bernie mentioned it twice during Tech, and even Jo couldn't resist reminding them in Theater History while they learned about early American plays.

"But this is one of my favorite days," Monty went on. "Because today, after spending this whole time trying to make things more real onstage? You get to completely blow that up."

He turned to the board and wrote SYMBOLISM in big letters.

"A symbol represents something else," he went on. "You remember when we were learning subtext, and we talked about how sometimes characters want to share something but don't have the words for it?"

Maren bobbed her head along with the others.

"Well, sometimes a playwright puts things that can't be said into a visual form—they make a character's emotional state actually *appear* onstage as a symbol."

Maren must not have been the only one looking confused, because he laughed.

"I know, it sounds complicated. So here, let's read a few examples."

He passed out the papers, and for the rest of the time, they read really weird scenes by real, adult playwrights. At first, Maren wasn't sure she liked them. For one thing, stuff didn't always make sense, but the characters frequently acted like strange things were totally normal. Sometimes the actors wore blindfolds or hauled giant suitcases onstage or fought with tiny swords. In one, a woman turned into an almond.

"You're overthinking it." Monty laughed after some kids groaned during the last one. "Stop thinking about what's happening or being said—symbols are there to make you feel the things words can't say!"

Most kids still looked doubtful, but Maren felt like she was beginning to understand. She thought about the scene with the giant suitcases—for some reason, this made her pity the characters, as if they could have set their baggage down at any time, but they kept hauling it around like they couldn't.

Their final assignment was to write a scene with symbolism. "Anything you want," Monty said as the other kids leaned over their papers. "And I hope to hear some of your scenes tomorrow before we say goodbye."

For half a second, Monty's eyes caught Maren's, but they were gone in a flash. This was another thing she didn't need to be reminded of—that, after their last class tomorrow, she wouldn't have the option of sharing her work.

At the beginning of rehearsal, Jo offered yet another reminder that it was the last week by talking through a new calendar. Tomorrow, Tuesday, they'd have their last day of classes, then Wednesday a tech rehearsal, Thursday the gala, and Friday the show.

"It's a lot to cover," Jo finished her explanation, "so you're going to need to be on your absolute best behavior this week. Any questions before we get started?"

Sal raised his hand.

"Yes, Sal?"

"Yeah, this isn't about the schedule or anything, but I

was wondering if there's somewhere I could get an instrument for the show?"

"An instrument?" Jo said, her mouth thoughtfully pursed.

"Yeah," Sal went on. "I mean, the script says playing music is how Feste makes money, so I just think he wouldn't be walking around empty-handed, you know?"

"That's an interesting thought," Jo said. "I think there's a recorder in the—"

"Actually," Sal interrupted, "I was kind of hoping I might pick my own instrument? Like, is there somewhere we would store instruments?"

Jo considered this. Maren held her breath. They had all agreed that, best-case scenario, Sal would be able to go and look for the clue during rehearsal; worst-case, they'd at least find out where instruments would be stored, then try to find a way to sneak in later.

"Why don't you check the orchestra pit?" Jo said finally. "Set crew is installing the backdrops, but you should be able to get in around them. Maren, why don't you go with him. Let Bernie know you two have permission."

Maren nodded and quickly gathered her things. This was even better than the best-case scenario: getting permission to go search the orchestra pit during rehearsal *and* getting to go with Sal. Mr. Cairn watched them go with his normal razor-sharp gaze, but if he knew about the clue, he made no move to stop them.

After Bernie gave them a flashlight and got them to promise to return in a few minutes, Maren and Sal made their way to the back of the stage, down a narrow set of steps, and through a stooped tunnel under the floorboards. They finally emerged in a space that looked like a basement: The floor was cement, an ancient-looking piano was in one corner, and old instrument cases were piled up all around. But unlike a basement, there was no ceiling, only a railing of curtain along the top that blocked the pit off from the seats. It was weird, seeing the auditorium from such a low angle. She could hear Jo above them, giving more instructions to the group, and then Greg started up with his lines again.

"Come on," Maren said softly, "and remember, people can see and hear us."

Sal glanced up at the railing of curtains and nodded. Quietly, they set to work searching. First, they lifted the piano lid and inspected the wires, but they saw no flash of white paper. Then they started in on the instrument cases. Most were empty and, though Maren dutifully felt along the velvet lining for any gaps or holes where a paper might be shoved, she found nothing. She worked her way through the pile, feeling more and more hopeless. But when Maren grabbed the last and biggest case—one that could have easily held a stand-up bass—she heard something clatter inside it. The case was almost as tall as she was and cumbersome to maneuver, but she managed to lay it on the floor and pop the clasps. The lid lifted with a squeal not unlike a coffin opening. She shivered and looked down. She expected to see the giant bass laid out before her like the body of a bizarre monster. But there wasn't a bass inside.

"Hey, cool, a violin," Sal whispered, appearing at her side. "Maybe I'll take that up for Feste."

"That's not a violin," Maren said, her voice breathy and excited.

"It's not? What is it?"

"A viola."

Even in the dim light, she saw Sal's bright white teeth gleam as he smiled. "Of course," he breathed. "Like the character!"

With trembling hands, Maren lifted the viola from the case. A folded piece of paper was carefully wedged in one of the curved cutouts by the strings.

"What does it say?" Sal said as she carefully pulled the paper free. "Read the clue!"

Maren turned to him, then closed her hand over the piece of paper. "Shh!" she hissed instinctively. But it was too late. Sal turned just in time to see Allegra's face riding over the top of the curtains, her expression victorious. She had heard everything.

But when in other habits you are seen,
Orsino's mistress and his fancy's Queen

Charlie

April 27, 1953
Los Angeles, California

The heat in the cramped editing room was stifling.
There was a small screen in front of Charlie, and wisps
and curls of cut film littered the floor around her. Next
to her, the projector whirred and clicked. She needed to
make cuts to the scene playing—the scene in which Viola
and Orsino listen to Feste's music—but she couldn't focus,
couldn't bring herself to watch. She had been working on
the *Twelfth Night* film for ages now, starting in the early
morning and going until late at night, but today she found
she had no heart for it.

Instead, her eyes kept getting drawn to a newspaper article laid out on her table. The headline, "President Clears Government of Lavender Threat," glared up
at her. The newspaper went on to explain that President
Eisenhower had signed Executive Order 10450, which set
security standards for federal employment. These security standards included a ban on homosexuals working for
the government. Homosexuals, the newspaper said, were
morally compromised. And, being morally compromised,
they were a threat. They could easily be manipulated by
Communists.

Still Communists, Charlie thought, though that was
just the name they used right now. Communists today,

homosexuals tomorrow, and someone else to hate next week. She had always imagined herself as fighting for the good guys. Meanwhile, everyone else imagined she was the enemy. She felt tears rise to her eyes as she thought of her father—America, he thought, was where you were allowed to be who you were and think what you want. But she wasn't sure she believed that anymore. There would always be some enemy name used, some excuse given to hate people who were different.

People like her.

The door to the editing room swung open. Charlie looked up in surprise but turned away quickly, swiping furiously at her eyes as Emma stepped in.

"I saw the news," Emma said softly. A moment later, Charlie felt Emma's hand resting gently on her shoulder. "Are you all right?"

"Of course," Charlie said. She tried to laugh, to put on a show of bravado. "It's not like I ever wanted to work in politics."

Emma was quiet. "Maybe not," she said after a moment. "But we both know you sympathize with all those people losing their jobs. Their secret is your secret, too."

"My secret?" Charlie was suddenly furious, that line between sad and angry crossed in a heartbeat. She turned and glared at Emma even as she felt more tears rise. "What about your secret?"

Emma blinked in surprise. Her hair was bleached unnaturally blond again—Wayman's preference, no doubt— and her makeup was expertly applied, but even in the heat she was wearing a jacket with long sleeves, a silk scarf patterned with honeybees wrapped around her neck. "My secret?" Emma said, obviously flustered. "What do you mean, my secret?"

"This secret!" Charlie stepped forward and grabbed Emma's wrists, pushing the sleeve back. There were bruises there, as Charlie had known there would be. Emma tried to squirm away, but Charlie held on. "You claim to be my friend, you keep my secret, but you won't even talk to me about yours?"

Emma made a sound of pain. Charlie realized she was squeezing Emma's wrist too tight. She dropped it, feeling unbearably ashamed. Emma wouldn't look at her. For a moment, neither one could speak, their breaths heavy and jagged with tears.

"Why are you engaged to him?" Charlie said finally, and she knew her voice was full of anguish. "Why do you stay with him when he does this to you?"

Gently, Emma took Charlie's hand. Charlie tried to pull away, but now it was Emma who held on, Emma who guided Charlie's hand over to her until it was resting on her belly. "This is my secret," she whispered. "At least... it's one of them."

Even through Emma's clothes, Charlie could feel a slight bump. Charlie looked at her and saw the fear written plainly across her face: Emma was pregnant.

"I've made my bed, now I have to lie in it," Emma said, her voice cracking a little. She cleared her throat and tossed her head. "Anyway, he's not so bad. He funded the movie, didn't he? At least we have the movie."

Charlie stared at her. "You stay with him because of the movie?"

"Not just for that, no." Emma wouldn't look at her.

"Then, for what?"

"Don't you mean, for whom?" She looked at Charlie finally, the tears she had been holding back breaking loose. "*You* are my real secret," she whispered.

When Charlie leaned in to kiss Emma, Emma kissed her back. It didn't feel wrong. It didn't feel like they were morally compromised. It felt like, after hiding for so long, Charlie had finally been found. There were tears in their eyes as they broke away, and they held each other for a long time afterward, not saying anything, just feeling safe in each other's arms.

"This can't happen. This isn't real life," Emma whispered into Charlie's shoulder. "This is just a dream. You can't live in dreams."

Charlie didn't answer, but she had already decided: If Emma were a dream, she was never going to wake up.

Maren

June 2015
Stonecourt, Massachusetts

Maren was in the middle of a dream that made no sense. In it, her sister was a rocking chair, using her wooden armrests to beat a bowl of raw eggs for an omelet. The wood creaked and creaked, louder and louder, like a ship in a storm. "Time to get up," came a sharp voice, cutting through the edge of her dream, and Maren turned to see the fierce, scowling face of Mr. Cairn. She screamed as he dissolved into a person made entirely of bees and then they swarmed, flying right at Maren—

"Maren!" And there was Theo, shaking her awake by the arm.

"What?" Maren sat up with a start. "What's happening?"

"We have to get up," Theo said, then stepped away.

Maren squinted, confused by the overly bright light in the cabin, and fumbled for her glasses. Eartha stood in front of the open door, her hair unbraided and wearing a shockingly frilly nightgown. Behind her, still on the porch, was Mr. Cairn.

"Up and at 'em, Miss Sands, thank you," Mr. Cairn said in his usual brusque way. "You may join the rest of your cabin over there."

She looked over to see Katie, Lorna, and now Theo standing against the far wall, looking as sleepy and confused as Maren felt. Katie was tugging at her pineapple-print pajamas, and Lorna was swaying slightly. Maren awkwardly disentangled herself from her sleeping bag. The wooden floor was cold on her bare feet, but she hobbled over to the others as fast as she could and stood next to Theo.

"Is this another anti-bad-luck superstition ritual?" Theo grumbled. "Because if so, theater people are just mean."

"I'm afraid not," Mr. Cairn said. "There's been a report of theft in the camp. Eartha, please begin the search."

Eartha crossed her arms. "I've told you, my loons are freethinking young women," Eartha said. Her normally breathy voice sounded harsh and angry. "This sort of tactic is undemocratic."

"A camp is not a democracy," Mr. Cairn said coolly. "We are guardians of their welfare, and that sometimes requires tasks we don't enjoy. If you please."

He gestured again to the room. With a cringe of apology, Eartha headed over to Lorna's and Katie's bunks. She made quick passes under the mattresses, flipped through the drawers, and felt tenderly along the massive photo mural they had created—all at Mr. Cairn's instructions, pointing and gesturing from the door. Theo and Maren shared a look when Eartha headed for their bunk. Eartha conducted the same search on Theo's bunk as she had on Katie's and Lorna's, and the only comment Mr. Cairn made was on the number of vests Theo had. When it was time for Maren's bunk, however, Mr. Cairn had a few extra instructions. First, he told Eartha to feel the lining of Maren's sleeping bag. Then, when she got to Maren's clothes in the drawer, he told her to take everything out, unfold it all, and check the drawer for a false bottom. Maren felt the tension in the room rise as everyone, even half-asleep Lorna, realized that something was going on. Maren kept her face studiously blank, though she felt her heartbeat rise when Eartha pulled out her play binder.

"Open it, please," Mr. Cairn said. "Check and see if there is anything that doesn't seem to relate to classes or the play."

Maren felt a bolt of panic, but Eartha had clearly had enough.

"Are thought crimes illegal here, too, now?" Eartha said in a very sharp, distinctly unethereal voice. "Are we going to police the opinions of children, Mr. Cairn?"

Mr. Cairn's expression looked even more sour than usual. "Very well," he said, turning to go. "Thank you, Ms. Trails, and thank you, students. Please get dressed and carry on to breakfast."

When he had gone, Theo gave a low whistle of appreciation. "All right, *Eartha*!" Theo said, raising their fist. "Forget loons, I think you're a *lioness*!"

"Oh! Do you think so?" Eartha's hand rose to her chest, flattered, and her voice fell back into its usual breathy waves.

"Definitely," Theo said. "I'm going to wear my safari vest today in honor of you."

Maren nodded in agreement. With her hair unbraided and tangled from sleep, Eartha even looked a little wild.

Eartha gave a wavering laugh. "I've always thought of myself as more of a gentle creature but, well, I am rather protective, aren't I...and I like that the lionesses do all the hunting; it's a very female-empowered species...." She straightened up and tossed her hair imperiously. "All right, cubs...to breakfast!"

⟡

Everyone was buzzing over the bunk checks when Theo and Maren arrived in the cafeteria. Sal and Graham were already sitting together at a table, though they were both attacking their muffins in silence.

"Do you believe us now, Graham?" Theo said softly as they and Maren sat down with their trays. "I thought you said bunk checks didn't happen at Goodman's."

Graham scowled at his plate.

"He still doesn't believe it's Mr. Cairn," Sal said.

"*What?*" Both Maren and Theo looked at Graham in shock.

"You told us that Allegra saw you two yesterday," Graham muttered. "She probably told Mr. Cairn or somebody. It was probably her fault."

Theo groaned, and Sal shook his head. Maren said nothing but watched as Ms. Green passed by the table. It seemed all the counselors were in the cafeteria this morning on some sort of patrol.

"It doesn't matter," Maren said softly, peeling an orange. "With *someone* closing in, we need to focus on finding the ring."

"Fingers crossed this clue's easy." Theo had their camera out and trained on Maren. "We don't have much time to be stumped again."

"Actually," Maren said slowly, "I think it might be the last clue."

The others stared at her.

"I don't know for sure," she admitted, "but these are the last spoken lines of the play before Feste's song. It would make sense if it were also the last clue to the ring."

"Thank goodness!" Theo huffed a sigh of relief. "Fingers crossed we figure it out fast."

"Well, actually..." Maren shrugged. "I think I *have* figured it out."

The others stared at her again. Then Sal nudged Theo. "Those are some magic crossed fingers right there!"

"Don't start celebrating yet," Maren warned. "*Queen* is capitalized, and there's only one queen around here that I know of."

She stopped talking and waited until Eartha had taken a seat a few tables down.

"Will you just tell us already?" Theo whispered. "My nerves can't take it!"

"I *am* telling you," Maren said. "*Queen* is the clue—the ring is hidden in the beehives."

There was a pause as the reality of this sank in. Then everyone looked at Graham.

"No way," Graham said.

Theo sighed. "We all know you can't go to the hives. You can sit this one out."

"This isn't about me being allergic to bees! You all can't go to the hives, either!" Graham said, his neck starting to flush. "Walcorp owns the fields on the far side now, remember! The boundary is right where the hives are!"

"That sucks," Sal said, "but if Maren says it's in the hives, then—"

"Maren hasn't been right about everything," Graham said. "There could be another queen, we don't know!"

Maren felt more than a twinge defensive—she'd been right about a lot of things, more than the rest of them. She glared at Graham. So much for his crush.

"That's true," Theo was saying, "but we should probably check the hives, just in case—"

"We're not going to risk getting caught by Renee Wallace to check *just in case!*" Graham hissed. "You promised." He glared at each of them in turn. "You all promised if it ever got dangerous, we'd go to Jo. If you won't, I will."

No one said anything, though Maren felt sure the other two were thinking exactly as she was: They couldn't go to Jo. Not now. Not after they'd gotten so close. Jo wouldn't believe them, Maren was still sure, and they would probably get in trouble for searching this long.

"Okay," Sal said finally, breaking the silence. He looked directly at Graham. "So let's say it's not in the hives. What do you think we should do?"

Graham blinked, the flush starting to fade from his face. "Do?"

"Yeah, I mean, any other ideas about what the clue could mean?"

Graham blinked again, then straightened up and tried to put some authority back in his voice. "Well, we need to think of other queens, right? Like maybe a queen in a play?"

"Good idea." Sal nodded. When he turned to Theo and Maren, his expression said clearly to go along with it.

"Sure," Theo said, shrugging. "Maybe we don't have to *tell* Jo about the clues, we could just *ask* if she knows anything about a queen."

"Yeah," Maren agreed, a plan starting to form. "And you know what? I think you should ask her, Graham."

Graham's eyes widened. "Me?"

"Well, yeah, someone is clearly onto the rest of us," Maren said. "Theo and I got busted for helping Miss Bradley and, if Allegra was the one to tell on us, then she would have told them Sal is involved. So far, you're the only one in the clear."

Sal was nodding along. "Plus," he added, "you've been here so long, they probably wouldn't believe you're in on anything even if you stood up, waved your arms, and shouted, 'Hey, I'm hunting for the ring!'"

Maren, Theo, and Graham all shushed him, but thankfully Mr. Cairn was at the other side of the cafeteria, and the nearest counselor, Rose, was several tables away.

"Okay," Graham said at last. "I'll do it. I'll ask Jo."

For most of the rest of breakfast, the four of them chatted on about nothing. Sal was in the middle of a story about one of his brothers when Graham stood to clear his tray. Sal waited until Graham was a few paces away, then leaned forward.

"Listen," Sal said in a hurried whisper, "if the hives are where the next clue or the ring is, then we have to get to the hives. We can't stop when we're this close. Agreed?"

"Agreed," Theo said. "And it's safe to say we all think that Mr. Cairn is the accomplice."

"Maybe we can use that," Maren said slowly. "If Mr. Cairn somehow learns that Graham is asking about a queen, maybe he'll get suspicious and start following Graham. We can send them both on a false lead, build a trap, and *prove* it's Mr. Cairn once and for all."

"Do we really want to do that to Graham, though?" Sal said hesitantly.

Maren shrugged, but there was a nagging discomfort tight in her gut. She didn't like the idea of lying to Graham, either, but she didn't see any other way.

"He'll understand, once we find the ring," Theo said confidently. "The real question is, when exactly are we going to find the real clue and lay a false trail for Graham and Mr. Cairn?"

Before Maren could answer, Graham was back, and they all stood to clear their own trays and head to class.

Maren didn't get a chance to talk to Theo or Graham during the whole hour of Tech class. At the end, Bernie thanked them for all their hard work and led them in a round of applause. His smile was wide and bristling under his beard, and Maren couldn't help but feel like she was in on a happy secret, knowing it came from Eartha the lioness. She made sure to keep her distance from Graham and Jo during Theater History, but she didn't have to pretend to be distracted when she left for Playwriting.

Today was the last day of class. Her last chance to share something she had written, if she was going to. She took her usual seat and pulled her bag into her lap, trying to keep the sadness and the fear she felt creeping up her chest at bay.

"Hey!" someone hissed in her ear.

Maren jumped and turned to find Allegra scowling down at her. "I know you hid that thing somewhere!" Allegra said.

"Really?" Maren tried to make her face as blank as possible. "That's funny, because I don't even know what you're talking about."

"Oh, please." Allegra rolled her eyes. "You're not nearly a good enough actress to pull off that lie. I saw you and Sal find something in the orchestra pit!"

As if summoned, Sal appeared at her shoulder. "What's up, Allegra," he said evenly. "You're in my seat."

Allegra turned her scowl at him. "You know, I honestly thought you were cooler than this, Sal."

Sal only laughed. "I'm not cool because you saw me and Maren in the orchestra pit? What's the big deal?"

"The big deal is that you choose to hang with rejects instead of *me*! We could have been the power couple of Goodman's if you had just liked me back!"

Instantly, Allegra's hand rose to her mouth, as if to snatch the words back and keep them trapped inside. Sal's eyes widened in surprise. Even Maren winced, but wasn't sure if she felt embarrassed for Sal, or for Allegra, or for all of them. It was such an honest, awkward thing that no one knew what to do.

"Hey…sorry, Allegra," Sal said, and he actually did sound sorry. "The thing is, I don't like…" Sal stood up straighter. Maren got the sense that he was about to say something important, and then he did: "I don't like girls that way."

Allegra looked at Sal, fresh wonder on her face, followed by a bright slap of pink on her cheeks. "Whatever," she said. "Just know that if you guys do anything—*anything*—to threaten the show, I'll make sure every last one of you is kicked out of camp for, like, *ever*."

With that, Allegra gathered her things and went to the other side of the room to sit. Sal took his seat next to Maren as if nothing were out of the ordinary. For a moment, they were both quiet.

"I'm sorry," Maren said eventually, keeping her voice as soft as she could. Sal looked up at her, his brows furrowed. "I mean, I'm sorry you had to tell us—or, I guess you didn't really tell *me*—but I'm sorry you had to come out like that—I mean, I don't know if you already were out or..." She felt her throat dry up as the words slowed to a trickle. Somehow, she had managed to take an awkward moment and make it even more awkward. So much for *her* crush. Maybe she was better off staying quiet.

Sal gave a soft laugh. "Maren," he said calmly. "I like boys. Consider me officially out, and now you know." He looked at her with his eyebrows raised, his expression wryly comical, but there was something serious in his eyes.

Maren took a breath. "Thanks for telling me," she said, but that wasn't exactly what she meant. "Thanks for *trusting* me," she said instead, and that felt truer.

She smiled, and Sal gave her a relieved, megawatt smile back. Then they turned and both started digging their notebooks out of their bags, and that was that.

Monty swept in, his jumble of hair bobbing elastically with each of his long strides. "Last day of class!" he cried. "And I can't wait to hear all the symbols you've written for me!"

The rest of class went by reading the symbolism scenes everyone had written for the final project. Sal's scene was, as expected, awesome, with two characters speaking in rhymes through masks and taking them off layer by layer, and even Allegra's wasn't entirely bad. She had written a scene with a mom and daughter fighting over a giant poodle, and it was pretty funny when the mom accidentally got squashed when the poodle sat on her. But as each new person raised a hand to read, Maren was intensely aware of the hour sliding past.

"Excellent work." Monty laughed after a monologue in which a kid couldn't lift his arm because of the number of fancy wristwatches he wore. "Anyone else who...?" His voice trailed off when he saw Maren.

Her hand was raised. It hadn't gotten higher than her ear. But it was raised.

"Maren?" Monty cocked his head, making his wild hair dance. "You ready?"

Maren nodded.

"All right!" He clapped his hands in excitement. "Maren's up! Let's hear it!" He leaned back in his chair, his arms folded on his belly, grinning.

Maren swallowed hard. Her paper fluttered as her hand shook. For an instant, the memory of reading her monologue for the teachers crashed over her. What if she cried? Or what if, even worse than crying, she just wasn't good? But she knew, no matter what, she wanted to share this one. She took a deep breath and started reading.

A girl, SEAWEED, stands in the middle of the stage.
SEAWEED
There's this fairy tale about two sisters and a godmother. The first sister doesn't help the fairy godmother when she's in disguise, and so that sister gets cursed. Every time she speaks, frogs and lizards and gross things fall from her mouth. The

second sister, though, helps the fairy godmother,
and gets blessed so that diamonds and pearls fall
from her mouth.

(Seaweed hiccups as a burst of fire roars out of
her mouth.)

I never really liked this story. The first sister
might have had a good reason for not helping the
fairy godmother. Sometimes you have to get home
because you're supposed to be babysitting your younger
sister. Or sometimes you're so busy with your own
stuff that you don't see someone else's needs.

(She hiccups fire.)

I also don't think the second sister has it all
that much better. I mean, yeah, they're diamonds
and pearls, but it must have been painful to have
sharp rocks fall out of your mouth.

(She hiccups fire.)

Anyway, I don't believe in blessings or curses,
and I don't think I was ever mean to any old
ladies, but I did get the flaming hiccups. Did you
know there's no real cure for the hiccups? All you
can do is wait, so…

(She hiccups again, and the fire burns every-
thing. She shrugs.)

Afterward, Maren didn't remember much about reading it. She just knew that at some point she got wrapped
up in the story, in the words. Even though Maren hadn't
exactly known what she was writing about when she wrote
the monologue, she felt something soften in her toward her
sister when she got to the end. She didn't want to be a little

sister who spoke diamonds any more than Hadley had to be the older sister full of snakes; maybe it was time to let go of the stories they had been telling themselves.

When Maren looked up again, Sal was grinning at her, and everyone clapped, and Monty said some nice things, and for the life of her, Maren couldn't remember why she had been so afraid. A few more kids shared what they wrote, and then the hour was over.

"And then we came to the end," Monty said. He clapped his hands and bounced on his toes brightly. "Can't wait to see you all in the show!"

The group applauded, and some of the kids crowded around Monty. Maren wanted to say something to him, too, but she wasn't sure what to say. When Sal asked if she was ready to go, she agreed, and kept her head down as she left.

Maren had no idea what dress rehearsals would be like, but for the rest of Tuesday and all of Wednesday, the camp functioned at a stressed-out, high-pitched frequency she hadn't thought possible. Every few minutes of rehearsal, Jo would shout for the actors to "hold!" and then the sound or the lights or something else had to be fixed, and then they'd have to "start from the top!" of the latest scene. The play moved forward at an agonizing pace, moment by moment, with kids running onstage half costumed or missing their cues. When it was finally time for dinner on Wednesday—after Nic had to be comforted when her headdress kept falling off—Jo and Maren only exchanged weary looks and laughed.

"We survived," Jo said, stretching out.

"Not yet," Maren warned. "We haven't even gotten through the gala yet."

"That'll actually be a nice break. You'll see." Jo had noticed Maren's doubtful look. "Every year I tell Vincent, there's no way we're going to be able to have a fancy fundraiser in the middle of camp, and each year he somehow manages to pull it off."

But Maren felt every inch of her go cold. "Mr. Cairn?" she managed to say. "He organizes the gala?"

"Of course," Jo said. "I don't know what I would do without him."

But Maren was stuck on something else Jo had said. "Fundraiser," she breathed. "*Levée de fonds*."

"What was that?" Jo was watching her, looking puzzled.

"Nothing," Maren said, trying to keep her voice level. "You said a bunch of people from the area come? Like who?"

"Oh, we have a lot of supporters," Jo spoke slowly. "Some local businesspeople, a lot of alumni—"

"Renee Wallace?"

Jo's mouth dropped open. "You know about—?"

"People say she's trying to buy the camp," Maren plowed on before she lost her nerve. "Is that true?"

"I had no idea the rumor mill was so active—or so accurate," Jo sighed. "Well, yes, the Walcorp store has been trying to buy more land for its parking lot—but don't worry," she said when she saw Maren's look. "She understands that the camp itself isn't for sale, and after the gala, we'll have enough money to make it another year."

"Right," Maren said weakly. She looked down at her

binder, thinking fast. "Did you want me to make sure the costumes are all hung up and labeled properly before we go to dinner?"

"No, I can do it." Jo stretched again. "Why don't you go ahead. We'll meet up tomorrow morning and—"

"Okay, see you then!" Maren was already halfway up the aisle and walking fast for the door.

When she got outside, she broke into a sprint and ran the whole way to the cafeteria. She almost wept with relief when she saw Theo and Sal alone at a table—she didn't think she could handle lying to Graham right now.

"Hey, settle something for us," Theo said as Maren arrived and struggled to catch her breath. They were spreading peanut butter directly on a banana with their finger. "If you had to eat one fruit for the rest of your life, what would it be? Sal says apple, but obviously it's—"

"It's the gala," Maren wheezed. "Renee Wallace is coming to the gala. She and Mr. Cairn are going to use that time to find the ring!"

"Slow down," Sal said. "What are you talking about? How do you know?"

"Theo, you said Renee Wallace was talking about raising money on the phone, right? What if *levée de fonds* literally translates to *fundraiser*!"

Theo's face went pale.

"Hey!"

Maren nearly jumped out of her skin and spun around to find Graham arriving with a tray and a huge grin.

"I figured it out!" he said.

"Figured what out?" Sal said, recovering first.

"The you-know-what!" Graham leaned forward, his

gaze bouncing eagerly across his friends' faces. "It's a chess piece! You know, like a queen? In chess, the queen?"

"Right," Sal said. "Cool. That makes sense."

"Any idea where there's a chessboard?" Theo asked.

"What do you think, Maren?" Graham turned toward her eagerly, but Maren felt so bad she had to look away.

"I don't know…" she forced herself to say. "Maybe…I mean, we didn't look for chessboards in the prop closet. It could be there."

"Makes sense," Sal said.

"We can sneak out and check during the scene at the gala!" Graham said. "It'll be like movie night, only the counselors will be ten times more distracted—"

"Ooh…actually?" Theo held up a finger half coated with peanut butter. "I have the scene to perform, remember?"

"Oh, right," Graham said. "Then the other three of us—"

But Sal was already shaking his head. "Sorry, man, but my aunt is going to be at the gala. I have to hang around so she can tell me how tall I'm getting."

"And I have to help Jo," Maren added. It was only a half lie, Maren comforted herself as Graham looked crestfallen.

"You can do it solo," Theo said heartily.

"By myself?" Graham's eyes went wide.

"Totally," Maren agreed. "We trust you."

"It's actually probably better that way," Sal said. "You can run up to the prop closet and be back before the scene is half over. No one will notice, and even if they do, they'd probably let you get away with anything."

"Well, I guess," Graham said hesitantly. "I guess I could go by myself—"

"Hey, speaking of everyone loving you, Graham," Theo

said, turning the empty eye of the camera to face him. Sometime during the conversation, they had managed to drop the banana and lift their camera. "Would you mind asking Chef Clarence for another fruit cup? I would, but the last time I asked, he said no, so I had to steal it, and our working relationship has been on the rocks ever since."

Graham laughed along with the others, then stood and headed for the food line. Maren felt another stab of treachery in her chest.

"Right," Sal said when he had gone. "What's the real plan? How are we going to get to the hives?"

Maren took a deep breath. "You're not," she said, looking at each of them in turn. "Graham is right about one thing: The only possible time everyone is going to be distracted enough to go is at the gala. I'll run out, check the hives, and get back as fast as I can—hopefully before anyone notices I'm gone, and hopefully before Renee Wallace gets there."

"Wait just a second," Theo said, their camera drooping so they could look at Maren directly. "That plan is bananas!"

"Completely loony tunes," Sal said. "It's one thing for Graham to go alone to the prop closet, but you want to go alone to beehives that are that close to Walcorp land?"

"I don't *want* to go alone," Maren said, "but it's the only way. Besides, it should be easier for one person to sneak out there than for three."

"Ba-nanas," Theo repeated emphatically.

"Completely," Sal agreed.

"I don't hear any other ideas," Maren snapped. She looked at them both, but Sal just shook his head and Theo muttered something that sounded suspiciously like "bananas" a third time. A moment later, Graham returned with another fruit cup.

"Hey, don't worry, guys," he said, taking in the pinched, nervous expressions on the faces of the other three. "I was worried at first, too, but it's a good plan. Everything will work out fine."

"You're absolutely right," Maren said, trying to make herself sound more confident than she felt. "Everything will work out fine."

On the morning of the gala, Maren woke with a dull throb of dread tightening like a fist in her belly. She had tried to sound confident with her friends but now, alone in the rising pink light of morning, the last thing she wanted to do was go close to Walcorp land to try to find a ring buried somewhere in a heap of stinging bees. There was so much that could go wrong.

Maren sighed. There would be no going back to sleep now. She stood and stretched and half glanced at Theo's bed, expecting to see them still passed out. But it was empty. They were probably already in the cafeteria, Maren decided—but when she arrived, there was no Theo in sight. Maren gathered a breakfast tray and sat where she could see the door, picking at a biscuit and trying not to worry. A few minutes later, Graham came in.

"Nervous?" Graham whispered as he slid in beside her with his tray. "Me too." But he sounded more exhilarated than nervous.

Maren didn't think she could stomach sitting around

for the rest of breakfast and lying to Graham's face, so she stood up and gathered her things. "I should get to the auditorium early," she lied. "Just in case Jo wants me."

"Oh, sure," Graham said, though he sounded disappointed. "I'll see you soon."

Maren nodded and headed for the door. There were a lot more students on the path now, stretching and yawning their way toward the cafeteria like good-natured zombies—but still no Theo. Maren started walking faster.

"Oh, thank goodness, Maren," Jo said when Maren arrived at the auditorium. "As soon as the cast is gathered, we're going to have to refigure the gala performance."

Maren took a step back in surprise. "What do you mean?" she said. "What's wrong with—with the scene you picked?" She had been about to say *Theo's scene* but caught herself. Jo seemed to read her mind anyway.

"Theo came to me a little while ago," Jo said in a hushed voice. "They're feeling sick and don't think they're up for performing this afternoon. Not sure what else to pick, though..."

Maren forced herself to nod as Jo went on about alternative options, even though she felt her blood starting to boil. It was obvious what Theo was up to—if they didn't have to perform in the scene tonight, they'd be free to go with Maren to the hives. Maren wasn't sure if she found the gesture touching or idiotic, but she knew she couldn't let Theo give up their chance to shine at the gala.

"Malvolio is in most of the scenes with Sir Toby and Sir Andrew, so those are out," Jo was saying as she flipped through her script, "but maybe we can switch to—"

"Sorry, would it be okay if I go see them really quick?" Maren interrupted. "Theo, I mean. I'd like to make sure they're all right."

Jo's face shifted. "Oh, Maren, forgive me, I forgot you were such good friends. Of course, I'm sure Theo would love a visit. They're lying down in the nurse's office."

Lying indeed, Maren thought as she quickly walked back up the aisle.

The nurse's office was on the second floor. The front part of it was barely big enough for a desk and the nurse sitting there, but behind her Maren could see a dim, cot-filled room. The nurse made a face when Maren, panting from running up the stairs, said she was there to see Theo.

"Theo's resting," the nurse said in a bored drawl. "They shouldn't be bothered."

"Jo said I could visit them," Maren hurried to say. "I need to talk to them about tonight."

The nurse sighed. "Fine. Just keep your voice down," she said, then gestured Maren through to the dim back room. Maren stepped tentatively inside, blinking to adjust to the light of the drawn shades. She could make out the shape of several cots along the wall; on one of the far cots was a lump that had to be Theo, curled in a fetal position with their back to Maren.

Maren carefully eased the door shut behind her so as not to alert the nurse, then stomped toward Theo's cot.

"Theo!" she hissed, her voice trembling with anger. "What are you thinking? You can't fake being sick and give up your chance tonight just because—"

But the rest of Maren's words evaporated when Theo turned over and she saw their tear-streaked face.

"I'm not faking," Theo hiccupped. "Someone stole my camera. I went to the cafeteria early this morning, and my bag was only sitting alone at a table for like five minutes while I talked to Clarence, but when I got back, it was gone!"

"Oh, Theo," Maren said, her anger instantly evaporating. "Theo, it's okay," she said, trying to be comforting. "I'm sure it's just another prank, probably Allegra again—"

"No, you don't understand," Theo groaned pitifully. "I'm not upset about the camera! I'm upset about the *footage!*"

"Why? What's so special about..." But Maren trailed off as understanding washed over her in an icy wave of dread.

"It was all the shots I got of us! All the times we were talking about the clues and the ring and Charlotte Goodman! Don't you understand? *Someone will know about our plan!*"

Rehearsal went until noon, and every minute of it was sheer torture for Maren. While Graham and Sal were getting their costumes fitted, she had to sit in the audience and watch as Jo directed a very nervous Piper and a very smug Allegra. Their act 1 scene had been chosen to replace Theo's. Just watching Allegra prance around made Maren want to throw up—or, better yet, throw something at Allegra's head.

At noon, Maren and the rest of the campers were shuffled into the cafeteria and given a quick lunch of prewrapped sandwiches and bagged potato chips. Chef

Clarence seemed especially beleaguered and had to keep steering kids through the lunch line when they paused to eye all the fancy treats being made for the gala.

"Can you imagine what Theo would do if they saw all this?" Sal said regretfully as he picked up one of the bags. He tossed a yearning glance toward the nearest tray in the kitchen, filled with tiny spinach-and-cheese quiches. "Good thing they're still resting in your cabin."

"That's *awful*, Sal! It's not a *good thing* poor Theo is stuck in bed!" said a voice so loud and familiar that Maren's teeth clenched automatically. As expected, Allegra stood behind them in line, smirking. "That's not kind!" She looked around, hopeful for attention, but she didn't get more than a cursory glance from Mr. Cairn. "Although," Allegra added under her breath when he looked away again, "it is a good thing they didn't bother trying to perform tonight. The fate of the entire camp staying open depends on these donors."

"Stop it, Allegra." They all turned to see Graham glaring at Allegra. "You may get to perform tonight," he said, "but you're only Jo's second choice."

Maren shared an amazed look with Sal. Allegra looked as if she had been slapped.

"I should have known you'd join team freak, Grahamie," she said, when she had recovered. "I'm sure your *moms* are so proud."

Maren felt a surge of anger, but Graham just shook his head.

"I can't believe I was friends with you for so long," he said, his voice as soft as ever but all the harsher because of it. He gave her one more contemptuous look, then turned to Sal and Maren. "Let's go," he said.

Sal joined him without a backward glance and, after a split second of shock, Maren followed behind.

She knew she shouldn't be glad but, if anything, Allegra overhearing and announcing that Theo was in their cabin was great news—because Theo certainly wasn't going to be there all night. The nurse had allowed them to go back to their cabin on the condition that they continue to rest, but as soon as the gala guests started arriving, Theo was going to go to the hives and hide nearby, their phone camera aimed and ready to catch Mr. Cairn or Renee Wallace in the act of searching the hives. "No one is going to be able to take *this* camera from me, at least," Theo had said viciously, gripping their phone. It was also a relief, Maren thought as she and Sal joined Graham at the table, that now they didn't have to use Graham as bait.

"Listen, forget Allegra," Sal was saying as Maren set down her tray. "She's not worth—"

"I don't care about Allegra," Graham interrupted. "I care because I should still be the one to sneak out and find the queen!"

Sal sat back with an annoyed sigh and shot Maren a look.

"We talked about this," Maren said quietly. "With Theo's camera missing, it's not safe. Someone knows all our plans."

Graham slumped over his sandwich. "But what if," he started, "what if I just *try* to go during the gala but stop if someone sees me?"

"No," Sal said bluntly.

"But what if—"

"It's too dangerous," Maren said. "There'd probably be an ambush waiting for you."

"But like you said, people know me here, they won't think—"

"And like *you* said," Sal interrupted, "we promised not to do anything stupid that puts us at risk. Right?"

Graham slumped even further in his seat. "Right," he muttered, almost inaudibly.

"Maybe we can go tomorrow," Maren tried to reassure him. "I'm sure, with all the counselors wrapped up in the show, there'll be a minute or two when we can slip away."

"But what if Renee Wallace goes there tonight?" Graham said miserably.

Maren didn't reply. She was worried about the same thing, except with the hives.

They were quiet after that, picking at their limp sandwiches. Toward the end of the hour, Maren heard hoots and catcalls start up, and she turned to see Jo and Mr. Cairn walk in looking very dressed up. Jo was wearing a silky dress of deep maroon with a sparkly black flower design. It looked like she had even made an attempt to tame her hair by twisting it behind her head into a twirly chignon, though the ends fluffed out at the top like a carnation. Mr. Cairn was wearing a starched navy suit, but his shoes were bright silver and matched the silver swirls in the ascot tied at his neck.

"All right, all right, thank you!" Jo announced when the whistling had died down. "Most of you know the drill, but just in case: The gala starts at five PM. You will be free to mingle with the guests for an hour before the scene performance starts at six PM."

Even across the room, Maren saw Allegra sit up straighter.

"Afterward, there will probably be some more mingling—"

There were a few more whistles and cheers, but Mr. Cairn glared around the room, as if challenging anyone who dared to mingle.

"But remember that you have a big day tomorrow, so make sure you don't get too distracted. And..." Here Jo paused, looking at each of them with that insistent faith that made the idea of disappointing her so tragic. "Remember that the guests are largely responsible for how the camp manages to keep its doors open. This year, we need their support more than usual."

The silence in the room was all-encompassing—a silence that Maren hadn't understood a few weeks ago, but now felt as deeply as anyone there. No matter what happened with the ring, Goodman's was a special place, and the thought of it closing its doors was heartbreaking.

"But also remember," Jo continued, "*you* are the reason we have survived this long, and *you* are the reason the donors come back year after year—so put your best foot forward and show them just how much we love this place!" She took a breath, then smiled. "If theater be a mirror to life..."

This time, Maren knew exactly what to say, and she felt no shame about joining wholeheartedly with the rest as they all cried: "THEN PLAY ON!"

Maren remembered Hadley having a minor meltdown a few years ago about what she was going to wear to the gala. "You don't understand, Mom!" Hadley had whined when their mother suggested packing an ordinary cotton green-and-white-striped summer dress. "The other girls get their mothers to buy them *prom* dresses for gala night."

Their mom had rolled her eyes. "Don't exaggerate, Hadley. I'm sure you'll look very nice in this."

But for once, Maren thought, Hadley hadn't been exaggerating. Out of nowhere, it seemed, girls were dragging full-skirted ball gowns and dresses with lace sleeves and silk sheaths pockmarked with crystals from their suitcases, then piling into the tiny cinder-block bathroom at the same time to get ready. The air was thick with steam as they screeched at one another for using up the hot water. The line to get to the sink mirrors was about five-girls deep, and those at the front still leaned over and elbowed one another to see their reflection.

"You're totally trying to sabotage me!" Piper shrieked at a first-year girl named Jamie who, in an attempt to get to a sink to brush her teeth, had accidentally knocked Piper's arm and sent a streak of black mascara down her cheek.

After a very quick, very cold shower, Maren put on the black jumper dress she had packed over a pink T-shirt and pair of leggings that had geometric patterns on them. She rubbed at her hair with a towel but, after seeing the frenzy to use the blow-dryer, decided she might as well wear it wet, behind a headband. As for makeup, she didn't see the point, but she did put on a pair of dangling silver earrings her sister had given her a few birthdays ago.

Back in her cabin, Lorna had already left, but Katie was just finishing zipping up a silky watermelon-pink dress.

"Hope you feel better, Theo," she said as she headed outside.

Theo smiled weakly from the top bunk. "Thanks," they said, their voice croaky with misery. "Have a good time for me."

Maren waited until she heard Katie's footsteps recede, then whispered to Theo, "All set?"

Theo nodded and hopped down, fully dressed in a vest patterned with sunglasses. They set to work stuffing old clothes into a vaguely person-shaped lump in their abandoned sleeping bag.

"You remember the plan?" Maren said, coming over to help.

"Hide by the hives and catch the thieves on this bad boy." They held up their phone. "Slightly off-topic question: How hard is it to get honey out of a hive?"

Maren rolled her eyes. "Don't try to do anything by yourself, okay? Don't go looking for the ring, and don't try to interrupt if Renee or Mr. Cairn find it first, and *definitely* don't try to get honey. Just get it on camera."

"Don't be seen or heard or enjoy tasty deliciousness, got it," Theo said.

"Right," Maren said.

They looked at each other in silence. Maren remembered that this was supposed to be Theo's big night, and here they were, throwing that away, all to help Maren.

"Theo, are you sure—" Maren started, but Theo waved her away.

"I should take off," Theo said, heading for the door. "You should head to the gala, too, or you'll be late."

"I'll see you as soon as I can get away," Maren said.

"I'll see you first," Theo promised, and they held up their phone.

❧

When Maren got to the auditorium, the lobby was already full of strangers wearing fancy clothes. Maren tugged at her dress self-consciously, edging past some cackling adults who stood at tall tables decorated with lace doilies and flickering tea candles. They all held tiny plates with the tiny food in front of their mouths. She imagined the look on Theo's face if they had seen the bacon-wrapped shrimp the guests were eating, and smiled to herself. She wound her way through the strangers until she found Jo, laughing with a pair of elderly women wearing matching dresses in seafoam green.

"Maren, wonderful," Jo said, and all three women smiled down at her. "These are the Manigotti sisters. They were friends of my mother's."

"Jo's mother was the most *beautiful* woman in the world," said one of the sisters. "She could have been famous, I'm sure of it."

"You have your mother's eyes," said the second sister, patting Jo's arm. "Her beautiful blue eyes."

Jo blushed at the compliment and thanked the sisters. After the two women moved off, Maren asked Jo if she needed any help.

"Nope, everything seems to be going off without a hitch or hiccup," Jo said, looking around the lobby with a satisfied sigh. "Enjoy yourself, and—"

"Jo!"

Maren turned and found herself face-to-face—or really, face-to-elbow, because of her high, high heels—with Renee Wallace. She wore a gown of icy-blue silk and a necklace with a single, giant diamond dragging heavily on its delicate chain.

"Renee," Jo said. She took a deep breath and seemed to work hard to gather a smile from herself. "Glad you could make it."

"Of course," Renee said, looking around. "And I must say, I'm utterly baffled by this surprising turnout. To think, there's this sort of culture up here? It's nothing short of shocking."

"I think this place could surprise you, if you gave it a chance," Jo said, and Maren was surprised to hear real earnestness in her voice. "I think we could."

Renee thrust out her steely laugh again. "Oh, Jo, that's a miracle beyond even your skill." With that, she tottered off, her normal clattering, high-heeled walk even more awkwardly restricted by the tight skirt.

Jo sighed, but she forced another smile when she saw Maren watching. "Go, enjoy," Jo insisted. "I'll find you if I need you."

Maren smiled back and watched Jo warmly greet an old man with more hair coming out of his ears than on his head.

"Hey," Sal said, appearing beside Maren. He wore a light purple button-down and had put a stud earring in one ear. He kept running one hand along the top of his head. "This is kinda wild, huh?"

"Totally wild," Maren agreed. "You look nice."

He gave her a dimpled grin. "Yeah, you too. Is Theo...?"

"Resting in the cabin," she said, probably louder than she needed to, just in case anyone was eavesdropping, but gave Sal a tiny nod. She added, "Have you seen Graham?"

Before he could answer, someone shouted, "And here's my savior!"

Everyone turned and watched as Miss Maxine Bradley, wearing an extremely flouncy white dress, launched herself directly at Maren. Maren gasped in surprise at the sudden collection of ruffles she was hugging, so big she could barely get her arms all the way around the tiny woman.

"It's good to see you, Miss Bradley," Maren said when she had finally pulled away. "Glad you're feeling better."

"Oh, please, call me Miss Maxine Bradley," Miss Maxine Bradley said, then giggled at her joke. "No, no, Miss Bradley is fine. People used to think I was stuck-up for hanging on to my 'Miss' title, but it was hard work, in my day, *not* to give in and get married!" Sal laughed, and Miss Bradley looked at him appreciatively. "And who is this fine gentleman?"

"Sal," Sal said, taking her tiny hand in his. "I've heard all about your adventures."

"Have you!" Miss Bradley looked delighted. "You know, when Maren found me, I thought—"

"Miss Bradley!" came a high screech as Allegra appeared. She wore a teal dress and a glittery tiara-like headband, her eyelids thick with a chalky silver eyeshadow.

"It's so good to see you, Miss Bradley! It's been *awful* not having Acting class to help shape my craft this summer."

"Oh, yes, nice to see you, too, Amanda," Miss Bradley said.

Sal and Maren both went into sudden coughing fits that didn't quite cover their laughter. Allegra glared at them. "I need to go prepare for the performance," she went on. "Did you know Jo chose my scene this year?"

"That's nice, dear." Maxine Bradley flipped a dismissive hand at Allegra, her focus turning back to Sal. "As I was saying, I owe Maren here a real debt. And where is my other hero? You know, the charming one with the themed vest?"

"You mean Theo." Maren looked right at Allegra as she said, "Their scene was chosen for tonight originally, but they got sick."

"Oh, that's too bad!" Miss Maxine Bradley clasped her hands in sympathy. "I'm sure they would have been brilliant."

Allegra glared and spun away, though only Maren seemed to notice.

"Like I was saying..." Miss Bradley started back in on her version of the night Maren and Theo had found her, with a few significant exaggerations. Maren was pretty sure she'd remember it if she'd had to wrestle a giant man wearing a Charlotte Goodman mask.

"Haven't lost your flair for dramatics, I see, Maxine," said a woman walking up in a slinky gold gown.

Her high, elegant cheekbones looked familiar—and Maren realized from where, when the woman planted a kiss on Sal's forehead, leaving behind a wine-colored lip-stick mark.

"This is my auntie Adelaide," Sal introduced her.

"Oh, Adelaide and I go way back," Miss Bradley said with a twinkle. "She's another fierce Miss from a day when everybody wanted to make her a *Mrs.*"

"I was a *Mrs.* a few times. It just never stuck," Adelaide said. She gestured at Miss Bradley's white dress. "Meanwhile, you're over here, dressing like a bride."

"Adelaide, you know I gave up my right to wear white a *long* time ago!"

The old women cackled, while Sal looked like he wanted to sink into the floor.

Jo appeared, playing a chime. "Time for the performance!" she announced, and the crowd began its slow, meandering tide toward the auditorium. Maren took a steadying breath. The hour had flown by.

"Be careful, all right?" Sal whispered.

She swallowed hard and nodded. He nodded back, then turned and, offering one arm each to his aunt Adelaide and Miss Bradley, headed into the auditorium.

"Oh, good," Maren heard Miss Bradley say as they disappeared in the crowd. "Let's go see if Amanda has improved since last summer."

Maren pretended she was following them, then swung to the side and ducked down the hallway beyond. Theo had described for Maren the door that went out onto a little patio—the patio where they had waited in the rain when their camera was stolen for the first time. Maren eased the door open and stepped outside. Like the rest of the lobby, the patio was set with tables and high barstool chairs, tea candles flickering from the center of each and lining the low brick wall. As Theo had promised, it opened directly onto the woods. Maren took another deep breath. At least she was alone.

"Maren?"

She jumped. Monty was standing in front of the path to the woods, his nice shirt already a little crumpled and rolled at the sleeves. He looked at her, puzzled. "You okay? What are you doing out here?"

"Yeah," Maren said, trying to think fast. "Yeah, I'm fine, just needed a little air."

"Tell me about it," Monty said, and there was an uncharacteristic note of bitterness in his voice. He turned away, looking out toward the woods. "I've hated this sort of *wear a tie and act rich* thing since I was a kid."

"You went to galas as a kid?" Maren asked, surprise leaking into her voice.

Monty must have noticed. He grinned. "Hard to believe, I know, but yes, shabby old me has been to galas."

"I didn't mean—"

"I know, I know, I'm just kidding." Monty waved away her apology. "Let's just say I'm the starving artist of the family. But you know all about family issues, I'm sure."

Maren nodded automatically, though she wasn't really listening. He was blocking the way to the woods.

"No matter what happens now," Monty went on, "I just wanted to say I'm really proud of you for writing about your sister in class. I just... I just wanted to say that."

"Thanks," Maren said awkwardly. She wished this conversation were happening another time—*any* other time—but right now she couldn't leave Theo alone at the hives. "I was gonna go check on Theo," she said, a half-truth. "They were supposed to perform tonight, and they're really disappointed. So…"

Monty blinked at her. "I don't know if Mr. Cairn would like you out without supervision," he said contemplatively. Maren's heart sank, but a second later he grinned again and added, "Good thing I'm not Mr. Cairn." He turned and headed for the door, winking at her as he passed.

"Thanks," she breathed. She waited until he was inside, then hurried into the line of trees.

It was cool and shady in the woods as she hurried along, hyperaware of the sound of her footsteps against the dry grass and leaves carpeting the ground. At every bend and fork in the path, she expected to run into someone, but everyone was up at the gala, she reminded herself—including Renee Wallace. Maren sped up, hoping Theo wasn't too late to catch whatever plans Wallace had put in motion, and didn't slow down until she got to the overgrown path behind the boys' cabins. There, she had to pick her way more carefully over tree roots and slippery, mossy patches. She figured she had maybe another hundred yards or so before she got to the edge of the woods where Theo would be hiding.

But she never made it that far.

Maren heard something ahead of her—the unmistakable sound of footsteps pounding closer. Quickly, she stepped back into the underbrush and ducked low into the thickest shadows. She held her breath as a figure hurried past, but when she caught sight of the floppy bowl cut of hair, she let it go in a sigh of relief.

"*Psst!* Theo!" she called softly to Theo's retreating back.

Theo yelped in surprise, and then there was a crashing sound.

"Theo!" Maren stepped out of the brush and ran forward. Theo was on the ground, holding one leg with a long scratch up their shin. "You're bleeding!"

"Never mind that!" Theo said, their voice frantic. "We have to get out of here! There's something coming!"

"Some*thing*?"

"We have to hide!"

Maren had more questions, but Theo was already scrambling to their feet, stumbling as they tried to limp off the side of the path.

"Here," Maren whispered. She wrapped one of Theo's arms around her shoulder and half dragged them into the brush, then helped ease them down to sit on the far side of a tree trunk. "You okay?"

"Yeah, but I think my ankle is sprained." They were breathing hard and winced as they readjusted their leg in front of them.

"What happened?" Maren pressed. "Did you see Renee or Mr. Cairn at the hives? Did you get them on camera?"

"It wasn't either of them..." Theo said through gritted teeth, their eyes closed. "You're not going to believe who it was."

"What? Why not? Who is it?"

Wordlessly, Theo held out their phone, a video pulled up on the screen. Maren took it. Her hands trembled slightly as she pressed play. It was hard to see—gray and grainy and empty except for a blocky white figure, moving slowly.

"They're wearing Jo's apiary suit?" she said.

Theo nodded. "But they lift the hood at the end. I saw their face."

Maren eagerly looked down at the video again. She watched as the figure searched one hive, then another. She saw them stop, their back turned, at a hive on the far left and fumble with something there. When they turned and started walking toward the camera, they reached for their hood and began undoing the latches. Maren held her breath as the veiled part lifted. . . .

"I can't see anything," she said to Theo, squinting at the screen. "It's too blurry—Theo, who was it?"

Theo started to answer, but just then they both heard it: another set of footsteps coming down the path. These were slow and a little bit shaky, but undeniably moving in their direction.

Theo's eyes went wide. Maren put a finger to her lips. Barely breathing, she edged closer to the path and then crouched behind a tree, checking to make sure she was still covered by shadows. The footsteps got closer, louder, and with them, the sound of Maren's heart.

A moment later the figure came into view.

Whoever it was still wore the apiary suit, which glowed a dull white in the shade of the trees. The person was wearing the hood again, but the veil had been pushed back so just their face was visible. Maren stared. She watched as the person got closer, then closer still. There was the sound of a stick cracking somewhere in the woods behind them. The person paused, cocking their head at an angle to listen. Maren held her breath, her brain unwilling to process what she was seeing. Something about the way the person held their head, that angle of concentration, seemed so familiar, unbelievably so....

Finally, the person kept moving away, down the path, back toward camp. But Maren was frozen in place. She couldn't blink, couldn't breathe, couldn't snap her brain out of it. She knew she couldn't have seen what she just saw, but there was no mistaking that face, that particular angle:

It was Charlotte Goodman.

⁓

"This isn't happening," Maren muttered, mostly to herself, as she and Theo hobbled back down the path. "This just cannot be happening."

"You think I don't know that?" Theo said between breaths. They were gripping their phone in their fist like they were never going to let it go. "But you saw Charlotte, didn't you? You saw Charlotte Goodman, just like I did. Just like Maxine Bradley did."

Maren didn't answer right away. She knew what she saw—or what she thought she saw—but she also knew it simply couldn't be. It could have easily been someone else who angled their head like Charlotte—couldn't it? Besides, Miss Bradley said she had seen a teenage, tomboy Charlotte, like the picture of her in the house, but Maren had definitely seen an adult in the beekeeper's suit. Hadn't she?

She shook her head. Now her memory, something she had always trusted about herself, was playing tricks on her, too.

"It can't have been," Maren said eventually. "Charlotte Goodman died a long time ago."

Theo gave a frustrated, disbelieving sigh. "Somebody better tell Charlotte that."

Maren ignored this. "Did…that person…whoever it was, did they see you?"

"I don't think so. I think Charlotte was too busy searching the hives—but there was this one super-weird thing, though, it looked like—" Theo stopped short, causing Maren to stumble. "Do you smell that?"

"Smell what?" Maren asked.

"It smells like barbecue," Theo said.

Maren gave a frustrated sigh. Of course Theo was thinking about eating, even now. "There's a lot of fancy food for the rich people. You can try some soon enough."

"No, I mean…" Theo sniffed the air again. "It smells like smoke."

Maren frowned. Now that Theo mentioned it, something did smell a little bit smoky. But before she had time to say as much, Theo took off ahead of her, trying to run with their one good leg while dragging the other behind them.

"Theo, wait!" Maren started after them. She was surprised at how fast Theo moved.

They were close enough now that Maren could just make out the shape of the auditorium in the distance, lit by a dull orange glow. Maren remembered the spectacular glow of the sunset against the front of the auditorium on her first night at camp. Was the sun setting already? How late were they? Up ahead, she saw Theo standing in the middle of the path, at the top of a small hill.

"Theo!" Maren called when she was within a few feet. She struggled up the last rise of the hill. "Theo, what are you thinking, someone might—" But she never had a chance to finish, overwhelmed as she was by the heat and the light and the unbelievable sight in front of her.

The auditorium was on fire.

Charlie

July 6, 1953
Los Angeles, California

"Rosalie?" Charlie asked into the grainy white noise. "Can you hear me?"

The connection over the phone was distant and staticky. Rosalie lived in western Massachusetts, where Jeremy's job had taken them a few years ago, and Charlie never had gotten used to the distance, even though they talked on the telephone once a week.

"I heard you," Rosalie sighed. Charlie could hear the anxiety in her sister's voice. "But... are you sure?"

"Yes," Charlie said firmly. "I'm sure."

Charlie was in the editing room again, only this time, the projector was turned off and still, the space eerily quiet without the hum of its motor and fan. Reels of unused footage were piled all around, while a few spare, half-cut strips of film hung like Christmas garlands. Right next to Charlie sat the eight canisters of finished, edited film, perfectly stacked. Charlie nervously tapped her fingers on the top canister.

"But what if things don't work out the way you mean them to?" Rosalie was asking. "What if it doesn't go according to your plan? What if—?"

"Rosalie." Charlie took a deep breath and pressed the receiver hard against her cheek, then winced. There was a bruise purpling under her eye that twinged every time she pressed the phone too close. She eased it away again and said, "The plan will work, but we need your help. Can we count on you?"

Rosalie was quiet so long, Charlie thought maybe the static meant the connection had been lost, but eventually Rosalie said, "Yes. Yes, I can help."

Relief flooded Charlie. "And you understand what we need from you? You understand what to do?"

"Yes, Emma filled me in on everything."

"Good." Charlie nodded and winced again, the receiver jarring the bruise.

She should have known her secret wouldn't stay hidden forever, and she should have known Wayman would get violent when he learned. She wasn't sure which had angered Wayman more: the idea that Emma was leaving him, or the idea that it was for Charlie, a woman. The studio would have already gotten a call from him. She could imagine the panicked meetings probably happening right now, the studio's frantic damage control. She'd never work as a director in this town again; her picture would never see the light of day; the dream she had cherished and worked so hard for would be lost to her forever.

But that dream meant nothing without Emma.

There was a hiccup, and then a moment later, Rosalie sobbed, "Are you sure about this, Charlie? Are you sure you want to—"

"I'm more sure of this than I've been of anything in my entire life," Charlie insisted. "I'm choosing who I want to be, Rosy. That has to be worth the risk."

"But what if—"

"Don't worry. I'll see you soon enough," Charlie said.

She swallowed the catch in her voice. "And just in case anything happens...I love you." She hung up before her sister had a chance to respond.

There was a tentative knock on the door of the editing booth. Charlie jumped, but when she turned, there was Emma peeking in. Just seeing her created a soaring feeling in Charlie's chest, as if she were suddenly full of air and light. She tried not to smile too much as she opened the door the rest of the way and pulled Emma inside.

"Hi," Emma said shyly. She was wearing brown tweed traveling pants and a silk blouse, a chic leather overnight bag gripped in one fist. Her brown lace hat matched her pants perfectly, but it also hid the dark roots of her hair growing out to her natural color again.

"Hi," Charlie said.

There was a pause as they seemed to be deciding whether or not to kiss, then they both leaned forward so eagerly they bonked foreheads. They laughed, then managed to kiss for real.

"Where have you been?" Charlie asked when they separated. "I thought you were going to be here an hour ago."

"There were some last-minute errands I had to run," Emma said. She tried to make her voice sound light. "There's a lot to do when you're about to run away from your entire life."

"Is that all you're taking?" Charlie asked. She gestured at the bag. "I thought for sure you'd have the matching set."

Emma pretended to be offended. "Naturally, I have the matching set, but a lady travels light."

They laughed again, but the silence that fell afterward was heavy.

"How are you feeling?" Charlie asked.

Emma blew out her cheeks and smoothed her trousers. "Nervous, I suppose."

"But...you still want to do this...right?" Charlie asked, feeling suddenly afraid. She could stand anything, anything at all, so long as she and Emma were together.

Emma smiled. "Yes. I do."

"Okay," Charlie breathed. "Okay, then we're all set up and ready, I think. Any news about...?" She tried and failed to say Wayman's name.

"Right." Emma straightened up. "I left the note for him to find. He normally gets home around nine or ten from the club. I'm sure he'll be here soon after...." She trailed off and took in the room regretfully, as if pained by the thought of saying goodbye to it.

"Don't think about it," Charlie insisted. "Think about tomorrow. Tomorrow, we catch a boat bright and early, and we're off to see the world! No one will be able to—"

But just then, there was a long screech from outside. Charlie and Emma both hurried over to the window and peered down. In the growing shadows and orange haze of sunset, they could see Wayman's car had just pulled up to the curb—or rather, pulled *onto* the curb, at a cockeyed angle.

"He's early," Emma said in a panicked whisper. "What do we do now?"

The driver's-side door opened, and Wayman wobbled out, a fat cigar smoking in one hand. He didn't bother closing the door behind him as he stumbled toward the front of the building. Charlie's heart sank. Not only was Wayman earlier than they had planned, but he was clearly drunk, and that made him unpredictable.

"It's okay," Charlie said, trying to sound more confident than she felt. "This doesn't change anything. We just need to hurry and—"

"He won't let me leave," Emma said, tears already sparkling in her magnificent eyes. "He'd rather see me dead than let me leave him, he told me."

Charlie pulled Emma to her and held her tight. "We're not going to give him the chance."

Emma nodded against Charlie's shoulders. When they stepped back, Charlie saw that some of Emma's steeliness had returned. Charlie offered Emma her hand, and Emma took it, the sparkling diamond glittering on one finger.

"Here we go," Charlie whispered, and she thought she could already smell the smoke of Wayman's cigar.

Maren

The sun was starting to set when the last of the fire trucks pulled away. Maren and Theo found themselves sitting on Jo's sofa. It was almost like the night they had found Miss Bradley, Maren thought. Except that time, they had done something good. This time? Maren wasn't so sure.

Overall, they were very, very lucky, Jo kept repeating.

The fire trucks had arrived early. None of the gala guests had been harmed. All the campers were safe and had been immediately gathered in the cafeteria, receiving ministrations from the nurse and a doctor called from town, while Eartha hovered around giving "spiritual cleansings."

But the auditorium hadn't fared so well. Most of the backstage was destroyed and, though the main stage itself hadn't caught fire, there was significant smoke and water damage to the equipment. It wasn't safe to walk inside, much less put a play up on the stage. There was no way *Twelfth Night* could be performed there on Friday. There might never be a play on the stage again.

Or at Goodman's, for that matter.

"We are very, very lucky," Jo insisted yet again, but her face hung heavily, and her beautiful dress had a scorch mark up one leg.

Nearby, Mr. Cairn's usual composure had fallen away. His hand trembled as he used his fancy ascot like a handkerchief to mop his face. Monty was also there, his rolled cuffs revealing soot-covered forearms, his expression deeply troubled. In the kitchen, Ms. Green was on the camp's phone, making endless calls to parents to let them know their children were safe. Only Jo's father, Lee, seemed as implacable as ever in his wheelchair. His eyes were heavy behind his thick glasses, and his faded baseball cap was pulled low on his forehead, but he sat with his hands crossed, as if waiting for a train.

"I need an explanation," Jo said, and it seemed to take an effort for her to raise her eyes from her wringing hands. "Maren? Theo? You missed the roll call we took when everyone evacuated. Where were you?"

Maren felt as if she were bolted to her seat. She looked at Theo and knew they were wondering the same thing Maren was: How could they tell Jo about the ring when Mr. Cairn was in the room?

"I'll tell you what happened," Mr. Cairn said, his voice trembling along with his hands. "These two have blatantly disregarded the rules since the moment they arrived!"

"It's not their fault," said Monty. He smoothed his hands down his pants and looked at Maren. "I'm sorry, Maren," he said. "I should have walked you to your cabin, or at least made sure you got through the courtyard safely. I'm so sorry you're part of this horrible accident."

Mr. Cairn made an irate cluck in the back of his throat. "*If* it was an accident."

"Vincent," Jo said warningly, but Maren suddenly understood.

"You think I set the fire?" Maren asked, astounded. And then, "You think I set the fire *on purpose?*"

Horrified, she looked at Jo, hoping to see some flicker of faith there. But Jo just looked back at her, waiting.

"I wouldn't do that!" Maren sputtered. "I wouldn't—I mean, why would I?"

"A pyrotechnic interest, perhaps," Mr. Cairn said.

"I told you," Monty said quickly, "Maren was only using a metaphor of fire in her scene, that doesn't mean anything."

Mr. Cairn made a dismissive sound and looked away.

"Maren wasn't even in the auditorium when the fire started," Theo suddenly spoke up. "She was helping me down the path by then."

Maren felt a wave of vindication, but Monty was already shaking his head.

"That may be true, Theo," Monty said gently. "But that doesn't mean Maren didn't accidentally start the fire when she left to find you." He turned to Maren, his eyes full of pity. "There were all those candles on the tables, remember? Maybe you accidentally hit one when you left, knocking a candle over?"

"But I didn't..." Maren said, racking her brain, trying to remember. She would have known if she had jarred a table or chair to knock a candle over. She would remember that—wouldn't she? The impossible face of Charlotte Goodman flashed before her. If she thought she saw Charlotte, could she really trust herself to remember anything else? She shook the thought away. There was a big difference between mistaking a face and not realizing she had set a fire—and she *hadn't* started the fire. "I *didn't* run into anything. I didn't start the fire, not even accidentally," she said more certainly, first to Jo, then to Monty. "I promise, you had gone inside by then, but I—"

"And I'll always regret that," Monty said, looking truly regretful. "I'll always regret that you had to be involved with this."

Maren opened and closed her mouth a few more times, but words never found their way out. The cold feeling of dread overwhelmed her, along with something else: something like disappointment. She had actually started to believe that Goodman's was a place where her voice mattered; she had let herself get comfortable in the idea that there was space for her to speak and be heard here. But no one was going to hear her now.

Theo cleared their throat. "Can we talk with you alone for a moment, Jo?" they said timidly.

There was a pause as everyone turned to look at Jo. Jo just looked tired.

"Please?" Theo asked.

"All right," Jo said with a sigh.

"You can't possibly be thinking of forgiving them, Jo, not now!" Mr. Cairn spoke at the same time Monty said, "Maybe I should stay, to verify their stories."

"It's fine," Jo said to both of them. "Really. Just give us a moment. Why don't you two go see if Ms. Green needs some help on the phone."

Mr. Cairn gave a furious huff, spun on one soot-streaked silver heel, and marched through the sliding door to the dining room. Monty followed, his footsteps hesitant and lingering. Jo's father was the last to leave, pausing and laying a questioning hand on her shoulder. She patted her father's hand and offered him a smile before he, too, wheeled into the dining room, sliding the door closed behind him.

Jo took a tired breath. "All right," she said. "What do you want to say, Theo?"

And then, to Maren's surprise, Theo began the whole story: about Maren finding the first clue, figuring out it had to do with lines from the play, following it to the other clues. Theo didn't bring up Sal or Graham, probably in hopes of keeping them out of trouble, but they told Jo all the ways they and Maren had broken the rules that summer.

"And then my camera got stolen," Theo said, "so we knew someone was—"

"Is *that* what all this is about?" Jo finally interrupted. "Your camera going missing again?" She looked at Maren, then back to Theo, then closed her eyes with an exasperated sigh.

"No! I mean, yes, but no!" Theo hurried on. "It's not that the *camera* got stolen, it's that the *footage* was stolen—all the footage about the clues, and our plans to go to the hives—"

"I really think I've heard enough," Jo said quietly, bringing her fingers to her temples and rubbing small circles there.

"—and then, today, while I was waiting to catch Mr. Cairn in the act? I saw someone else searching the hives, searching for the ring!"

"Someone," Jo said slowly, her eyes still shut, "searching for the ring."

There was something dangerous in her voice that made

Maren apprehensive, a warning note that they were right on the razor's edge of going too far. Maren tried to catch Theo's eye. But too late:

"I know this sounds impossible," Theo finished, "but... it was the ghost of Charlotte Goodman."

Jo's eyes popped open. She shook her head slightly, as if dazed, her mouth moving around, searching for half-finished words. Then she seemed to expand, to grow larger in her anger. "How—how *dare* you!" Jo stammered. "How dare you!"

"But!" Theo started.

"No!" Jo stood. "I refuse to hear another lie tonight. First, you tell me the same old nonsense about your stolen camera, and then this ridiculous search for a ring. Then you accuse Vincent Cairn, the most trustworthy, loyal man I know, of trying to go behind my back. And now you repeat what you heard Miss Bradley say when she came in here injured? I'm very disappointed in you, Theo, very disappointed in you both to make up such a *selfish* story to try to excuse your behavior."

"It's the truth!" Theo seemed shocked. "I have it on video—well, sort of—but, just, here!" Theo fumbled with their phone, then held it out and pressed play. Jo crossed her arms and watched the few seconds.

"What I see," Jo said, "is someone wearing my bee-keeping suit. Which could be either of you—and, at this point, I fully believe it could have been."

"It wasn't, though!" Theo insisted. "I saw Charlotte's face, it was—"

"Enough!" Jo said, her voice commanding. "If I go my

entire life without ever hearing again about this ring or clues or a ghost, it won't be long enough!"

There was a tapping sound nearby.

"Knock knock," said Renee Wallace, drumming her long, pointed nails on the doorframe. She was still wearing the icy-blue silk dress, but unlike everyone else Maren had seen, she still looked pristine, not a smudge of soot on her. She slunk in, swaying on her stilettos. "Sorry to interrupt, but I thought you might need to *reassess* a few things about your financial situation now."

In that moment, Jo seemed to age several years before Maren's very eyes. She grew smaller as her anger left her, and smaller still as it was replaced by a weary sadness. "Please, Renee, have a seat in the dining room," she said, her voice barely audible. "I'll be right with you. I need to finish this, and then we can—we can talk business."

"No rush, I'm only here to help." Renee clattered away down the hall.

Jo waited until she had left, then sat heavily in her chair, letting her head fall completely into her hands. She seemed to forget for a moment that Maren and Theo were even there.

"You can't sell her the camp," Maren said, surprising herself. "Even if you don't believe in the ring, Renee does. That's the reason why she's doing all this. She's Wayman Wallace's daughter."

Jo lifted her head, her eyebrows raised, and gave a weak laugh. "I suppose I should be impressed you found out about Wayman Wallace," she said, though she didn't sound impressed. "You certainly did your research while breaking all the rules, didn't you?"

"You can't sell the camp to her, you just can't!" Theo said, close to tears.

Jo smiled sadly. "I don't have a choice now."

"But—!"

"And it's really none of your concern." Jo sighed. "I'm sorry the summer has to end this way. But you both have broken too many rules for me to ignore."

Maren braced herself, knowing what was coming next. Theo's lip started to wobble. Jo took a breath.

But just then, an argument broke out in the other room, loud voices shouting nonsensically over each other. Theo and Maren exchanged a startled look. A moment later, the door from the dining room flew open and Mr. Cairn strode in, Renee Wallace a half second behind.

"Vincent, what is going on?" Jo said, standing.

"Jo," Mr. Cairn sounded a little breathless, "the alumni have been ringing the phones off the hook. When they heard that the camp was in danger of closing, they wanted to help. They've been promising donations right and left—"

"It'll hardly be enough to pay for the land *and* to fix the auditorium." Renee tried to laugh dismissively, but a hint of panic had snuck into her voice. "Even if every camper who ever went here donated, it won't be enough to—"

"Ms. Green says we've been getting messages nonstop!" Mr. Cairn's voice rose and drowned out Renee's. "She's still on the phone now, and there are emails and texts—everyone wants to help save the camp!"

"If they could have saved the camp, then where have they been this whole time?" Renee's voice rose higher. "Why haven't they helped sooner, why haven't they—"

"Jo, you cannot seriously be considering selling to this vile woman!" Mr. Cairn stamped one sooty silver-shoed foot. "You cannot!"

Jo held up both her hands, and the bickering fell silent.

"Vincent, tell Ms. Green we need to keep the landline open for parents," Jo said.

"Jo—" Mr. Cairn began.

"Exactly—" Renee said.

"*So*"—Jo interrupted them both again—"Vincent, you and I will go into town and answer the calls on our cell phones. I'm afraid I agree that it seems unlikely our generous alumni can do much, but—"

"Name your price!" Renee shrieked, her voice high and sharp and brittle. "Name an amount and it's yours, if you accept it right now! One time only!"

She pulled a checkbook out of her thin silver clutch and waved a pen like a knife. Everyone gaped at her.

"Renee," Jo managed, sounding both astonished and gentle, as if handling an upset child. "You can't honestly—"

"One time only!" Renee's face was pale and sweating, her knuckles white where she gripped the checkbook and pen. "Now or never, Jo, what's it gonna be?"

Jo looked at her for a long moment. "I'm afraid I don't see the difference a single day can make," she began gently. "It's too late for the banks to be open right now—"

But Renee was already shoving away her things. "You'll regret it!" Renee trembled dangerously. "You'll regret not taking this offer now—you will regret it!" She turned, her icy-blue dress flaring behind her like a chill breeze, and went out the front door with a slam.

Jo sighed into the silence that followed and rubbed at her temples. "Vincent, let's go. Maren, Theo, stay here. Dad, can you look after them for an hour or so?"

Lee August, who had placidly rolled into the room in the wake of Renee and Mr. Cairn's screaming match, nodded.

"Thank you." Jo grabbed her keys from a dish and a sweater from a hook by the door. "And Maren, Theo, you need to call your parents, please. Let them know...just tell them to get here as soon as possible."

With that, she and Mr. Cairn were gone, the front door slamming again. Mr. August wheeled back into the kitchen. Quiet fell.

"Isn't it weird that Mr. Cairn *didn't* want Jo to sell the camp to Renee Wallace?" Theo said under their breath.

Maren didn't answer.

Mr. August reappeared with an old house phone on his lap. He held it out to Maren and she took it, but he held on another second. For an instant their gazes met, and his expression seemed apologetic. Then he let the phone go and mimed dialing.

"You want me to try my parents?" Maren said.

He nodded and then wheeled away again, maybe to give her some privacy. Theo was leaning back, half buried in the squashed cushions, a contemplative expression on their face. Maren dialed her father's number first. No answer; no surprise. She dialed her mother's number. It rang and rang but also went to voice mail. She must be with Hadley.

Maren hung up and held the phone out to Theo. They didn't take it.

"So," Theo whispered, "what do we do?"

Maren just stared at them.

"Come on," Theo said impatiently. "If we don't do something quick, Renee Wallace is going to find the ring!"

"It doesn't matter," Maren said dully. "The ghost already got it, remember?"

"No, that's what I was trying to tell you!" Theo said. "Whatever they found, they put it back!"

Maren blinked. "What?"

"The ghost! I saw them on the camera—they found something, looked at it, then *put it back*!"

Maren stared at Theo. "Why would the ghost...?" she started, then angrily shook the thought away. "It doesn't matter."

Theo's eyes bugged out. "It doesn't *matter*?" they repeated incredulously.

"Don't you get it, Theo?" Maren's voice rose. "There's nothing we can do! We're about to get kicked out of camp, and someone made it to the hives before us, and we've already lost!"

Theo seemed about to say something else, when there was a sound outside the window. "Hey!" came Sal's voice. "You two in there?"

Theo gave Maren a vindicated look, then hurried over as fast as their bad leg would allow. "We're here," they whispered. "Though probably not for long."

But Sal seemed too distraught to process what Theo said. "Graham's in trouble."

"What do you mean?" Theo asked.

"The hives," Sal said. "He's gone there himself."

Theo gasped. "He couldn't. He *wouldn't*."

"He did!" Sal's words spilled out in a worried rush. "He

heard what happened to you two and was going to sneak out to the prop closet, so I told him the truth about the hives because I thought he wouldn't dare try to go there, but he snuck out when I wasn't watching, and then it took me *forever* to have a chance at sneaking out after him and—and he's probably there already!"

"We have to stop him," Theo said, and they felt around the windowsill. "Maren, help me pop out the screen, and we'll climb out."

They paused when they had the screen unlatched, then looked over their shoulder. Maren hadn't moved.

"Come on!" Theo said. "Forget the ring, this is about Graham! Remember, Graham—your *friend* who is *allergic* to *bees*?"

Maren just crossed her arms and turned away.

Sal looked back and forth between the two of them. "Maren—" he started, but Theo cut him off.

"Forget her," they said, their face pinched into an ugly look of disgust. They lowered the screen down to Sal, then threw their hurt leg over the windowsill first. "Come on, we have to hurry."

They scrambled the rest of the way out the window and disappeared into the growing dark. Sal hesitated a second longer, shooting Maren one more look of hurt and confusion, before following. Soon enough, the sound of their footsteps had faded. Maren leaned deeper into the sofa, her breath suddenly shallow, her throat full. This was all her fault. But if she went to help, she'd only make things worse. She only ever made everything worse.

Just then, the home phone trilled to life in her hand. It would be her mother, Maren knew, or Ed with the worst timing as usual. She closed her eyes and braced herself, then answered: "Hello?"

"Hey!"

Maren's eyes flew open. "Mom?" she said, even though she already knew it wasn't her mom.

"No, it's me, Seaweed!" said the voice, sounding delighted.

"Hadley," Maren whispered.

"Yeah, Mom is driving us home and just saw she missed a zillion calls from camp, so she told me to call you back," Hadley said, and now Maren could hear the white noise of the road beneath her voice. "I get to go home today! My doctors say I'm ready. Isn't that great! And just in time to see your show tomorrow! Didn't you get my email? I wrote you all about it!"

"I—" Maren said.

"Anyway, I've been dying to hear about your summer!" Hadley interrupted. "Do you love Goodman's? Have you made friends?"

"I don't know," Maren said, her voice still dulled with shock. "Maybe."

Hadley squealed. "Oh yeah? Tell me everything!"

There were a million interesting things Maren could have said about Theo, about Sal and Graham, about camp and the play and the hunt for the ring, and here was Hadley, finally offering her the space to share, to tell her all about it. But Maren found she couldn't. "I don't want to," she said honestly.

There was a slight pause, the roar of the road filling the phone.

"Oh," Hadley said.

"I don't want to tell you anything," Maren said. "You've missed a lot."

For once, Hadley was quiet.

"This whole year, you've missed a lot," Maren repeated, and she felt herself tearing up.

"I know," Hadley said, and Maren thought she could hear Hadley tearing up, too. "And that sucks, Seaweed, really, I wish I could—"

"I didn't know you were sick," Maren blurted out, unable to keep the words or the tears back now. "I didn't know you had a problem! I should have figured it out, Hadley, I'm the one who figures things out—but I didn't!"

"It's not your fault," Hadley said.

"But I should have known!" Maren felt tears drop free from her eyes. "I should have seen the clues, I should have done something, I—"

"Maren," Hadley cut her off, and there was something sturdy in her voice—a strength Maren hadn't heard in a long time. "Maren, it isn't your job to take care of me. It's *my* job to take care of *me*."

Maren took a surprised breath.

"I forgot how to do that for a while," Hadley went on. "And I'm so, so sorry I hurt you in the process. Can you please forgive me?"

Maren rubbed her eyes. She didn't have an answer to Hadley's question, because it wasn't Hadley she hadn't forgiven. It was herself. She had never forgiven herself for not knowing.

There was a creak on a floorboard behind her. She turned to see Mr. August, watching her from his chair.

"I'm sorry," Maren said, both into the phone and to him. "I have to go."

She hung up. Mr. August made no move to stop her as she clambered through the window and set off at a run.

⟡

It was fully dark as Maren ran along the paths. She felt as if she were flying, ready for every rise and fall this time, every knobby root and overgrown limb that tried to impede her path. She said a silent prayer that Theo and Sal had stopped Graham before he did something stupid and reckless. She didn't care about the ring anymore, just that her friends didn't get hurt. Finally, she caught a glimpse of the greenhouse, but she didn't see anyone there. Her heart soared with relief, and she burst with full speed into the clearing with the hives.

"Graham?" she called across the hive boxes. "Theo? Sal?"

For a moment there was no answer but the low drone of the bees.

"Well," said a satisfied voice. "Here's another one come to join the party."

Maren turned. There was Renee Wallace, just inside the shadow of the line of trees. Her frost-blue dress was now streaked with dirt, but she looked particularly pleased with herself. One hand was gripping Graham's shoulder. The other was holding Theo's camera.

"I suppose you'll have to hold on to this one, too," Renee said, and she turned to look at someone behind her. There was the sound of footsteps from deeper in the trees, and a moment later a cluster of people emerged. There was

Theo. There was Sal. They were both being held by someone wearing large work boots.

Monty offered Maren a sad sort of smile and shrug.

"Meet my cousin," Monty said with a flick of his head. "Things are always complicated in families."

Maren stared at him, unable—*unwilling*—to process what was happening. The realization came slow and creeping and cold, like jumping into freezing water and only feeling the sting of it later. Monty? Monty, who had been so kind to her? Monty, who had been so encouraging of her writing? Monty had been the collaborator all along? Had everything he'd said and done just been an attempt to get to the ring?

"*Absolument, Montague,*" Renee purred, putting a French flair onto Monty's name. "But you can hardly claim you don't care about a payday."

Monty shot an annoyed look at her, but he addressed Maren and the others calmly. "Look, kids, it's not a big deal—just let Nene get the ring and we'll be on our way, okay? No one's going to get hurt."

"Don't make promises you can't keep, *mon petit cousin,*" Renee said, digging her talon fingernails into Graham's shoulder. He winced under the pressure. "I heard the other two shouting about how this one is allergic to bee stings. It'd be such a shame if one happened to buzz buzz buzz its way over here and—*zzitt!*" She made a stinging sound and buried her forefinger deep into Graham's shoulder. He tried to squirm away, but she gripped him tighter.

"You did all this for Charlotte's stupid ring?" Theo said furiously.

"*Charlotte's?*" Renee spun on them. "It belongs to me!

My father never got over its loss and what his first fiancée did to him—not even when he had Mama and me!"

"The ring's also valuable," Maren said. "And your father needed the money, didn't he? He needed the money when the company almost went under."

Renee's face softened for a moment. When she spoke, there was something childish about her voice. "Poor Daddy. If we had had the ring then, we could have sold it. He wouldn't have had to..." She trailed off.

In spite of everything, Maren felt a flash of pity for Renee.

"I understand," Maren said softly. "But hurting people like us, like Miss Bradley, won't make things better."

Renee eye's flashed, and any softness there disappeared. She laughed. "Oh, I've done much worse than kidnap that bitter old hag! I've bought out almost this entire town, and Monty and I burned down the one good thing this lousy camp had going for itself!"

Monty made a sound.

"Oops!" Renee put her fingers to her lips playfully. "I suppose that was a secret, wasn't it? Like the secret that we set up your little friend here to take the blame."

Monty looked at Maren, ashamed. "Sorry, Maren," he said. "It wasn't personal. You just happened to be there at the wrong time."

"The *right* time for us, more like," Renee chirped. "He kept telling me how lucky it was that you had walked by, because you had written about all your troubles, hadn't you? He knew no one would believe you weren't responsible— meanwhile, all we had to do was wait, and you'd lead us to the clue, he said. You'd lead us right to it, and you did."

Monty glared at his work boots. So it had all been an act. It must have been. Maren was aware this hurt her, but it didn't matter right now. None of it—not Monty, or the fire, or even the ring—mattered now. All that mattered was getting her friends away from this malicious woman. All that mattered was figuring out a way to get everyone to safety.

"So," Renee sighed and forced her face back into her tight smile. "Who's going to fetch the ring for me from the hives?"

She gave Graham's shoulder a shove. Theo made a squeaky sound, and Sal strained against Monty's grip on his arm.

"Hey," Monty said, "I thought we agreed—"

"Shut up, Montague," Renee said. "I want them to know I mean business."

"I'll get it," Maren heard herself say.

Everyone looked at her.

"From the hives," she said. "I'll get it. Just leave Graham alone."

"Fine," Renee said. "But know that if you try anything stupid like running away...there'll be consequences." She gave Graham another shove forward.

Maren took a breath and looked at the hive boxes, trying to remember what the person in Theo's video had done— she was pretty sure the person had found something in the box on the far left. With slow, careful footsteps, she started around the edge toward that one. The droning sound of the bees grew louder as Maren got closer. A few bees zipped by her, but they hadn't started stinging yet.

When she got to the hive, she paused, trying to think

clearly over the rising panic she felt. If you were going to hide something in a beehive, where would it be? It couldn't be anywhere near where the honey came out, as this would make it easy to find. It couldn't be near the queen, either, since that might have endangered her and the hive. But it also couldn't be exposed along the outside; it would have to be somewhere protected from the elements.

Maren's eyes fell on the metal supports bracketing the wooden legs. There was probably enough of a gap between the wood and metal to be able to slip something in. It was someplace to start looking, at least.

She took a deep breath. Slowly, she took a step forward, then another. The droning got louder in her ears, and bees hovered closer to her, no doubt inspecting her as a possible threat. She fought hard to keep her panic down. They wouldn't bother her so long as she didn't bother them... right? When she was close enough, she slowly reached out and felt along the nearest leg of the box. The first one had nothing there. Neither did the second one. Some bees crawled curiously over her hand, but she hadn't been stung yet. She started feeling around the third leg.

"Hurry up already!" Renee shouted, and Maren jumped. She felt a sharp pain on her shoulder and looked over to see a bee crouched there, its stinger disappearing into her T-shirt fabric. She winced but forced herself not to run away. The sting hurt, but it wasn't that bad, and the rest of the bees still hadn't taken notice of her yet. She reached out for the final leg and felt around it. Her fingers brushed against something.

"I feel something," Maren called out, excited in spite of herself.

"Je le savais!" Renee said. "Bring it here!"

Maren tugged until something came loose. Then she turned and walked back as carefully as she had come.

"What's that?" Renee said, a sour look on her face as Maren got closer.

Maren didn't answer. She just held out the piece of gold-edged paper.

Love's night is noon.

"What?" Renee shrieked. She rounded on Monty. "Where's the ring? I thought you said that other one was the last clue!"

"How should I know?" he said sullenly. "And I didn't say it, they did."

Renee glared at him, then thrust the paper back at Maren. "Well?" Renee snapped. "You figured out the others. What does this one mean?"

Maren took the clue and stared down at it, not really reading the words but trying to think quickly. The second

Maren had seen the clue, she knew exactly what it meant—she had been surprised, in a way, that the hunt for the ring hadn't sent them there earlier. The problem was, Maren couldn't think of a lie. What she needed was to lead Renee somewhere close to camp, somewhere adults would be, so that someone, anyone, might find and help them. But would Renee believe her? She stayed perfectly still, as if this would force her brain to work faster.

"I'm waiting," Renee sang. "And so is your little friend."

She gave Graham a shove closer to the hive. He whimpered.

"It's the ghost light," Maren stammered. When she saw Renee was looking at her, she went on. "A ghost light in a theater stays on all the time. It would give light even at night. Plus, the one here is a real antique."

"So?"

"So it would have been around sixty years ago," Monty threw in, nodding. "I guess that makes sense."

Renee looked back and forth between them, but Maren didn't dare look at Monty. She wasn't sure if he really believed her, or if he was playing along for some reason.

"Where is it?" Renee said.

"The auditorium," Maren said.

Renee frowned. "The auditorium at camp?"

"Yeah, but no one will be there right now," Theo jumped in.

"That's right," Sal said. "Everyone left because of the fire."

"Maybe we should go over there and check?" Graham said.

For a moment, Renee actually seemed to believe them.

She cocked her head, looking at each in turn, and Maren could see she was willing to be convinced. But when her eyes landed on Maren again, they shrank to mean slits, like a trap sprung shut. "You wouldn't be lying to me, would you?"

"No," Maren's voice quivered.

"Because if you were trying to trick me"—and here, Renee started walking Graham steadily and surely forward—"then that would be really stupid."

"Come on, Nene, stop," Monty said.

But she didn't take her eyes off Maren. "If you are lying," she said, holding Graham out in front of her. They were within an arm's reach of the hives now, and Graham's face was full of terror. "I'll tell you this: It won't work."

Everyone was talking now, shouting their protests as Renee held Graham's hand by the wrist and began to stretch it out, closer and closer to the hives, and then everyone was yelling—Graham in fear, Theo and Sal in fury, Monty still trying to reason with his cousin. Maren heard a sharp ringing in her ears, felt her stomach rising in panic, until she couldn't keep it in any longer:

"It's the clock!" Maren screamed. "It's the clock in the village church!"

Everyone else fell silent. Renee grinned victoriously.

"What about it?" she snapped, still holding Graham's arm outstretched.

"It's stuck on 12—noon and midnight—it has been for years!" Maren felt tears pouring down her face. "It's where Charlotte Goodman is buried."

Renee let Graham's hand down to his side but kept her

gaze pinned on Maren. "How do I know you're not lying this time?"

"I'm not, I promise." Maren's voice came out cracked and jagged with tears. "I promise. Just please don't hurt him."

"*Pour l'amour de Dieu*, Nene! Obviously, she's telling the truth!" Monty shouted. "Just let the boy go. I didn't sign up for hurting the kids!"

But something in Renee's face went from hard to harder. "There's only one way to make sure of it," she said.

"Don't!" Monty said.

"No!" Maren screamed, but it was too late.

Renee had pushed Graham's bare hand, palm-down, on top of the hive swarming with bees. It only took a moment. Graham's face twisted in pain, then panic. He looked at Maren, and she saw the truth in his scared expression: He had been stung.

"Graham?" Theo squeaked.

Graham looked at them and tried to smile. "I'm okay," he said, his voice already a little wheezy. "It's not that bad."

"It's gonna be okay, Graham," Monty said, letting Theo and Sal go and fumbling in his pockets. "I've got an EpiPen here. We'll just—"

"No!" screeched Renee. "Not yet!"

Monty looked up, appalled. "He needs a shot, Nene, or he'll literally die!"

"He'll get his shot just as soon as I get my ring!" Renee snapped. "I'll call you when I have it." She shoved Graham at Monty and grabbed Maren's arm and pulled. "You're coming with me to the church, just in case—and we better hurry," she added nastily as Graham's breathing began to grow more labored.

The drive to the church was surreal in how ordinary it was. Maren sat in the passenger seat, her seat belt buckled, her palms burning damp circles on her knees. Renee drove, gripping the wheel with white-knuckled claws and humming almost manically along to the radio. The village of Stonecourt was mostly dark when they arrived, but Maren could see lights on at the coffee shop, and Jo's van parked in front. For a brief, wild second, Maren considered throwing the door open, running as fast as she could, and begging Jo or the coffee shop owner, Gabby, for help—but she pushed the idea away. Even if she did manage to make it, it would take too much time to explain, and they might not believe her. She was on her own.

"You have no idea," Renee muttered—to herself or to Maren, it didn't seem to matter—as she parked in front of the church. "You have absolutely no idea how long I've waited for this...."

Renee got out, slamming her door, and Maren followed suit, walking toward the church. She could hear Renee mumbling behind her, sometimes cursing as her skinny heels kept sinking in the grass and making her stumble.

"There," Maren said, pointing to the broken clock over the front door when they arrived. Both the clock's hands were still stuck at 12: *Love's night is noon.*

"How do we get up there?" Renee said, peering at the clock as if a diamond ring might fall on her forehead.

Maren hadn't thought about that. They probably couldn't do anything from the outside, especially not without a ladder, but the church had an old bell tower above the clock. "Let's go inside," Maren said. "There's got to be a stairway or something."

Their footsteps echoed as they stepped into the quiet vestibule and then into the chapel beyond. Maren felt goose bumps rise on her arm. There was something about churches, even empty, dark ones—or maybe *especially* empty, dark ones—that made her feel like she was being watched. She walked up the aisle, trying not to let the spooked feeling distract her. At the front was the stained glass, though it was hard to see the image now that it was dark outside.

"Now where?" Renee said from behind her.

"I don't know," Maren said, taking in the size and shape of the church. "There has to be a door…some stairs…"

"Like this one?" Renee was standing in front of a small arched doorway. Maren hurried over as Renee pushed it open, revealing a set of winding, extremely dusty stairs. Maren could just make out the first few steps before the rest disappeared into the darkness above. The feeling of being watched intensified.

"Well, that's creepy," Renee muttered.

Maren took a deep breath. "Got a flashlight?"

Renee fumbled with her phone, then held the beam up and into the darkness to show a few more stairs.

"Thanks," Maren said, and held out her hand to take the phone.

Renee pulled it out of reach. "I don't think so," she said, then made a shooing motion. "After you."

Maren started climbing, the wood squealing in protest with every step. It was clear it had been a long time since anyone had been up there. The wood smelled damp and musty and definitely half-rotten. Dust plumed with every step, twisting and sparkling in the beam of light. Finally, Maren's feet hit a platform of solid wood—she'd reached a landing. On the far side of the platform, the stairs continued up, probably to the bell tower, but right in front of her was a small wooden door that came up to Maren's chest. Maren went to it and pulled, but nothing happened. She tugged a few more times, harder and harder, trying to heave the little door open.

"Ticktock, your friend's running out of time," Renee said, appearing behind her. Then laughed. "Oh! Like a clock! How appropriate!" She laughed again at her own joke.

If Maren had had the spare thought—and wasn't terrified out of her mind—she would have rolled her eyes. Finally, she managed to drag the little door open just wide enough that, kneeling on the floor, she could get most of her torso inside the gap. Renee stepped right up behind her to better aim the flashlight beam over Maren's head.

"Well?" Renee demanded. "Where is it?"

Maren didn't answer. In the stark blue-white glow, she could see all the ancient gears, their still teeth glinting dully but emptily. There was nothing hidden there. No clue. And no ring. "I thought it would be here," Maren muttered, sliding her fingers over the naked dusty gears. "I really thought it was here." Maren's heart thudded in her ears, as if it were counting seconds in place of the still, silent clock.

"Well, you better start thinking of something else," Renee said. "And quick, or I know of another clock that's about to run out."

Run out... What would have happened when this clock struck 12? Maren dropped to her belly on the floor, lying flat to feel along the bottom of the clock. "I think it's like a cuckoo clock," she said. "It would have had some sort of decoration that would have come out when the clock rang 12...." Her fingers brushed against a small wooden figure. "Yes! I feel something!"

She felt Renee wedge closer, and a moment later there was more light over her head. It was even dustier down there, but as Maren's fingers swept over the figures, recognizable colors and shapes started to appear. "It's a sheep... and a shepherd," Maren said as she uncovered each enough to be identified. "And I think that's a person riding on a donkey.... It's the Nativity scene again!"

And it was. There was the story of Christmas, with the usual barnyard animals and men come from afar, all lined up and ready to circle around the clock. Joseph and Mary were at the end, and in the manger—

"There's a box," Maren called over her shoulder. "There's a little velvet box."

Renee screamed, and a moment later Maren felt herself yanked back and away from the door. She scooted out of the way, wincing and rubbing at her shoulder where Renee had gripped her, while Renee threw herself into the place where Maren had been, flailing her arms around the mechanical figures. When she sat back up, a very dusty velvet ring box was in her hand.

"Finally!" she cooed at it, stroking the top of the box as if it really were a baby. "Oh, *mon coeur*, I've waited so long, and now I finally have you!"

Maren cast a sidelong glance at the stairway leading down. If she left right now, she might just be able to make a break for it while Renee was distracted. She *should* make a break for it, she decided, she *would* make a break for it... but still she hesitated. The truth was, after all her hard work, she wanted to see the ring, too. She couldn't help it—some part of her needed to know it was real. That there really had been a ring. That she hadn't gotten in trouble and endangered her friends and ruined the camp for nothing. She held her breath as Renee peeled back the lid and stared down at the contents.

For a moment, the victorious smile lingered on Renee's lips.

But then... it was like Renee's face was suddenly made of wax, as if it had started dripping down on itself, collapsing and crumbling from its shape.

"What?" she whispered. She pulled out a white note-card with gold edges and unfolded it, ripping the paper slightly in her rush. Her eyes flew over the words, but whatever she read there only made it worse. "No," Renee said, real anguish in her voice. "No, it can't be!" Her eyes flew up, too bright in her head, and latched onto Maren. "Read it!" she shrieked. She flung the little white-and-gold card at Maren's chest. It bounced off harmlessly, landing in her lap, but Maren made no move to reach for it. "Go on!" Renee voice scaled even higher, even louder, and Maren flinched. "Go on, read it, and tell me what this one means!"

Hands trembling, Maren reached for the card. She unfolded it carefully and read.

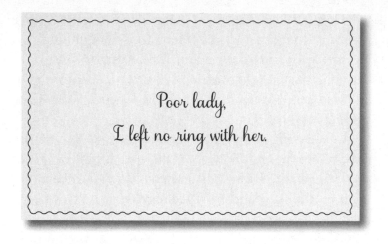

Poor lady,
I left no ring with her.

"No!" Renee paced back and forth on the creaking wooden platform, her heels sounding thunderous with each step. "No, no, no!" She said it over and over, as if the more she said it, the more she could make it true. "No, it—it has to be some trick, some sort of a—some sort of a something!" She swooped down suddenly, grabbing Maren's wrist. "You have to tell me what this means! Tell me where we go now!"

"You know what it means!" Maren cried as Renee started dragging her toward the stairs. "It means there's no ring! It means—"

"NO!" Renee shouted. "You're lying to me! You're just trying to keep it for yourself! You're—" But her words fell away in a scream of surprise and outrage.

Instinctively, Maren had grabbed on to the hand railing at the top of the stairs and held on with all her might. When Renee tried to pull again, she lost her grip and stumbled backward. Her cell phone flew out of her hand, the light leaping high and then arcing away, bouncing down the stairs. Maren could see Renee's arms windmilling, trying to regain her balance. She almost managed to catch herself...but she was wearing very, very high heels. She followed her phone bumpingly all the way down the stairs, landing in a heap with a heavy *oof!*

In the dark, Maren hurried after her, stopping a few steps before the bottom to see if she was all right.

"Stupid girl," Renee groaned from the tangled mess she made on the floor. "I think I've broken my arm, you horrible child...."

Maren wasn't sure what to say to this, but thankfully, she didn't have to say anything. Just then, there was a loud squeal, as the door to the church opened wider. A man in a baseball cap was standing there, looking first at Maren, then at Renee, then at Maren again. Maren squinted. She couldn't see his face in the shadow.

"You have to help me," Renee groaned. "This girl attacked me for no reason. She's dangerous. She—"

But the man had taken a slow, shuffling step forward, into the light from Renee's fallen cell phone so that they could see him clearly. Maren's jaw dropped.

It was Lee August, Jo's father.

He stooped to pick up the phone, then reached across Renee, holding out an old and gnarled hand to Maren. His fingers, she thought as she took his hand and he helped her down the last of the stairs, were long and slender and strong. At the bottom, Renee made a weak swipe at Maren's ankle, as if to keep her there, but Maren easily side-stepped her and joined Mr. August in the doorway.

"You can't just leave me here," Renee moaned.

It was true. Mr. August seemed to be considering what to do. Then one hand still tight in Maren's, he held Renee's cell phone out to her with the other. Maren didn't need him to gesture what to do this time. She was already dialing the police.

Maren and Mr. August sat on the curb out front and watched as Renee, flanked on both sides by police officers, was brought out of the church on a stretcher and loaded into an ambulance. She was shouting the whole time, mostly about how she was going to sue everyone, but they ignored her, and soon enough the ambulance doors were slammed shut, her wails drowned out by the siren.

Some police officers went over to the coffee shop and got Jo and Mr. Cairn, while another told Maren and Mr. August that they'd have to give statements, but that they were going to do it at Jo's house, where everyone would be waiting for them. Maren stood and, together with a police officer, helped Mr. August stand. He seemed stiffer and older now that the rescuing was done, and for the first time Maren remembered: Mr. August used a wheelchair. She studied him as the officer helped ease him into the back of the police cruiser, and she kept studying him on the ride back, taking in his face in the flash of blue from the police light, imagining what it might look like without the glasses and the baseball cap, a little younger, a little taller, a little different....

And then, just like that, Maren figured it out.

The ride was as short as ever, and soon enough they pulled up at Jo's house. Maren was surprised to see that the driveway was full of cars—including another police car already there, her mom's car, and an old junker that she recognized instantly as Ed's. She and Mr. August were just climbing out of the police car when the front door to the house was thrown open and someone came racing down the walk.

"Maren!"

Before she could react, Hadley slammed into her and wrapped her in a hug so tight Maren felt the bruises from her time with Renee Wallace twinge. She must have made a sound, because a second later her sister released her and stepped back.

"I was so scared," Hadley said breathily, blinking fast. "They told me some lady had basically taken you hostage, and I was so, so scared something was going to happen to you!"

She went to hug Maren again. Instinctively, Maren took a step back. She saw hurt flash across Hadley's face, replaced by a calm resolve.

"I'm so sorry," Hadley started to say again, but Maren discovered she didn't need to hear it. She stepped back into Hadley's arms and hugged her tight again, even though it hurt.

Mr. August touched her lightly on the shoulder, and Maren turned to see a whole crowd of people waiting for them in the entryway.

"We should probably go in and explain," Maren said to Mr. August, and he nodded.

It took a while, and a lot of hugs, for everyone to be convinced Maren was really all right. Both her mom and

Ed—her dad—had to hug her, and then Theo and Sal needed a turn, and then—

"Graham!" Maren cried.

He was sitting between his flustered but relieved-looking moms. "I'm okay," Graham said on reflex, then turned very red when Maren bent down and hugged him.

"Monty brought us here as soon as you were gone," Theo said. "He gave Graham the EpiPen and called the police himself. He said he never meant to hurt anyone, but the cops still took him in for questioning because he confessed to starting the fire. And he returned this!" They held their camera up—already recording the moment.

Maren nodded, feeling a twinge of something bittersweet. Monty hadn't been who she thought he was, but it was a relief to know he wasn't all bad, either.

"Maren?" Jo was standing behind her father, who was sitting in his wheelchair again and smiling at her. "I think we all want to hear how it is that *you're* okay."

"Okay," Maren said, taking a deep breath and a seat between Theo and her sister. "But it's kind of a long story."

Maren told them everything she could. About finding the first clue and thinking someone left it for her to figure out. About realizing it came from the play and following it to the next clue and the next after that. About realizing it was connected to Charlotte Goodman and the ring. About realizing they weren't the only ones searching for it, and that Renee Wallace was the heir to Walcorp, Wayman Wallace's company, and that was why they were working so hard to buy the land.

"But I didn't really start to put it all together until today, starting with when Theo and I went to the hives," Maren said, turning to Theo. "Remember who we saw there?"

Theo shifted uncomfortably. "Well…I'm pretty sure… I mean, I think I saw—"

"We saw Charlotte Goodman," Maren said confidently. "Theo recognized them right away, but even I didn't believe it."

"Because it can't be," Jo said, though her voice was gentler now than it had been earlier. "I'm sorry, Theo, but I'm telling you, there is no ghost."

"How are you so sure?" Maren asked.

Jo didn't answer, just shook her head.

"You know there's no ghost—because you know Charlotte never died, don't you?" Maren said. "Because Charlotte Goodman is very much alive."

Jo, and everyone else in the room, stared at her.

"Of course Charlotte Goodman is dead," Mr. Cairn said dismissively. "Everyone knows the story of—"

"A fire that burned so hot no remains were found?" Maren finished his sentence. "It's very clever, isn't it? A perfect way for Emma and Charlotte to disappear."

"But why?" Hadley asked. "Why would they want to disappear?"

"Because they loved each other," Maren explained. "They loved each other and lived in a time when that love wasn't allowed, when their *lives* weren't allowed, so they faked their deaths to start over."

"But what does all this have to do with the clues?" Theo asked.

"Actually, Theo, you're the one who made me realize that, too," Maren said. She turned and explained to the rest of the room, "See, Theo said the hunt for the clues seemed like it was meant for someone special, someone who would know the answers. Someone who was loved. It was Emma who set up this whole treasure hunt with clues from *Twelfth Night*. It was Emma who wanted Charlie to find something she hid here for her."

"How could Emma have hidden anything at the camp?" Sal asked.

"Because she was here. For years and years. From the very beginning," Maren said, and she turned to Mr. August, Jo's father. "Isn't that right, Charlotte?"

Lee August smiled.

Then he—she—*they* reached up and took off their glasses, where warm, intense eyes sparkled underneath.

"Call me Charlie," they said.

There *was* a ring, once.

A ring worth enough money that—after they started the fire and snuck out the back door while Wayman was still out front—it bought two tickets on a ship that traveled around the world. A ring worth enough that it paid for a few years living abroad. A ring that, finally, bought *three* tickets back to the United States when a safe place in a small town had been set up for them.

"It saved our lives," Charlie said. They—and they did prefer "they," they said, now that it was an option—gestured at Jo. "We lived in Europe for a few years—there were places there that were much more understanding about who and what Emma and I were, even back then. My sister, in the meantime, set up the camp and helped us get different identities. We arrived in Stonecourt as the August family, as Lee and Violet and Jo. No one here suspected us, especially not with a little kid."

"But Mr. August," Graham piped up, then swallowed and corrected himself, "I mean, Charlie—why did you keep living as Lee for so long?"

"For a while, it was because we weren't sure how safe we were from Wayman," Charlie admitted. "But even after he was gone and we knew we were safe...well, the honest answer for why I stayed hidden is I was scared. I was scared of losing everything we had built here." They took a breath, held it, then let it leak slowly out. When they spoke again, their voice shook with effort and emotion. "All my life, I had a secret that gave me freedom, but that same secret also created the danger of exposure. I was afraid of being rejected as the real me. And then, when I lost Emma... well, I wasn't sure who the real me was anymore."

Charlie gave Jo a small smile, and she smiled back at them, tears bright in her eyes, before addressing the rest of the room: "I always knew my father was someone else. But I also always knew Charlie was my dad." She reached out and took their hand in hers, holding their gaze. "I've always known the real them—no matter what name they use."

"So that's why you didn't believe me about seeing Charlotte Goodman's ghost," Theo said. "You knew Charlotte hadn't died."

Jo nodded. "And I was tired of talking about a legend

that could potentially expose my dad, with Miss Bradley telling everyone she had seen Charlotte Goodman. I lost my temper, and I'm sorry for that."

"Wait! Miss Bradley!" Theo looked at Charlie, confused. "Did you really make her fall down the trapdoor?"

"No," Charlie said firmly. "No, I would never. I have no idea who did that."

"I think I do," Maren said. "Miss Bradley said she saw a Charlotte Goodman as they looked when they were in the picture—much younger, with short hair. I think she must have seen Monty's reflection. He would have looked warped and distorted, but probably reasonably like Charlotte used to look."

"And to think we thought Mr. Cairn was working with Renee Wallace." Theo shook their head.

"Me?" Mr. Cairn sat up straighter and pressed an elegant, indignant hand against his chest. "Why on earth would I work with that revolting woman?"

"You mean besides threatening to kick us out?" Maren said.

"And shutting down the library and instituting bunk checks?" Sal added.

"And talking to someone on your cell phone up in the prop closet?" Theo said.

"Well!" Mr. Cairn sniffed. "Perhaps I am a *bit* adamant about the rules."

Theo gave Maren a look, while Sal snorted at the understatement.

"But the prop closet—not that it's any of your business, but that's the only place high enough on campus for me to get reception. My partner has been unwell for some time. I need to be able to contact him, but because we are unmarried, his family can block my phone calls and visits."

"That's terrible," said Graham's mom, putting her hand on Mr. Cairn's arm.

He nodded tightly, then sat up straighter. "And even if I didn't have a good reason for being there, the prop closet is yet another place campers are not allowed to go!"

Maren looked away, remembering that she was still, technically, kicked out of camp, when she heard a strange honking sound. Mr. Cairn was *laughing*.

"Honestly," Mr. Cairn said, doing his honking laugh again. "Me—*honk*—work with—*honk*—Renee Wallace!"

Theo gave their squeaky-wheel laugh, and Maren had no choice but to join in.

"Perhaps I should have given Miss Sands a bit more of the benefit of the doubt," he allowed when his laughs had settled down.

Maren couldn't respond. Her mouth was hanging open.

"But I'm not sure what you thought you would find," Mr. Cairn said. "Charlie, if you knew there wasn't a ring to find, what did you think you were looking for this whole time?"

"Can't say I knew." Charlie shrugged. "Some years ago, when Emma got her diagnosis, she came to me with the first clue."

"The *be not afraid of greatness* quote," Maren explained to the other listeners. "With the *Wear this jewel of me* envelope."

"That's right," Charlie said. "I begged Emma to explain it, but she never did, only told me that she had liked the legend of a hidden treasure so much, she decided to make me a treasure hunt. She said I should start looking. She died soon after that—too soon—and I still hadn't found anything. I considered the clue, and kept considering it, and probably would still be considering it if it weren't for you, Maren."

Maren felt her heart rise. "So you did leave the clue for me!"

"Oh yes. I heard how quick you were, helping Jo find her phone, and remembered Hadley bragging for years about her clever sister."

Maren blushed as Hadley gently elbowed her.

"I thought maybe you could figure it out," Charlie went on. "And you sure did. After you realized the first one was about the Black Box, it was pretty easy for me to figure out the others, but I kept putting them back for you to find after I read them, just in case I got stuck again."

"I have to admit," Jo said ruefully, "not even I thought the clues led to anything. My mom wasn't well in the end, and I assumed she had forgotten to do whatever she meant to do."

"Speaking of clues," Sal said, "Maren, you still haven't told us—what was the last one? What did you find in the town church?"

Maren took a breath, but Charlie answered for her: *"Poor lady, I left no ring with her."* They gave Maren a sad smile. "I heard Renee Wallace scream about it."

A confused, disappointed silence fell around the room.

"So...is that it, then?" Hadley said, looking around. "This whole search just ended up being...nothing?"

Charlie shook their head. "It wasn't nothing to me,"

they said. "I never expected a ring, but this was a walk down memory lane—our favorite things, our inside jokes, the way we decorated the grid in the Black Box, her beehives, even that silly clock! Emma used to love Christmas. It was one of the reasons why *Twelfth Night* was her favorite play. I know it might be hard for you all to understand, but I'm not disappointed. If anything, it was like getting to talk to Emma, laugh with her, years after she's gone."

Another silence fell—but this one solemn, and warm, and comforting.

"Actually," Maren said slowly, "I don't think your walk is over yet."

Everyone looked at her. Charlie blinked, surprised, and Maren smiled.

"*Poor lady*—it's another clue," Maren said. "In the play, it doesn't go before the line *I left no ring with her.* It goes before another line. One that made me realize where the clues really point..." She paused and looked around at the eager faces looking back at her. *SUSPENSE*, she thought of Monty writing on the board, and smiled. *No matter what happens now*, she remembered him saying when she was sneaking into the woods, *I just wanted to say I'm really proud of you*. Maybe that, at least, hadn't been an act. Maybe it was enough that she could remember him now for what he had offered her—had offered all of them—instead of what he almost took away.

"Well!" Hadley finally exploded in a very Hadley-like way. "Will you tell us where already!"

"No," Maren said. "But when it's light outside I'll show you."

And so it was, early Friday morning, that Maren and Charlie and Theo and Sal and Graham and Jo and Mr. Cairn and Hadley and Maren's mom and dad and Graham's mom and mommy and even the police officer who didn't want to be left out of the last adventure piled into cars and drove the slow mile back into town. When they had all pulled into the parking lot, Jo started pushing Charlie's chair—which they had taken to again, exhausted after the excitement of the night before—toward the church.

"Actually," Maren said. "We're going this way." She pointed to the graveyard.

Charlie's eyebrows rose, and Jo shrugged.

"Lead on," Jo said, and Maren started across the soft grass through the rows of gravestones. It grew warmer as they went, the sun high enough now to see that it was going to be a beautiful day. After a few minutes, Maren drew up to the mausoleum they were looking for: Charlotte Goodman's. Maren had asked the police officer to make a call for her, and a graveyard worker was waiting for them when they arrived.

"Can you read the inscription?" Maren asked, turning back to Charlie.

Charlie shook their head. "It's in Latin. I never understood why my sister and her husband used Latin."

"Emma probably asked them to," Maren said. "She couldn't make it too easy." Maren turned to Theo. "Remind us what it says?"

"I don't know exactly," Theo admitted. "But it's something like, if I'm sleeping, let me sleep?"

"Or maybe: *If it be thus to dream, still let me sleep?*" Maren suggested.

"Hey! That's Sebastian's line!" Graham said.

"That's right." Maren turned to the group and explained: "See, the *Poor lady* part didn't go with *I left no ring with her.* The real quote is supposed to read, *Poor lady, she were better love a dream.*"

"Emma used to say something like that," Charlie said slowly, remembering. "She used to say our love was like a dream."

"And I bet she wanted to save your other dream," Maren said. "The one you were willing to sacrifice for her."

Charlie looked at Maren, their eyes full of emotion, too much to speak. Maren nodded at the graveyard worker, who stepped up and cut the lock from the mausoleum door.

"You sure about this, Seaweed?" Hadley whispered to her. "This could be pretty gruesome if you're wrong...."

But Charlie was already standing up from their chair and reaching for the door. It still took some work to get it open—Mr. Cairn and Jo and Ed all helped pull—but finally, with a jagged, rusty shriek, the door gave.

Inside it was cool and dry. There was no coffin or urn, no body or skeleton, nothing in the least bit gruesome. Only a small chest, like a lady's traveling footlocker. On top of it sat another white-and-gold calling card.

"She knew how sensitive it was," Maren said softly. "How it had to be stored in the proper conditions."

Theo gasped, understanding what they would find inside, as Charlie reached down and opened the last clue.

Here, wear this jewel of me,
'Tis my picture.

Maren

Inside the chest were the eight reels of Charlie's movie.

Their "picture."

The movie they thought had gone up in flames in order to trick Wayman Wallace.

"But how..." Charlie kept asking, tears streaking their face. "Why...?"

Maren didn't answer. She couldn't answer the exact details of how, but as for the why, it was only too obvious. It was because Emma loved Charlie. And because, since Charlie was willing to give up everything for Emma, Emma was willing to do anything for Charlie, too. She had probably replaced the celluloid movie reels with other reels of the same material—which would go up in the fire just as fast but wouldn't take Charlie's dreams with them. She worked with Rosalie to make sure the film was hidden, especially from Wayman, and she put it somewhere that, once they really were safe to be themselves, Charlie could find.

Everyone was crying and holding on to one another after that—Jo rubbing her eyes with one hand and her father's back with the other, Mr. Cairn honking his nose into a tissue, Graham's mothers hugging each other, Maren's parents laughing at each other's tears, Theo and Graham and Sal smiling and smiling with damp eyes. Even the police officer kept sniffling before he told them that, as far as he was concerned, everything had happened too far past the statute of limitations to prosecute any false-identity claims.

"How did you know?" Hadley asked Maren softly, sidling up to her. "How did you know it would be here?"

Maren smiled at her sister. "The newspaper said no bodies were recovered," she explained. "At first, we thought this mausoleum was just a memorial constructed by Rosalie, but...it's a pretty big memorial. I started to wonder if maybe it had another purpose."

"That *is* totally gruesome." Her sister nodded in approval, then hugged her. "And totally awesome."

A hand appeared on Maren's shoulder, and she turned to find Jo there. "You've made us all very, very happy," Jo said. "I can't thank you enough for giving the camp its best year ever."

Maren smiled, but her heart sank a little at the thought of the camp. "I wish that were true," she said sadly. "But it can't be its best year ever without a show, and the auditorium—it's still wrecked."

"What?" Hadley sounded aghast. "The auditorium is wrecked?"

"There's too much fire damage," Jo said. "We're not going to be able to put on a show this year."

"I can't believe you'd give up so easily, Jo," Hadley said, her voice rising with her usual Hadley theatrics. "The show must go on!"

Jo laughed. "As much as I admire your spirit, Hadley, there's not a lot we can do. It's not safe to take anyone, much less a bunch of kids, into the auditorium."

"Auditorium, schmauditorium." Hadley waved an arm over her head in a dramatic, Miss-Bradley-esque gesture. "Since when do we need fancy things like an *auditorium*? Someone once taught me that the Greeks didn't even have a roof over their heads!"

Hadley gave Maren a look, as if waiting for Maren to put something together, and a moment later, Maren did.

"The amphitheater!" Maren cried. "We can do it outside! Can't we, Jo?"

Jo made a considerate face. "I don't know, girls, it would take a lot of work to change everything in time...."

"We're up for the challenge," Mr. Cairn said, appearing at Jo's side. He gave a thin smile. "The parents will be here to pick up their kids anyway, might as well give them some kind of show."

"Well..." Jo shrugged, but she was smiling. "We're going to need our Malvolio back. Can you think of anybody up for the job?"

Maren looked over at Theo, who was crouched next to Charlie and looking at the film reels as if they were even more precious than diamonds. "I have someone in mind."

"That's good," Jo said. "How about a stage manager?"

It was incredible, Maren thought as she worked backstage, how the Greeks had had it right all those centuries ago. True, the amphitheater's stage wasn't fancy like the auditorium—the seats weren't plush, the sets weren't elaborate, and they had no microphones. But here they all were: the actors decked out in costumes streaked with soot, performing to music Ms. Green played on a portable keyboard, standing in Bernie's last-minute lighting arrangement, and delivering their lines to the shining faces of proud families.

There were some parts, Maren thought, that were even *better* in the outdoors—the storm at the beginning, in which Viola and Sebastian get separated, was all the more frightening with a real breeze rattling the blue sheets they used for water, and the love scenes were more romantic in the light from the setting sun. Plus, it seemed as if all the campers had decided that they were going to give their best performances ever. Greg mooned about like a heartsick duke, Nic's boredom was funny as sassy Maria, and Piper seemed to enjoy squirming away from Allegra in the moments when Olivia tried to grab hold of Viola. Even Allegra was tolerable, Maren admitted. Once, Maren caught Allegra staring at her backstage, but instead of whispering something snide, she just stuck her chin out and looked away. Maren smiled to herself. From Allegra, that was practically a *thank you*.

Even so, none of the others held a candle to her friends. Graham seemed like a true leading man as Sebastian, and Theo as Malvolio recited the lines they had worked so hard to memorize, getting the biggest laughs from the audience. But it was Sal's Feste that brought everyone to their feet. In the very last scene at the very end of the play, Sal grinned out at the audience and started his rap:

> *All right, I've got a story*
> *'Bout the Wind and the Rain*
> *With a heeeeeey! Hoooooe!*
> *With a heeeeeey! Hoooooe!*

And every day it was the same
For the Rain, it raineth every day
With a heeeeeey! Hoooooe!
With a heeeeeey! Hoooooe!

The rest of the cast came out and joined him in a dance until the audience was on their feet, clapping and screaming along at the end.

The bows and applause seemed to last long into the evening.

No one wanted to say goodbye after that—to the show, to the night, to the summer—and a bunch of people Maren had barely spoken to gave her hugs and told her they hoped to see her next year. Afterward, while her friends were still getting out of their costumes, Maren went out into the audience and found Hadley and their parents.

"You were the best stage manager ever," her dad said, giving her a high five. "I think I'll have you manage some of my shows when you get older!"

"That would probably help them go a lot smoother than ever before." Her mom winked. "And you know, she gets those management skills from me."

Hadley pulled her close. "I'm so proud of you."

"Is this how it was when you were here?" Maren teased Hadley.

"Nope." She grinned. "It's even better."

Theo came over to introduce their parents—their father was silent behind a giant mustache, but probably just because Theo's mama outtalked anybody and gave Maren a squeeze so tight Maren thought she saw stars. Graham and Sal and their families joined them, and while Sal's aunt chatted with Maren's dad about jazz, and Graham's moms beamed and showed off their engagement rings in celebration of the Supreme Court decision legalizing same-sex marriages earlier that day, Maren snagged Graham and tugged him over to her sister.

"Hey, Hadley," she said. "Not sure you recognized him in all the chaos today, but you remember Graham, right? He was in the elementary camp when you were a counselor."

"Oh, of course." Hadley beamed at him. "How are you, Graham?"

Graham only managed to turn bright red.

"Plot twist," Theo whispered so only Maren could hear. They were once again behind their camera, capturing the celebrations on film. "Maybe it wasn't you that Graham had a crush on after all."

Maren just laughed.

"There's the girl who saved Christmas." Maren turned to see Jo walking over, helping Charlie by the arm. "You are absolutely a queen among stage managers," Jo said, stooping down to give her a hug.

"Thanks," Maren said. "But who knows, maybe I'll try out for a role next year."

"Next year?" Jo said, and she let out a long breath. "We've got a lot of rebuilding to do before then. Not to mention we still have to figure out a way to fund it all."

"I'm sure we'll find a way," Charlie said, smiling at Maren. "We're good at finding things."

Epilogue

Maren had never seen Theo so nervous as they watched a dusty electric car bump its way down the long lane toward Goodman's.

"Relax," Maren teased. "It's only your hero."

Theo made a squeaky sound in the back of their throat. They tugged their vest straighter—this one decorated with popcorn for the occasion.

"Don't worry, Theo," Charlie said in a much kinder voice. "I'm the one who should be nervous."

"Why aren't you?" Theo asked seriously.

Charlie shrugged. "Too old to bother."

Theo nodded seriously and muttered something that sounded suspiciously like, *I wish I was too old.*

"No one should be nervous," Jo said, nervously, as she adjusted, for perhaps the tenth time, the blanket across Charlie's legs. "No one should be nervous at all."

Charlie was in the wheelchair all the time now, and Maren could tell by the way Jo kept fussing with her father that Charlie's health was declining. Maren looked at them with concern, but Charlie just jutted their chin and grinned, their eyes as sharp as ever.

Finally, the car pulled around the drop-off circle, and the guest of honor hopped out. After watching as many of Quigley Forrager's horror films as she could manage—mostly from between her fingers—Maren wasn't quite sure what she was expecting, but it wasn't the lanky, glasses-wearing, balding man who eased himself out of the small car.

"Hey-o!" he called out to the welcome party, waving one long arm enthusiastically. He was wearing dirty white sneakers, jeans that looked as if they had been ironed, and a windbreaker that swished as he jogged up.

"You made it," said Jo, a little breathlessly. "We're so pleased you could join us, Mr. Forrager."

"Oh, please"—he flopped his hand—"call me Quigs!"

Theo looked as if they were going to spontaneously combust from the possibility.

"You must be Jo," Quigs went on, taking Jo's hand. "And you're Maren, of course—I feel like I know you already from watching all the footage," Quigs said, shaking Maren's hand as well. "And *you*!" He beamed at Theo. "You must be Theo. I have to say, your documentary footage was very, very impressive. And what is this vest? *Fabulous!*"

Theo's mouth moved up and down but—for perhaps the only time in their entire life—absolutely no words came out.

"That's Theo," Maren said. "You're their hero."

Theo made another squeaky sound but still couldn't manage actual words.

"Well, I'm meeting a hero here myself." Quigs looked at Charlie and brought both hands up to his face, making a tent with his fingers over his nose. "Charlie Goodman, I can't tell you—I'm just—gosh, I'm just such a big fan!" he babbled. Maren even thought there were some tears glistening in his eyes. "I just think about what it would have been like for me, starting out, if I had known there was someone like you making movies—and what it'll mean to young filmmakers now!"

He beamed at Theo, who looked as if they might faint at being called a "filmmaker."

"I'm just so happy you're letting your film join my archive." Quigs turned back to Charlie. "I mean, for years, everyone assumed it was destroyed!"

"Including me," Charlie said. "I'm happy it wasn't, and happy it's managed to do some good." They swept an arm at the new auditorium, gleaming in the summer sun.

Quigs made a delighted sound. "Oh, it looks amazing!"

"By buying the film, you allowed us to rebuild it," Jo said. "Not to mention make some expansions to our normal camp offerings." She looked at Maren.

Maren nodded. "There's a festival of new student works tomorrow," she said. "We'd love if you came to see it."

The new Playwriting instructor, Ms. Lauren, had been very eager about the idea of staging a reading of the plays the students wrote in class. It wasn't in costumes or anything like the main show, but Maren's short play would be among those read onstage this year.

Quigs beamed. "Of course! I want to see it all!"

"Perfect. Our teaching intern, Hadley here, would like to give you a tour," Jo said, and Hadley stepped forward with a smile. "The rest of us will head down and meet you at the amphitheater for the screening."

Quigs agreed, and he and Hadley took off together down the path.

"I love you!" Theo croaked when Quigs was out of earshot.

Maren couldn't help laughing. "What was that? Why didn't you just talk to him?"

"I'm working up to it," they said defensively.

"That's what you say about learning your Puck lines," Maren reminded them about their role in this year's play, *A Midsummer Night's Dream*.

"Don't remind me!" they groaned.

"Don't worry," Jo said, "I'm sure Titania here can prompt you from offstage if you forget any, the way she did through the last rehearsal."

Maren blushed guiltily but felt herself grinning, too.

"As well she should. What else are fairy queens for?" said Charlie, and they all laughed.

Together, the four of them set off down the path for the amphitheater, Jo pushing Charlie. As they went, they were joined by clusters of parents and former campers, some stopping to shake Charlie's hand and thank them, others talking excitedly about the viewing. Charlie had agreed to let their film be shown in the amphitheater before it went to join the archives of Quigley Forrager, who had given the camp a handsome payment for the rights to the original film and was even talking about releasing a digital version to cinemas.

The sun was just beginning to set as they all arrived at the amphitheater and took their seats near the back with Sal and Graham. At the projector, a very happy Bernie was finishing setting up with the help of a very pregnant Eartha, while nearby Mr. Cairn and his husband, Carlos, were listening with remarkable patience to one of Miss

Maxine Bradley's stories. A still from the movie—Emma, dressed as a tattered, shipwrecked Viola and looking stoically out across the flat expanse of the ocean she had just been rescued from—was projected on the screen.

"Well, Charlie," Theo said, stretching out in their seat with a contented grin, "you're finally getting to see your movie on the big screen—is this just your absolute dream come true or what?"

Charlie smiled, but their eyes stayed on Emma's image. "You know, when I was your age, this would have been *exactly* my dream come true. But after living the life I got to live?" They reached up and took Jo's hand, who beamed down on them. "Just goes to show you, I was dreaming too small."

"Wow," Theo said, sounding awed. "I hope watching my movie someday makes my dreams feel small."

Now Charlie laughed. "Oh, I think you'll know the feeling," they said. "Tell me, how's your next film coming?"

"I'm still looking for inspiration," Theo sighed. "But I'm definitely thinking my focus will be social justice films. Things were just getting better for people like me, but now, with the election coming up and all, who knows what's going to happen?"

"It'll work out," Charlie said with certainty.

"You're not worried?" Theo said, their brows still pulled tightly together in concern. "You're not at all worried about the election or politics or the future at all?"

"There are always more battles to fight," Charlie said. "But we keep fighting them. Maybe we don't win right away or in exactly the way we want to, but we always win in the long run."

"How are you so sure?" Maren said, looking into Charlie's lined face, their eyes bright even behind those smudged glasses.

"Because I know that the fight is in capable hands," Charlie said. "Yours."

Some Facts in the Fiction

$\backsim$

Charlotte Goodman is named in honor of Charlotte Cushman (1816–1876), a stage actress and opera singer who played both male and female characters in Shakespeare's plays, including famously appearing as Romeo to her sister's Juliet.

Dorothy Arzner was a woman film director in the 1920s to 1940s who challenged preconceived ideas about women in Hollywood, frequently collaborating with her partner, Marion Morgan. Perhaps her most famous film, *Dance, Girl, Dance*, starred Lucille Ball and Maureen O'Hara as two showgirls.

The Fox vault fire happened on July 9, 1937, in Little Ferry, New Jersey. As Theo explained, nitrate film was highly flammable, and the decaying film produced gases that caused a spontaneous combustion. It resulted in the loss of a lot of silent films produced by the Fox Film Corporation before 1932, but the fire, among others like it, ultimately led to a greater interest in, and understanding of, film preservation.

The "Red Scare" is the name for a time during the 1940s and 1950s when there was a deep and widespread societal fear of Communist influences. Because of this collective prejudice, many personal civil liberties were threatened by the House Committee on Un-American Activities hearings. "The Hollywood Ten" was a group of screenwriters and directors who refused to testify at these hearings, several of them serving jail sentences as a result. *Hollywood Fights Back* was a real radio program in which celebrities showed their support of the Hollywood Ten and others on the blacklist who were refused work because of personal and/or political prejudices.

Helen Gahagan Douglas, a former actress who served in the House of Representatives from California, did lose the Senate race to Richard Milhous Nixon in 1950. His smear tactics included targeting her liberal Democratic politics, labeling her as soft on prosecuting Communists, and exploiting prejudice against her Jewish husband, the prominent actor Melvyn Douglas.

In 1953, President Dwight D. Eisenhower signed Executive Order 10450, which barred homosexuals from working in the federal government. This act of extreme prejudice resulted in mass firings and would later be referred to as the "Lavender Scare."

On June 26, 2015—the last day of camp in the story—the Supreme Court of the United States ruled in a landmark civil rights case, *Obergefell v. Hodges*, that the right to marry is guaranteed to same-sex couples on the same terms and conditions as the marriage of opposite-sex couples and must be recognized in all fifty states.

Like many people, Hadley Sands struggled with depression. If you or someone you know needs help with depression and/or suicidal thoughts, please don't hesitate to reach out. The National Suicide Prevention Lifeline is 1-800-273-8255. The Trevor Project is a national organization providing crisis intervention and suicide prevention services to lesbian, gay, bisexual, transgender, queer & questioning (LGBTQ) youth. You can learn more at thetrevorproject.org or by calling 1-866-488-7386.

Bonus Material

A Conversation on Gender Diversity
with Jennifer Feldmann, MD

AUTHOR: Would you introduce yourself to our readers?

DR. JENNIFER FELDMANN: My name is Jennifer Feldmann, and I am a physician. I'm board-certified in both pediatric and adolescent medicine and have a master's in public health. My official title is Service Line Lead for Adolescent Medicine and Gender Health and Wellness at Legacy Community Health in Houston, Texas. We're working on not only the clinical care but also improving the entire clinic experience for gender-diverse people, from the call center to the forms they complete and the signage on the restrooms. We try to make sure everything is consistently and thoughtfully welcoming for everyone of all genders.

AUTHOR: Just so we're all on the same page, would you go ahead and define some of the terms for us, like transgender, cisgender, and nonbinary?

DR. JENNIFER FELDMANN: Gender has four parts.

There's your *biological sex*, which is when a baby is born, they look at the genitals and say, "It's a boy" or "It's a girl." Your biological sex is what your body or your chromosomes show.

Your *gender identity* is the gender of your brain. That

is how you feel: your innate sense of self. That is, if you feel more like a masculine person or a feminine person or something else.

Gender expression is how you show your gender to the world. If I wear dresses, for example, my gender expression would be seen as feminine.

Your *sexual orientation* is related to gender identity, but it's not the same. While gender identity is your internal sense of self, sexual orientation is external; it's who you're attracted to.

You have to first know those terms to talk about what genders *are*.

Cisgender means that your gender identity and your biological sex are the same. More easily put, your brain and your body match. So if you're identified female at birth and your brain feels feminine, you're a cisgender woman.

If you're not *cis*, you fall under the umbrella of *gender nonconforming* or *gender diverse*. For example:

A *transgender* person's gender identity and biological sex don't match. That is, if they're identified female at birth, but have a masculine gender identity or masculine brain, that would be a transmasculine person. We identify by the brain. The brain is what we share with people, what people know about us, whereas our crotches or genitals should be very private.

Now, that implies that gender is a binary—that you're one or the other. But gender, like everything else in the body, is not a binary. So if someone doesn't feel like they fall into the masculine or feminine category, but somewhere in between or a little bit more of one than the other, that is very normal and often called *nonbinary*.

But there are lots of terms for genders outside of the binary—genderqueer, two-spirit, or simply gender nonconforming—that can apply to everyone who is not cis. *Agender* is another gender-nonconforming identity, when you don't identify with any particular gender. Those are the main categories.

AUTHOR: Readers might hear about gender-diverse people in the news in relation to bathroom rights and pronouns. Could you share a little bit about why those issues are so important?

DR. JENNIFER FELDMANN: Pronouns are important because everyone should be seen for who we are. The biggest challenges in being gender diverse are a consequence of stigma and discrimination. People are often seen as *less than,* or their identities are not seen as valid, so they are not treated as who they know themselves to be. Using correct pronouns means you respect who people say they are; you see them truly.

Bathrooms are important because we all use them all the time! I mean, you go into the bathroom, you do your business, you wash your hands, you walk out. It's very private. It's not usually an issue. But for someone who may be gender nonconforming, it can be very nerve-racking. First of all, you're using a non-affirming place, and you feel unsafe or endangered in that place. The most unsafe person in the bathroom is actually the gender-diverse person.

So bathroom rights have become a really hot-button issue and, in fact, unnecessarily so. If you look at all the data in cities across the nation that have protections for people to use the restroom that is consistent with their identified gender, there's been *no* increase in crimes or risks or harm to anyone in a restroom.

AUTHOR: For a reader who might feel like they are gender questioning or gender diverse, do you have any recommendations on how to start a conversation with their friends and family?

DR. JENNIFER FELDMANN: Coming out is really difficult. I want to commend all of the youth who have done so, because it takes a lot of strength and courage, and also send support to those of you who don't feel safe doing so. It really depends on the family and the friends, but I think creating support with friends, gauging your parents' potential reaction, and then laying some groundwork of information for them, so they can at least know what the terms are and know what you're talking about, can be helpful.

I think a lot of folks end up telling their friends first, just because it's safer; theoretically, you can get new friends, but you can't get a new mom. So a lot of times, people try out a new pronoun or a new name with their friends first, in person or online, to see how it feels.

If your parents seem open to talking about gender, you can just ask them: say, "Hey, I'm not entirely sure who I feel like, can you help me explore that?" For some parents, it comes out of the blue, and that's okay. The more out of the blue it seems, the more discussion might be needed to help them understand.

For parents who might be more rejecting, have a history of conservative religious views, or have even made negative comments about trans people before, it can be more difficult. That doesn't mean you shouldn't do it, but I think shoring up your support with friends first is a really good idea. Maybe you talk about Caitlyn Jenner or watch Jazz Jennings's show, or maybe you put out materials for them to read or leave things up on the internet to help them understand. Many families come around, but it takes time.

Keep in mind that often what's perceived as parental rejection comes from a parent's fears. Whenever anyone is different, it makes them a little less safe; you're at risk of bullying or people being mean to you. And unfortunately, even though being transgender is 100 percent normal, the world doesn't get it yet, and that does put you at higher risk of bullying and harm. A lot of parents worry that if they support their child's identity, it will make them *more* trans or *more* nonbinary, and that will make them *more* unsafe. Understanding that point of view can be really helpful when it comes to talking to parents about what's going on for you.

Sometimes they also don't understand gender identity and how people know who they are when they're quite young. They think, "How can you know at twelve who you are?" It's a fair question—until you flip it around and ask the parent, "Well, Mom, if at twelve years old I had called you 'Matthew' and 'he' forever and ever and ever, would you ever become Matthew and he?" And the answer is no. It's true both ways. It's true for a cis person and it's true for a trans person.

AUTHOR: Does a gender-diverse young person need parental consent to get medical care?

DR. JENNIFER FELDMANN: The adolescent consent laws vary greatly by state. In most states, to get gender-affirming hormone therapy (that is, testosterone or estradiol), you would need to have parental consent. If parents are divorced, it depends on the divorce decree who has medical decision-making. There are things that you might be able to do, though. If you're transmasculine, you can have your period stopped with birth control without parental consent. Hormone replacement therapy almost always requires parental consent, though.

AUTHOR: For someone who has the support of their family, what would a first appointment with a gender health specialist like you be like?

DR. JENNIFER FELDMANN: I just spend the first visit getting to know the young person and their family. I ask about their history.

I ask about how they discovered their true identity.

Some people have always known. You don't have words for that when you're a kid, but they can remember the feeling of it. A lot of times, it's when they're young, but sometimes clarity about their gender happens at puberty, so I ask how it happened for context.

I ask about who supports them.

I ask about any history of psychiatric needs (like depression, anxiety, or suicide attempts), which are unfortunately disproportionately common among gender-diverse young people—*not* because they're gender diverse specifically, but due to stigma and rejection.

I ask how school is going, because we can help them be supported at school.

From there, we identify family and patient needs and goals. We might start medicine to pause their period, or work toward hormones, or find them a therapist or a support group, or work with their school to get them more affirmed there.

My goal is to have them be supported.

If parents are unsure, we talk about what support looks like. We talk about starting reversible interventions, things like name and pronoun, and if it's a transmasculine person, stopping their period. Those are all things you can start, and if you stop and they go away—there's no permanent impact.

Usually, once the parents start doing supportive things, they realize how powerfully helpful it is.

AUTHOR: Will you share some resources you give to patients here?

DR. JENNIFER FELDMANN: Gender Spectrum (genderspectrum.org) is a great website for info and for support groups for everyone, in English and Spanish.

HRC—Human Rights Campaign—(hrc.org) has a really great booklet for families about supporting trans youth, in English and Spanish. They also have "coming out resources" for various cultural backgrounds.

The Family Acceptance Project (familyproject.sfsu .edu) also has a lot of really good information on the power of support and the consequences of rejection.

There's Q Chat Space (qchatspace.org), a community for LGBTQ+ teens.

For parents, there's PFLAG (pflag.org), Gender Spectrum (genderspectrum.org), and HRC (hrc.org). All have meetings for parents of gender-diverse youth. There are also Facebook and Discord groups, which all host supportive groups for youth as well as parents. Parents really benefit from support, too, as they have unique questions and concerns that parents of cis kids won't understand.

AUTHOR: For a cisgender reader, how might they better support their trans or nonbinary family members and friends?

DR. JENNIFER FELDMANN: The main things are supporting them and having their backs.

If they haven't told you that they have a preferred name and pronoun, ask them, "Is there something you'd rather me call you, and what pronoun do you use?" Then use that pronoun.

Also ask them if, when someone else misgenders them or uses the wrong name, you can help by correcting the person. For a gender-diverse person, constantly correcting people about their name and pronoun is like being sandpapered each time. So if they want your help, it can be such a relief to not have to correct people themselves, plus they feel supported.

Also, be a safe space. If things at home aren't great, can they maybe stay at your house?

Something all cisgender people can do is state their pronouns when they introduce themselves, on their email signature, Zoom name, and online. This both models respecting other people's pronouns and shows gender-diverse people that you are an ally.

AUTHOR: What mistakes do you commonly see, and are there easy ways to fix them?

DR. JENNIFER FELDMANN: Common mistakes include asking for a pronoun and then not using it. That's honestly just awful, because you've asked but then validating them just didn't seem important enough to you. So use the name and pronoun that's been requested.

When you make a mistake, don't stumble and apologize a ton of times, because it makes it a really big deal, which is also really unpleasant for the gender-diverse person. Just say, "Oh, I'm sorry," and correct yourself. Briefly, quickly acknowledge it, and move on.

AUTHOR: What are your hopes for gender-diverse youth in years to come?

DR. JENNIFER FELDMANN: I hope people, instead of thinking gender diversity is odd, can actually think it's wonderful and normal. The Youth Risk Behavior Surveillance System by the CDC [Centers for Disease Control and Prevention] found in a national study that about 3.5 percent of youth who are currently in high school identify as non-cis. That's a lot of people! It's more common than being redheaded, more common than having an IQ of 150. We value redheads; we value high IQs. I'd like it if we valued gender as something cool and unique, one of the differences that makes our world better instead of challenging.

And I'd like to see more gender-diverse people in media. I'd like to see it be not *a* trans character, but just another person who happens to be a nonbinary person or a trans person in books and movies and ads. I'd like to see gender-diverse people just being people, and represented doing everyday things as everyday people.

Acknowledgments

Twelfth was inspired by my youth as an unapologetic theater nerd at Houston's Theatre Under the Stars and the High School for the Performing and Visual Arts. Growing up is never easy, but if you have to do it, make sure to surround yourself with people who accept you unconditionally, insecurities and all, and just want to make art. Eternal gratitude to my graduating theater class and all my wonderful teachers, with special thanks to Robert Singleton, who taught me to love Shakespeare, and in loving memory of Terry Ogden, my playwriting teacher.

The setting of the fictional Stonecourt, Massachusetts, was inspired by my time spent in the Berkshires first as the Stonecourt Writer-in-Residence in Stockbridge, and later as resident at MassMOCA in North Adams. Big thanks to David and Julie McCarthy, who served as the most generous hosts—and took me to the theater!—and to the other residencies that gave me time to write.

Thanks are due to the extraordinary Little, Brown Books for Young Readers team, especially my excellent editor, Liz Kossnar, and my agent, Heather Rizzo—the Monster Goddess!

To the brilliant readers who helped make this book stronger: Blair Ault, inspiration for Theo's undimmed awesomeness; Schaeffer Nelson, pen pal and soul speaker; the delightful Stuart Rodriguez; Ray Stoeve, sensitivity reader extraordinaire; Matthew Modica and Patricia Grace King, for their fresh eyes and big hearts; and Bonnie Metzgar, for her kind and amazing insights.

To many fellow writers and dear friends whose support I relied on along the way, especially Asako Serizawa, Claire Jimenez, Marysa LaRowe, Rebecca Bernard, Jill Shepmann, Jenna Williams, Lee Connell, Reid Douglass, Maggie Zebracka, Matthew Baker, Edgar Kunz, Cara Dees, Dallas Woodburn, Lauren Baran, Taya Kitaysky, among many, many others, and to the village of writing instructors who raised me, including Aimee Bender, T. C. Boyle, Marianne Wiggins, Paula Cizmar, Velina Hasu Houston, Lorraine López, Nancy Reisman, and Tony Earley.

To my family: my mom and dad, for sharing their love of stories and their unwavering support in writing my own; and Rick and Claire, who didn't question why I was writing about Massachusetts while living with them in Hong Kong.

And finally to you, reader—I waited a very long time to meet you, and I can't tell you what an honor it is. Thank you.

When **JANET KEY** was twelve, she sang and danced onstage in the background of musicals, stayed up too late reading Shakespeare, and had a closet full of themed, hand-sewn vests. This is her first novel.